Midwives' Miracles: Unexpected Proposals

ROBIN GIANNA

TINA BECKETT

MARGARET McDONAGH

MILLS & BOON

First Published in Great Britain 2022
By Mills & Boon, an imprint of HarperCollins*Publishers*, Ltd
1 London Bridge Street, London, SE1 9GF

www.harpercollins.co.uk

HarperCollins*Publishers*
1st Floor, Watermarque Building,
Ringsend Road, Dublin 4, Ireland

MIDWIVES MIRACLES: UNEXPECTED PROPOSALS © 2022 Harlequin Books S.A.

The Prince and the Midwife © 2016 Harlequin Books S.A.
Her Playboy's Secret © 2015 Harlequin Books S.A.
Virgin Midwife, Playboy Doctor © 2008 Harlequin Books S.A.

Special thanks and acknowledgement are given to Robin Gianna for her contribution to *The Hollywood Hills Clinic* series

Special thanks and acknowledgement are given to Tina Beckett for her contribution to the *Midwives On-Call* series

Special thanks and acknowledgement are given to Margaret McDonagh for her contribution to the *Brides of Penhally Bay* series.

ISBN: 978-0-263-30438-1

THE PRINCE AND
THE MIDWIFE

ROBIN GIANNA

CHAPTER ONE

GABRIELLA CAIN ABSENTLY raked her fingers through her hair and stared at the messy room, fighting the deep fatigue that crept quietly into every aching muscle. Her second double shift of the week might be officially over, but as the labor suite department head she wasn't about to leave the disarray for the next midwife to clean up.

Thinking about the twins she'd just delivered to a Hollywood actress and the new mother's proud, beaming husband gave her an energy boost. The suite was a mess for a great reason—the birth of two healthy newborns. After all, just like a kitchen that was never cooked in stayed clean, a spic-and-span labor and delivery suite would mean no new little babies, and wouldn't that be a sad thing?

Gabby finished putting new sheets on the bed, wishing her own at home were as nice as the luxurious Egyptian cotton sheets The Hollywood Hills Clinic provided for its demanding patients, then topped it off with a fresh down blanket. The room was strewn with the various supplies she'd just used, and she figured it made sense to clean that up last so she could note what inventory she might be running low on and get them ordered tomorrow.

She folded clean blankets and stacked them inside the toasty warming cupboard. Crouching down to finally gather the things on the floor, the sound of the double

swinging doors banging open and a gurney being hurriedly wheeled into the room had her pausing in surprise. The other, even more alarming sounds? A woman's moans and the receptionist shouting her name.

"Gabby? Gabby! Are you in here?" Stephanie called.

"I'm here." She stood and stared in dismay when she saw it was Cameron Fontaine lying on the gurney being steered by the hospital's uniformed EMTs, who had doubtless brought her here by helicopter. The famous A-list actress, who was one of Gabby's most difficult patients, and whose baby wasn't due for months. "Cameron? What's wrong?"

"I don't know. I think the baby's coming. It's way too soon, though, isn't it? Oh, God, I'm so scared." She jabbed her index finger toward Gabby, her blue eyes somehow wide with fear and imperiously demanding at the same time. "You've got to do something!"

Gabby's stomach plunged. Yes. It was too soon, and she sent up a deep prayer that Cameron wasn't in labor. That her baby would be fine. That her infant would be born healthy and alive. Her hands suddenly cold, she rushed over to wrap her fingers around Cameron's. "All right. Try to relax. Let's get you into the bed and see what's going on, okay?"

"Just get it stopped! The baby has to cook in there a little longer, right?"

Somehow, Gabby forced a smile, wishing it were that easy. "I believe the proverbial bun in the oven actually bakes, not cooks," she said lightly, proud that she'd managed to keep her tone joking and relaxed. "Let's see what we can do to make sure she gets to rise a little longer, hmm? Try not to worry until we learn more. Maybe baby is just in a mood, wanting a little attention?" She hoped

that was the case, and resisted adding that would mean the infant was a chip off the old block.

Cameron's hand squeezed hers tightly, and Gabby frowned when she realized the woman's breath seemed short and gasping as the EMTs carefully moved her to the bed. Thirty-two weeks along was definitely not the optimal time for a baby to decide to come into the world.

"Stephanie, get in touch with whichever OB's on call and get them here, please."

Stephanie gave a nod and ran out, and Gabby barely noticed the EMTs leaving too as she grabbed the blood-pressure cuff. "I'm going to get your vital signs, then do an internal exam, okay?"

"Will you be able to tell if the baby's coming?"

"If you're dilating, yes. Tell me why you think you might be in labor. Are you in pain?"

"Not…not exactly pain." Cameron's hands cupped her belly and her face scrunched up in an unflattering expression Gabby was sure hadn't been seen on any movie screens by the actress's many fans, which proved how distressed she was. "I felt a little crampy, kind of like the Braxton-Hicks contractions you talked to me about. And my belly got sort of hard, and when it didn't go away I knew I had to do something right away and called the clinic."

"You did exactly the right thing, calling for the helicopter to come get you."

"Well, it seemed to take them forever!" She swiped her elegantly manicured hand across her frowning brow. "It was at least five minutes longer than when they came to get me after I hit my head, and every second that passed I got more worried. I called three times, and I think that made them finally hurry."

A smile touched Gabby's lips, as it was pretty easy to

imagine how those conversations had gone. "Let's see how baby is doing, all right?"

Gabby pressed her stethoscope to Cameron's belly, and the sound of the baby's steady heartbeat sent the breath she was holding right out of her lungs. Thank God, baby was still alive and moving. She snapped on exam gloves and what she found during the examination was a mixed blessing. "The good news is that your membranes are still intact, so no rupture there. Which means your labor's not advanced, which is also good news. But your cervix is dilated two centimeters, so we're going to have to do something about that."

"Like what? And what do you mean, labor's not advancing? Dilating means labor, right?"

Cameron's voice had gone a little shrill, and who could blame her? Gabby knew she had to help her stay calm—the situation was scary, yes, but with luck it could be managed. "Dilation means early labor, yes, but it can be slowed or sometimes completely stopped with medication. I'm going to get an IV set up to give you a mag sulfate drip right away, and also keep you hydrated with saline and lots of water to drink. We'll do a urinalysis to make sure there's no infection, just to be safe. Then we'll give you steroid injections to help baby's lungs develop in case she decides she just can't wait to get here. Please, try not to worry, okay? We'll be doing all we can to keep her healthy."

"I want to see Dr. Crane. When is she coming?"

Gabby had learned long ago to not be insulted by that demand, which she got from a lot of patients and their husbands. And when it came right down to it, she wanted the obstetrician to get there, too, in case the situation got worse instead of better. "I'll find out." She patted Cameron's shoulder and smiled. "Try to relax. Easy to say, I

know, but you don't want your blood pressure all out of whack and make things tougher for baby, do you?"

"Could you get me something to drink before you leave? My breath's been so short for what seems like hours, and I'm beyond parched." She wrapped her fingers around her throat, little gasping sounds coming from her mouth that this time sounded a little forced. "I'd love some artesian sparkling water with a squeeze of lime. You have that, of course, don't you?"

Gabby wanted to say it was more important to get going on the medications she needed first, before wetting her whistle, but figured it would be just as fast to get what Cameron wanted as to point that out.

The small stainless-steel refrigerator in every room was kept well stocked, and Gabby ran the lime wedge around the rim of the crystal glass like a Hollywood Hills nurse who'd been a former bartender had taught her to. Cameron grabbed it like she'd been walking miles through the desert, and Gabby was glad after all that she'd taken a moment to get it for her.

"I'll be right back, okay?" Gabby hurried out to find Stephanie, passing through the halls and out past the beautiful fountain in the center of the glass atrium that made the place feel like a luxury hotel, and breathed in the calming scents of lavender and sandalwood. Except at that moment it didn't do much to slow the current surge of adrenaline that had replaced all her prior fatigue.

"Is the doc on the way to see Cameron, Stephanie? Who is it?"

"Well, as I was about to see who's on call, James phoned. He told me Cameron contacted him while she was on the helicopter to tell him to send her own doctor, because she's convinced Dr. Crane is our best. But she's

out of town, so James asked a good friend of his who's in L.A. visiting to come see her. A Dr. Rafael Moreno."

"What?" Gabby stared at her, not comprehending. "Some friend of his? What do you mean?"

"I guess he's some world-renowned OB, and not only that but the prince of some Mediterranean principality, if you can imagine. Isn't that exciting?" Stephanie's eyes were shining, which seemed ridiculous to Gabby since the woman saw superstars in this hospital all the time. "Said he has privileges in hospitals all over the world, including here in California, and thinks Cameron would appreciate the status of having a prince taking care of her."

Gabby gaped. *What in the world?* A *prince* OB? Just visiting the U.S.? *That* was who James thought was the best person to care for this very demanding and famous patient?

She loved working at The Hollywood Hills Clinic but just might have to point out to James Rothsberg that, exclusive and prestigious or not, the number one focus at this hospital still had to be on premier medical care and not the royalty status of some doctor from another country he happened to be besties with. And, yes, she knew James had founded this hospital with that philosophy, demanding every patient receive the best medical care available, but had to wonder about this particular decision.

"Well, send him in as soon as he gets here, please." She headed back to the room, pondering if she should call James right then to talk to him about the seriousness of Cameron's situation and ask about this doctor and his qualifications—if he was really "world renowned," or just famous for being royal.

"The doctor's on the way, Cameron," she said as she got the items she needed. "I'm going to start your IV now." For the moment, she had to ignore the last of the mess in the

room she hadn't finished cleaning up yet until the doctor arrived and she was certain Cameron had been stabilized.

"It'd better be Dr. Crane," Cameron said, looking away at the wall with a dramatic wince and yelp as Gabby got the IV needle placed in her arm. "She already knows all about me and my past health scares and situation and I only want to see her."

"I know you do." Gabby tried to find reassurance in the fact that Cameron's voice had become the petulant one she often used when she felt normal. At least she wasn't getting real contractions yet or freaking out. Gabby conjured her own acting skills and infused her voice with enthusiasm, bracing herself for the woman to get upset at the news her doctor was unavailable. "Unfortunately Dr. Crane is out of town. But this doctor is a personal friend of James Rothsberg and is not only an excellent OB but apparently a prince too."

"A prince?" Surprise lit Cameron's face before it relaxed into a pleased smile, thank heavens, instead of outrage. "Well, how nice. If Dr. Crane can't be here, at least a prince will understand how important my baby is to the world."

Because a prince and a self-absorbed actress's baby were more important to the world than most other human beings? Emotions crowded Gabby's chest—disbelief that Cameron obviously genuinely believed that. Annoyance with that attitude. And deeply buried pain. Because every person's baby was the most important child on earth to them.

She swallowed before she spoke. "I'm not sure when Dr. Moreno is going to get here, and we shouldn't wait to get your mag sulfate drip started. Is your belly still hard and tight? Still feeling crampy?"

"Well, yes. But not too bad. I think we should wait for this prince-doctor." She picked up the television remote,

clicked to a movie channel, and beamed the famous mega-watt smile she normally reserved for the cameras. "Oh, look, it's one of mine! I loved this one!"

"Cameron." Gabby worked to keep her patience. "Giving you the sulfate drip certainly isn't going to hurt, regardless of what Dr. Moreno has to say, and timing can be critical. Up to three courses of steroids are recommended for the baby's lung health, but have to be given at least twenty-four hours apart, and the sooner we give the first one, the sooner we can give the second one."

"I admit I'm still nervous. I know you're good at what you do. If you think you need to start it now, then let's do it." Cameron's smile disappeared, and Gabby's frustration with her patient evaporated when she saw the tension etched on her face. Probably her wanting to wait and watch the movie, all smiles, was some coping mechanism, telling herself everything was fine now that she was here at the clinic. Deluding oneself was all too easy to do, as Gabby knew firsthand.

She patted Cameron's arm, then gave it a gentle squeeze. "I'll get it started right now. And I bet the doctor will be here any moment." As though her words had willed it, a brisk knock on the door sounded, and she turned as it opened.

To reveal the most physically beautiful man she'd ever seen.

His dark hair was cut fairly short and impeccably groomed, and his olive skin was tanned a golden brown which looked even more swarthy in contrast to his white doctor's coat. The blue dress shirt he wore was crisply starched but left open at the collar without a tie, and it was obvious that beneath it lay a very well-built physique. But the most riveting thing about him was the startling color

of his eyes, nearly the same hue as springtime in Seattle after rains had turned the landscape a vivid green.

She felt a little as though all the oxygen had been sucked from the room as those eyes met hers. Though the contact was brief, his gaze seemed to both assess her and dismiss her at the same time. Then his attention moved around the room in a careful scan of the space before finally focusing on their patient.

A smile transformed the aloof expression on his handsome face. *"Buenos días."* He stepped to the bed, reached for their patient's hand and, to Gabby's astonishment, lifted it to his lips. Since when did doctors kiss their patients, even if it was just on the hand? "I do not have to ask if you are the famous Cameron Fontaine. I would recognize your stunning face anywhere. I am Dr. Rafael Moreno."

"It's wonderful to meet you, Doctor," Cameron practically cooed.

"I understand your very special baby is demanding some unexpectedly early attention. I'm told your little one is a girl—what a lucky child. She'll no doubt be as beautiful as you are." Lord. Gabby had to wonder if he'd intentionally ratcheted up the charm, or if it just oozed naturally from the man. "Let us see what she has in mind, shall we?"

"Yes. I'm so anxious to hear what you think is going on and what to do about it."

Cameron's expression could only be described as coy and flirtatious, and Gabby caught herself about to shake her head at the whole scene. Dr. Moreno had instantly sized the woman up, that was for sure, and Gabby was torn between admiration and disgust at how quickly and easily he'd had her eating out of his hand. While not even bothering to introduce himself to Gabby or ask who she was. The man was royal, all right. Royally rude.

"Tell me what's been happening." He sat and directed

his attention solely to Cameron, as though Gabby wasn't even there, and the actress told him all about her symptoms as he looked at the vital signs Gabby had recorded. He took his time speaking with her, acting more like they were at a cocktail party than in a hospital room. But of course Cameron, who was always more than happy to talk at length about herself, basked in the attention as he asked all kinds of questions about her life and career in addition to the ones related to her health.

As the minutes stretched on, Gabby fidgeted, wondering when in the world he was going to get on with what needed to be done and have her administer the meds Cameron needed. At the same time, she had to grudgingly give him credit for completely relaxing their patient.

Then that credit evaporated when he reached for gloves, obviously planning to give her an internal exam.

"Excuse me, Dr. Moreno, but did you see in the chart that I just gave her an exam about thirty minutes ago? That she was already dilated to two centimeters?" Gabby asked.

He turned to her with one eyebrow quirked. "And you are…?"

"I'm Gabriella Cain, head midwife here at The Hollywood Hills Clinic."

"Now that I am here to care for Ms. Fontaine, I will take care of future internal exams. I'm sure you know they need to be limited in cases of early onset labor."

What the…? Anger began to burn in Gabby's chest. "Yes, I am aware of that, Dr. Moreno. Which is why I feel you should wait to do another. I was about to get the mag sulfate drip started, followed by the steroids, then do an ultrasound."

"I prefer to not rely on others' examinations and opinions, as that normally isn't in the best interests of my patient. However, if you've done an internal exam, I won't

do another at the moment." He turned away from Gabby again, and she stared at the back of his silky dark head, hardly able to believe his arrogantly dismissive attitude. *His* patient? She'd worked with some doctors with domineering attitudes before, but this guy got first place for jerk of the year.

"It's good that you're dilated to no more than two centimeters," he said to Cameron as he looked at Gabby's notes. "Although that is clearly an indication of pre-term labor, there are things we can do to try to make that cease, and at the same time give baby a chance to grow more."

"So it is preterm labor. I was so hoping it wasn't." Cameron's white teeth worried her lip, her eyes wide. "Do you think whatever you do to try to stop it will work?"

"It often does, so we will hope for the best." He lifted his tall frame from the stool he'd been perched on, moving to stand beside the bed and hold Cameron's hand between both of his, a smile on his face some people might think was charming. "And if baby says, *Oh, no, Mama, I'm coming anyway*, we will at least have time to give you steroids to help her little lungs function better when she arrives. So we will do that without delay. Okay?"

"All right. Whatever you think," Cameron said, all grateful smiles. "Thank you so, so much, Doctor."

"Please, call me Rafael."

Whatever you think. Thank you so, so much... Gabby gritted her teeth and told herself she couldn't feel bothered by Cameron's immediate agreement to the same treatment she'd initially refused to agree to when Gabby had told her exactly the same thing. It was no secret doctors got more respect than midwives from many patients, and an über-handsome doctor who, by the way, happened to be a prince too? Jerk or not, it was no surprise that status-

conscious Cameron was all too happy to go along with whatever he suggested.

"Bien." He stood and turned to Gabby, and his warm expression cooled to one of professionalism. "I'd assume you have the mag sulfate and steroid ready?" Those startling green eyes slowly scanned the area again before pinning hers again with one dark eyebrow raised. "Except perhaps I should not assume that. When I first walked in I was shocked to see the state of this room, which is, well, I must say, terribly disorganized. I'm frankly very surprised by this, considering the stellar reputation of The Hollywood Hills Clinic and knowing James Rothsberg's perfectionism."

The irritation that had been simmering in her chest burst into a full conflagration of anger that surged through her blood and made her brain burn. Who did this guy think he was? Friend or no friend of James, prince or no prince, he had no right to waltz in like he owned the place, give it his version of the white-glove test, then criticize her without knowing a thing about the patients and medical situations she'd been taking care of for the past ten hours.

"I was in the process of cleaning and reorganizing it from an earlier, lengthy delivery when Cameron arrived in what might have been an emergency situation. I deemed taking care of her and her baby was a lot more important than tidying and prepping a room that could be tidied and prepped later. And the meds *are* ready."

She stalked to the counter, gathering the items together and wishing she could throw them at his arrogant, judgmental face. He reached for them, his hand briefly touching hers, and it ticked her off even more that the feel of his skin brushing hers sent some kind of weird electric shimmer up her arm. The sensation could have been mis-

taken for attraction, if there had been anything attractive about the man.

Well, there were all those superficially attractive things, but she wasn't a woman interested in slick, glossy men. Or any kind of man anymore, really.

With grudging respect, though, Gabby did have to admire how quickly and efficiently his long fingers administered the drugs, all the while keeping up a smoothly distracting conversation with their patient.

"All set," he said to Cameron, giving her a warm and reassuring smile. "Now we wait, keep you comfortable, and check baby periodically through ultrasound and monitoring."

"Thank you, Rafael. I'm *so* glad you and Gabby are the ones taking care of me."

And Gabby was glad the next shift midwife would be arriving soon to deal with Cameron and Dr. Moreno. Not to mention that she was way overdue for a major nap.

"How about deciding what you'd like to have for dinner?" Gabby said as she brought her another sparkling water, along with a menu of options for her meal. The onsite Michelin-starred chef was amazing, and even the pickiest patients loved the elegant and trendy foods he prepared. "The midwife on the next shift will be checking on you throughout the night to make sure you're comfortable. Then tomorrow morning I'll be back to take care of you. In the afternoon it'll be time to administer another steroid dose."

"But I don't want another midwife," Cameron said, a twisting pout on her lips that had Gabby wondering how in the world she managed to still look so pretty doing it. "I want you to stay here with me tonight, Gabby."

The fatigue Gabby had felt earlier was back in spades. She had a feeling if she closed her eyes she might fall

asleep on her feet like a horse, and the vision of curling up in her own comfy bed and getting a solid night's sleep nearly had her moaning, but she knew Cameron. And Cameron's expectations. The Hollywood Hills Clinic was known for its exceptional medical care, and that included going above and beyond in every way.

Which meant she'd be spending the night here again.

"I appreciate you wanting me with you, Cameron. I—"

"Your staying here is important, since you are familiar with our special patient and her physical condition and worries," Rafael interrupted smoothly. "Here is my contact information. Please don't hesitate to get in touch with me for any reason."

Did the man think he was boss of the world? Gabby felt like smacking that seemingly sincere smile from his handsome face as he handed her an elegantly embossed card, then turned to give one to their patient. When Cameron reached for hers, she clasped his hand along with it for a lingering moment, practically batting her long lashes at him as she smiled back.

"Thank you so much, Rafael. I can't tell you how much I appreciate your help and expertise during this terrifying time."

"It's beyond my pleasure. It is my calling to help mamas and their babies, whether a pregnancy is smooth and uneventful or high risk and worrying. I promise to take care of you and *bebé* to the best of my ability."

Whereas Gabby and most other nurses and doctors didn't? The guy was pure egotistical arrogance in a white coat, absolutely no doubt about that. And Gabby intended to tell him so, though somehow she'd have to tone down the strength of the language she'd really like to use when she did.

"As I started to say a moment ago, Cameron, I'm more

than happy to stay," she said, giving Dr. Moreno a pointed look she hoped he interpreted correctly—which was to tell him to keep his guest-in-this-hospital nose in his own business. "I'll sleep better knowing I can check regularly on how you're doing, and hopefully me being here will help you sleep better too."

"Thank you, Gabby. I will sleep better."

"Why don't you rest now and watch a little TV? I'll be back in a few minutes to find out what you've decided to order for dinner." She turned to Dr. Full-of-Himself and somehow kept her voice cordial. "May I speak to you privately in my office, Dr. Moreno?"

He inclined his head again, and she sensed him following her from the room and down the marble-tiled hallway, past large windows with beautiful views Gabby normally enjoyed, but not at that moment. Right then, she had only one thing on her mind, which was giving Rafael Moreno a piece of it.

She stopped in front of the open door of her office and gestured for him to go inside but he stopped with her.

"Ladies first," he said as he mirrored her gesture.

A man with good manners was usually appealing, but this didn't feel like good manners. It felt more like he was just being controlling again, wanting things to be the way he wanted them and not giving her respect for the fact that it was *her* office. Which meant she should be calling the shots at that moment, even if it was something as simple as who entered the room first.

The smile she stuck on her face was stiff and fake and she didn't care if he saw through it. While part of her knew it wasn't something worth arguing about, he'd irritated her so much already she found herself digging in her heels. "No, I insist. You are a guest here at the clinic, after all." And if that didn't give him a strong hint that

he'd overstepped his bounds, she was about to tell him so much more directly.

Those silky eyebrows rose at her, and their gazes clashed for several heartbeats until he inclined his head and stepped into the room. She shut the door behind her, not wanting anyone to overhear their conversation, and when she turned to look at him she had that oxygen-sucked-from-the-room feeling again. His height and the breadth of his shoulders made the room seem to shrink, and his erect posture and the utter self-assurance of his demeanor compounded the effect until she felt she couldn't breathe.

Except breathing was necessary to give him a piece of her mind. Her mouth suddenly dry as sandpaper, she hoped he couldn't sense her discomfiture as she stepped behind her desk instead of having them sit in the two chairs side by side, wanting to send another message that she was in charge of the maternity wing and its midwives and he should treat her accordingly.

"Please sit," she said as she perched herself in her swivel chair.

But of course he didn't. He simply stared down at her, and she suddenly felt like a bug-eyed hamster being eyed by a hawk. Rafael Moreno, standing there all confident and imperious, had utterly ruined the message she'd tried to send by sitting behind the desk, so now what was she supposed to do? Sit there craning her neck up at him while giving him a dressing-down? Or bob back up like a jack-in-the-box? Either one would make her look foolish and, worse, completely lacking in power and authority.

Damn the man.

"What is it you wish to discuss with me, Ms. Cain?"

She huffed out a breath, trying hard to regain some semblance of equilibrium, and slowly stood again to look him

in the eye. Or as much as that was possible, considering he still had a good six or seven inches in height on her. "I know you are James's friend, and I'm told you are good at what you do. Also that you are part of a royal family, which is perhaps why you feel you can do as you please."

"I can do as I please."

The arrogance of the words wasn't diminished by the even modulation of his deep voice. Her heartbeat upped its tempo to double time, and that burning sensation prickled her scalp again. "Maybe you can in a lot of places, but not here, Dr. Moreno. I may be a midwife and not a physician, but I assure you that I'm the person in charge of the day-to-day operation of The Hollywood Hills Clinic's maternity ward. While I am grateful you came quickly to see Cameron when James requested you to, I don't appreciate you walking in and just taking over. Completely ignoring the notes I made on Ms. Fontaine's chart and utterly dismissing my medical opinion and recommendation. Even worse, you said and did it all in front of the patient. That was insulting and rude, and frankly could have very well undermined her confidence in me, my knowledge, and my skills."

The expression on his smooth, angular features didn't change, but in the depths of his eyes there was a sudden, dangerous glint. Her breath caught and held in her chest during the long pause that crackled between them before he finally spoke. "Anything else?"

"Yes, actually."

Gabby slowly walked around from behind the desk, taking that moment to get the air moving in her lungs again, hoping to calm both her tripping heart and her frustration. For the first time in her life she wished she was taller than her five feet six inches, but was so angry she came to stand nearly toe to toe with him anyway.

"I resent you saying that room was a mess, that it was substandard, and by association that *I'm* substandard. Even worse that you said it in front of our patient as well. I work very hard to keep my ward immaculately clean, organized and running smoothly, to keep these rooms as luxurious and beautiful as James insists they be, and our patients expect. But as an obstetrician you should certainly know that when there's any kind of medical emergency, like the difficult twin births I was dealing with prior to Cameron arriving, it tends to mess up a hospital room. Is it possible that you never give that a thought, though, since an OB can often run in, catch a baby, play hero, then leave the cleanup to someone else?"

"I assure you," he said in a silky-soft voice at odds with that glint sparking in his eyes, "I am well versed in hospital room chaos, having worked in all kinds of clinics around the world. *I* resent *your* implication that I'm a spoiled and selfish man unwilling to take on any task required of me. That is an unacceptable insult. Who and what I am is a doctor who prides himself on paying attention to every detail, and the fact is that the disarray of that room was obvious evidence that I had to take control of the situation."

The small gap between them closed, and with his narrowed gaze so close, so intense Gabby found she had to break their eye contact before she got dizzy from it. Which then had her staring at his mouth, at lips that were hard and uncompromising, and somehow at the same time so soft and sensually shaped that her stomach did a strange little flip that didn't feel at all like the anger pumping through her veins.

"And I assure you that was a misconception, and you *taking control of the situation* was both unnecessary and unwelcome." Gabby resisted the urge to stroke her hand down her throat, swiping away the sweat she was sure

must be forming there. Why did it suddenly seem so hot in this room? Was it her anger making her heart quiver, and was it her imagination that all that heat seemed to be shimmering right between them, practically pouring from his big, masculine body? "If you end up coming back to see Cameron, and I frankly would prefer a different physician do so, I would appreciate you showing me respect in front of our patient, and I will continue to show you that same respect."

"Oh, I'll be back, Ms. Cain, have no doubt about that. Whether you like it or not. When I make a commitment to a friend like James, and to a patient, I always see it through to the end." His eyes were still narrowed, his words still spoken in that silky, soft tone that sounded odd, coming from lips that had been firmly clamped together the whole time she'd spoken. Then, to her utter shock, he reached for her hand and lifted it to those beautiful lips, pressing them to the back of it.

Both soft and firm, he kept them there for three long seconds, causing that weirdly disconcerting spark to fly up her arm again. Then he released it and, without another word, turned and strode out the door.

Gabby stared blindly at the wall beside her door, absently running her palm from the back of her other hand up her arm, feeling the gooseflesh still making all the little hairs stand at attention. "Well, Gabby, that went well," she muttered to herself, barely able to catch her breath. "When it comes to verbal sparring to handle a problem, that man is clearly way out of your league."

Which left her with a very difficult question. What she was going to do next to keep him from taking over her entire ward?

CHAPTER TWO

"You've always been a workaholic, but your schedule seems insane to me," Rafael said as he sat across from James, glad his friend had finally found time to stop by the cliffside home Rafael was renting. "I thought I might be moving on from L.A. before we had a chance to share another drink."

"Hey, I do things other than work."

"Like what? Are you taking up golf?" Rafael asked with a grin, since he knew the man had zero interest in spending that much time on a game.

That drew a return grin from James. "No, but I do have a date in about…one hour," he said, glancing at his watch. "And what do you mean, you might be moving on from L.A. soon? Is rolling stone Rafael already thinking about leaving? I thought you'd come here to go into hiding for a while."

"Doesn't seem to have worked too well. One or the other of my parents calls me practically daily with disapproving updates on the photos and completely exaggerated stories still showing up in the gossip magazines about me."

"If you didn't date strippers, maybe you wouldn't have that problem."

"I didn't even know she'd been a stripper until it was splashed across all the papers." He shook his head, won-

dering why everyone had to make such a big deal out of it anyway. "But if I hear one more word from my family about having to find a 'suitable' girlfriend, I may just become a monk."

"Like there's any chance of that," James said with a smirk. "One of the reasons I always liked hanging out with you was because women flock around a prince like ants to a piece of candy. A good way for me to meet the cast-offs."

"Because you have such a problem with meeting women," Rafael said dryly. "Didn't you just tell me you have a date tonight?"

"Yeah." James's face instantly settled into an oddly serious expression, and it struck Rafael that his friend might be getting back into a relationship with Mila Brightman, his former fiancée.

"I heard you're having to spend time with Mila now you're working with her charity," he said casually, hoping James would talk to him about it if he felt a need to. "Are you seeing her again?"

"No. That was over long ago." James seemed to be studying the condensation droplets on his iced-tea glass very intently, and Rafael wondered if it was to avoid looking him in the eye. "But I do think dating someone new is a good idea to, you know, distract me from thinking about the past."

Rafael frowned. He knew their breakup had been hard on both James and Mila, but it had been James's idea, after all. How much was he still bothered by it? "Maybe you and Mila—"

"I don't really want to talk about it." James set his glass down and put on the cool, professional face Rafael had seen many times when James wanted to put distance between himself and others. "Tell me about how things went

with Cameron Fontaine. And by the way, I don't think I've told you how much I appreciate you seeing her."

"I'm glad you asked me. It's what I do. Not to mention that not working and having to lie low in L.A. has been getting a little tedious, so I'm happy to be at the clinic." Oddly, the first thing James's question instantly brought to mind wasn't his patient but a certain gorgeous midwife who was an all-too-attractive combination of warmth and smarts and toughness.

Thinking back, he realized he'd deserved the one-two punch she'd given him in her office. He should have shown her immediate respect instead of making her earn it, but in some of the places he'd worked, it had been important to make sure everyone knew what they were doing before you trusted them to. In spite of the chaotic condition of the room, it had been obvious that she was an expert when it came to the medical care of the patients. And wasn't afraid to point it out in no uncertain terms to anyone who doubted that.

"What's with that smile on your face?" James asked, quirking his eyebrow. "Did you fall in lust with Cameron?"

"No." That would be a snowy day in the desert, and he practically laughed at the question. Cameron Fontaine was the kind of self-absorbed woman he met all too often and had no interest in even for just sex.

He wouldn't admit to James that the woman he'd felt a stirring of lust for had been the clinic's head midwife. A woman with a fiery temper to match the golden fire of her hair. The last thing he needed was the complication of dating someone he had to work with. Not to mention that dating anyone at that particular moment was asking for more trouble from the press and anger and disapproval from his family.

After the tabloids had blown up again with the juicy

story of his latest girlfriend, his parents had insisted he stop embarrassing them. It all seemed so ridiculous since he'd dated the woman barely a month before they'd stopped seeing each other, which was how he liked to keep it. Any longer than that and a woman had a tendency to start thinking long term, and he had no intention of doing forever after with anyone. His brother had taken care of marrying to provide heirs, and saddled himself with a woman who didn't even like him much. And the picture-perfect partnership of his parents' arranged marriage? It didn't hint at the cool distance between them, or question why they were on different continents half the time.

No, Rafael was never going to get stuck in some passionless marriage. He liked his freedom and planned to keep it, thank you very much. Lying low to let his parents simmer down a little was the price he had to occasionally pay for that freedom. With any luck, they'd soon stop throwing "suitable" women his way, wanting to torture him with the kind of loveless marriage they had.

"I'm not sure we're going to be able to stop Cameron's labor," he told James, "but I'm hoping to be able to get her at least a second steroid dose before it happens. I'm heading over there soon to see how she's doing."

"Good. You're the best at what you do, and I hope she knows that. I'm guessing she doesn't mind that her doctor is a prince either."

Probably true, but his royal status was something Rafael found to be a far bigger burden than a benefit. "I'll text you with an update after I see her."

"I'd appreciate that." James stood, so Rafael did too. "I'd better get cleaned up for my date."

He had to wonder how Mila would react to seeing photos of James with a doubtless beautiful woman in the media

that followed him around as much as they followed him, but it wasn't any of his business.

No, his present business was to keep a low profile and his own face out of the tabloids for as long as possible.

Gabby poured herself another cup of coffee, desperate to somehow keep her heavy eyelids from closing. During the night, when Cameron had slept, she'd managed to grab an hour or two of rest, but had jumped to attention every time Cameron had woken up, both worried that her labor might be advancing. That, combined with her recent double shifts prior to Cameron's arrival, had left her without much in the way of reserve energy.

Gulping at the dark, hot liquid, Gabby moved to Cameron's bedside again. "Any changes in the way you're feeling?"

"No." Cameron folded her arms across her chest and pouted up at Gabby. "And I'm awfully tired of just lying here. The only thing that makes it bearable at all is the good care you're taking of me."

"That's nice of you to say." Her words managed to fractionally perk Gabby up since, inside, she'd become a little tired of catering to the woman's every whim. At least she apparently appreciated it. "I'm doing everything I can to keep you comfortable, and hopefully help baby stay in there a little longer."

"I know I should apologize for being a tad complaining. Even grumpy occasionally. It's just so tiresome being in this bed, but I know you understand that."

"I do understand. Would you like your pillows plumped again?"

At her nod, Gabby complied, thinking it was good the pillows were faux down to prevent any allergens from being in the room, as real down would have been plumped

to death by now. Cameron's word "tad" was an understatement, but Gabby was pretty sure the woman truly didn't realize that "Diva" should be her middle name.

"It's not easy getting comfortable, sitting in a bed all day, or to keep from getting bored. I'll bring you another book to read, if you like."

"Maybe later." She leaned back against her pillows with a long-suffering sigh. Just as Gabby was about to creep away, Cameron opened her eyes and started talking again. "And of course the other thing making it bearable to be here is Rafael. He's just the sweetest, dreamiest thing, don't you think? And he's obviously a wonderful doctor."

Dreamy, maybe, when it came to his looks. But sweet? Definitely not. It was an effort, but Gabby managed to keep a smile on her face and sort of agree. "He has an excellent reputation. I'm glad you like him."

"Like him? I just love him! Adore him!" Cameron gushed. "I feel so lucky that he happens to be in Los Angeles right now. It seems like fate, doesn't it?"

Privately, she didn't think it was fate, unless the universe had decided to challenge Gabby by making life at the clinic difficult, having to work with someone as full of himself as Rafael Moreno. But she was a professional and could handle it, no matter what. And, to look at the positive, at least Cameron was happy.

She glanced at her watch. "If you're not going to sleep right now, I'd like to get another ultrasound of baby, then give your next steroid injection."

"Should we wait for Rafael?" Anxious blue eyes met hers. "He said he'd be here this afternoon, and I'm sure he will be."

Damn the man for insisting he be in charge of everything, and basically telling the patient not to trust her. "I believe Dr. Moreno was simply being cautious because

he doesn't personally know me. But midwives are highly trained in all aspects of pregnancy and delivery, including caring for high-risk patients. You can trust me completely."

"Of course I trust you. In fact I'm— I— Oh, my God!" Cameron sat bolt upright in bed, her eyes suddenly wide and scared as she stared at Gabby.

Her heart picked up speed because the look on Cameron's face didn't seem like overdramatic acting this time. She reached for Cameron's hand. "What? What is it?"

"I think…I think my waters just broke!"

Oh, no. Gabby immediately checked to be sure Cameron wasn't experiencing some other sensation that made her think it was her membranes breaking, but there was no doubt about it.

Heart sinking, she prayed the steroids had gotten baby's lungs developed enough for the premature infant to be all right. She perched on the side of the bed and reached for Cameron's hands again. "You're right. Your waters have broken, which means your amniotic sac is no longer intact. And that means baby has to be born, otherwise there's risk of infection. I'll call Dr. Moreno and get him here right away."

"Oh, yes, you must!" Cameron's manicured nails dug into Gabby's skin. "Tell him it's an emergency!"

"I'm sure he'll get here as quickly as possible. Try not to worry, okay? With luck, you'll have a smooth, uncomplicated delivery, and baby will be just fine. I'll be right back."

Gabby managed to extricate her hands from Cameron's grip and made a quick note of the time her waters had broken and an estimation of the amount of fluid before she moved into the hallway to pull up Dr. Moreno's number on her cell. Hopefully, he wasn't at lunch with some bigwig, or with a woman after a date the night before and not

answering the phone because of it. And why that thought would make her tummy tighten uncomfortably, she had no idea. Must just be concern for Cameron, because she knew the woman would worry about having a different doctor come to deliver the baby.

But he answered after only two rings, and Gabby let out a relieved breath. "Dr. Moreno, it's Gabby Cain. Cameron's waters broke a few minutes ago and—"

"I'll be right there."

She stared at the now dead phone. Now, there was a man of few words. And questions. Which was probably a good thing since the sooner he arrived, the sooner he'd wield his potent charm on Cameron to keep her calmer in a way Gabby wasn't always able to accomplish.

Back in Cameron's room, she plumped her pillows yet again and checked her vital signs once more. "Dr. Moreno's on his way."

"I knew he'd come right away. I'm just praying he gets here before my baby does!"

"It usually takes a while for contractions to get strong enough for baby to be born. Are you feeling any yet?"

"I…I can't tell for sure. I feel very crampy, like there's a fist inside my belly. It doesn't feel good. And my back really aches. Is it going to get worse? I hate pain! I don't do well with it at all!"

The famous blue eyes staring at her were so scared and anxious Gabby gave her hands another reassuring squeeze. "How contractions feel varies a lot from woman to woman. Some go from feeling cramps that become more intense as labor progresses, and others experience pretty intense contractions. But all that is helping your baby be born, so it's nothing to be afraid of."

"How long will it take?"

"That varies too." Gabby wasn't about to tell her it could

be just a few hours or as long as twenty-four or more. If Cameron was stressing now, that would probably send her into a panic. "I'm going to check your cervix to see how much it's thinning and dilating, which may give us a clue how far along you are."

"Okay, but I want an epidural, because it already hurts a lot! So please call whoever does that right away. Unless Rafael will do that himself?"

"Epidurals are done by an anesthesiologist. We'll let Dr. Moreno decide when that should happen." Since he'd wanted to be in charge, Gabby was more than happy to pass the epidural discussion on to him.

It seemed Gabby had barely plumped Cameron's pillows a third time and gotten ice for her to suck on when Rafael Moreno strode into the room as if he owned the place. All tall and powerful and regal, his mere presence seemed to electrify the air. His gaze trapped hers, and everything in the room seemed to fade away except for that intense connection. Suddenly she felt a little unsteady on her feet, but that was probably sheer exhaustion.

"Thank God you're here, Rafael!"

Cameron's voice snapped her back to reality. *Focus on your job and patient, silly, not the handsome prince.* Um, what had she been about to do just then? "Hello, Dr. Moreno. As I told you, Cameron's had PPROM. I was about to check her cervical thinning and dilation."

"What's PPROM?" Cameron sounded alarmed, and Gabby gave her a pat.

"Sorry, I was talking to the doctor. It's just an acronym for preterm premature rupture of membranes, which just means your waters broke before baby is full term."

"Let's check how far along you are, Cameron, okay?" he asked. Rafael donned gloves and began the internal exam, smiling at their patient and asking questions as he

did. Somehow he managed to have her smiling back and laughing at a few of his remarks, and Gabby had to grudgingly admit he had a wonderful bedside manner, obviously used to dealing with even the most nervous and difficult kinds of patients.

When he finished the exam he snapped off his gloves and seemed to take a moment to think of how he wanted to present his findings. "Your special little one is, as we know, very anxious to arrive. You are already dilated to six centimeters, which is a bit surprising for a first baby, though of course your *bebé* has been impatient for some time, hasn't she?"

Gabby stared at him in surprise and had to bite her tongue to keep from blurting out something like *You're kidding!* Six centimeters was way further along than she'd expected, and she had to admit she was glad Rafael was already there, or she would have been concerned that he might not get to the clinic in time, which would have worried Cameron at a time she didn't need more worries.

"Oh, my Lord, then I need to get an epidural right now, don't I?" The blue eyes staring at Rafael quickly became panicky as she apparently experienced a contraction. Panting for a moment, she leaned forward to grab his hand. "I hate pain. You can make sure I don't have any more pain, right? Fix that for me, please."

So used to addressing laboring mother's worries, Gabby opened her mouth before realizing Cameron had asked Rafael, not her. And much as it rankled a bit, since she was used to either delivering babies on her own or being part of a team with the obstetrician, she managed to let him answer instead.

"I have already spoken to the anesthesiologist, as I know you want to be as comfortable as possible," he said in that soothing voice that was also, damn it, incredibly sexy.

"Now that we know you're dilated enough to receive the pain relief, we'll get the anesthesiologist here pronto."

He turned the power of his smile on Gabby, and she had to admit to a warmth filling her chest that he'd included her with the "we" word. Though why she should care if he did or didn't give her that lip service, she had no clue.

"Gabriella, would you please ask Dr. Smith to come now?"

"Yes, Dr. Moreno."

"Please, call me Rafael. You and Cameron and I are all friends trusting one another here to bring baby into the world, yes?"

"Um, yes." No. Not friends. Colleagues. Co-workers. But that simple word—*friends*—made her chest feel warmer even as it contracted with pain as she went to phone the doctor. Her last relationship had taught her that counting on true friendship and closeness with a man was a mistake. That trust was a mirage. An elusive shimmer of light that could disintegrate and disappear in an instant when times got tough.

Briefly closing her eyes, she willed away the hurt, stuffing it down into the deep, dark corner where it usually resided, until unexpected moments like this dragged it to the surface. But this moment wasn't about her past. This moment was about helping a mother who would soon hold a new life in her arms, a precious child she obviously wanted with all her heart.

Tears unexpectedly stung her eyes, and she angrily swiped them aside. She delivered babies for a living, and usually felt nothing but joy for the new parents, new families. So what was it about this moment, this delivery that was bringing memories to the surface that were better left behind?

The question made her wonder if, somehow, some way,

for some bizarre reason, it was Rafael's presence that was making her feel so strange. But, of course, that made no sense. She didn't even know him. Didn't want to.

She kept her life simple. Worked a lot of hours, taking on as many double shifts as possible. Went out with friends occasionally, but that was pretty much it. Could it be that after such a long time of keeping to herself, being around an exceptionally attractive man, annoying or not, had her neglected hormones all charged up or something?

Yes. That had to be it. And knowing that was all it was helped her get her equilibrium back. Time to quit thinking and remembering and start working. She quickly contacted the anesthesiologist, then headed back to Cameron's room.

"You checked Cameron for her group B beta strep culture, yes?" Rafael asked from his position by Cameron's bedside, holding her hand the way she would have, in a way she couldn't remember ever seeing an OB interact with a patient.

"I did. Status was uncertain, so I gave her a second dose of antibiotics in case it's an issue."

"Good." He nodded and stood, and Gabby found herself fixated on the way his broad shoulders and chest filled out his scrubs, how his tanned forearms looked more like they belonged to an athlete than a man who caught babies for a living. Thankfully, her inappropriate perusal was interrupted as Dr. Smith strode in. Face heating, she turned away, hoping to heck no one had noticed her staring.

The doctors shook hands before the anesthesiologist introduced himself to their patient. "Cameron, I promise I'm not going far, just giving Dr. Smith and Gabriella some room," Rafael said. "I'm sure Dr. Smith will take good care of you, and of course you are in Gabriella's excellent hands as well. See you shortly, okay?"

And Gabby sure as heck needed a little space and a

breather from Rafael Moreno. She did her darnedest to focus on only Cameron, but as he walked by her she found it impossible to not be aware of the pull of his green eyes, the angular shape of his smooth, golden features, and the sheer masculine force of his presence.

To cover up her confusion over this odd discomfort, she nearly asked tartly if it was okay for her to do an internal exam now, but resisted the urge. She was pretty certain that antagonizing him would just ratchet up this peculiar sizzle between them, and whether it was animosity or something else, Gabby wasn't sure anymore.

Rafael left her to monitor Cameron's labor progress and take care of her, checking in only occasionally, which Gabby was glad about on more than one level. She couldn't deny feeling pleased that he'd obviously come to trust she knew what she was doing, then inwardly scolded herself for that. He should have assumed she was competent at her job, not the other way around, especially knowing James Rothsberg and what he demanded of everyone who worked at the clinic he'd founded.

Rafael not hovering around the room, monitoring everything she did, was another good thing, though why she kept finding him so distracting she had no idea. The man was an expert at turning his charm on and off at will.

"How long is this going to take, for heaven's sake? I thought she was coming soon." Cameron's voice had gotten steadily more frustrated as her contractions got closer together, and Gabby prayed for both their sakes she was close to being ready to push.

"Your baby has a mind of her own already, Cameron, doesn't she?" she said, keeping her voice light. "First she's in a hurry, then she takes her time." A bit like her mother. "The good news is her heart rate looks perfect on the moni-

tor. Let me check your dilation again. Looks like the epidural is keeping you comfortable, isn't it?"

"I guess. If you can call starving to death comfortable." Cameron sighed dramatically as she crunched another of the tiny round ice cubes Gabby had replaced in her cup three times now. "You'd think that with modern medicine, giving birth could be completely pain-free."

"A few decades back, women were given morphine and scopolamine to put them into a twilight sleep. They'd hallucinate, then not remember the birth at all afterwards. I don't know about you, but I'd want to remember forever the moment my baby arrived in this world."

It wasn't the kind of memory she'd wish on anyone, but it was still hers. To rail against, to shrink from, to cherish.

She could see him as clearly as if he were even now in her arms. Stillborn. One simple word that perfectly described a lifeless infant.

Motionless. Quiet. Angelic and beautiful.

Every detail of that day was burned into her very soul. And she prayed it wasn't a memory Cameron would ever have to share.

"I suppose," Cameron said grudgingly. "So, how many centimeters dilated am I?"

Grateful for the distraction, Gabby checked and was surprised and more than happy at what she found. "Guess what? You're at ten centimeters and fully effaced. Time for baby to come into the world."

"Oh, my gosh—really? Don't you need to call Rafael? What if she comes out before he gets here?"

Gabby wanted to remind Cameron that she was a qualified midwife, fully capable of delivering a baby on her own, but managed to keep her mouth shut. Besides, she'd

be lying if she didn't admit she kind of wanted to see Rafael at work. "I'll give him a call right now."

"No need. I'm here," a deep voice said, and Gabby glanced up to see Rafael looking relaxed yet wired, obviously ready to get to work. "I had a feeling your little *bebé* had finally made up her mind."

"That's because you and I are *simpatico*, don't you think? How much longer?"

"Time to be the strong woman you are and get pushing with the next contraction, *si*?"

Cameron nodded, and Gabby was surprised at how quickly her next contraction came. Rafael was calmly encouraging as long minutes passed, stretching into a half hour, with their patient becoming more frustrated and impatient with each push.

"My friend had her baby sucked out with something. Can't you just do that?" she gasped.

"Ah, 'sucked out.' That's a funny way to put it, though accurate, I suppose." Across their patient, his amused eyes met Gabby's and she felt her lips curving. "But it is not a good idea to use the vacuum on a premature infant, and you're doing well. Isn't she, Gabriella?"

"Wonderful. Just remember to breathe with the next push, okay?" She reached for Cameron's hand, stroking it. "Puff, puff, puff. In and out. Tuck down your chin when you push to give it some extra oomph, okay?"

"Extra oomph." Rafael's laughing eyes met hers again. "You Americans use amusing words. I must take notes."

"Well, do it some other time," Cameron said tartly. "I'm more interested in getting this baby out than helping you write a thesaurus of American words."

"Just trying to distract you from your hard work, Cameron. Another push now, please."

He turned those green eyes back to their patient and

Gabby realized she'd been briefly mesmerized—again—
by that gaze. She glanced at the monitor wrapped around
Cameron's belly as she pushed again, and the reading
jerked her mind back to work. "Fetal monitor is showing
a decreased variability, Dr. Moreno."

He glanced at it, too, and his expression turned serious.
"Keep an eye on it during the next contractions."

"What? What does that mean? Is something wrong?"
Cameron nearly moaned the questions as she pushed again.

"Baby's heartbeat is a little flat. But that may just mean
she's sleeping."

"Sleeping? How could she possibly be sleeping when
she's about to be born?"

"She's warm and cozy inside her mama, and also tiny
because she is early. So sleeping is a possibility, though I
agree it seems odd that babies sometimes are sleep before
being born, doesn't it?"

His eyes met Gabby's, and she read the message in
their serious depths. He wanted her to pay close attention
to the monitor, and she gave him a small nod. She pressed
the intercom around her neck as she watched the baby's
heartbeat. "I'll give Neonatal a quick call to get them here
and ready."

As Gabby spoke soothingly and encouragingly, Rafael
interrupted. "Baby's head is crowning, Cameron! Not too
much longer now. You are doing such a good job."

"Yes, a few more good pushes and hopefully she'll be
here! Tuck that chin in again and give us another push,
okay?" Gabby wiped Cameron's forehead at the same time
she glanced again at the monitor and froze for an instant.
"Heart rate's flat on the monitor, Dr. Moreno."

"Stop pushing, Cameron," he said in a sharp tone.

"Stop?" The woman looked at him, her tired eyes wide.

"What do you mean? I thought you said her head was crowning!"

"The cord is around her neck. I need to get it off before she can arrive."

CHAPTER THREE

CAMERON LET OUT a long cry full of dismay and fear, and Gabby held her hand tighter. "Hang in there, Cameron. Rafael's getting his fingers under the cord."

Gabby kept her voice calm and quiet but her chest squeezed hard when she saw the cord wasn't just around the baby's neck, it was wrapped round a full three times between her collarbone and her tiny chin. Dear God, this was the last thing a preterm newborn already bound to be in distress should go through.

Throat tight, she watched Rafael carefully wiggle his fingers between the cord and the baby's neck. Gabby was pretty sure she didn't breathe at all as the long, tense seconds passed while he worked gently to loosen it.

"What's happening?" Cameron asked in a high-pitched voice. "Is...is she okay? Oh, God."

"Working on it. Hold on."

His fingers finally loosened the cord enough to slip it over the baby's head, and air spilled from Gabby's lungs in a relieved whoosh. "Cord's clear now, Cameron. Get ready."

"Looks like she's been doing synchronized swimming in there to get so tangled up," Rafael said as he flashed a quick grin.

How he managed to look so completely collected,

Gabby wasn't sure, and hoped she always exuded the same calm confidence whenever she had to deal with a tricky situation. "Rafael has her head and shoulders now. One more big push, okay?"

"Good. Perfect. And…here she is!" Rafael had the infant in his hands, his dazzling smile lighting up the room as he held her. "You were *magnifico*! *Bravo!*"

Gabby quickly laid a towel on Cameron's chest so Rafael could briefly place the baby there for Cameron to see her for just a moment as the neonatal team swooped into the room. Cameron looked down at the tiny little face, not a good color yet, still too purple, but Gabby's heart lifted when she saw the infant was already pinking up.

"My sweet precious," Cameron whispered. Two wide eyes stared back at her, and the new mother promptly burst into noisy tears that pulled hard at Gabby's heart. "I love you so much. Please be okay. Please be healthy and normal and not damaged because I didn't eat enough and worked too much and squeezed my belts too tight when you were growing. Worrying about myself instead of you. Please, Skye. Please be the perfect angel I dreamed you would be."

Skye. Cameron had airily claimed she had no idea what she'd name her baby, but Gabby had always suspected she just hadn't been ready to share it. And as she looked at the tiny, scrawny baby's blue eyes, she got choked up herself, knowing so well the guilt Cameron felt. Worries she hadn't shared with Gabby. And she understood. Because she, too, didn't share her guilt with anyone.

Skye was exactly the right choice for the new life in front of her. A pure and precious gift, like any baby was to its mother. Even those who never had their chance to grow up.

"Skye is a beautiful name." Gabby gently wiped Cameron's perspiring brow once more, thinking how the woman

looked more beautiful at that moment than all the times her makeup was immaculate and her hair perfectly done by her professional stylists. Having worked so hard to bring her baby into the world, she looked vulnerable and scared and more like a real person than Gabby had ever seen her—not at all the ultra-confident screen persona and diva actress she projected to the world most of the time.

For a moment, she let herself watch a little longer. To see Skye whisked to the heat lamp by the neonatal team, a bulb suction quickly clearing her nose before the small oxygen mask was placed over her head. To marvel at the little body being cleaned up and swaddled tight as Gabby would have done if the baby hadn't had the stress of the cord scare added to her being so premature.

Then she didn't want to watch anymore. She turned to focus back on Cameron and caught Rafael's eye. An eye that seemed to be searching right into her very soul, seeing far too much, and she quickly turned away from that unnerving green gaze.

"She is so beautiful, Cameron," she said, wishing her voice wasn't tight with unshed tears. "Hard work bringing her into the world, I know. But now she's here, you can spoil her rotten."

"Yes," Cameron said in a wobbly voice as she watched the neonatal team take Skye from the room to the NICU. "Yes, I plan to do just that."

"You did great," Rafael said. "I'm not surprised that the real Cameron Fontaine is even more of a warrior than the parts you play." The smile he gave the actress looked so sincere, Gabby wasn't sure if he meant it or if he was as good an actor as their patient.

"Thank you," Cameron said, but without the preening

she usually responded with when given a compliment. "But what if she's not all right?"

"No worries until we have to worry, right? What is it you Americans say? Don't borrow trouble?" Another flash of white teeth. "I will get you fixed up, then we'll see if we can sneak you in to see your *bebé*, and ask the doctors how she is doing. Okay?"

Cameron simply nodded, her lip trembling, and Gabby wanted to distract her from her worries. Maybe distract herself a little too. "You must be hungry after all that hard work. How about I get you a bite to eat? What sounds good?"

"Just crackers or something. And maybe juice. Do you have orange juice?"

"You want it, we've got it." Which was pretty much true, as the clinic had more different kinds of food and drinks to offer patients than the biggest restaurant in L.A.

Trying to think about food instead of everything else occupying her mind, Gabby could hear Rafael's deep voice chatting with Cameron as she left the room. She'd already seen he was good with patients, seeming to know when they needed to be firmly told what to do, and when they needed comfort or distraction instead. And, yes, she'd also seen he wasn't *all* arrogant, full of himself princely fluff. That might be a part of him, but there was no denying he was an excellent medical doctor too.

Which, dang it, were all unfortunate realizations, because it had been much easier to ignore the man's overwhelming mojo when she'd thought he was just a handsome, royal jerk.

She concentrated on figuring out what might appeal to Cameron, to focus on *work*, which was how she always coped when something happened to yank her back in time. But how could she deny that concentrating on

Rafael Moreno for a moment instead was an awfully appealing distraction?

Promising herself she wouldn't look at said distraction as she walked back to the room with a tray, she stopped dead in the doorway. For one heart-stopping moment she thought Rafael and Cameron were in an embrace, and she stared as a horrifying thought followed. Which was that the man was taking advantage of his beautiful patient at a vulnerable time.

Then her heart jerkily started up again when she realized that Cameron was sobbing, tears streaking down her cheeks as she rested her head against Rafael's broad shoulder, her hands clutching his scrub shirt. That his large hand gently stroking her damp hair back from her face was meant to comfort and soothe. Soft and beautiful Spanish words were coming from his beautifully shaped lips, and though Gabby's knowledge of the language wasn't as good as it should have been, she recognized them as words of praise and reassurance.

Oh. My. In her years as a midwife, working with doctors of all kinds, she'd seen many who were wonderful with patients. But this? This was something entirely new to her experience. This man was one lethal combination of excellent medical skill, patient care, and soothing empathy, with movie-star good looks on top of it all.

A sudden vision of his big, tanned hand pushing back her own hair, cupping her jaw before lowering those sensual lips to hers nearly stopped her breath. At that moment, he seemed to realize she'd come just inside the door and looked up. Still holding Cameron, patting her shoulder, his attention somehow seemed to be one hundred percent on Gabby as his eyes met hers. His lips curved in a slow smile, and his head inclined toward her ever so slightly in

a subtle but obvious compliment. Giving her his respect and silent kudos that he thought she'd done a good job.

Somehow she managed to break that mesmerizing eye contact, breathe, and get her feet moving to the side of the bed. Her heart pounded hard in her ears, but thank heavens he couldn't hear it. Could he?

She shook her head at herself and tried to keep her attention on just Cameron, but that was nearly impossible since her face was buried in Rafael's neck, and she was hanging on to him like a barnacle to a rock. "I brought you a few different things to eat." Other than Rafael. Gabby found herself momentarily distracted, wondering how, exactly, his neck smelled. Tasted. She'd bet pretty darned good on both counts. "Try a few, and if you think of something else you'd like to have, I'll be happy to get it for you."

Cameron slowly eased away from Rafael, her hands releasing his scrub shirt to swipe at the tears on her face. Rafael reached for a tissue to hand her and she gave him a grateful smile. "Thank you. Both of you. You've been just wonderful to me through all this, and I really, truly appreciate it."

"It has been a privilege to be a part of it, Ms. Fontaine." Rafael stood from his position by the bed. "I need to make a few notes and talk to the pediatrician about when we can see *bebé*. I'll be right back."

Gabby watched Cameron dig into her food with surprising gusto, considering how emotional she'd been a moment ago, and how she'd mostly picked at her food before then. "I'm glad you're eating. It'll help you get your strength back faster."

"I'd thought I'd felt starved before, all the times I'd hardly eaten, trying to stay skinny to get into my costumes. But this time I'm honest to goodness famished!"

"Anything else you want, just let me know."

"I want to see Skye." She put the fork down and tears welled in her eyes again. "Rafael said he'd get me there as soon as possible."

"I'm sure they'll let you go to see her very soon. They know how important it is for a new mother to be with her baby."

"I hope so." Cameron sighed, and this time it sounded less worried and more dreamy. "Rafael's the sweetest, isn't he? Just wonderful. Gorgeous. Edible."

Edible? Apparently, Gabby wasn't the only one who'd had that passing thought. Then immediately had a vision of Cameron nibbling on the man's sexy lips. Lips she couldn't deny any woman would like a taste of.

Was Cameron planning on making a play for him once she was out of the hospital? Gabby had to wonder if he'd be more than happy to take the A-list actress up on anything she might offer. Then again, she'd just given birth, so they wouldn't...

She drew herself up short and stuffed down those ridiculous and plain awful thoughts. What in the world would make her start thinking about the sex lives of either one was beyond her. She didn't do relationships anymore. Sex either, and maybe that was why it had come to mind at all. It had been a long time and, hey, she was only human, right? What warm-blooded woman wouldn't think about sex at least briefly when sharing the same air as Rafael Moreno?

Thankfully, the man entered the room at that moment, so she didn't have to respond to Cameron's comment. Or maybe she wasn't thankful, because her wayward thoughts sent her gaze straight to his lips and, yes, she couldn't deny they looked very edible indeed. She quickly moved her attention to the bronze color of his throat visible in the V of

his scrubs, then on to the broad, powerful chest stretching his scrub shirt taut.

His eyes met hers with something unnerving glimmering in that startling green, and she had that *can't breathe* feeling again. Lord, did he know, somehow, she'd been thinking about his nibble-worthy lips?

"Has our patient had a bite to eat?" he asked in a low, rumbling voice meant for Gabby's ears only. Also meant to make women swoon, if the shivers currently skittering down Gabby's spine were any indication.

"Um, yes." Gabby cleared her throat. "Did NICU say she could see Skye now?"

"*Sí.* They've given us the green light, and transport is coming to get her as we speak." He turned to smile at Cameron, speaking louder now. "Ready to see your beautiful girl now?"

"Yes, I'm so ready!" Cameron shoved aside her food. "Is she okay? Is she going to be fine?"

"Be prepared that she is in an incubator, being given extra-special care. So don't be scared when you see that a few tubes are attached to her. The neonatal specialist will talk with you, but I can tell you she is optimistic."

Gabby noted that he stopped short of committing to the baby being fine, which was wise, considering how premature Skye was and the multiple wraps of the umbilical cord around her little neck. He moved to the bed to pat Cameron on the shoulder again, leaving his backside turned to Gabby's view. A tight, prime backside that filled out his scrubs all too well. Not that she was looking.

"Well, what's taking them so long to come get me so I can see her?"

Gabby hadn't thought she'd ever welcome Cameron's demanding tone, but this time she was glad to hear it. Far

preferable to how upset and vulnerable-sounding she'd been earlier.

As if her imperious voice had commanded it, transport arrived seconds later. Gabby moved to help Cameron down from the bed into the wheelchair, but to her astonishment Rafael simply lifted their patient up and gently deposited her in it, as though she weighed little more than her newborn.

"Are you coming with me, Rafael?" Cameron asked, clutching his arm. Her blue eyes were wide and imploring, and her lips were quivering again. Gabby had spent a lot of hours with Cameron, and had a sneaking suspicion the woman was pulling out her acting skills.

Curious to see how Rafael would react, Gabby nonchalantly glanced at him out of the corner of her eye.

"I will join you as soon as Gabriella and I finish up here."

It must have been Cameron's exhaustion that had her simply nodding instead of arguing. An evil part of Gabby that she hadn't even known was inside her had her smiling, wondering how Cameron would react if she said, *I'll join you and Rafael as soon as possible too!*

Then felt horribly guilty about that when Cameron reached for her hand, holding it until the transport guy had to stop wheeling her. "You've been so wonderful in every way, taking care of me and my little Skye long before she was born, and I'm so grateful. I hope you know that."

"Oh, Cameron." The sweet words touched her, especially coming from someone who'd seemed oblivious to many of Gabby's ministrations throughout these long hours. "It's been my pleasure and honor. And of course I'll be checking on you and Skye while you're still here at the clinic."

Cameron squeezed her hand, and she squeezed back

just before the wheelchair moved on out of the room. She thought of the new mother seeing her baby again, touching her small body through the incubator ports, and knew exactly how overwhelming that maternal love felt. The only kind of forever love, no matter what the circumstances.

She turned to see Rafael Moreno studying her, his eyebrows twitched together questioningly. She wondered what he was seeing, and put on a bright smile. "Congratulations, Dr. Moreno! You dealt with everything very impressively. So scary that the cord was wrapped around her neck three times—I've rarely seen that. She pinked up fast, though, so I think you got it handled before she'd suffered any oxygen deprivation."

"I hope so. We'll see what the blood gases show."

"Are you worried?" The man looked oddly serious, and Gabby wondered for a second if he'd seen something more alarming than she had.

"No. I agree with you that she looks remarkably good, considering everything. But I owe you an apology."

"For what?" The intense way he was staring at her made her stomach feel strangely twisty and her skin warm and tingly. Hoping he wouldn't notice, she tried for a joke. "Telling me I'm a lousy housekeeper?"

A slight smile alleviated some of the ultra-seriousness from his face. "Yes. And also that I implied you were incompetent."

"Less of an implication than a statement, Dr. Moreno. I believe you said the condition of the room was obvious evidence you had to take control of my ward and care of my patient."

"And I was wrong. Something that rarely happens." His smile grew wider. "I have seen you are excellent at what you do, both with patient care and medical care. I was glad to have you working with me today, keeping me

informed of the variables on the monitor, which had me looking for complications when baby's head had barely crowned. Cameron and Skye have much to thank you for."

"Well." What was it about this man that sent her breathing haywire with a simple compliment? Or was it more the way those green eyes caught and held hers? "I appreciate you saying that. And I've seen you are an excellent doctor."

And wasn't standing there giving one another kudos beyond awkward? Gabby quickly turned to tidy the room. "I'd better get to that housekeeping before you report me to James," she said lightly, hoping to get back the equilibrium he seemed to throw out of whack every time she was near him.

"What I will report to James is that you are exceptional at dealing with patients like Cameron Fontaine. He did well to hire someone like you for a clinic catering to the rich and famous."

A club he doubtless belonged to very comfortably. "Thank you again. Likewise." Fumbling with the equipment, she managed to drop the suture kit, and items skittered in every direction across the floor.

Lord. She crouched to gather everything, feeling like a teenager hanging out with the high school football star, utterly clumsy and tongue-tied. When would the man leave so she could finish and go home to finally get more than a couple of hours' sleep? Maybe then her brain would function better around Rafael Moreno, instead of strangely short-circuiting.

Then she had a complete brain freeze when he crouched next to her, his thick shoulder bumping hers as he helped her to pick things up. "Do I make you feel nervous, Gabriella? If so, I'm sorry."

The soft rumble of his voice drew her gaze to his. She couldn't move as she stared at the closeness of his lips. At

the sculpted cheekbones and jaw. At the interesting gold and brown flecks within the green staring back at her. As she breathed in the scent of him—a mix of masculinity and antiseptic soap that on him smelled so sexy, her mouth went dry.

"Nervous? No, of course not."

"I think that's a lie. That needs to change, though, as it looks like we'll be working together for the foreseeable future. So we will have dinner together, and you can educate me more about how the clinic and the maternity ward run." He dropped the items onto her tray, then gently stroked his fingertip beneath her eye. "See if you can get in a short nap before your shift ends. That's at six, *si*? I'll be back here at seven."

Before she could formulate a single response to his astonishing suggestion he was gone, leaving her to stare openmouthed after him. When she'd gathered her wits, she stood and studied herself in the mirror, twisting her lips as her finger slowly traced the skin he'd just touched. Nothing like being told, basically, that you looked like a baggy-eyed wreck.

A wreck completely unready for a dinner date with a prince.

CHAPTER FOUR

Rafael studied the woman sitting across from him, nearly smiling as he watched the gusto with which Gabriella attacked her meal. No Hollywood starlet starving herself here, or one of the many jet-setting socialites he knew who ate as little as possible to save their calories for a martini or three. Not that she wasn't every bit as beautiful as those kinds of women, just harder working, spunky, and no-nonsense. Far more down to earth than the women he usually dated.

How had he never noticed the appeal of a woman like Gabriella?

"I trust that your dinner was tasty enough to overcome your doubts about sharing it with me?" he asked.

"I'm sure you've noticed that I'm practically licking my fork, and it's so yummy I'm not even embarrassed about that. So you know the answer is yes."

"Good. James recommended this restaurant, and I'm happy it lives up to its billing. And also happy that I now know the best way to persuade you is through your stomach."

"As opposed to your overbearing insults of the past?" The twinkle in her light brown eyes belied the words, which he hoped meant they'd sent their first impressions of one another into the past. "And the recent one too. And

here I thought you were supposed to be a suave sophisti-
cate with a vast knowledge of women."

"What makes you think I'm not?"

"No smart man wanting a woman to go on a dinner
date tells her she should take a nap first because she has
bags under her eyes. Then at dinner implies she's making
a pig of herself."

He had to laugh. "I apologize profusely if that was how
my words came across. Even after several long days of
work, you still look amazingly beautiful. And as for the
pig part, if that is you, it's now my favorite type of creature. Watching you take pleasure in your dinner has made
mine that much more enjoyable."

Even in the candlelight he could see her luminous skin
turn pink, which was something else attractive about her.
He couldn't think of another woman he knew who would
blush at a simple compliment.

"Thank you. For the dinner and the flattery. Both of
which have me wondering why you invited me here tonight. What exactly are you wanting from me?"

What did he want from her? He'd thought it was simply
a cordial working relationship, learning from her the nu-
ances of how The Hollywood Hills Clinic worked. But her
words suddenly had him thinking about something entirely
different, and his body stirred with a surge of testosterone.

There had to be legions of men who reacted to her the
same way. He had to wonder if she had a man in her life. If
she didn't that would be surprising, but perhaps he'd caught
her between boyfriends. Except he couldn't be "catching"
her at all, since the whole reason he was in L.A. was to
steer clear of women and keep his face out of the papers
until the heat from his parents cooled off. Their attitudes
annoyed the hell out of him, but he still cared about them.

It was probably part of his duties as a son to avoid giving either one of them apoplexy.

"All I want is for us to work well together, the way we did with Cameron this afternoon. And to learn a little about the clinic from you." He stuffed down the wayward thoughts pushing him to ask about her personal life and sent her a smile he hoped was blandly professional. "Tell me why you became a midwife and where you trained."

"I'm from a family of several generations of midwives, which isn't as common here in the U.S. as in some other countries. I always knew that was what I wanted to do. Trained at a nursing school, then a midwifery program near Seattle, which is where I'm from."

"And you came here after training?"

"No. I worked at a private midwifery unit there for quite a while. Came here two years ago."

Was he imagining the shuttering of her eyes? That the relaxed smile on her face just moments ago had stiffened into something else? "Was it the appeal of working with famous people that drew you here?" He didn't think so—she just didn't seem like the type to care about that, but it wasn't as though he really knew her.

"No. They'd approached me a few years before I came, then I…decided I wanted a change, and let them know I was available. How about you?" Her brown eyes held something—sadness maybe?—along with a clear determination to change the subject. "I have to admit it's surprising to me that someone born a prince would decide to become a doctor."

"Unless that prince is the second born. My parents saw my role within the kingdom as leading charity work, and while that's worthwhile, I felt there were plenty of others who would happily take on that job. I wanted a career helping people in my own way, and my parents never under-

stood that. Also, they got very annoyed the times I ducked out of various superficial royal duties."

"What kind of royal duties?"

"Number one would be cutting a ribbon for the grand opening of a museum or concert hall or school. I was taught from a young age how to keep my scissors sharp."

He was glad she laughed at his joke, but there was a nugget of truth to it. His parents couldn't fathom why he'd become a doctor, and Gabriella no doubt wouldn't be able to understand that attitude, since she was a medical professional too. God knew, he'd spent years trying to figure out why they disapproved of him and his choices, and he had finally given up worrying about it.

"Since you could be anything you wanted to be, how did you decide to go into medicine?"

"From the time I was small, I was fascinated with anatomy, dissecting worms and frogs with my tutors. Later, I insisted on studying the animals butchered on our land to feed the royal household and its guests, much to my mother's horror."

Her dazzling, real smile came back, lighting the darkness of their corner table. "I can imagine that might be alarming. Did she think you might grow up to be an axe murderer?"

"Probably. Or, worse, a livestock farmer. Facing the options of her son's occupation being murderer, farmer, or doctor, she reluctantly accepted the latter."

"A wise woman. So how did you decide to become an OB/GYN? Or is that something personal I don't want to know?"

Her soft laughter had him staring at her mouth, and he wished that, just once, he could taste it. Just to see if it was as soft and sweet as it looked like it would be. "My reputation isn't as bad as you might have heard, so it's not the

reason you're thinking. You of all people should know the amazement and joy of assisting a new life. I had that experience totally by accident, when I was visiting a sheikh friend whose wife went into labor unexpectedly. Being there with my friend and his wife to bring their newborn into the world was such an amazing experience, I knew that was what I wanted to do."

"That's a wonderful story. You could have just spent your life traveling the world in search of fun, but instead want to make a difference in people's lives. I really respect that."

The way her eyes shined at him in genuine admiration had him nearly confessing to the many failings he was all too guilty of, but letting her think he was wonderful was far preferable. "I went to medical school with James Rothsberg. We learned what hard work and drive could accomplish, no matter which world you're born into." Especially when that world always looked to find the worst in you, instead of the best. Set examples he had no interest in following, like tethering yourself to a permanent marital relationship for no reason other than convenience.

Her expression turned even more admiring, and as she opened her mouth to ask another question he realized he'd already said too much in terms of true confessions for the night. "Would you care for coffee? How about a look at the dessert menu? I'm guessing you're still not quite full."

"Again, your comment could be interpreted as an insult instead of an offer. But I'll let it slide, since I did put teeth marks on my spoon."

"And the price of a replacement spoon will doubtless be added to the bill, but just this once I'll take care of it. So, dessert?"

"No, thank you." Her fingertips covered a small yawn that morphed into a big one, until she laughed about it.

And what was more adorable than a woman who could poke fun at herself? "I'm sorry, but I'm really, really tired. Worked several double shifts, then stayed with Cameron for the past two days. And she needed a thing or two over all those hours that interrupted my dozing."

"I can only imagine," he said dryly, picturing Cameron wanting any number of luxuries as she'd lain in that bed. "And can also imagine you giving her the best of care, regardless of the way it was requested."

"Do I deserve all that credit if I was sometimes secretly irritated in the midst of it?" Her grin was interrupted by another yawn, this one audible. "Oh, my gosh, I'm so sorry. I need to get home to sleep."

"Yes, you do." He quickly scribbled on the check and rose to take her elbow, helping her from the chair to guide her out the door. It was apparent she'd been pushing herself past her limit for days, and he was struck with a sudden, surprising desire to take care of her. A wish that he was close enough to her to have the right to tuck her into bed for a long, well-deserved rest.

But he wasn't and couldn't be. Problem was, only moments after she settled into the leather seat of his car, she fell fast asleep.

So what was he supposed to do now? He drove toward the clinic, the original plan being to drop her off so she could drive her car to her own home. If he had any idea where that was, he would simply drive her there himself. But he didn't have a clue if she lived east or west or north or south of the clinic.

He glanced at her for the tenth time, noting the way the peach-blonde fire of her hair had slipped across her face. Tangling in her long lashes, the silken strands caressed her cheekbones and lay across the corner of her lush lips. Pulling to a stop in the clinic lot, he reached over to gen-

tly smooth her hair back, letting his fingers linger on the softness of both her cheek and hair.

"Gabriella? Gabby?" For the first time he used her nickname and found he much preferred her given name, which he'd enjoyed the sound of the moment it had first rolled off his tongue. *Gabriella.* It suited her. Beautiful and feminine. Strong and intelligent. "Wake up. Do you want me to take you home, instead of you driving there? Where do you live?"

No response at all. Just the sound of gentle breathing through slightly parted lips. He did the usual things. Shook her slender shoulder. Asked the same questions louder. And when she still slept like an angel, he made up his mind.

Instead of rousing her enough to get her in her car to drive home, possibly still dangerously half-asleep, he'd take her to his house and tuck her into one of the comfortable guest suites. That way, she'd be sure to get the long sleep she obviously desperately needed. After all, it was his fault she wasn't already in bed, having insisted she dine with him tonight.

Hopefully the paparazzi weren't lurking around the house he was renting. He was pretty sure they'd only watched him the first couple of weeks after he'd arrived in L.A., then moved on to more exciting prey when he'd behaved himself.

He studied her delicate profile. Her straight nose and a slightly stubborn jaw that suited her. The appealing dip above her pretty lips, soft and sweet in sleep. Yes, getting her to his house was the best way to handle the situation. Gabriella would sleep well and be grateful in the morning, ready to tackle her day at work with her usual energy.

But, a little later, as he swung her soft, warm body into his arms, carrying her fast asleep into the house, that surge of testosterone hit him even harder than before. The

feel of her sweet curves pressed against him shortened his breath and sent his heart rate into double time, and neither had anything to do with the exertion of carrying her dead weight. It was then he realized, too late, the big downside of his decision.

Gabriella would get a good night's sleep. But he had a feeling she'd be the only one in the house who did.

The sensation of silky-soft sheets and light, cozy down wrapped Gabby in a snug cocoon as her senses slowly came to consciousness. Feeling more comfortable than she'd ever felt in her life, she lay there in tranquil warmth, a small smile on her face. Feeling wonderful. Feeling indulged and pampered, but why that was, she wasn't sure.

Her palms slowly stretched across the linens, over the fluffy comforter enveloping her, eventually wrapping her arms around herself, savoring the sensation.

Where was she? Not in her little apartment. On a vacation in some exotic place? No, she hadn't been vacationing. Obviously this was some hedonistic dream and she'd be waking soon.

Somehow she managed to crack open her heavy eyelids. And realized it wasn't a dream. She really was in this ridiculously comfortable bed, but where that bed was, she had no clue.

Abruptly, her eyelids shot wide open and, heart tripping, she sat up, trying to get her eyes accustomed to the darkness. Trying to figure out whether or not her beautiful, comfortable dream was really some horrible nightmare.

And realized this was, for certain, most definitely not her bed. So whose was it? Dragging in a rattling breath, she uttered an involuntary shriek and leapt out of the bed, blindly stumbling toward the shadowy door she thought she could see across the room. Fumbling with the latch,

she yanked it open, through it into freedom, only to smack right into something large looming across the threshold.

Something hard but smooth. Something warm to the touch, with a rough covering that felt like hair. Something immovable that grasped her arms, holding her. Imprisoning her.

A full-fledged scream tore from her lips. "Let me go!" She writhed to free herself from the monster, to no avail. "Let. Me. Go!"

"Good Lord, Gabriella." The words were tense but soft as the hold on her loosened. "It's me, Rafael. Please stop screaming. It's all right."

Another scream about to rip from her throat, she blinked up to see a sculpted jaw, and though the mouth above it was tightened into a thin line, they were obviously the sensually shaped lips of Rafael Moreno. Relief had her sagging against him. "Oh, my heavens. I woke up and… didn't know where I was." And still didn't, and that realization brought her fully alert. "So…what in the world happened? Where am I?"

"In my home. You were sound asleep in my car. In a near coma really—I couldn't rouse you."

His lips had softened into a smile, and his eyes gleamed at her through the darkness. The bizarreness of the situation finally sank in, and she started to get suspicious then angry. What grown woman would fall asleep so completely she wouldn't wake up when someone tried to, as he'd said, "rouse" her?

She realized her palms were pressed flat against his hard pectorals and soft, hair-roughened skin. Heat seemed to pump from that wide, masculine chest, enveloping her and making it hard to breathe. She yanked her hands off like she'd touched the sun, flinging them to her own chest to do a quick check of what exactly she was—or wasn't—

wearing, then jerked out of his hold completely. Relief that she still had on the clothes she'd worn on their dinner date didn't temper the anger making her start to physically shake.

"I can't believe you brought me here, then inside your house to…to put me in bed like a child. Why would you do that? I thought for a minute you must have drugged me or something. And…and taken advantage of me."

Infuriatingly, instead of looking contrite or insulted, his arrogantly amused smile widened. "Believe me, *belleza*, I don't have to drug women for them to wish to come home with me, nor do I have to take advantage of them. They are, instead, quite happy to take advantage of me."

She parted her lips to say something caustic in response, but nothing came out. Because she'd just realized he stood there not only shirtless but was wearing only boxers on his bottom half. Boxers that hung low on his hips, and even in the darkness she could see the ripples of muscles across his middle and the big, sculpted quadriceps of his legs beneath the hem that stopped well above his mid-thigh.

It had been a long time since she'd been with a man. And never one with so much potent masculine appeal, it should be illegal. She sucked in a breath so she could finally talk, but unfortunately brought his scent inside her nose and nearly felt dizzy from it. "Well, I'm not one of them."

"Sadly, I'm aware of that. In fact, you've crushed my ego. Never have I had a woman fall asleep in my company unless it was after a long night of making love."

The rumble of his voice combined with his deliciously drawling accent and his inappropriate mention of lovemaking sent shivers across her skin. Or maybe she was just cold, having left the comfortable bed and the heat of his body. A peculiar tension curled through her body, and

she had an almost irresistible urge to snuggle up against that firm, warm chest, imagining how good it would feel against her.

Which was ridiculous. The man had all but kidnapped her. "I doubt if anything could crush your ego, Dr. Moreno. But now that I've woken from my *coma*, I'd appreciate it if you'd take me home."

"If you insist." The polite inclination of his head was regal, despite the fact he stood there practically naked. "But it's four a.m. and I, for one, would like to get a few more hours of sleep before work. Surely it would be best for both of us to go back to bed for a few hours."

Back to bed. What in the world was wrong with her that his words made her think of something very different from sleep? Involuntarily, a slightly hysterical giggle left her lips.

"Something amusing?"

"Just that I was thinking that, since you're a prince, you should have tried kissing me when I was asleep. I wonder if that would have worked, like in the fairy tales?"

Lord, she must be delirious. Appalled that she'd blurted her thought out loud, the feeling faded as their eyes met. His seemed to blaze at the same time his lids lowered in a look that made her quiver. "Excellent question, *bella*. Next time, I'll try that to find out, hmm?"

"There won't be a next time. But I guess you're right about it being silly to go home right now." She gulped, searching for her common sense. Time to shut down this sensual back and forth between them that she had a feeling could easily get out of control. "I'll just get back to sleep and we can leave for work in the morning. I always keep extra clothes there, anyway."

He inclined his head again. "*Bueno*. We will leave here at eight. Sleep well."

And then he was gone, taking all that heat and testosterone that had shimmered in the room with him.

Gabby shoved her fingers through her hair with a sigh and sank back into the bed, pulling the covers to her chin. She should be glad the bizarre interaction between her and Rafael was over with. Instead, she felt revitalized but at the same time there was an odd hollow in the pit of her stomach. A disappointment that he hadn't responded to her ridiculous remark about a prince kissing her awake with an actual kiss. And why had she said it, anyway? Probably because, unconsciously, she'd been thinking about it all evening as she'd stared across that candlelit table at his beautiful lips.

She flopped onto her side, trying to ignore the tense, letdown feeling around her heart, deciding not to make too much of it. The man was physically gorgeous enough to make any woman swoon, right? And she was a woman who hadn't felt much of anything for a man besides disillusionment in a long, long time.

CHAPTER FIVE

"Ready for work?" Rafael asked, breaking the silence between them as he drove them to the clinic in the powerful car she barely remembered getting into after dinner last night, which made her blush all over again. "I trust your middle-of-the-night awakening didn't interfere too much with the sleep you obviously needed."

"No, thank you. I slept well." Which was a total lie. She hadn't gotten a wink after he'd left her room, imagining how awkward it would be in his house together in the morning and on the way to work. And awkward was an understatement. She'd taken the world's fastest shower in the stunning bathroom attached to the room she'd slept in, wondering if the man might not be the gentleman he seemed but instead a prince who thought he had the right to walk in on her. Then, nervous and uncomfortable, she'd stood in his kitchen, nerves twitchy, clutching her purse and ready to go, while he'd sat relaxed, drinking coffee and having a croissant.

She'd steadfastly declined his invitation to join him, partly because she'd wanted to get going and partly because he'd had a vaguely amused expression on his face. Obviously he wasn't used to women wanting to dash out his door. She didn't doubt it was usually quite the opposite.

He swung out of the car, looking smooth and hand-

some and not even remotely tired, like she knew she unfortunately still did. She pushed open her own door, about to get out and hurry inside as fast as she could, when he appeared, holding out his hand to her, eliminating any chance of a quick escape. She tried to walk fast, but he simply kept pace with her at her side. As they walked together to the clinic's big double doors, she blushed scarlet from head to toe.

The walk of shame. This was what friends of hers had talked about in the past! Out on a date, spend the night, and show up somewhere wearing the same clothes for all the world to see. Except she hadn't even enjoyed what people would think she had, damn it. Shamed without reason.

"I'm late for work. I'll…um…see you around." She walked faster, trying to get inside and to her locker fast, praying no one had paid attention to what dress she'd worn the night before.

Rafael caught up with her. She stared straight ahead, but he dipped his head to look at her, drawing her gaze to his. To green eyes that now danced with amusement. "Are you worried people will talk, *bella*, if they see us arrive together?"

"Yes!" she hissed. "So please go wherever you need to go and goodbye."

"Not goodbye. We're seeing a patient together in twenty minutes. Until then." He reached for her hand, his eyes twinkling above it as he pressed his lips to it. She snatched it away and practically ran down the corridor toward the women's locker room. The imprint of that quick kiss still tingled on her skin, and she had a bad feeling that meant she was in for a very long day.

Freya Rothsberg, the clinic's PR guru and also James's sister, raised her eyebrows at Gabby as she tore down the hallway, and she forced herself to slow down.

"Good morning, Gabby," Freya said.

"Good morning." Was it her imagination, or was Freya's voice a little questioning? Or was she just being completely paranoid? "I...need to get into scrubs to see my first patient. Have a great day."

Finally able to hide in the locker room, Gabby flung off her dress, quickly hung it up, then got her scrubs on. Breathing a sigh of relief, she leaned against her locker door. Clearly she wasn't up for middle-of-the-night adventures, innocent or not.

Ten minutes later, she felt almost normal and composed, putting a smile on her face as she went into her patient's room. Then every ounce of composure slid away when she saw Rafael standing there, talking with the woman.

"Ah, Gabriella." His eyes met hers, and that darned twinkle still lingered, making her feel embarrassed all over again. "I hope you don't mind, but I took the liberty of seeing your patient before you arrived, as my first patient isn't here yet."

She could feel hot color rushing into her cheeks again, annoyed as all get-out at her reaction to seeing him there. Somehow she bit back the words she wanted to say, which were, *Yes, I do mind, as a matter of fact. I'm trying to stay away from you!*

"Of course not. How are you feeling, Megan?"

"Absolutely great! I was just telling Dr. Moreno that my yoga instructor is so impressed with my workouts. I mean, I'm doing every bit as much at eight months along as I did before I got pregnant."

"As long as you're feeling good when you exercise, that's very healthy for you and your baby." She made herself turn to Rafael, and the power of that green gaze nearly choked her.

"I'm sure I'll be fit enough for the minor role Daddy

has in mind for me in the film he's starting this summer. I told Rafael he should come to the set."

"Megan's father's films are among my favorite thrillers," he said. "I particularly enjoyed that scene in his last movie where one of the main guys showed up in the heroine's bedroom, and she didn't know until then that he wasn't her friend but the terrifying killer instead. Scary stuff."

The wicked glint in those green depths was both irritating and unnerving, since it sent her thoughts right back to what she'd been trying so hard not to think about. Which was the feel of his hard, warm body against hers, and how he'd looked in those boxer shorts.

"So," she said, desperately trying to change the subject, "have you examined Megan yet, Dr. Moreno?"

"I thought I'd leave that to you, along with getting her vital signs. Just wanted to introduce myself before the big day arrives."

"Surely you won't still be working here in another month, will you?" If her voice held a trace of panic, she couldn't help it. "I thought this was a brief pit stop in your life."

"I expect I will be staying a while. I'm enjoying my time in L.A. and here at The Hollywood Hills Clinic. The staff is most…interesting, and I hope to get to know everyone much better."

Gabby dropped the blood-pressure cuff on the floor, then had to take the reading twice she was so distracted by Rafael's teasing. Which she knew full well it was—for some reason, he was enjoying yanking her chain and making her blush again.

"I'm about to do your internal exam now, Megan, okay?" She turned to Rafael with a saccharine-sweet smile, hoping her narrowed eyes told him exactly how irritated

she was without showing, again, how he rattled her. "So you're free to see if your patient has arrived, Dr. Moreno."

"Why do I get the feeling the boss is tossing me out on my ear?" He turned that lethal grin on Megan. "See you next time you're in. You have my contact information if you need me."

Remarkable how the minute the man was out of the room, Gabby was able to focus on her patient and her job without dropping or forgetting a single thing. Pitiful. Which meant that, if Rafael was really going to be sticking around for a while, somehow, some way she'd have to get a handle on her ridiculous, distracted hormones.

Chuckling to himself as he walked down the hallway to see his patient, Rafael reflected on how easy it was to get under Gabriella's skin, and how much fun it was. She was such a complex mix of characteristics combined in a fascinating way, all bundled up inside a beautiful, touchable package. Sweet and smart, feisty and a little shy all at the same time, he wanted to spend more time with her. Learn a lot more about what made her tick.

He might have gotten off on the wrong foot with her initially, but he knew she found him attractive now as well. Last night when he'd held her in his hands and her wide eyes had looked up at him in the dark bedroom, he'd seen the way her lips had parted; had felt her quickened breaths skating warm and fast across his skin. The rise and fall of her chest had been less about her fear and more about sexual attraction—he knew because he'd felt the same hot vibration. Then she'd tried to cover up the zing happening between them with pretend indignation. Zing that had been a two-way street—it had taken all his *won't*-power to resist the urge to pull her closer for a kiss, to see where all that heat shimmering between them might lead.

Except he'd then figuratively smacked himself with the reminder that he was supposed to be lying low in L.A. "Behaving himself," to quote his parents, and dating "appropriate" women, whatever the hell that meant. Apparently not strippers, or those whose faces graced the gossip magazines, and why any of that was a big deal, he didn't understand.

It wasn't as though a single one of them would ever get an engagement ring from him. Seeing the various loveless marriages in his family, not to mention what James's parents' relationship had been like, Rafael figured that kind of commitment would be sheer purgatory. Why in the world would he want to handcuff himself to one woman forever if he didn't have to?

Short-term handcuffing, though? Now, that he was all for. Thinking about something short, sweet and hot with Gabriella put the smile back on his face, only it quickly faded because, damn it, he couldn't let that happen, with the media and his parents breathing down his neck.

Seeing his next patient got his thoughts back on track, and as he was about to go to the nurses' station to discuss her chart, the sound of his name on the large, wall-mounted television in the patient's room stopped him in mid-step. He looked up at the screen to see what ridiculous, untrue story was being spread on the TV gossip shows now.

To his shock, the photos were of the cliffside mansion he was renting, with two people in front of it. Pictures of him carrying a sleeping Gabriella inside, then of the two of them leaving in the morning, with sensationalized questions and speculation about who Prince Rafael Moreno's late-night booty call might be this time.

Damn it to hell. What had he just said about his parents breathing down his neck? This time they'd probably be belching pure fire. He glanced at his patient and her

nurse, glad they were too busy talking to pay attention to the stupid television. He wiped his suddenly sweaty hands on his lab coat, thankful the photos were distant and grainy enough that nobody would likely be able to figure out who the woman was. He hoped Gabriella didn't get wind of the story, and hoped even more that she wouldn't suffer any embarrassment from it. Already, he knew she wasn't the kind of woman who would appreciate being part of a media frenzy, which was one of several good reasons he'd been telling himself he had to keep his hands off her.

Anger surged into his veins on her behalf. The hard-working, exhausted woman couldn't even fall asleep in his car without untrue rumors being spread, and he wished he could contact the TV programmers with a vehement rebuttal, telling them to lay off.

But experience had taught him that kind of thing just inflamed the gossipmongers even more. With any luck, the hounds would back off when they couldn't figure out who she was, and the story would die a quick death.

For Gabriella's sake, and for his too, he hoped like hell that was exactly what would happen. Seeing the photos in his mind again as he strode from the room to update the charts, he nearly ran into Freya.

"Rafael." A smile played about Freya's lips and she lifted an eyebrow. "I hear your patients love you, so thanks for stepping in. Also sounds like you're very much…enjoying your time in L.A.?"

"Not as much as I'm given credit for, I can tell you that," he said, somehow keeping his voice cool and amused, even as his stomach felt a little queasy. "The story of your life and mine, isn't it?"

"Stories aren't always fiction." Her smile widened, and she walked away without another word.

Trying to get the annoying voice of the TV host out of

his head, along with the blurry images he hoped Gabriella wouldn't have to see, he concentrated on the computerized patient charts until his phone interrupted him.

Then he knew the day was going downhill even faster when he saw it was his mother, and his gut clenched with the certain knowledge that their palace spies had informed her of the latest gossip fest.

"*Buenos días,* Mother. It's wonderful to hear your voice." Or would be, if their conversation was going to be about the palace horses or her latest fundraiser or something else pleasant and benign, but he was pretty sure he wouldn't be that lucky.

"Rafael. What do your father and I have to do to make you understand your position in life? Your responsibilities? We might not have liked that you chose to do something like doctoring instead of accepting your traditional role here, but we have learned to live with it. That doesn't give you the right, though, to disregard your family's status completely and do whatever you wish! I thought the latest scandal had taught you that. You said that's why you went to L.A. for a while, to behave! And yet here you are, the subject of gossip again. When are you going to marry a nice girl and be done with this? When—?"

"Mother." He'd gritted his teeth and held the phone from his ear during her long diatribe, but finally managed to cut her off when she took a breath. "If you're talking about the stupid TV news, I can assure you it's nothing. I'm working for a time in James's clinic, and a co-worker and I had work to discuss. She fell asleep and…" This time he cut himself off. Why the hell should he have to defend himself to anyone, including his mother, about something completely innocent? Was it his fault he'd been second born into a royal family, and because of that was a chronic disappointment and annoyance to his parents? His fault that

the paparazzi liked to stalk him? As for getting married, she might as well save her breath, because that was never going to happen. "You know, I'm done with this conversation. Is there something else you'd like to talk about?"

"We need to get this ironed out first. If you—"

"Goodbye, Mother. Call me if you want to talk about something besides how much my being a doctor and a heathen embarrasses you."

Under normal circumstances, he would have felt bad hanging up on his mother, even when she was scolding him. But this subject had been beaten to death for months, and he'd moved here to escape the gossip his parents despised. He couldn't handle one more minute of being accused of something he hadn't done. Hadn't he been doing his best to be the outstanding representative of his country his parents wanted him to be?

Anger and frustration had him wanting to punch something, and he knew he needed a calming distraction. And the one thing that always gave him perspective and helped him remember what was really important was spending time with innocent new babies, some of whom were struggling with far more serious problems than he had. Much more important than parental disapproval and gossip and damned fabrications that shouldn't be more than an inconvenient annoyance to be ignored.

Just three steps into NICU he stopped, struck by the picture in front of him. The beautiful profile of Gabriella Cain as she sat next to Skye's incubator, her fire-streaked golden hair tucked behind her ears. Unaware that anyone was looking at her, every emotion was visible. Her eyes and lips, her posture, and the way her fingers gently stroked the infant's tiny arm exposed a mix of emotions so raw his chest tightened to see them. Sadness and anguish.

Guilt. And a longing so naked he knew this was far more than a woman simply looking at the miracle of a newborn.

What had happened to Gabriella to bring this kind of pain to her life?

He watched her for long minutes, uncertain whether to approach her with comfort or quietly leave her alone. His feet seemed to make the decision for him, and he found himself right next to her, his hand reaching to slowly stroke down her soft hair then rest on her slumped shoulder with a gentle squeeze.

She didn't react immediately. It seemed to take her a moment to emerge from whatever dark and private place she was in. Then she turned and looked up at him. Her professional mask slipped across her face, covering all that starkly haunted emotion.

"Have you come to see Skye? She's doing really well." Gabriella stood to give him room to move closer to the incubator, and his hand fell from her shoulder. But he didn't want to see the baby now as much as he wanted to be there for Gabriella. "I left Cameron a short time ago," she said. "She's resting, but asked me to check on Skye and report back. Not that she hasn't gotten reports about every fifteen minutes from various members of the nursing staff. But she isn't quite convinced that's enough."

Her smile seemed forced and it didn't banish the sadness from her eyes. He wanted to reach out to her. He wanted to hold her close and console her for whatever hurt she was holding inside. He wanted to tell her it would be okay, that all pain faded and nothing was forever. And as his eyes met her somber brown ones, he knew.

He wanted to know Gabriella a whole lot better, and to hell with lying low and living like a saint. He couldn't care about gossip or stupid photos or even his mother's embarrassment and worries. Right then, the only thing he cared

about was spending time with Gabriella and finding a way to make her smile again.

"My updates from the pediatricians have been good enough that I think we can move Skye into her mama's room," he said. "That would keep Cameron happier and save some time and footsteps by the nursing staff, don't you think?"

"Yes. But of course I don't mind checking on the baby. She's beautiful, isn't she? I'm so happy she's all right."

That wistful look crept across her face again, and Rafael found himself reaching for her hand before he even realized it. "I have a favor to ask of you."

"A favor?"

"Yes. Freya told me that all the recent high-profile operations for Bright Hope patients have the cream of L.A. society lining up to hold exclusive fundraisers, so she's asked if I can attend a charity ball. Since I'm new to Los Angeles and have no one to ask to go with me, would you please come? I'm sure you know all the great things the clinic does for people who don't have easy access to good medical care. Including pregnant women. Wouldn't attending the fundraiser together be a great way for both of us to help continue creating awareness for a good cause?"

The eyes staring at him were wide and stunned. Why, he wasn't sure, since they'd dined together the night before. Surely if she'd heard about the photo and gossip, she would have said so. Still, she just stood there, her lips parted but mute.

"Is my English not as good as I think it is? I asked if you'd attend a party with me. Did I accidentally ask you to eat worms?" he teased, hoping to get a real smile and a yes from her.

"Um, no. Your English, as you well know, is better than most who speak it as a first language." The smile she gave

him was strained, but it was a start. "But I'm afraid I can't come with you."

"Why not?"

"It just…wouldn't be right. Excuse me while I check back with Cameron."

He watched her tear from the room as though that gorgeous hair of hers was actually on fire and not just shimmering with flaming hues. He wasn't used to being turned down flat and wondered if it just might have to do with her running from the barely banked-down heat they'd shared last night.

Remembering that the whole reason he'd come to NICU had been to find some inner calm, he turned to little Skye, sweetly and innocently lying in her crib. But he wasn't really seeing her. He was seeing Gabriella's expression as she'd looked at the infant, and he knew without a doubt that whatever had caused that anguish was something she'd been carrying for too long.

Yes, he'd been given orders from headquarters—which meant his parents—to hide from the past, unwelcome limelight for a while. And maybe it would be a mistake to expose Gabriella and whatever secrets she carried to the heavy weight of that microscope along with him. But thinking about her somehow told him with absolute certainty that hiding wasn't the answer. Not for him, and not for Gabriella. It was time for both of them to put their pasts behind them, and the first steps to making that happen would take place at a certain charity ball. A ball with plenty of supporters. Allies who'd be more than happy to convince her to attend with him.

CHAPTER SIX

"Everything looks great, Freya, with baby the perfect size for a healthy fetus, four months in gestation," Gabby said, smiling. "And you look wonderful too. Your skin is positively glowing. Can I admit to being jealous?"

She'd said the words to make Freya happy, but right after she'd spoken them, the unpleasant, unexpected, and unwelcome cloud weightily slipped over her head again. Why were the memories becoming more frequent, instead of more distant? She had no idea, but dwelling on it accomplished nothing, and she did her best to shake off the gray gloom, because Freya deserved the true joy Gabby felt for her friend and employer.

"I do feel wonderful, honestly." Freya's smile was big enough to banish some of Gabby's moping and make her smile too. "Though several friends have told me to enjoy it while it lasts, because after it arrives I'll be so sleep-deprived I'll forget the baby's name."

Freya's words dashed the final remnants of gloom, and Gabby had to laugh. "Maybe not quite that much. But no matter how many times I warn new mothers that a lot of babies refuse to sleep, no one really hears it until they're living it."

"Well, either way, sleep or no sleep, I'm beyond excited." Freya sat up and adjusted her exam gown. "Half-

dressed isn't the way to talk business, but since we're both so busy I'm going to take advantage of this time alone to chat."

"About?"

"The charity ball. Rafael Moreno told me he asked you to go with him, but you told him you didn't want to." Her voice became chiding. "Really, Gabby, why in the world would you say that?"

Her stomach plunged and tightened as she stared at Freya in surprise. How was she supposed to answer that? *Oh, I find him too sexy and attractive, that's all, and my life is devoted to my work now.*

"Well, he's a little overbearing, don't you think? And arrogant."

And unbearably hot.

"I think it's confidence more than arrogance," Freya said with a smile. "But you don't have to be best friends with him, or even particularly like him, to attend the ball with him, Gabby. The purpose of the fundraiser is to raise awareness and money for the Bright Hope Clinic. When one of our own obstetricians, temporary or not, who happens to also be a *prince* attends the ball, that's news. Like it or not, that's the way the world works. Rafael pointed out to me that if the head midwife at the hospital is the prince's date for the night, that's even bigger news, and exactly the kind of public relations opportunity I'm always looking for."

How weird was it that Freya's words sent Gabby's stomach sinking in dread at the same time her chest lifted in excitement and her darned subconscious immediately imagined what kind of dress she should wear to such an event? Clearly Rafael Moreno's arrival at The Hollywood Hills Clinic had sent her sanity a little off-kilter, since she really should be annoyed that he'd gotten Freya involved,

using that kind of manipulation to get her to attend with him. Another example of the man's colossal ego!

But even if her entire body had been filled with dread instead of that peculiar mixture of emotions, it wasn't like she could say no. She believed in what the Bright Hope Clinic was doing, and if she could contribute in any way, big or small, she wanted to.

"Fine. I'll go." She hoped Freya didn't notice that her gruffly sighed answer was charged with anticipation too. After all, what woman in her right mind—or even confused one—wouldn't want to be Cinderella for just one night, attending a ball with a handsome prince?

She'd just have to be sure to leave her glass slippers buried deep in her closet at home.

When Gabby had decided to install a new top-to-bottom door mirror in her closet, she'd never dreamed that she'd be needing it to look at herself in a long gown. A gown she'd be wearing to attend a ball with a handsome prince. Gabby snorted and shook her head at herself, wondering how a grown woman could feel so wrapped up in thinking about a party and what she'd be wearing, like a teenager going to the prom. Ridiculous.

She studied the lines of her dress. Turned side to side, looked at the back, then the front again. And sighed. Because she knew full well that the majority of women attending the ball tonight would be wearing designer dresses that cost more than her month's rent, not to mention that there wouldn't be a single one there who'd made her own gown.

Filled with jitters of doubt now, she worried that maybe she shouldn't have done that. Why had she been so convinced she shouldn't just buy one off the rack? The answer was because she knew anything she could afford would be

made from substandard fabrics, compared to the glamorous, designer dresses the rich and famous would be wearing tonight. And she knew how to sew, didn't she?

Her strong, female ancestors had not only studied midwifery and spent their lives helping others, they'd been talented seamstresses. Hadn't learning at her grandmother and mother's knees given her the skills to pull this off? Staring at her dress now, she wasn't so sure. The ring of her doorbell…a loud, silly horse whinny the previous avid horseracing fan tenants had installed…made her jump. Then laugh out loud. Clearly Cinderella's carriage had arrived, except the prince was already on board, not waiting at the ball.

Resisting the urge to wipe her suddenly sweaty hands down the emerald-green fabric of her gown, she opened the front door. Then stared, her breath hitching.

She'd thought Dr. Rafael Moreno had been attractive in the scrubs that showed his strong physique? In a dress shirt and pants at the clinic, and when they'd gone to dinner? Those Rafael Morenos had nothing on this one, who exuded royal arrogance from head to toe in a tuxedo that fitted him so perfectly she knew it had to have been tailor-made for him. His shirt was so white it was practically blinding, his classic black bow tie perfectly placed beneath his strong, tanned throat. The late evening sun gleamed on his dark, glossy hair and sculpted jawline, and a slow smile curved his lips.

She gulped. There was one perfect way to describe how her body was reacting to his mouthwatering beauty.

Tuxedo libido.

She fought down a nervous giggle. How had the room gotten so warm? Clearly, May in Los Angeles meant it was time to adjust the thermostat.

"Hi," she said, knowing she sounded a little breathless,

but since she *was* breathless it was the best she could do. "I'm ready. I just need to grab my purse."

"I'm relieved, I have to say."

"That I'm ready? Is that another comment about what you think of my organizational skills?"

"No. As I drove here, I wasn't sure what to expect, having several scenarios that came to mind. In the first, I was afraid you'd open the door wearing sweatpants, planning to ditch me to lounge at home instead, since you hadn't wanted to come with me tonight."

"I wouldn't ditch you, even though you'd have deserved it if I did, since it was pretty sneaky of you to get Freya involved as your date planner. However, I always honor my commitments. Though I admit that lounging in sweatpants holds a certain appeal."

"To me as well. You would look very sexy in sweatpants."

"Uh-huh. Pretty sure sexy and sweatpants are mutually exclusive."

"Not true. I'm picturing you in them right now." Something about the way he was looking at her had her wondering exactly what he was picturing, and her breath hitched all over again. "The other, even worse scenario I envisioned was you wearing a more casual dress because you were planning to go on a date with someone else. In which case, I'd have to fight him when he came to pick you up, and my parents rarely appreciate that kind of scene."

Despite the absurd words, there was something serious in the gleam of his eyes that had her laughing in surprise. "I can't see you fighting over a woman. There are too many fish in the sea who'd fall at your feet for a date, because they don't know what a shark you are."

"But you're willing to risk a date with a shark for a good cause, hmm? And there's only one woman as beautiful and

interesting as you are. That dress is exquisite on you, by the way. My mother would be impressed with your designer."

She laughed. and at the same time a bubble of satisfaction and relief that she didn't look ridiculous filled her chest. "Don't tell anyone, but the designer is someone who works for a dress-pattern company, and I made it myself."

"You made it yourself?" The astonishment on his face was comical. "That's incredible! Beautiful, compassionate, and talented as well. Every man at the ball tonight will envy my good fortune to have you on my arm."

It was a line, she knew, but her stomach flipped inside out anyway. "They'll probably envy you for a lot of other reasons, like that whole prince thing that makes you think you can do whatever you want whenever you want." Okay, she didn't really think he was an overbearing jerk anymore, but it was probably a good idea to keep up that charade.

She also wouldn't add all the other reasons men would envy him. Like his incredible good looks and confidence and sense of humor and everything else about him that made every part of her body tingle a little. She turned jerkily to grab her evening bag from the chair, willing herself to act normal and calm. After all, this wasn't a real date. The only reason he'd asked—no, manipulated—her to join him tonight was because it was good PR for the clinic, and more publicity about the ball would result in more donations.

His grasp on her elbow was light, but Gabby still felt the warmth of it clear to her toes as he tucked her into the car. Her heart seemed to thunder as much as the car engine as it accelerated around the mountain curves. Excitement pumped through her veins, and she realized she hadn't felt this…this *alive* in a very long time. Not since her life, which she'd thought had been so steady and planned out, had been obliterated with one, selfishly bad decision.

She determinedly squelched those thoughts. No point in dwelling on something she couldn't change when she had a few hours to enjoy what she knew would be a very special evening. She stole a look at the man sitting so very close to her and he must have felt her gaze because he glanced at her with a smile that suddenly faded.

"There's one thing I must warn you about," he said, turning his attention back to the road. "I'm frequently followed by the press, looking for a juicy story. I would guess there will be photographers outside the hotel anyway, wanting to get pictures of the various stars attending this event. Some will doubtless take pictures of us too, so don't let it worry you."

"Do you often give them juicy stories?"

"If you asked my parents, they'd say yes. In fact, I'll tell you the truth. I came to stay in L.A. for two reasons. To see James and to hide from the press after an unfortunate incident."

"I can't imagine you hiding from anyone."

"I don't like to. But there are times that even I have to bow to family pressures, and this was one of them. But I've decided I don't care. That being out with you tonight is important to me—and I hope you won't let any media coverage bother you either."

"The media won't care who I am, so I'm not worried about it."

"Don't count on that."

His expression looked almost grim as he pulled the car up to the front doors of the hotel. Gabby stared in shock at the swarm of people wielding cameras and standing on both sides of the huge double doors, kept back by red velvet ropes curving between golden stanchions. A valet opened her door and in mere seconds Rafael appeared by her side, reaching for her hand. The camera flashes were so bright

and constant it was like being hit in the face with a strobe light, and she blinked and instinctively reeled back. Rafael's hand dropped hers to move to the small of her back, firm and steady. He seemed unfazed by it all, leading her forward in an even, unhurried pace until they were safely inside the hotel doors held open by employees.

"Oh, my Lord, you weren't kidding!" She stared at him. "Is it like this wherever you go?"

"Not always. When there's an event they know I'll be showing up for, yes. But sometimes, as you saw when we had dinner the other night, they're not around. Or it can seem that way, though sometimes I'm wrong about that."

As they moved farther into the room, she quickly looked around, expecting cameras to be closing in on them at that very moment. Thankfully, all she saw was a room filled with beautifully dressed men and women, all smiling and talking against the gorgeous backdrop of an old-style hotel, built in the days when Hollywood had been all glitter and gold and extravagance.

"Gabriella, there is something I need to talk to you about regarding the paparazzi," Rafael said.

She turned to him, wondering what was causing that crease between his brows, but whatever he'd been about to say was interrupted by the arrival of several people eager to talk to him. Then others. More as they wandered through the crowds, taking bites of amazing hors d'oeuvres and sips of champagne, and it was obvious that more than one woman admired her date for the night, and were looking at *her* with envy, not the other way around, as Rafael had flatteringly predicted.

"Rafael, Gabby, I see my sister nudged you into coming tonight," James Rothsberg said as he appeared next to them. Held in the curve of his arm was the stunning

woman Gabby had recently seen photographed with him in a few tabloid spreads.

"Does Freya ever nudge anyone into anything?" Rafael said with a grin. "Strong-armed is more like it, but I'm glad to be here for such a great cause, and I know Gabriella cares a lot about underprivileged children too."

"I'm so happy to be helping spread the word about the Bright Hope Clinic," Gabby said. "Not to mention getting to eat all the wonderful food here tonight." She stopped there, even though she would have liked to note that Rafael was pretty good at strong-arm tactics himself.

"Freya's a force of nature, for sure. I'm glad you were able to make it." James grinned and introduced them to his date, who seemed to study Rafael with extreme interest before glancing at Gabby.

"Such a pretty dress," she said with what looked like an oddly amused smile, and Gabby froze, wondering if it was obvious she'd made it herself. "Did you choose the color of it to go with your date's eyes? Quite a striking color."

Well, that was even worse than noticing it was homemade. Embarrassment streaked through Gabby's whole body, ending with her cheeks scorching as she realized her dress really was almost exactly the same color as Rafael's eyes. Would anyone else think she'd done it on purpose, like they were attending a high school homecoming dance together or something? Or, worse, had she chosen the fabric unconsciously thinking of his mesmerizing gaze?

"My goodness, you're right! I hadn't even noticed that," she managed to say, struggling to make her tone sound light and amused too. "My mother drummed into me that people with strawberry blonde hair like hers and mine should wear green whenever possible and avoid red so as not to look like a spark plug."

"She looks amazing in green, doesn't she?" Rafael

said smoothly, before turning to Gabby. "Though there's no possibility that tall, slender you could ever resemble a spark plug."

The seeming sincerity joining the gleam in his eyes made her blush all over again. "Thank you."

"You probably know how lucky The Hollywood Hills Clinic is to have her running the maternity ward, James. She's not only a skilled midwife, she has a way with patients that makes every one of them more than glad they're there. Thanks for giving me the opportunity to work with her."

"Gabby's the best. And you'd better not think of stealing her away to some hospital in the Mediterranean when you leave, Rafael, or I'll have to tell secrets about you that you wouldn't want shared."

Obviously just kidding, James's eyes twinkled as he spoke, but Rafael seemed a little more serious when he looked down at Gabby. "We all have secrets, don't we? Sometimes sharing them is a good thing, don't you think?"

Heart skittering, she didn't answer, wondering what he meant. Could he somehow know about her past and her mistakes?

No. Impossible. Freya knew she'd had a bad breakup before coming to work at the clinic, but not the reason for it, and that was the way Gabby wanted to keep it.

"Sometimes. But usually it's best to keep our secrets to ourselves." James's smile had flatlined too, as he and his date said their goodbyes and went to mingle with the crowd.

"Let's dance, shall we?"

Oh, goodness. Dance? Close to him? "I don't think—"

But in typical Rafael fashion he didn't wait for her to finish her answer before setting his glass on the tray of a passing waiter then wrapping his hand around hers to

move to the dance floor. When he turned to face her, his other palm slid from her waist to the small of her back. She slipped her hand up the soft fabric of his jacket to rest it on his shoulder, and her breath caught in her throat as she looked up at him.

The orchestra struck up a new tune, and they began to move. "Thank you for coming with me tonight."

"Thank you for inviting me. It's been lovely."

"Even though you didn't want to at first?"

"Even though." She wasn't about to tell him why, and at the moment that seemed unfathomable. Because being so close to him, with all that heat from his body skimming across her bare arms and décolletage, felt wonderful.

On a slow turn, he brought her close enough that her breasts brushed his chest, and he lowered his mouth closer to her ear. "So why didn't you want to, Gabriella?"

"Because you're arrogant and bossy."

"Yes. Among other things." The chandelier cast light and shadows across his chiseled face and the bow of his lips as he smiled. "I thought we worked out a few of those issues when we went to dinner together. Which reminds me, I have to tell you something."

"What?"

His smile had disappeared and when he opened his mouth to answer he hesitated. Then, to her surprise, the words that came out were, "Uh-oh," and his attention seemed to be grabbed by something behind her.

She turned to see James standing mostly hidden at the back of the room behind the band. With him, instead of his date, was Mila Brightman and even from this distance it was obvious that Mila was hopping mad about something, and giving it to James with both barrels.

"Oh, dear. What do you think is wrong?"

"I don't know. I hope it's not— Never mind." A deep

frown creased Rafael's brow as he shook his head. "I was about to tell you—"

But before he could finish, the band stopped playing and Freya stepped onto the platform to speak into the microphone about the event and why they were all there tonight. After thanking the hosts and giving some details about the Bright Hope Clinic, she advised everyone to enjoy desserts and drinks as there would shortly be a video presentation about some of the patients who'd been helped there.

"I don't know about you, but I think we've done our duty," Rafael said, leaning close to speak in her ear. "What do you say to a little dine and dash?"

"Dine and dash? Do princes do that? I have to admit the mental image of you gobbling food then furtively sneaking out the door is hard to picture." Since she hadn't seen him any way but tall, proud, and very visible, that was an understatement. "But I can't say I'd complain about leaving soon. I'm about talked out."

"You know how it is, trying to say goodbyes and exit an event like this. Takes at least another hour, so let's get the process started."

She didn't, really. If she walked out the door that second, she was quite sure not a soul would bother her, but she'd already seen the attention Rafael garnered, and could well believe he'd be stopped by half the crowd en route.

Which was exactly what happened. And each time he was stopped he took pains to draw her into the conversation. Not only did he introduce her to everyone with glowing compliments about her skills as a midwife, stating again how lucky The Hollywood Hills Clinic was to have her, there was something else in his eyes and expression as he did so.

Something that didn't seem like simple professional admiration. Instead, it felt much more personal.

That odd mix of excitement and dismay rolled around her belly all over again, which was dangerous. Yes, it was a magical night. But she couldn't let the magic of it allow her to forget. She couldn't risk a relationship with any man, even one as amazing as Rafael. And, yes, she knew a man like Rafael Moreno would want only a fling, but even that would be too much.

Why was she even thinking he'd want that, anyway? Must be the Cinderella feeling she'd had all evening, wearing a dress far fancier than she'd ever worn before, on a date with pretty much the world's most handsome bachelor prince. The feel of his big, possessive hand holding hers or resting on her lower back. The compliments. The way he looked at her for long moments as though they were totally alone.

She shook her head fiercely at herself. The man doubtless acted like that with all women at parties, and especially those on a date with him, and to read anything more into it was plain foolish. Probably flirting came to him as naturally as the charm he'd exuded all evening. As naturally as the arrogant rudeness he'd bestowed on her when they'd first met.

Any woman would be intrigued by a multifaceted man like Rafael Moreno. None of it meant a thing—not his flirting and not the googly eyes she caught herself making at him. Tomorrow she'd be wearing her scrubs again, they'd go back to their normal, cordial working relationship and tonight would be forgotten.

Trying to bring her mind back to the conversation, she watched his mouth move as he talked to friends of James he obviously knew, and the sensuality of his lips pretty much obliterated all her previous self-scolding. Her ability to converse. Her thoughts instead drifted to all wrong ones that gave her tummy a different kind of funny feel-

ing. A feeling that she'd give her next paycheck to kiss him once, just to see how it would feel. Just once. Once before the strike of midnight—was that so much to ask?

She stared in fascination as he took a sip of his drink and his tongue licked a tiny drop from his lip. And with breathless certainty she knew. The man would be one amazing kisser.

"You probably agree with that, don't you, Gabriella?"

Rafael had turned fully to her, the slight curve of his lips fading as their eyes met, and she foggily realized the people he'd been talking to had moved on. Several beats passed as they just stared at one another, and Gabby wished she had some idea how to answer him but had no clue.

His lids lowered slightly, and something hot and alive flickered inside that deep green. "You weren't listening at all, were you, *bella*?" He stepped closer, his voice a low rumble. "Something else on your mind?"

Yeah. Oh, yeah, but I'm not saying what. Except she had a bad feeling it was written in red neon on her forehead for him to see anyway. Frantically trying to come up with an answer that wasn't incriminating, she managed one word. "Sweatpants."

A slow smile creased his face and made his eyes gleam. "Mine too, Gabriella. Let's get out of here."

"I don't believe you even own sweatpants."

"Not true. I have all the latest designers' versions in every color, like any prince should."

"Now you're making fun of me. I wasn't saying you wouldn't have any because you're a prince, it's because…because…oh, never mind." He might have been saying sweet and complimentary things about her all night, but it still felt strange to tell him what she'd been thinking. Which was that he exuded a regal confidence all too well suited by the tuxedo he wore. Then again, that same pres-

ence filled any room he was in at the clinic, even wearing scrubs, so clearly it had nothing to do with what he wore.

Or what he didn't.

Shocked at the sudden fantasy of what he might look like naked, which she sort of, kind of almost knew, she pinched her lips closed so she wouldn't say anything completely embarrassing as he opened the car door. So focused on her thoughts and, well, truthfully, on *him* and his sheer, breathtaking masculinity as he held her hand, she barely noticed the dozens of flashbulbs lighting the night. His big body shielded her from the cameras as he tucked her into his car before sliding into the driver's seat.

"Seat belt on?" The engine roared to life as he turned the key in the ignition, pausing to look at her with one eyebrow quirked.

"Yes."

"Good." The car rolled slowly forward for about ten feet, then took off like a rocket down the curve and onto the main road.

CHAPTER SEVEN

THE GROWLING SPORTS car's sudden acceleration shoved Gabby back into the sumptuously curved leather seat, and she gasped then chuckled. "You must be in a hurry to get into those sweatpants."

He didn't answer. Just looked at her with that glint in his eyes. A gaze so unnerving she felt like he might be seeing something clear down in her soul she didn't want him to see. He was close, so close to her inside the small confines of the car it seemed he'd sucked every bit of oxygen completely out of the space, making it very hard to breathe.

"Um, you're making me nervous," she finally said. "If you're looking at me, that means you're not looking at the road, and if I have to die, I want equal billing in the headlines."

"Equal billing?" His gaze finally moved to the road, and she let out a relieved breath. "What do you mean?"

"You know, instead of 'Prince Rafael Moreno and some other person die in car crash,' I'd like to at least get 'Joe Schmoe and Gabby Cain plunge into a canyon to their deaths.'"

He laughed. "And here I would have thought you didn't crave publicity, like most of our patients do."

"I'm kidding, of course. Believe me, the last thing I would ever want is my name splashed in the papers for any

reason." Not that it would ever happen to her. But she'd seen enough times when patients got publicity they'd originally wanted, only to have it result in reporters digging deep into details of their lives they didn't want shared.

"I've been in the media since the day I was born. You get used to it."

"I didn't get what that might be like, not really, until all those cameras flashed in my face. It may be just a part of life for people like you and Cameron Fontaine, but I bet it's still not fun." And suddenly it struck her that someone just might want to put a name to *her* face. Some unknown woman attending tonight's party with a Mediterranean prince. Her stomach tightened at the thought, until she remembered that Freya had made a big, public deal out of her being a midwife at The Hollywood Hills Clinic. Surely that's all they would report. Probably no one would feel a need to look beyond that.

The car ground to a halt against the curb in front of her apartment. Rafael turned off the engine and the sudden quiet seemed to ring in her ears along with her rapid heartbeat. He had that look in his eyes again. The one he'd had all evening, as though he thought she was special. Beautiful, which he'd said, but men so often didn't mean what they said, she knew. Sometimes their words were a thoughtless, casual compliment, or a tactic to get sex, or a way to distract a woman from starting important conversations.

And yet when Rafael complimented her, it didn't feel like any of those things. It struck her that, other than the appreciation she often got from her patients, she hadn't felt special to anyone in a very long time.

The last time she had, it had proven to be a mirage. Evaporating when she'd messed up so badly. Her mistake had broken her heart. Then, along with being heartbroken,

she'd been suddenly alone, just when she'd needed support and love more than at any other time in her life.

She drew in a breath, shoved the pain of those negative memories aside, and stomped on them for good measure. Wasn't she Cinderella, just for tonight? Maybe she didn't really deserve happiness, but this evening Rafael had made her feel wonderful and carefree, and she wasn't quite ready for the evening, and those good feelings, to end.

"Would you...like to come in for coffee?"

The eyes that seemed to be studying her with questions in them warmed, crinkling at the corners as he smiled. "I'd like that very much."

Once inside, she ushered him to sit down, and her belly quivered with a maelstrom of nerves and excitement. She'd lived in L.A. for two years but had never had even one man in her apartment. There'd been good reason for that, and there still was, but tonight was a fairy tale, right? One evening before her life went back to normal at midnight.

"Feel free to change into those sweats so you're more comfortable," he said, slipping off his tuxedo jacket and settling himself onto one side of her sofa. "I would if I could."

She watched his long, tanned fingers pull the end of his bow tie, sliding it off before slowly unbuttoning his top shirt buttons, revealing a bronzed throat. Then realized she was just standing there motionless, practically mooning over the man.

Yep. Tuxedo libido all right.

"I think I'll do that. Be right back."

Alone in her room, she felt a twinge of regret at having to take off the dress that had made her feel like she was floating as they'd danced around the ballroom. But it would feel silly, not to mention uncomfortable, to be sitting in her living room in a long gown. As she slid off her

clothes, the brief thought of Rafael walking into her room and sweeping her into his arms shortened her breath, but at the same time she laughed at herself. Definitely too much fairy-tale fantasy going on in her head tonight! One thing she was sure of—arrogant or not, playboy reputation or not, he wasn't the kind of man to do something inappropriate like that.

She quickly slipped into a T-shirt and the shapeless, comfy sweatpants they'd joked about, feeling even more unisex in them than the scrubs she wore most days. But if she put on jeans to look at least marginally attractive, he might know why. As the thoughts pinged around in her brain she rolled her eyes at herself and snorted. "Get a grip on yourself, Gabby. He's probably just here to be polite."

But when she emerged to walk across the living room, the way his gaze tracked her made her feel like she still had that gown on after all. Heart thudding, she made coffee in her small kitchen that opened to the living room so she could still see him, watching her in a way that was unnerving but exciting.

"Do you take cream or sugar?"

"Just black."

She handed him the cup, hyperaware of the feel of his fingers sliding against hers as he took it. Then stood there hesitating, probably looking like a fool, as she pondered whether or not to sit next to him on the sofa or several, discreet feet away in a chair.

The decision was made for her when he reached for her hand and gave it a gentle tug. "Sit by me. You can curl up in comfort a lot better here than over there."

"How did you know this is my curling-up corner? Was I eyeing it longingly?"

"You could say that."

Oh, Lord. Maybe he'd spotted her eyeing *him* long-

ingly. Breaking eye contact with that amused green, she took longer than necessary to slide her cup onto a coaster before scrunching up in the corner as far away from him as possible. Which was still just a couple feet from him. She needed a distraction, and picked her cup up to take a sip, eyeing him over the rim, wondering if the heat radiating through her body was from his nearness or the coffee. She had a bad feeling it had nothing to do with her drink.

Despite loosening his top shirt buttons, there was no way he could be described as being able to "curl up in comfort."

"I feel bad you're still in your starched finery, but I don't think anything I have here would fit you."

"Which is a good thing, as I always feel a little strange when I'm at a woman's home and she opens a wardrobe of men's clothes for me to choose from."

"Does that really happen?"

"More than you'd guess. Which is one of the many reasons spending time with you is like breathing in fresh air."

"Does that line usually work for you?"

"It's one I haven't used before, because I meant it." His eyes gleamed. "Maybe you can tell me how well it works."

She gulped. Should she tell him that just hearing that deep, sexy voice of his recite the alphabet might make her jump into his lap? If she'd been a different kind of woman, that was. A woman interested in being with a man. "I'm not much of an expert on lines men use, so I'm not a good person to ask."

"If that's true, the men in Los Angeles must not be very bright. You're not only beautiful, in the short time I've known you I've seen you're smart and caring and feisty and damned special. And I promise that's not a line."

The amusement had left his face, and his expression was utterly serious as he looked at her. Gabby felt her

heart melting and thudding and had no idea what she was supposed to say in response. Maybe compliment him too?

"And I've seen that you're not the arrogant jerk I thought you were. Just a doctor who does what it takes to make things right for a patient, whether it's good medical care, empathy, or humor. Princely attitude notwithstanding."

"Thank you. I think." He smiled again. "Is that what's called a backhanded compliment? But I probably deserve both the good and bad from it. So tell me. Why do you work so much? So many double shifts? And when you're not working, why do you keep mostly to yourself?"

Startled by the turn of the conversation, she found herself hesitating, for a split second feeling a shocking need to share her past, her mistakes. Her pain. But that was ridiculous. She didn't talk to anyone about it. She barely knew Rafael, and he probably wouldn't want their evening together to be spoiled by a depressing conversation. Not to mention that the last thing she needed was for everyone at the hospital to know who she really was. "I love my job. And who says I keep mostly to myself?"

"Freya. James. Even if they hadn't, I've seen it just in the short time I've been here. Seen a sadness that you carry with you." He reached to grasp her hand again, his touch warm and comforting and somehow arousing all at the same time. "What makes you sad, Gabriella?"

"I… Nothing." Just the bittersweet part of her job, bringing babies into the world to loving parents who wanted them. Praying they never had to know how it felt to lose one. "How about you? What makes Rafael Moreno travel the world, working hard and playing hard?"

"Different reasons. But one I just found out? Once in a very long while I'm lucky to meet someone remarkable I enjoy being with." He moved closer, his fingers slipping beneath her chin to bring her gaze to the darkening green

one staring at her. "Someone who makes me feel strangely happy in a way I didn't even realize I wanted to."

She stared in breathless fascination as his mouth slowly lowered to hers, giving her time to protest or pull away, but she found she wanted his kiss. Wanted it with a desperation new to her experience. Had wanted it, if she was honest, all the hours they'd spent together.

His lips touched hers, warm and soft and gentle. Not demanding or insistent or aggressive, as she would have expected a man like him to kiss. No, it was the sweetest kiss she'd ever experienced in her life, his mouth moving slowly and surely on hers, giving and taking, and the longer it went on the more her heart liquefied into a puddle of want for him.

The fingers beneath her chin slipped across her jaw, his wide palm cupping her cheek as the kiss deepened, heated, and Gabby was glad she was half lying down or she was sure she'd have fallen down.

"Gabriella." His usually almost nonexistent accent thickened slightly as he spoke against her mouth. "I knew you would taste *delicioso*."

"It's…the coffee."

She could feel him smile even as he kept pressing soft kisses to her lips. "No, *belleza*, it's most definitely you."

A sigh of pleasure left her lips as the kiss went from slow and sweet to hot and wet and so earth-shattering she found herself clutching his muscled shoulders and hanging on for dear life. His palms had moved from her face to tangle in her hair, turning her head to the perfect angle for a deep, mind-blowing kiss. Dazed, she realized one hand had moved down to slip beneath her T-shirt, tracking across her skin in a slow caress that made her shiver, finally resting on her breast through her bra.

"I…see now why you wanted me to change out of my dress."

"I was just thinking of your comfort. And I still am." He surprised her by moving his hand off her breast to caress her ribs again, pressing another soft kiss to her mouth, and she quivered at the tenderness of it. "Obviously, I want you. But not if the Gabriella who mostly keeps to herself will regret it tomorrow. You know I'm here for only a little while, and I have a feeling you're not a woman comfortable with making love with a man who's not able to stick around long."

"Not normally, I admit." But she'd learned not to expect someone to stick around, hadn't she? And as she looked into the green of his eyes, dark and questioning and filled with the same intoxicating desire she was feeling, she knew with certainty that tonight was the one time to change that. "I'm content with my life as it is. But I want you, too. And tonight I feel like being Cinderella, making love with you before I turn back into plain old Gabby Cain at midnight."

"That's the worst description of you imaginable." He seemed to study her a long moment, and she wasn't sure what he was seeing, or looking for. His fingertips traced her cheekbone as his thumb caressed her bottom lip. "You, Gabriella Cain, take my breath away."

Then he kissed her again, slowly and deeply, taking her breath away, too. The kiss held so much promise of delicious, incredible sex she uttered a sound of protest when he stopped. "Are you absolutely sure? Because I need to know now or it might kill me to stop."

"I'm sure, okay?" He appeared so suddenly hesitant she was afraid he'd leap up and leave, which might kill *her*. "Take my word for it. The last thing I want is to end up in a Mediterranean prison for killing a prince."

He chuckled against her mouth. "The prisons at home

don't have as many rats as they used to, but it's probably still wise to stay out of them."

"That's my plan."

"Good. Coincides well with mine." She gasped as his lips moved to her jaw, down to her throat, touching the sensitive spot beneath her ear as he deftly flicked the front clasp of her bra open. "I'm wondering if you're perhaps overly warm. I know I am."

Before she could even form an answer, he'd somehow managed to slip her T-shirt over her head and her bra straps down her arms and was staring at her nakedness. His eyes were dark and slashes of color rode high on his cheekbones as his gaze scorched her. Her heart thumped so hard against her ribs she thought he might actually be able to see it pounding.

"You are even more beautiful than I envisioned, *mi ángel*." The glide of his touch across her breasts felt nearly reverent as his gaze returned to hers, and even as she was shocked that she was doing this, letting herself be with a man again, with *this* man in particular, she wanted him more than she could ever remember wanting anyone.

He kissed her again, hotter and more intense, lying nearly on top of her now, pressing her into the cushions, and the small groan that left his mouth and swirled into hers just about set her on fire. Knowing he was as aroused as she was had her arching her back for more, pressing her breasts against him, only to discover it wasn't enough to feel his shirt there. She wanted his skin against hers, and fumbled to get the shirt open and off.

Except she hadn't done this for a long time, and never with a tuxedo shirt, which she was learning had aggravatingly difficult buttons, and couldn't manage to make it happen. Her sounds of frustration made him smile against her mouth before he leaned back.

"Let me, *bella*."

In a slow striptease, he worked the buttons one by one, his lips curved at the same time his eyes smoldered, intently focused on her as she watched him. Inch by torturous inch, he exposed a chest even more muscled than she remembered, his bronzed skin covered with dark hair that looked as soft and silky and outrageously manly as the rest of him.

Mouth dry, she knew with certainty that this was truly a Cinderella night. That she'd never again be with a man as physically perfect as Prince Rafael Moreno, and she still couldn't quite wrap her brain around the fact that he wanted to be with her as much as she wanted to be with him.

Then she couldn't admire his chest anymore because he lowered himself to her, his bare and scorchingly hot torso pressed against hers. He kissed her again, and she practically drowned in the deliciousness of it all. Her bones turned to utter liquid when he skimmed that talented mouth down her throat, across her collarbone, then on to her breasts. Gasping, her hands burrowed into the thick softness of his hair as he ministered to one nipple, then the other, and she didn't care that she was making little sounds and moving beneath him and pressing against him because control had gone out the window and all she wanted was to experience the incredible way he was making her feel.

Vaguely, she was aware of wide, warm palms slipping inside her sweatpants to cup her rear, then more aware of his hot mouth tracking from her breast down her belly as the pants and panties disappeared off over her feet, leaving her naked. Strong hands slid back up her legs to caress her thighs, his mouth following.

"Rafael." She didn't know what she was going to say,

exactly, and wasn't sure she could talk at all—her breath was so choppy she feared she might hyperventilate.

"Gabriella." His teeth nipped her knee, followed by a teasing lick, moving up to her hipbone, and she jumped with a laughing gasp. "Shall we take this to the bedroom?"

"No. I might combust before then."

A low, masculine laugh full of satisfaction swept across her skin. "*Bueno.* Me as well."

Licking across her quivering belly, he touched her right where she wanted to be touched, and she gasped and wriggled against his talented fingers, until finally she couldn't wait any longer. She reached for him, only to realize his darned pants were still on and completely in the way, just like his shirt had been. "What are your pants doing on? Get them off, fast."

He gave a short laugh. "And you call me bossy?"

"I'm assertive when I need to be. And, believe me, right now I need to be."

His eyes blazed at her with both amusement and heat. "My pants are on because I keep a condom in them. But not for long."

"I appreciate a prepared prince," she managed to say.

Another husky chuckle left his lips as he shucked his pants and took care of the condom, thankfully seeming to be in as much of a hurry as she was. He lowered his body to hers, and she gasped at the amazing sensation as he gently, slowly joined with her body, arching helplessly as they began to move together.

"*Cariña. Mi ángel.*" His whispered words had her blinking open her eyes, and his were the greenest she'd seen them, focused and gleaming and locked on hers. More Spanish words left his lips, first in whispers then louder as they rocked together until she cried out, and he joined with her in a long, low groan that reverberated in her chest.

The way he gathered her against him, tangling his fingers in her hair to tuck her face against his warm throat, felt tender and protective, and Gabby let herself absorb the intimacy and wonder of it. She tried hard not to think about how good it felt, how right, and how, when midnight came, Cinderella would be back in her corner all alone once again.

CHAPTER EIGHT

RAFAEL LISTENED TO the sound of his footsteps echoing across the marble-tiled foyer and wished he'd worn his scrubs and crepe-soled shoes instead, planning to change out of his regular shirt and dress pants if he'd needed to deliver a baby. Then cursed lightly under his breath at himself as he caught himself glancing around guiltily.

When was the last time he'd felt like a boy trying to sneak around undetected? Not since he'd been in primary school, since even before high school most people in authority hadn't felt comfortable disciplining the second-born prince of their country. It was no wonder he'd run a little wild at times.

His various sports adventures, dating adventures, and foolish errors in judgment had been so well documented by the press over the years, he'd believed he was immune to caring about it. And he was immune, really, except that he had to care for Gabriella's sake.

Yes, there were the occasional non-sensationalized stories. Ones that talked about medical school, and the years of study he put in to become a doctor and his actual work. But articles like that didn't seem to hold as much interest for most people as the simple fact that he'd been born under the blessing and curse of royalty.

Not that it was only the public who felt that way, since

his own family was pretty uninterested in his accomplishments. There were those times when he was happy about the press coverage, if it brought attention to the needs of the many women around the world who were underserved by proper medical care—or didn't have access to care at all. But those kinds of stories were unfortunately few and far between.

As he skulked through the clinic, he felt ridiculous. And selfish. Spending time with Gabriella while he was in L.A. was more than good for him, but for her? Not so much. Being out in public with him definitely exposed her to potential embarrassment, with the media sniffing around. To having things publicly spread about her, and whether they were truth or lies wouldn't matter.

He'd dated plenty of women who liked having their faces in the tabloids, holding on to his arm. But Gabriella wasn't like other women. In so many ways. Something about her had grabbed his insides and tugged hard at his soul from the first second he'd met her. Her fiery temper had matched that beautiful hair of hers, then the next second she'd been endearingly sweet and caring with their very difficult patient. Add to that a sexiness she seemed barely aware of and a sadness in the depths of those brown eyes, and she was fascinating with a capital F.

The vision of the smile in her eyes and on her lips as they'd danced last night, the sight of her beautiful naked body as they'd made love, the memories of how her skin had felt against his, had him closing his eyes to hold it all inside. Had him wanting to find her right then, pull her into an empty room, and kiss her breathless.

But she deserved better than him. Deserved more than a man who would only be around for a month or two. Deserved the kind of man who was capable of offering her

a commitment and a future, if that was what she wanted. And he wasn't that man.

No. For her sake, he should steer clear of her from now on. Let last night be one great memory for both of them. The last thing he would ever want would be to add to the sadness in her eyes after he'd moved on.

He sighed and, feeling a little bruised, rubbed his chest. Knew that the bruising was inside, not out, but it would heal. At least, he assumed it would. He'd never felt quite like this before, so he couldn't be sure. But it would be far worse to keep seeing Gabriella and bruise her, too.

Time to stop moping and get to work. He stopped at the computer outside one of the nurses' stations to check some charts, and decided to see Cameron Fontaine first. Medically, she was absolutely fine. But she'd wanted to stay at the hospital a little longer, both so she could be near baby Skye and because she didn't want to be seen in public while she was losing her "baby fat."

Rafael and everyone else had reassured her it was hardly noticeable, though he knew many of the new mothers giving birth at the clinic worried about the same thing, having to live in the very close scrutiny of the public eye. Cameron was happy to be eating healthy spa food specially prepared to have the nutrition she needed, while helping her lose weight as she worked with personal fitness trainers. And, Lord knew, a happy Cameron made the lives of everyone in the clinic easier.

Including Gabriella's, and he again marveled at her amazing patience and even empathy with a woman who could be pretty demanding. Then realized his every thought seemed to lead right back to Gabriella. How had his head become so consumed with her in such a short period of time?

Deep in thought on his way to Cameron's room, the

woman on his mind seemed to practically materialize out of thin air. She'd probably come out of the door he'd been about to walk by, but since her face had been what he'd been seeing and not the hallway, it gave him a start to see her actually there.

From the expression on her face, he'd startled her, too. Her face seemed to flush as she stared at him, and she swept her hair behind her ears in a nervous gesture he'd only seen that night in his house when she'd run into his naked chest. The night he'd wanted to kiss her to see how she'd react.

Which reminded him all over again what it had been like to kiss her the night before. Along with all the other things they'd done together over the course of the night, and he had a feeling his face was flushed, too, but not with nervousness. With a heat he'd had a hard time banking down every time he'd thought of her since leaving her in the wee hours of the morning.

"Good morning, Ms. Cain."

"Um, good morning, Dr. Moreno."

Her voice was husky, and her tongue flicked out to lick her lips, and he was damned if all his resolutions to the contrary moments ago didn't fly straight out of his brain. Replaced by that desire to grab her up, take her to the nearest empty room, and kiss her until neither of them could breathe.

"I was about to see Cameron Fontaine," he said, forcing his mind away from the thoughts that were actually making his body hard as they stood there in public. "Have you checked on her this morning?"

"Yes. She's in the gym with the fitness trainer right now, so you'll have to see someone else first. Speaking of which, I have a patient waiting in my office. She's feeling

nervous about some pain and wants to talk to me about it. Excuse me."

She turned without another word and hurried down the corridor. He watched her slim rear in her scrubs swaying slightly, which immediately took his thoughts back yet again to last night and how she'd looked in her sweats. Then out of them. Which he'd sworn to himself he'd stop thinking about.

Maybe he needed to hit the clinic gym himself for a long workout, then a nice cold shower.

"Dr. Moreno! Rafael!"

Gabriella's urgent voice had him turning to see her running back in his direction. "What's wrong?"

"We have a precipitous delivery. My patient thought she might be imagining things, but she's already eight centimeters dilated. Would you go and see to her while I get the pre-cep pack? My office."

Rafael strode to the room. Knowing Gabriella knew what she was doing should have prepared him, but he was still surprised to see a woman lying on the floor of Gabriella's office, practically wedged between the chairs in front of her desk, writhing and moaning, with blood beneath her on the floor. He cursed under his breath, because it was pretty obvious it was too late to move her to a birthing suite. He gave her knee a quick, reassuring pat. "It's going to be all right. I'm Dr. Moreno, and Ms. Cain is getting what we need to help you, okay?"

He shoved the desk against the wall then grabbed the chairs. As he carried them into the hallway to give them all room, he could see Gabby tearing toward him with a big bowl in her hands.

"Everything should be in here. Clamps, scissors, bulb suction, sutures. Syringe for delivering intramuscular Pitocin. Blankets."

"IV bag?"

"Yes."

He and Gabriella shared a look. It was clear she'd experienced this before, and also knew the potential hazards of delivering a baby under these conditions. A shriek of pain drew their attention to the patient, who was gasping and clutching her belly.

"I want…I want an epidural now."

"I'm afraid it's too late for that," Gabriella said in a gentle, soothing voice. "The baby's coming fast, Trina, but that's good news, because it won't hurt for long, right?"

"Then let's get the C-section done fast. But you can't do the C-section here, can you?" Trina sucked in a few heavy breaths. "I…I don't think I can walk. Can you get me moved to wherever you do that, maybe in a wheelchair?"

"C-section?" Gabriella glanced at Rafael with a question in her eyes, obviously asking if he'd somehow had a conversation with the woman about a Caesarean in the minute she'd been gone. He shook his head but since it was her patient kept quiet to let Gabriella handle it as she saw fit.

"Yes. I talked to my doctor about a C-section so I wouldn't have any changes in my, you know, down there, and he agreed."

"Trina, a vaginal birth is always preferable to a Caesarean section, both for the baby and for the amount of time your body needs to heal."

"I don't care. That's what I want. I know the scar would be low and not noticeable."

The mulish expression on her face contorted into pain as she had another long contraction. Rafael placed his hand on her belly. He could feel the muscles pushing hard, and was sure the baby was on its way. Gabriella must have

thought the same thing, as she efficiently set up an IV line in the woman's arm.

Deciding that nature was making the decision for this woman about how her baby would be born, he figured an argument was unnecessary.

"Let's see how much you're dilated now, Trina," he said, giving her what he hoped was a comforting smile. "Do you want me to do the internal exam? Or would you prefer Ms. Cain to?"

"You, please," the woman gasped.

He glanced at Gabriella, and had a hard time not grinning at her narrowed eyes and the expression on her face that was just about the equivalent of her sticking her tongue out at him. But there was a twinkle in those eyes too so he knew she wasn't going to yell at him again.

He snapped on gloves and knelt in front of the woman. "All right. You'll feel a little pressure as I check. You're doing great." Gabriella got the IV taped down, then moved to hold one of Trina's knees.

Then their eyes met in surprise, and the plan changed again. Because the top of baby's head was clearly visible— as he'd guessed, nature had decided when this baby was going to be born. "Guess what, Mama? Baby's decided the time is now. We can see the top of its head. Push hard next time you have a contraction."

"Oh, God! No! I'm… I don't want it to be this way."

Gabby had turned to speak into the microphone around her neck, presumably to call Neonatal and get the troops ready, but now reached to squeeze Trina's hand as she moaned again. "I know, I'm sorry. But, ready or not, here he comes. Breathe now, it's going to be just fine. Give us a push, okay? Another one."

"Great job. Here he comes! I've got his head now." He

gently grasped the infant's head, sliding his fingers up to hold the tiny shoulders. "Another push."

As the mother labored, Gabriella kept up her encouragement. "You're doing an amazing job, Trina. Remember to breathe. Puff, puff, puff. One more. Oh, my, you've done it! He's here, and so beautiful!"

The baby was a good color and seemed to be under no stress at all, and the usual, spontaneous satisfaction hit Rafael square in the chest. He grinned at the mother then at Gabriella. Their eyes met for the briefest moment, but it was long enough to see she felt exactly like he did, which was that he wanted to pump his fists in the air that all had gone smoothly, despite the not-very-normal situation.

"You can be front-page news if you want to be, Trina," Gabriella said as she did a quick bulb suction on the baby before handing him to his mother. "I think you might be the first woman to give birth on the floor of the clinic midwife's office."

Trina, obviously tired but now beaming, laughed. "Being on the front page is always one of my goals."

Something Rafael couldn't imagine, and he'd be glad to have her take his place the next time it happened.

Neonatal arrived to take the baby and get him cleaned up and swaddled.

"Your body was obviously perfectly made for this, Trina, with baby coming so fast and easy, and with no complications at all." Rafael had learned that it was always good to distract his patients with chitchat and jokes while he took care of post-birth necessities. "You might consider doing it another ten times or so. What do you think?"

Predictably, Trina laughed at the same time she scowled at him. "Easy for you to say when you're not the one who went through the pain or got your body all stretched out. Besides, every woman's body is made for birthing babies,

right? It's our curse in life, though I have to say he just might be worth it."

He smiled at the happy, adoring look she was giving her baby, then glanced at Gabriella, wanting to enjoy her smile, too.

Except she wasn't smiling. Her eyes held the sadness he'd seen in them before. No, this time he'd even call it anguish, and her slender shoulders were slumped with the weight of something heavy but invisible. Seeing her pain, that same heavy weight seemed to settle in his own chest as it ached for her, and he knew that, damn it, he had to learn what was making her feel this way.

To hell with keeping his distance. With keeping her safe from him. He might not have much to offer her other than the here and now and an ear to listen and a shoulder to cry on, but he could at least offer that. Or whatever it was she needed from him.

God knew, he was well acquainted with what it felt like to not have anyone close who particularly cared who you really were.

Dios. He wanted, right then, to take her in his arms and kiss away that sadness. To whisk her off somewhere to talk about it right now, to find out the source and show her that, whatever it was, it would be all right. Except they were at work, caring for a new mother and a new life. Waiting wasn't his strength, but patients had to come first.

Gabriella must have felt that he was watching her, maybe even sensed the intensity and turmoil inside him at that moment, because she turned to look at him. Their gazes fused for a long moment of charged connection before she blinked, then turned away. He saw a smile force its way to her lips as her face became a smooth mask. She chatted with Trina as she was helped onto a gurney to

transport her to a room, and cooed over the baby the neo-natal team had placed back in its mother's arms.

Anyone who hadn't been looking at Gabriella exactly when he had might have seen only the pleased, warm mid-wife caring for her patient. Giving them the kind of heart-felt attention and empathy any pregnant woman would be lucky to receive from her nurse.

Gabriella seemed to be pointedly directing her atten-tion to anywhere and anyone but him as she and a techni-cian got the room cleaned up. Just before the new mother was wheeled out, she thanked him and he turned to smile at her, chucking the little newborn under his chin but still thinking of Gabriella busying herself behind him. He pon-dered how exactly to approach her. His phone rang, and the screen told him it was James.

He stepped into the hallway, keeping an eye on Gabri-ella's office door to make sure she didn't escape before he had a chance to talk to her.

"Hello, James, what's up?"

"Can you take a couple of days to go to a special des-tination?" James asked.

"Depends on the destination."

"A sheikh friend and his wife and extended family are staying in Vail, Colorado. He came here to take care of some business in L.A., and they were planning to leave the U.S. day after tomorrow. Except it looks like she might be close to delivering earlier than expected. Any way you can head to the mountains to see what's going on?"

He didn't have to ask why they didn't just go to the local hospital or see a doctor there. He knew a number of Middle Eastern princes, and they didn't "do" local hospi-tals without having some connection, along with a guar-antee of privacy.

"Any way they can get here?"

"No. He's worried, and doesn't want her to travel. So, can you?"

"Yes." For the first time in half an hour he felt like smiling. "Though I'd need assistance, which means you'll have to adjust Gabriella Cain's schedule so she can come with me."

"Those are your terms?" A low laugh came down the phone line. "Fine. But I hope you know what the hell you're doing, and why you're doing it."

Rafael wasn't too sure he knew either of those things, but he was going with it anyway.

CHAPTER NINE

SWOOPING DOWN THEN back up and around on the winding road that had been cut through sheer rock cliffs, the
powerful rented sedan effortlessly handled the mountain
curves Gabby was sure her own little car would have struggled with mightily. With any other driver at the wheel, she
might have been a little nervous at the speed with which
he was taking the sweeping turns, but Rafael's supreme
confidence was evident, just like it was at work. Or anywhere else, for that matter.

She couldn't help but wonder if her coming along on
this work trip had been James's idea or Rafael's. Somehow,
she had a feeling it was the prince wielding his powers of
persuasion, which was a nice way to say he was manipu-
lative. But how could she be sorry about that?

She glanced at the man and his gorgeous profile, a smile
playing at the corners of his mouth.

"Spectacular, isn't it, Gabriella?"

"Yes." And she wasn't about to tell him she was thinking of his looks as well as the scenery. "But I'm surprised
you wanted to take the time to drive from the airport, instead of using a helicopter. I thought the Sheikh was worried to death."

"The chopper would only cut about twenty minutes off
the trip. And I talked to both the Sheikh and his wife on

the phone. Between you and me, I'm almost positive this is false labor, and maybe not even that. She's taking every twinge or odd feeling as something catastrophic. But of course we need to confirm that, which is why we're here."

Gabby stared out the window, suddenly not seeing the craggy rock cliffs and tumbling river below. She was remembering the odd twinges. Peculiar, off sensations that she too had assumed were nothing, focusing on her patient instead. A stupid error in judgment that had ended up being catastrophic indeed. "I hope we're seeing her as soon as we get there. Just in case."

"Don't worry. We are."

He must have sensed something in her response, because his voice had changed from pleased at enjoying their drive to more serious.

"If you think it's unlikely to be labor, why did you want me to come?"

"I don't know this man, and some sheikhs can be difficult to deal with. Traditional attitudes being what they are, it can be helpful to have a woman who's an experienced midwife helping care for his wife."

"I guess I can see that. How often has Dr. Jet-Setting OB run into problems with that?"

"A few times. When I do, I put on a wig and a dress. Solves everything."

He flashed her a quick grin, and Gabby laughed at that amusing and absurd vision. As though putting on those items would in any way disguise the potent masculinity that exuded from the man.

The road flattened and soon the wilderness gave way to houses and large apartment buildings alongside the highway, then the town of Vail itself came into view. Rafael swung the car through a roundabout and on into the village, where cobbled walks and charming buildings lined

the streets, many designed to look like they belonged in an old Swiss town.

"Like I said, we'll stop at the hospital first, then check into the hotel."

Unable to shake the unease she felt about the pregnant woman's condition, Gabby was just about to ask how far it was to the hospital when she saw signs for it and they swung into the parking lot. "Wow, I'm surprised the hospital is so close to the main town. And how did you know where it was?"

"I've been here a few times. It's a good gig to combine skiing with working."

"I'd think you'd do that in Switzerland and Austria."

"There, too. Among other places. Like I said, it's a good gig." That grin again, then he was out of the car and coming over to her side to open the door, reaching for her hand.

"You don't have to open my door, you know. I'm an open-my-own-door kind of woman."

"Sorry if it bothers you. But as you noted the first day we met, I do as I please. And it pleases me to be a gentleman."

The words held a tinge of that arrogance that was just part of him, but his eyes were warm and sincere. Even as she rolled her eyes a little, she had to laugh. "I guess it's impossible for a prince to not believe he can do as he pleases. And since you haven't asked me to kiss your ring, I guess I'll indulge you by letting you assist me out of the car."

"The only reason I haven't asked you to kiss my ring is because I don't wear one. But I would like you to kiss something else." And with that, he leaned into the car and pressed his mouth to hers.

For a split second she stared into half-closed moss-green eyes before her own flickered shut. And just like that her

heart began to pump in slow thuds as she savored the taste of him in her mouth, as she breathed in his scent, letting herself slowly sink into the kiss until he broke the delicious contact and pulled back.

The eyes staring at her this time had darkened, and it seemed his chest rose and fell in several deep breaths before his lip quirked at one corner. "Air's thin up here, isn't it? Let's go."

He held out his hand, and she didn't say a word as she slipped hers into it. Then kept it there as they walked into the hospital, and she had the same bad-good feeling she'd had when James had first told her she needed to come on this trip.

She'd never get truly involved with a man again. Never fully trust that kind of relationship. But if she had to briefly fall off that wagon, wasn't Rafael the perfect man to do it with? Okay, yes, she already had, figuring it would be just that one time. But she was beginning to see that, as long as he was still working at the clinic, there was no way she could resist letting their professional time together turn personal.

She wanted him. Again. And it looked like he wanted her the exact same way.

Her lips hadn't stopped tingling, and she willed herself to look normal as they stopped at the front desk to get directions to the seventh floor. Still holding her hand, he led her to the elevator. "I didn't hear what the room number was."

"That's because there's no need to know it. They've paid big money to basically rent out the whole floor."

"The whole floor?"

"Not uncommon. The Sheikh wants privacy and discretion. He'll likely have flown in his own staff to prepare food for everyone and to tend to his wife. Possibly

brought comfortable furnishings for their stay here. I had one patient in Morocco whose family brought twelve place settings of fine china from their palace to the hospital."

"Wow." That was about the only thought she could conjure, though she wasn't sure if it was because she was so amazed or because her brain could only focus on one thing at a time, and at that moment it was still thinking about his lips and the feel of his hand wrapped around hers. About the rest of their stay here together and where it all might lead.

Rafael punched the elevator button and the doors closed. Alone in the enclosed space, their recent kiss sizzled in the air between them, so hot she could practically feel it burning her skin. And from the slight flare to his nostrils, the way his skin seemed to tighten over his cheekbones he felt every bit as much heat as she did.

The elevator pinged open just in time, since her fantasy of grabbing him and pushing him back against the wall to have her way with him was making her feel a little woozy. Their eyes met, and she saw his lips curved in a half-smile and realized hers were, too. Then he gave her a quick wink, and it was so unexpected from autocratic Prince Rafael Moreno she gave a little breathless laugh.

"We'll hold that thought until later, hmm, *bella*?" he murmured.

They walked down the corridor, and Gabby couldn't help but stare at the number of people around. Some wore uniforms, and others were dressed in elegant clothes. There were even quite a few children, and while some occupied themselves quietly with a board game, several boys were tearing down the hall, kicking a ball and shouting.

"This looks like a hospital, and yet not," she said to Rafael in disbelief. "Does the hospital director know this is going on?"

"I'm willing to bet he's done this drill once or twice so, yes. Also planned ahead and put away any equipment that could be damaged by an errant kick." His eyes twinkled. "Let's see how our patient is doing. I'll find out where she is."

He stepped toward a small group of women and started speaking in some language Gabby had never heard, amazed at him and his various skills. Though she shouldn't have been, really. Probably a prince grew up learning any number of languages. She felt embarrassed all over again at her very rudimentary knowledge of Spanish, vowing to study it more. She hadn't needed it too much in Seattle, but speaking the language even halfway well would come in very handy in California.

"This way," Rafael said. He didn't lead the way, having her follow. Instead, he waited for her to join him, then pressed his hand against her lower back as they walked together.

"More of your gentlemanliness? Waiting for me?" she teased.

"Or maybe I just wanted an excuse to touch you."

The gaze that met hers was twinkling, but hot, too, and Gabby sank her teeth into her lower lip to make sure nothing came out that shouldn't. Something along the lines of *You don't need an excuse, which I'm pretty sure you know.*

Acutely aware of that wide hand on her back, she had to wonder when she'd gone from being an efficient workaholic uninterested in dating to a woman with sex on her mind in the middle of a hospital. Though she knew the answer, and it was standing right next to her in all its six-foot-plus gorgeous glory.

When they went into the patient's room, Gabby was in for yet another unexpected sight. The place looked more like a plush hotel room than a hospital room. Even more so

than The Hollywood Hills Clinic rooms—and, since she'd always thought they seemed right out of a five-star hotel, that was saying something. This had to be one of those situations Rafael mentioned where they'd brought in furniture for their stay. A portable wall between two rooms had been removed, creating a huge space, and comfortable furniture filled the area. The bed was still a hospital bed, but it had beautiful linens, and the bedspread looked like something from a high-end furnishings magazine.

An exotic-looking woman lay in the bed, which surprised Gabby a little. Since she wasn't connected to any monitors or IV at this point, Gabby would have expected her to be sitting in one of the deep, upholstered armchairs, but maybe she felt more comfortable lying down. Or maybe, since Rafael had said her husband was worried, everyone thought she should stay in the bed to be safe.

Rafael made introductions, then focused his attention on speaking with the Sheikh, which also surprised Gabby. Normally, getting information and history directly from the patient was important, but since Rafael knew that, it must be part of the typical protocol in this very atypical situation. Maybe this was exactly why he'd wanted her to come, so she could speak directly to the patient without going through her husband first. If she spoke English, that was.

Of course, she couldn't deny that she hoped Rafael had wanted her along for another reason, too. Then scolded herself for having that sex subject dive back into her mind when she had work to do.

"Hello, Amala, I'm Gabby Cain, a nurse midwife from The Hollywood Hills Clinic. I understand you're having some pain, and are worried about the baby?"

"Yes." Thankfully, Amala spoke excellent English, and

Gabby smiled in relief. "I keep having pains. Contractions, I think."

"Have you timed them at all? To see how far apart they are?"

"No. But they happen often."

"Okay. I'm going to take your pulse and blood pressure to check those—is that all right?" She pressed her fingers to the woman's delicate wrist. "Tell me about the pain. Where is it, exactly?"

"My belly. Low. And down…there as well."

The woman seemed uncomfortable even using a euphemism, and Gabby smiled wider to hopefully relax her. "The good news is that your pulse and blood pressure are normal. So, are you feeling any pain in your back? Up high in your belly?"

"No. Not my back. I am not sure about how high. But they go away sometimes if I lie down."

Sounded like Rafael might be right about this being false labor, but it was too soon to say for sure. She glanced up to see him finishing his conversation with the Sheikh, then he came to join her on the other side of the patient's bed.

"I'm Dr. Rafael Moreno. It's my privilege to come see you today. I understand you're thirty-four weeks pregnant. Can you tell me about your symptoms?"

Amala repeated what she'd told Gabby, and more as he asked additional questions. Finally, he nodded. "Let's take a look at what baby is doing inside you, using ultrasound. You have it ready, Gabriella?"

"Yes."

"Good." He reached to lift the patient's shirt over her belly, but she stopped him.

"I'd like Gabriella to do it. Please."

The surprise on his face was gone in a blink, replaced

by a calm smile. "Of course. Gabriella is excellent with ultrasound, and I can read them later as well, if you want. I'll be back in a little bit."

His gaze lifted from their patient and his eyes met Gabby's. She absolutely could not control the gleeful little smile quivering on her lips that the tide had turned, and this time the patient trusted her to do the job instead of him.

Gabby slowly ran the wand through the warm jelly she'd squeezed on Amala's abdomen, and carefully studied the pictures on the monitor. Seeing that everything looked one hundred percent normal, and that baby seemed healthy in every way, Gabby's knees got a little jelly-like, too, as relief for the woman swept through her. "Baby looks absolutely perfect in there, all snug and happy. I'm going to go over my findings with Dr. Moreno, but I'm confident that the pain you've been experiencing is false labor, which can be very hard to distinguish from true labor."

"Oh, I hope so. I want my baby to be born at home, so this is good news. Thank you so much."

"So glad to be here to help you." And she was. Glad, in a strange kind of way, that she knew exactly how this pregnant woman had felt, which made her a better caregiver. A better nurse and midwife. She cleaned off the gel and got the patient's top back in place. "Let me see what Dr. Moreno thinks, okay?"

She found him sitting at a round table, playing the board game with the kids there, all of them laughing. Struck by how boyish he looked, too, so unlike the arrogant prince or the dashing date, she slowed her steps and just looked at him, her heart feeling all warm and squishy and starstruck.

He glanced up and grinned at her. Unfolding himself from the chair, he came over to her. "False labor?"

"Yes." She cleared her throat and went over the results

with him, and for the first time in her professional life a tiny corner of her mind was on something other than her patient and her work. It was on him, and the scent of him, and how close his head was tipped to hers. Afraid everyone in the room could see how she was feeling and what she was thinking, she again went for a joke to cover it all.

"So, Dr. Prince Rafael Moreno, how does it feel to have your patient doubt your skills and send you out of the room, leaving someone else to do the tests?"

"First, she did not doubt my skills. I'm sure she just knew her husband might be jealous because I am so handsome."

The gold flecks sparkling in his green eyes showed he was teasing, and didn't believe that for a minute. Probably it had been more about modesty, but Gabby was going to rib him about it anyway.

"Uh-huh. All I can say is it made me pretty happy for you to get a taste of it, considering how mean you were the first day we met."

"Mean?" All humor left his face as he looked at her searchingly. "You thought I was mean? I'm sorry if that's how I came across."

"Okay, mean isn't the right word." A man as empathetic as he was didn't have a mean bone in his body. "Dismissive. Disrespectful."

"And for that I apologize too. Only a fool would disrespect or dismiss someone like you, and sometimes the fool in me comes out when it shouldn't."

"Never mind." Lord, she'd meant it really as a joke, and now he looked so contrite, ashamed, even, she was sorry she'd even mentioned it. Who would have thought the man was even capable of feeling that way? "I'm teasing you, really. Like you do me sometimes."

"I know exactly how to make it up to you in about…"

he glanced at his watch "…half an hour. Let's talk to the Sheikh and his wife, hmm?"

Walking beside him, she couldn't help but glance up at him more than once, wondering what he'd meant about making it up to her, and her toes and a lot of other things started to tingle as she imagined what it could be.

You're at work, Gabby! she scolded herself. And work was not the place where her mind could be wandering to bad thoughts.

She stood on the opposite side of the patient's bed as Rafael recommended they stay one more day. He told Amala to write down when she had contractions and how long they lasted, and to be ready for Gabby to do one more ultrasound tomorrow. Gabby tried to listen, but since she knew everything he was going to say, watching his lips move seemed far more fascinating. As did wondering what in the world he had in mind to "make it up" to her.

Those darned thoughts of sex came right to the forefront of her brain again. When in the world was that going to stop?

Probably only after Rafael Moreno was long gone back to the Mediterranean or wherever he was headed next. Her life could get back to normal. The life she'd chosen where she worked a lot and stayed relationship-free. Since it was apparent that she couldn't seem to help but be dangerously distracted by him, she knew that day couldn't come soon enough.

Yet she also had a bad feeling it would also come far, far too soon.

CHAPTER TEN

ADVENTURES IN THE sky were nothing new to Rafael. He'd enjoyed hang gliding, glider planes, and skydiving many times all over the world. At the time, he'd thought every one of those adventures was enjoyable, but nothing came close to the evening he'd just spent with Gabriella.

Holding her close as they'd stood in the basket of a hot-air balloon, able to see for miles across the awesome expanse of the Rocky Mountains, they'd floated through a quiet so deep he'd felt it all the way to his soul. Filled with a tranquil contentment he couldn't remember ever feeling in his life.

Listening to her cries of delight as she'd pointed at beautiful blue-green lakes below, at the snow still covering the jagged peaks, at mountain goats picking their way across vertical rocks in a feat that seemed nearly impossible, he'd smiled and laughed and held her closer.

Her hair had blown across her face, and he'd tucked it behind her ears more than once, both to feel its softness within his fingers and so he could better see the joy on her face and in her eyes.

Joy he'd wanted to see there from the moment he'd observed them shadowed with sadness when she'd sat next to Skye's incubator. Joy he'd known was a big part of who

she was, or had been until something had chipped away at it. Minimized it. Maybe even crushed it.

As the balloon had sunk back to earth, they'd watched the sun set in a blaze of glorious red and gold behind the mountains. Colors so vivid they'd almost rivaled the strands highlighting Gabriella's beautiful hair.

He'd wanted to have her to himself for a little while longer, away from L.A. and whatever was there that might be the reason she carried that sadness around. Again, he knew that was damned selfish of him, but he'd been having a tough time battling it. And since fate had seemed to give him exactly what he'd wanted, did he really have to fight it?

All he knew was that he didn't seem to have a lot of fight left in him when it came to keeping away from Gabriella.

He opened the door of the hotel restaurant, sliding his hand around hers before they meandered out onto the huge stone patio, warmed by several fire pits surrounded by cushioned chairs. And, lucky for him, it was nearly deserted.

"Would you like to sit out here? Or are you too full to sit after you ate a steak big enough for two people?" he couldn't help but tease.

"Haven't we already discussed how not at all suave it is to talk about how much I eat?" Her eyes gleamed up at him. "All women need iron in their diets. The occasional steak is good for me. But I'm not sure what your excuse is, because you ate even more than I did."

"Fresh out of excuses." That was true for pretty much anything he did around Gabriella, and he didn't care anymore. "Where would you like to sit?"

"By the fire. It's getting chilly, don't you think?"

"We can go inside if you like."

"No. It's so beautiful, I want to stay out here." He fol-

lowed her gaze over to the timeless mountains, silhouetted by the darkened sky that was still slightly lit with pale pink streaks. Across the creek covered with small chunks of ice and snow, slowly melting in the springtime temperatures. "I can't believe there's no one around to enjoy this."

"May is off season for Vail. Too late to ski and too cold for most other sports."

"Except hot-air ballooning. Bundling up in a ski coat, gloves and hat were part of the fun." Her eyes smiled at him through the darkness. "And since I don't even own a coat, it's a good thing the hotel keeps winter stuff guests have left behind for people like me to borrow."

"I'm sure you're not the only Southern Californian to come here unprepared."

"Unprepared?" He nearly laughed at her indignant expression. "I was a Girl Scout. Believe me, I know how to be prepared."

"If you say so. How about we sit here?" He tugged her down to a thickly pillowed settee, and he could feel the warmth of the fire reaching out to him. Much like Gabriella's warmth did, touching him in ways he couldn't remember being touched before. "I'm glad you liked it."

"I loved it. It was the most special thing I've ever done. Thank you."

"The most special thing I've done too. So thank you." And the reason it had been so special was because he'd done it with her. How he felt about her was something he couldn't quite figure out, but he suspected that feeling might not happen again for a long time. Or maybe ever.

"I know that can't be true, but it's sweet of you to say so." She laughed softly. "You've been all over the world, but I haven't left L.A. in two years."

"You haven't?" He couldn't wrap his brain around not getting out of town even once in all that time. "That's got

to be a record. I haven't *stayed* in one place more than two months since I graduated from medical school."

"Yours is more likely to be a record than mine."

He saw her shiver a little in the crisp mountain air, despite the orange flames licking upward, ending in gray smoke that disappeared into the starlit sky. He wrapped his arm around her shoulders and tugged her close to his side, and the way she snuggled against him felt damn good. "Cold?"

"A little. My Washington State blood, used to damp, chilly weather, must have thinned after living in California."

"I've been wanting to ask you something." If she was feeling even a little of the closeness, the intimacy he was feeling right now, sitting next to her in this beautiful place, maybe now was the right time to learn what secrets she might be keeping to herself. Secrets she might need to unload.

"What?"

"I've noticed that sometimes when you look at newborns, or after you've helped bring a baby into the world, that there's a sadness in your eyes. Why?"

"Sadness?" She made a sound that was probably supposed to be a laugh but didn't get there. "I don't know what you're talking about. There's nothing more joyful than a successful delivery and healthy baby, and you know it."

"But sometimes a pregnancy doesn't end successfully. Or with a healthy baby," he said quietly, his gut telling him there was some kind of history for her that was tied to that reality.

"True."

She stared fixedly at the fire, her relaxed expression more tense now. He hesitated, wondering if asking her more questions would ruin her evening. And his too. But

he'd wanted to provide an ear in case she wanted to unload on him, so he'd try just once more. "Why did you leave Seattle to come to L.A.?"

More staring into the fire, and just when he was regretting ruining the intimate comfort they'd been feeling by digging into her life, instead of keeping it light and superficial like he usually did, she sighed and started to talk.

"I was engaged to be married. Thought I had it all—a job I adored, a family who supported me, a man who loved me. But it turned out he didn't love me, at least not enough. Something…bad happened, and he left me. I decided to start fresh in L.A., and that's it in a nutshell."

He wanted to say that any man who had her in his life, planning on forever, then left was a fool and an idiot. But he knew that was just the way relationships turned out most of the time. Unfortunate for people who believed in that kind of love, but it was reality. Either someone left, or a couple stuck together long past the time they should have gone their separate ways.

Her boyfriend's abandonment, causing her pain, was just more proof that relationships weren't meant to last for the long haul, and that planning to get married was just a road leading to unhappiness.

"I'm sorry. That must have been hard for you."

"It was. But I'm over it now."

Somehow he didn't believe that. But he knew her well enough to know she was done talking about it, even though he was sure it couldn't be the whole story. He slipped his fingers beneath her chin, tipping her face up to his, and all he could think of to do for her was kiss away the sadness on her face, replacing it with the desire he'd seen there on and off all day. Desire that he'd battled with a whole lot of effort, because he didn't want to hurt her. A battle he had to win now that he knew her ex had already caused her pain.

But just as he was about to draw back and start some unimportant chitchat, she wrapped her cold hand around his nape, brought his face close, and pressed her mouth to his.

He could see her eyes closing just before his own did, and the way she sighed and sank into him knocked every good intention out of his head and had him gathering her close. He cupped her soft cheek in his hand, angling her mouth to his, and when she sighed again it felt like a siren song, driving him a little crazy. He couldn't help but deepen the kiss. The wet slide of her warm tongue against his felt as erotic as full sex with any other woman, and it was only through some miracle that he managed to remember that, deserted or not, they were in a public place and pulling off her clothes right then and there wasn't an option.

Or a good idea. He absolutely was not going to be the next man to hurt her.

"Gabriella." He sucked in some much-needed air. "It's too cold out here to be comfortable. Let's go inside and talk in the lounge."

"I'm very comfortable."

Well, damn. What was he supposed to say to that? She pressed her chest to his, and while he couldn't really feel her breasts against him, knowing what softness lay under all the layers of clothes they wore nearly made him moan. Her cold hands cupped his cheeks and she brought his face to hers again for another mind-blowing kiss that had him thinking about risking arrest and getting naked with her right there after all. Thank God the murmur of other voices on the patio cut through his fog and helped him get his libido at least marginally in check.

Which then helped him remember the paparazzi and how he needed to keep Gabriella safe from the media.

While he hoped they hadn't gotten wind of them coming to Vail, he'd learned not to count on that.

He dragged his lips from hers and sucked in a deep breath of chilly mountain air that barely cooled the heat pouring through his veins. "Bad idea to do this out here. Cameras, you know?"

The brown eyes that met his looked a little dazed, but she nodded. "Cameras. I remember. How about we go to the room?"

Knowing she wanted that, too, made what he had to say nearly impossible. But he forced himself. "Gabriella, it's better if—"

"Stop." She pressed her fingertips to his lips. "You asked me things. There are things I want to ask you too."

He braced himself, not being in the mood for true confessions. Mostly because he hated to see her shock and disappointment and disapproval. But she probably had a right to know.

"Ask away."

"Why are you hiding out in L.A.?"

"What makes you think I'm hiding? I'm visiting."

"I don't live under a rock, Rafael. I know there was a scandal with some woman."

The way she smiled and cupped his cheek in her hand relaxed him a little. At least she knew that much, and was still there with him. He turned his face to press his mouth to her palm for a moment, deciding what he wanted to say.

"Then you know I dated a woman who some people thought was not the kind of person a prince should be dating. It wasn't as though we had anything more than a casual relationship, but the media hounds ran with it, as they love to do. Since my face had been plastered on television and tabloids quite a lot the past couple years, there was more uproar than usual back home."

"Do you care about it? And if you do, why do you do things you know the media will have a field day with?"

At first, he thought she was judging him, and the pain of that stabbed his chest. But when he looked into her eyes, really looked, he could clearly see that she was just asking, not judging. Her hand still softly caressed his cheek, and the touch weakened him. Or made him stronger, he wasn't sure which. Either way, he realized he actually wanted to talk to her about it, which surprised the hell out of him.

He drew in a fortifying breath before he spoke. "First, half the stuff said about me isn't true. Or is greatly exaggerated. Second, if I read that stuff and worried about it, I'd spend all day doing it and I have more important things to think about."

"So why hide out at all?"

Good question, and one he wasn't sure how to answer. "My parents get upset about it. And this time the hubbub was so loud they demanded I lie low and keep my face out of the press. And since I'm a grown man and can do as I please, my only explanation of why I did so is that I care about their opinion of me. Because their opinion's been pretty low for a long time, and I guess that's always bothered me."

His words rang in his ears, and it was like being given a good whack on the side of the head. Apparently there was some part of him deep inside that was still that boy who was the second prince. The spare heir. The one who didn't always follow rules and had embarrassed his parents when he'd left the kingdom to become a doctor. The one who refused to ever marry, despite having very good reasons for that.

The son they were always disappointed in, whether he lived up or down to his reputation in the media. Pathetic that it hurt that they felt that way, but there it was. The truth.

"What do you mean, their opinion of you is low? That's ridiculous."

"Not ridiculous." He pressed his lips to her forehead and let them stay there, because the simple connection felt good. "I told you before that they wanted me to stay in the family business, so to speak. They never understood or approved of my wanting to be a doctor, and were more than disappointed when I did it anyway."

"Rafael." She grasped his face in her hands, and he felt a little like he was drowning in the sweet sincerity of the brown eyes staring into his. "I don't know your parents. But I have to believe you're wrong about a lot of this. Maybe they wanted you to do more traditional duties at home, but surely they're proud of the hard work you put in to be a doctor. Of the lives you save and the good you do. When you go home, promise me you'll talk to them. Share how you've felt, and clear the air. I bet you'll be surprised at how they respond."

Gabriella knew a lot about human nature—hadn't he seen it first hand in so many ways? That didn't mean she knew a thing about his family situation, but he realized he didn't have anything to lose by talking things over with his parents. Who knew, maybe they could come up with a relationship less full of stress and more full of the kind of closeness he'd seen in other families. Including royal ones like those of the Sheikh they'd met today, who obviously cared deeply about his extended family.

"I don't expect anything would change, but for you I'll think about it."

"Not for me, for you. Because after another week or so we won't see each other again."

A good thing for her. Not so much for him. She was the most special woman he'd ever known, and he wished they could spend more time together. But he was a man

who generally disappointed the people in his life, and she was a woman who'd already been badly disappointed by someone else. She deserved someone who believed in love and happy-ever-after. He definitely didn't, but maybe she'd somehow find that one day.

The thought made his chest feel oddly tight and he stood to end the torture of being with her when he shouldn't be. "We have an early morning. The Sheikh wants to get going as soon as we check once more that his wife's not in labor."

Her gaze stayed on his as she slowly pushed to her feet. Searching. Questioning. Not a surprise, since moments ago he'd been kissing her like a man on a mission to get horizontal with her as soon as possible.

Much as he still wanted that more than his next breath, she deserved better.

They walked in silence to their rooms, which were connected by an interior door, and Rafael knew he wouldn't get much sleep, thinking about her warm, soft body curled into a bed so close to his. The same way he'd been unable to sleep the night he'd tucked her into the guest room of his house, and he hadn't even known her then.

Now that he did, now that he knew the attraction was mutual, staying away from her would require Herculean strength, but for her sake he could do it.

Stopping at the door to her room, he somehow managed to kiss only her cheek, though he knew his lips lingered there too long. "Good night, Gabriella."

"This is totally unfair, you know."

"What is totally unfair?"

"Getting James to include me on this trip, then making me sit close to you, look at you, feel the touch of your hand while we drove, and it was all so distracting I barely noticed the gorgeous scenery. Then you took me on a romantic balloon ride with your arms around me, which was

the most incredible thing I've ever done. More romance and kissing and touching by a fire under the stars. And now you dump me like a hot rock in front of my door?"

The flash of fire in her eyes, the annoyance in her voice and her words were so surprising and adorable he couldn't help but laugh, even though having to leave her now wasn't in the least amusing. "Dumping is a strong word. I'm simply dropping you off after a wonderful day together."

"Why?" A challenge in her brown eyes joined that single word.

"For the reasons we just talked about outside, Gabriella," he said quietly, hoping she'd understand. "You deserve so much more than someone like me can give you. I'm leaving soon, and I don't want to be another man who disappoints you."

"You can't disappoint me if I'm not expecting anything." Her fingers slid up the front of his jacket to grasp his neck again, on up to trace his jaw and cheekbones, and even that simple touch made him want her even more. "You've made me see that I've been living in a cocoon this past two years. Hiding. But unlike you've had to do in these past weeks, I haven't been hiding from outside forces. Haven't been hiding because someone asked me to. I've been hiding from myself, and now I know it's time to change that." Her eyes softened, and her voice dropped to a whisper. "Being with you tonight is all I want. Breaking out of my shell to enjoy just one more incredible night with an incredible man. Is that so much to ask?"

He didn't even realize he'd wrapped his arms around her until his hold tightened and he couldn't make himself let her go. He warred with himself about the right thing to do. "Gabriella—"

She rose on tiptoe and buried her hands in his hair.

Pulled his mouth to hers for a kiss so long and sweet and hot it fried every last working brain cell he had left.

He somehow broke the kiss and stared into her beautiful eyes. "You promise you won't regret it when I leave? That you won't feel hurt that I can't stay?"

"I won't regret it. I won't be hurt. Unless you walk away this second. In which case I'll have to become like autocratic Rafael Moreno was the first day we met and 'take control of the situation.'"

How a woman's eyes could be amused, sensual, and flashing all at the same time he had no idea, but it was an irresistible combination. He loved how Gabriella made him smile and laugh and want her so much he ached. "You already know I hate to give up control of any situation, *mi ángel*," He touched his mouth to hers and began to walk her backwards ten feet down the hallway to his own door. "So how about we take control of it together?"

"I like that idea a lot."

And with that she plastered her body close to his, wrapped her arms around his neck and kissed him, which was so distracting he had a hard time remembering in which pocket he'd stuffed his room key. "Can you wait for just two seconds while I find my key?"

"I don't know. But I'm happy to help you look."

She peppered kisses on his face at the same time she put her hand caressingly into his pants pocket, obviously looking for something other than his room key, and he laughed then nearly moaned.

"I'd never have dreamed that charming midwife Gabriella Cain could be such a vixen." Thank God he finally found the key in his jacket pocket, because she was driving him crazy and they were both still fully clothed. He shoved the door open and nearly stumbled as he backed her inside because now that they weren't in a public hallway

and he'd abandoned all worries of hurting her, he couldn't get his hands and mouth on her fast enough.

"I've never been a vixen, I don't think." She pushed his jacket off at the same time he was unzipping hers. "Apparently, you bring her out in me."

"I'm about to show you what you bring out in me. Didn't you say you felt like Cinderella at the charity ball? I think I may be turning into the Beast." And while it was a joke, it wasn't far from the truth. He'd already stripped off her sweater and was in the process of unbuttoning her pants, and couldn't remember a time he'd felt as desperate to make love with a woman as he felt right now.

"You're mixing up your fairy tales. But since you are a prince, I guess that's okay."

She lost him on the conversation because he'd gotten her pants off and he took a moment to look at her, holding his breath at the vision before him. At her slim body, her luminous eyes, her hair a little tousled and her beautiful lips parted. He reached to unclasp her bra and as she stood there in near-naked perfection, he felt humbled. Incredibly lucky to be the man she'd chosen to break out of her shell with.

"Gabriella." He drew her close and kissed her, drinking in the taste of her and the sweetness of her, then scooped her up against his chest. A couple of steps to the bed and he'd deposited her in it, stripping off the last of his clothes to slide in next to her, loving the feel of her skin against his.

He captured her wrists in his hands and raised them above her head, letting his other roam in a gentle touch over her breasts and down her ribs as his mouth captured her nipple.

"I guess you were serious about taking control." She gasped. "How can I touch you if you're holding my hands?"

"Later. First, I want to make you feel good." So good,

so special for her that she'd never feel regret. Just memories of what it had been like between them, which he knew he'd never forget.

He moved his mouth back to hers, slipping his hand between her legs to feel the wetness there, caressing her for long minutes, and with any other woman he might have joined with her right then. But this was Gabriella, and he wanted to touch her all night. Could listen to her little moans forever as she writhed and gasped, but finally her hands broke free of his hold and she reached for him.

"I thought we agreed we were going to share control tonight, hmm?" she said, grasping and stroking him until he was the one moaning.

"Take pity on me, *bella*. The truth is I have little control around you."

He could feel her smile against his lips. "That's what I like to hear, Dr. Moreno. And remember how I said I was a Girl Scout? Always prepared?"

He laughed when he saw she had a condom in her hand, and where she'd grabbed it from he had no clue. Didn't care either, because after she slid it in place she rose up and sheathed herself on him. Rafael had never seen anything so beautiful in his life as this woman moving gracefully above him, looking down at him through eyes shining with the same intense desire that clawed into his very soul, leaving him weak. He held her hips, moving faster, wanting to see her expression as she came undone. When she did, arching her back and crying out, he was again filled with awe that he'd been privileged enough to be the one to put that look of ecstasy on her face. Then he followed her with his own cry of rapture as he gathered her close to his pounding heart. A heart he knew would never be quite the same again.

* * *

Rafael awoke to the feel of a slender shoulder pressed against his collarbone and a round, firm bottom spooned against him, and instantly began to harden at the sweet sensations and memories of last night's incredible lovemaking. Never had he experienced something so beyond the physical with a woman. Something that had demanded engagement from his heart and mind and soul every bit as much as his body.

He softly kissed Gabriella's hair, the hair he so loved to look at and touch. The golden fire that was such a part of who she was both inside and out, feisty and angelic, determined and dazzling. He moved his lips to the soft curve behind her ear, which he'd learned was a sweet spot she particularly enjoyed him kissing, but she didn't stir. Apparently she felt as worn out by their time together as he did. Worn out by the emotion of sharing their secrets with one another as much as their late-night lovemaking.

Finally hearing her story about her ex had been satisfying. Not completely, because he had a feeling there was more to the story than she'd wanted to talk about last night. But knowing she'd trusted him enough to share at least part of the reason she confessed she'd hidden away the past two years felt good. He wanted to be the person she danced with in the sunlight now that she'd decided to come out to play.

But he couldn't be that person, couldn't risk hurting her, and that reality blasted his sense of triumph to smithereens. He wouldn't be here for her. Couldn't be her forever love, because such a thing didn't exist.

He tucked her warm, captivating body closer, closing his eyes to breathe her in, and the ache in his chest told him one thing for certain. At least one person would hurt like hell when he moved on from L.A., and it would be the

first time in his life that ending a fling would make him feel anything but guilt or relief.

The muffled tones of his cellphone had him searching for it in the bed, finally finding it when he slid his hand beneath Gabriella's pillow. This time she did stir, and his good morning murmur in her ear got cut off in mid-word when he saw who was calling.

His brother.

What could he possibly want? His brother's life was full of responsibilities that Rafael was more than happy to not have. Also more than happy that his brother rarely called, because when he did it was usually to scold him for embarrassing the royal family, as if it wasn't enough to hear it from both his mother and his father.

He nearly ignored the call, but finally swung his feet to the side of the bed and stood, striding to the bathroom so as not to disturb Gabriella. "To what do I owe the honor, Alberto?"

"Unfortunately, I have bad news. Mother has had a heart attack, and you need to come home right away."

CHAPTER ELEVEN

GABBY DID HER best to focus on work but, despite repeatedly yanking her attention back to her job, she kept making silly mistakes. Thankfully none had been too important, but still. How often did she normally drop things? When was the last time she'd walked into the storage room before completely forgetting what she'd needed? It had happened twice already. And giving a patient still water when she'd asked for sparkling…? Never.

And she knew it was because Rafael and his family were weighing on her mind. When he'd told her he had to leave and why, he'd sounded very matter-of-fact, but she knew him now. Knew that behind that suave and confident exterior was a man with a sensitive heart who cared passionately for others. No matter what he'd said about his family, about his conviction that they were disappointed in him, that he'd let them down when he'd decided to take a different path than what they'd planned for him, she could see he wasn't indifferent to it. That he cared about that more than he'd ever let on. And when she'd looked into his eyes after he'd told her his mother was ill, the calm mask on his face hadn't concealed the worry in his eyes.

Of course he'd been worried. No matter what kind of relationship anyone had with their parents, they were still important. Still loved.

She stared, unseeing, at the tray of supplies in her hands. Love. Such a complicated and confusing thing. She'd been so sure she'd loved Ben, had made a baby with him and had been planning to marry him. But now? Now she knew the truth. That it had all just been easy. They'd dated, he'd seemed like a good, stable man, and when she'd gotten pregnant had figured it was time to get married. Wasn't that what most people would have done?

But she'd never really loved him.

She knew that now. Knew because she was crazily in love with Rafael Moreno. Arrogant prince, excellent doctor, and tender lover. The knowledge balled her stomach, and her heart swelled at the same time it pinched tight. How had she let herself fall in love with the man? A notorious playboy, an international jet-setter who didn't stay in one place very long, and a man who freely admitted he didn't believe in forever-after love.

Truth was, though, she couldn't blame herself. It hadn't been a question of letting herself fall for him. It would have been like trying to stop an ocean wave as she swam in the Pacific, because Rafael was a force of nature every bit as mesmerizing and powerful.

She loved him. And when he'd kissed her goodbye, she'd known there was a good chance he might never be back.

The ball in her stomach rolled and her knuckles whitened on the tray, but she lifted her chin as she picked up her pace down the hallway. Somehow she had to focus on what she did best, which was work. It wasn't Rafael's fault she'd fallen so hard for him. If he called to report back about his mother, which he'd promised to do, she'd do everything in her ability to listen like a friend would and not let him know how much she missed him. How much she

hoped he'd come back to L.A., but at the same time part of her hoped he wouldn't.

The love, the connection she felt with him seemed huge and overwhelming and uncontrollable. But the thought of having a real relationship with someone again? Something more than the short fling she'd decided to allow herself with him? Just the idea of it scared her to death.

"Why do I even care, Freya?"

Gabby hesitated at the sound of Mila's upset voice, not wanting to walk by the open lounge door while she was obviously having a personal conversation. "He already broke my heart once—shouldn't that have been enough to make my feelings turn to stone where he's concerned?"

"We can't just turn our feelings on and off like a faucet, Mila," Freya said in a soothing tone. "It's okay to feel the way you do."

"I mean, it almost seems like he's flaunting his new girlfriend, doesn't it? Like he's deliberately waving her in my face to upset me."

"I think James...well, he might be having his own struggles, Mila. He's never been one to let emotions control him, you know? Maybe his behavior is some unconscious reaction to seeing you again. I don't know what else to say, except you should tell him what you just told me and give him some time to think about it."

Now tearful, Mila continued to talk, and Gabby pivoted, deciding to go back the other way so as not to embarrass her. Her already aching heart hurt a little more, feeling bad that Mila was so upset. Why did life have to be so hard? Why did love have to hurt?

Giving your heart to someone made you horribly vulnerable, she knew. So where, exactly, did that leave her when it came to Dr. Rafael Moreno?

* * *

Everyone walking the hospital hallways drifted toward the walls to leave an open path as Rafael strode through, murmuring to one another and bowing as he passed, and his lips twisted at the sure sign he was home. He'd grown up with that kind of deference. Hadn't really even noticed it until he'd left the country. Now most people just saw him as a doctor, and it struck him how much he greatly preferred that to this kind of respect, based only on his birthright and not his accomplishments.

Something his parents and brother still didn't understand.

He pressed his lips together and forged on until he got to his mother's room. Then surprised himself when he had to stop outside it to inhale long calming breaths, fighting for composure. It wasn't as though he didn't practically live in hospitals. Between medical school and residency and working around the world, doing basic medicine and not the specialized obstetrics he did elsewhere, he'd seen thousands of sick people. Had seen plenty of them die. Had seen patients make miraculous recoveries too.

But none of them had been his mother.

Yes, she aggravated him, insulted him, berated him and lectured him. But she was still his mother and, damn it, he loved her. She'd been so angry about the recent press brouhaha and the various photos and lurid details, half of which had been made up, and he wasn't proud of the things he'd said back to her when she'd scolded him about it. He couldn't remember what they were, exactly, but he knew his words had hurt her feelings.

All that felt pretty unforgivable now that she was lying in a hospital bed in Intensive Care. Even though her heart attack had been fairly mild and the prognosis was good, he also knew things could go downhill fast.

Bracing himself, he forced his feet to go through the doorway. Then stood feeling slightly off balance at the end of the hospital bed, gripping the railing tight, because the pale woman hooked up to machines, with an I.V. in her arm and an oxygen hose in her nose, didn't look like his mother at all. She looked a good ten years older than the last time he'd seen her, and in that very second he vowed to never let so much time go by again between visits.

He swallowed hard then looked past the scary things to the one thing that seemed normal and familiar. Her hair was remarkably well coiffed and tidy for someone lying in the ICU after a heart attack, and it helped him manage a smile. Yes, this woman was his mother after all. The vain queen of the land who was always perfect and regal from head to toe.

Her eyelids flickered open and took a moment to focus on him. Then she smiled and slowly extended her hand. "Rafael."

The heavy tightness in his chest loosened at the way she said his name. At the way her smile, weak as it was, lit her tired eyes. He quickly stepped around the bed to grasp her hand. "Hi, Mother. Your hair looks nice. I'm surprised, though, that you're not wearing lipstick."

Her smile widened into a slightly wheezy chuckle. "Had one tucked under my pillow, but I think the nurse took it when they changed the sheets." The squeeze she gave his hand was weak but stronger than he'd expected, and he began to relax.

"Isn't this a rather drastic way to get me to come home?"

"You make me do drastic things. You've been like that since you were a little boy, and you're apparently never going to change, even if it kills me."

"And apparently you aren't going to change either, scolding me while flat on your back in a hospital bed."

Her acerbic tone was that of the queen and mother he knew well, but her eyes held a new vulnerability that made him feel guilty as hell for all the things he'd done wrong in his life that had caused her anxiety and stress. He leaned over to kiss her cheek. "I checked all your test and lab results. Has your cardiologist been in to talk to you about it?"

"Yes. But I'd like to hear what you think."

She wanted to hear what he thought? Since when? "You have some mild blockage in your right coronary artery. They're going to do angioplasty to cross through the area that's narrowed by cholesterol plaque, and put in a stent to bridge that narrowing. The procedure has been done for years now, and results are usually good. So, assuming it goes well, you should be your old, bossy self soon."

"I'm never bossy. I'm simply assertive and direct."

"Rafael!"

He turned at the sound of his father's booming voice to see him striding into the room. Unlike Rafael's mother, he looked exactly like he always did, posture erect and the picture of health with his skin tanned from golfing and his silver hair thick and wavy. But his eyes held a worry Rafael had never seen before.

His father's arms enfolded him in a hard hug. "What do you think about your mother? Is she going to be all right? Is what they want to do a good idea? I've talked to the doctors here, but I trust you to know what's really going on."

Rafael stared at him in shock. Again, this was entirely new. He couldn't remember the last time they'd trusted him about anything, let alone his doctoring skills.

"I was just explaining the test results to Mother." He repeated what he'd told her, and as he stood there, beyond surprised at the intent interest on both his parents' faces as he spoke, Gabriella's words came back to him. Saying that he should talk to them, should share how he felt about

their opinion of him. He'd told himself for years he didn't care if they respected him or not. But the peculiar mix of emotions filling his chest as he stood there looking at them told him loud and clear he'd been lying to himself.

Maybe Gabriella was right, and it was time to see if the air could be cleared between them, at least a little. "But I have to be honest. I'm surprised you're asking my opinion. You've expressed nothing but disappointment that I decided to become a doctor."

"I admit we wanted you to stay here and help your brother with various royal duties, but when you became a doctor? That wasn't a disappointment, Rafael." His father grasped his shoulder in a strong grip. "We were proud of you."

"Always, Rafael. And I'm sorry we never really told you that," his mother said. Her eyes held some look he couldn't be sure of—guilt, maybe? Contrition? "As I've been lying here, I've thought about you. Realized that perhaps we've been wrong to object to you living your life the way you want to."

"I'm sorry, too," his father said. "In case you don't know, your mother regularly brags about your work. When she's not apologizing for the stupid things you do sometimes, that is." His father's grin took any sting out of his words, and he squeezed Rafael's shoulder before releasing it to hold his mother's hand tight. And when his parents' eyes met both were filled with softness, an obvious connection that he'd never seen between them before.

That rocked him back on his heels as much as what they'd just said. They were proud of him? Even *bragged* about him? He found it nearly impossible to believe, but it was becoming clear he'd been wrong about a lot of things, so maybe it was really true.

His mind filled with a vision of Gabriella and her in-

sight about his family that he hadn't truly thought was a real possibility. Insight that had been pretty incredible, since she hadn't even met his parents. She'd figured out something in just a few minutes of conversation with him that he hadn't seen in thirty-one years.

She was one special woman, no doubt about that. Someone who understood human nature in a way he was obviously still trying to figure out, which was just one reason she was an amazing midwife.

Just one reason why he'd been so attracted to her that very first day they'd met.

A need to talk to her that moment, to call her and tell her he'd taken her advice, had him opening his mouth to tell his parents he'd be back in a short time when a nurse came into the room.

"Time to check your vital signs, Your Majesty," she said, before coming to a dead stop to stare at Rafael.

A good excuse to make his exit. "Then I'll leave you for the moment, Mother. I'll be back in a little while."

He scooted past the nurse, who still hadn't moved, on down the long hallway to an exit door so he'd be sure to get a good signal on his phone. Just the thought of hearing Gabriella's voice made his chest feel lighter than it had since the second his brother had called him in Vail.

Gabby wandered restlessly out of her kitchen with a cup of tea in her hand and plopped onto her sofa. The sofa where she'd made amazing love with Rafael, and thinking of it made her breath short and her heart heavy. If she was going to feel this way every time she sat on it, she might have to sell it and buy a new one. Something a completely different style and color. Maybe rearrange the whole room while she was at it.

Then again, her memories of being in Vail with him—

their hot-air balloon ride, their intimate conversation beneath the stars, their lovemaking there too were all etched in her mind forever. And since being hundreds of miles away from Colorado didn't seem to be doing much to dim those memories, rearranging her living room probably wouldn't help much either.

She grabbed the TV remote and skimmed through some channels, not finding much that grabbed her attention. Why hadn't she taken on a third shift instead of just a double to keep her mind occupied? To keep her mind off Rafael and his mother and wondering how she was and if he was upset and if he'd ever come back to Los Angeles.

Wondering if she'd ever hear from him again.

If she did, she'd try to act normal. Cool. Like the kind of woman he usually dated, who didn't expect anything more than a quick fling. Not that she did expect more than that, or even wanted more than that, and had to somehow make sure he knew that, but still.

Lord, she was a confused mess. She sighed at the same time her phone rang and her heart nearly flipped over in a loop-the-loop when she saw it was him on the line.

"Is your mom okay? Are you okay? Is everything all right? Where are you?"

She winced even as the last words were coming out of her mouth. So much for being calm and cool.

"I'm at the hospital. I've just left Mother for a bit and am glad to say she's doing well. They'll be doing an angioplasty later today, and hopefully that will go smoothly and she'll be heading home soon."

"That's wonderful news! Thanks so much for letting me know. I've been so worried."

"I knew you would be, *bella*, because you care about everyone, even people you've never met. In fact, I have to tell you I took your advice and I'm impressed with your amaz-

ing insight. How is it you understand the inner workings of my parents' brains when you don't even know them?"

"What do you mean? What advice?"

"You told me you thought I must be wrong about them not being happy that I became a doctor. And you were right. I just about fell over when they were asking my opinion about Mother's health and the upcoming procedure, and decided then to ask them, to tell them my perspective on it. Only because you'd suggested I do, so I thank you for that. They assured me they aren't unhappy that I became a doctor, and I suspect my relationship with them will be a little less…turbulent now."

"Oh, Rafael. I'm so glad you did." She'd known his parents had to be proud of who he was. How could they not be?

"Me too."

Gabby bit her lip, feeling the silence stretch awkwardly between them but not wanting to say anything that showed how much she'd been missing him. Definitely didn't want to ask what his plans were, and prayed he'd tell her so she wouldn't have to either ask or stay anxiously in the dark about it.

"Anyway, I just wanted to give you an update," he said, his voice low and warm and not all that different from the way it had sounded when they'd made love, and she quivered in spite of herself. "I'm not sure exactly when I'll be back. I'll be staying here at least until she's stabilized from the procedure—I'll let you know how that goes."

"I'd like that. And I'll be thinking of all of you."

"And I'll be thinking of you, Gabriella Cain, both when I'm awake and asleep. You can be sure of that. *Adios* for now."

"Bye." She hoped her voice wasn't shaking at his words as much as her heart was. "Talk to you soon."

She hugged the phone to her chest and grinned like an idiot. Then, seconds later, a niggle of fear jabbed her in the solar plexus. When he came back, would she ready to put herself out there again? Let herself be in a relationship with a man, if that was what he'd been hinting at? Risk getting hurt all over again? There was a part of her that said no. The scared, wimpy part Rafael didn't know about. He thought she was feisty and brave and wasn't that who she wanted to be? Who she used to be?

Rafael had risked his family's disapproval to go for what he wanted, which was to become a doctor. Wasn't the chance to maybe, possibly be happy with him worth even more of a risk?

Yes. There was absolutely no doubt about that. It was worth that and a whole lot more.

She didn't have to be at work for another eight hours. She felt beyond antsy, but it was a little too late to go out somewhere. How in the world was she going to fill the time?

Forty minutes of cleaning her apartment left it unfortunately immaculate. Chewing her lip, she had an *aha* moment. "My knitting stuff and the DVD on how to do it!" Surely learning something new would take up at least an hour, wouldn't it? Then, with any luck, she could get some sleep.

Like that was going to happen.

She pulled the knitting things from a drawer she'd stuffed them into and was crouching down to stick the DVD into the player when one of the shows featuring stories about musicians and movie stars came on the TV. About to switch it off, she stopped dead when Rafael Moreno's face filled the screen.

"And in other news, remember Prince Rafael Moreno and his former stripper girlfriend? Looks like he's gone

to the opposite end of the spectrum, dating a wholesome nurse midwife."

Heart pounding, Gabby's legs felt so wobbly that she tumbled back onto her rear as she stared at the bubbly blonde host of the show. How had they found out about her?

"But wholesome and midwife might not always go hand in hand, at least when it comes to Gabriella Cain, who works at the famous and prestigious Hollywood Hills Clinic.

"Our reporters have been busy doing in-depth research on the prince's newest fling and found out that just two years ago she was not only pregnant with another man's child but her utter disregard for her health led to her child being stillborn. A tragedy that could have been avoided, sources say, if she'd been focused on her unborn child instead of herself.

"Not something you would expect from a midwife who takes care of pregnant women every day, is it? We're the first to bring you this breaking report and we are pretty sure that Rafael's parents, and many others in the palace, will be furious all over again about his taste in women. After all, someone like Gabriella Cain isn't the best choice to be the prince's girlfriend or future wife, is she?"

A sickening, icy numbness crept across every inch of Gabby's skin as she watched and listened. Saw the photos of her and Rafael together coming out of his house the morning after the night she'd fallen asleep. Photos at the charity ball. Photos in Vail. Heard the lies, and the truth too, about her mistakes and her loss and how Ben had left her because of her terrible choices. There was even a photo of her baby's grave marker, and seeing it made her feel like she was dying inside.

She was shaking so badly it hurt physically, but she found she couldn't move to turn it off. Had to watch the

entire train wreck of her life unfold in garish Technicolor for all the world to see. And just when she was sure it couldn't get any worse, it did.

Because some person, she had no idea who, was offering a loud opinion that someone like Gabby, a woman who'd neglected to pay attention to signs there might be a problem with her own pregnancy and baby, was totally unsuited to be a midwife anywhere, let alone at The Hollywood Hills Clinic, where patients had come to expect the very best.

Dear God.

She should have told Rafael. Should have told him their night together in Vail, when she'd only touched on the truth, telling him about Ben. Had decided she would when the time was right, if there'd been a time that was right. If she'd seen him again.

And now he'd find out this way. In this horrible, lurid, appalling way with exaggerated detail that made her sound like a monster. Not a woman who'd made a bad mistake and had had her heart broken because of it.

She had no idea if Rafael had planned for them to possibly be together as a couple, but it didn't matter. Even if he had, after he heard about this he'd drop that thought fast and run as far as he could. And as she stared at the screen, the nasty things being said about her sounded very far away. A light year's distance.

The same distance she now felt between herself and Rafael.

It made her realize that, even though she hadn't let herself admit it, deep inside her stupid, lonely heart she'd thought maybe, possibly the two of them had something special. Something that might bud into a real relationship, even bloom into a forever-after. But her pathetic heart

should have known better than to keep clinging to those Cinderella dreams.

As a prince, the man would surely need an heir. And even if, somehow, he still wanted to be with her after all this, it would be impossible. She could never go through the nightmare of losing a baby again. Never get pregnant again. Because the pain ripping through her heart at that moment felt, impossibly, even more torturous than the day she'd held her beautiful, lifeless baby in her arms.

A damp saltiness touched her lips, and she realized tears were streaking down her cheeks in stinging waterfalls. With shaking hands she slowly swiped them away.

Somehow she had to start a new life. She'd done it two years ago and, as hard as it had been, she could do it again. After this horrifying media exposure she couldn't imagine a single patient would trust her anymore. She didn't want James and Freya to feel bad about having to let her go. And even if, somehow, they didn't want her to leave, she couldn't face the looks and secret whispers about her past and her baby from patients and staff alike, whether it was criticism or sympathy.

No. It was time to cut the cord, so to speak, and be reborn. Again. Start over someplace where people didn't know her past and, somehow, try for a new future.

A future that could never include Rafael, and of all the things ripping out bleeding pieces of her heart that was the very worst.

CHAPTER TWELVE

"Rafael!"

His father's bellow carried all the way down the hospital hallway, and Rafael took off in a dead run to his mother's room, fearing the worst. His heart practically stopped when he saw the bed was empty, and his father was pacing the room like an agitated grizzly bear.

"What? Has something happened to Mother?"

"She's all right, for now at least. They took her to prep her for the surgery. I hate to think, though, how your damned latest scandal is going to upset her. The woman has already had a heart attack, Rafael—how is it that you don't care how your actions will affect her recovery? Why don't you give a damn about anyone but yourself?"

"I don't know what you're talking about, but I wouldn't be here if I didn't care about Mother and her health and recovery." He fought down his anger, which was rising to match his father's, because he didn't understand what had enraged the man again.

"You told us you'd go to L.A. to stay out of the news for a while. And now this! Who knows, maybe the last few scandals were part of the reason your mother had her heart attack in the first place. Maybe you should think about her health and recovery first instead of last."

"Again, I don't know what you're talking about, so

please enlighten me." He wanted to add, *Before I put a fist through this wall, or even your face.* Which, of course, he'd never do, but visualizing how good that would feel after being accused, again, of something he doubtless hadn't done helped calm him down.

"This." His father flicked on the TV, and a news station blared with chatter and photos. Rafael stared in horror. These pictures weren't dim and blurred. These showed him holding Gabriella's hand as he'd helped her from the car outside the charity ball. The two of them going into her apartment afterwards. The two of them kissing—hotly kissing—by that fire pit in Vail.

Damn it to hell.

"So I dated a woman? A nice woman. A few casual dates. Since when is that an embarrassment that would give Mother another heart attack?" He tried to keep his voice cool, but it was hard with his breath short and his anger flaming higher. Did his parents expect him to stop living?

"Nice? Not according to this. This shows why she's not a good choice for you. Are you ever going to find someone to settle down with and marry who's appropriate? Who would make your mother happy and proud?"

Proud. There was that word. They'd said they were proud of him for being a doctor, but obviously it stopped there. They weren't proud of his private life, of who he was outside the hospital. He'd told himself he didn't care but, like the rest of it, knew now that wasn't true.

He shifted his gaze back to the TV monitor and listened to the story in all its garishness, his gut burning and his heart feeling like someone had driven a scalpel straight through it.

A stillborn child. This was the source of the pain he'd seen on Gabriella's face as she'd watched little Skye in the incubator. When new mothers had held their infants close

to their breasts. And now all that pain was being blasted out there for all the world to see. Lurid details he knew had to be killing her to hear and see splashed in the media, and even unbelievable, nasty comments implying she was unfit to be a midwife.

And that it was happening at all was completely his fault.

His fault. There was no doubt he'd made the torment she obviously carried inside even worse. And as bad as that felt, there was something else digging a hole into his chest. The fact that she hadn't told him any of this, hadn't shared it when they'd been talking about their pasts and their secrets, made him wonder if there were other things in her past she didn't want to share. Other things she wanted to keep hidden.

It seemed most everyone he got involved with had a past that was better left buried. Over and over, his notoriety ended up causing whatever it was to become unearthed. And that hurt everyone. His mother, now ill and fragile. His father, angry about that, and who could blame him? Whatever woman Rafael had been seeing at any moment. And even his career, when a few scandals had threatened to derail his reputation as a doctor, making a few people see only that part of him, and not his skills as a physician.

No wonder he ended up being a disappointment to some of the people closest to him. And not only because of the media. Because he'd never wanted to commit to anyone. Still didn't believe in love and forever-after, though for a brief moment being with Gabriella had made him wonder if he could possibly be wrong about that. He had learned not to fully trust anyone, and felt ashamed that a small part of him felt that way about Gabriella, wondering what might come out next that would upset his mother while she

was in Intensive Care. And what kind of son would risk his mother's health and recovery for a fling?

God. What did it say about him that he would even let that cross his mind about Gabriella? Obviously, he couldn't see her anymore. For her sake. For his mother's. The damned selfish man inside him argued with that decision, but Rafael resolutely struck him down. Gabriella had already been through so much terrible heartache. She deserved someone who knew how to trust completely. Who wouldn't expose her to public scandal. A man who could offer her something she might believe was real love, forever wiping away the pain of her old boyfriend leaving just when she'd needed him.

"No, Father, I'm never going to settle down and get married, which I've told you before. I'm sorry that's a disappointment to you and Mother, but that's just the way it is. I'm going to stay here for a while, though, until Mother gets well. Because I do care about her, even though you've thought some of the things I've done make it seem like I don't."

He turned and left the room, heading back to the door opening to the outside, needing to suck some air into his lungs that wasn't vibrating with anger. And to call Gabriella again.

His last promise to his father would be the easiest to keep. Staying away from women wouldn't be an issue, because he had no desire to date anyone besides Gabriella or make love with anyone other than her. And he knew that would be true for a long, long time.

Rafael wasn't sure how long he stood there on the small hospital balcony, staring across the landscape of the place where he'd grown up. The place he'd left for too long, searching for something. When he'd met Gabriella, a part of him, an unconscious part, had felt a little like he might

have found it. But that part was the selfish part, and he was kicking that guy out of his life for good.

He knew he needed to stay here for now. Lie low. Really lie low this time, being the poster boy for a good prince doing his duties. Even embrace the good that might come of that, bringing his knowledge of healthcare needs around the world to charitable work here at home. Be here for his mother, keep an eye on her medical care as her health improved. Not upset her. Be here for his family.

He held his phone in his hand, staring at it, but couldn't make himself phone her. He'd ended things with a woman more times than he could count, but it had never felt painful like this did. Nearly impossible, in fact. But he couldn't be the man she needed. He couldn't be his old, selfish self.

He made himself phone her number. It went straight to voice mail, and his heart fell when he realized he wouldn't get to hear her voice again. At the same time, the cowardly part of him felt relieved to be able to just leave a message.

He hesitated over what to say, then decided to keep it short. Without detail, or comments about her pain that he'd just learned about. Anything that might hurt her more, or make her try to contact him. Weaken his resolve to keep her safe from him.

"Gabriella? Rafael. Listen, I'm... Mother is so far still fine, so don't be worried about that, but...well, I don't think I'll be coming back to L.A. I need to stay here until she's stronger. It was great knowing you, and I wish you only the best for your life. Truly." His voice shook on that word, but he couldn't help it. The last ones he whispered, so she wouldn't know. *"Adios, mi bella."*

Gabby sat on the damp, green grass in the Seattle cemetery, not caring that her pants were getting wet and cold.

She couldn't care about her clothes or anything else when she'd lost everything she cared about all over again.

Her baby lay under this earth where she'd just placed a small bouquet of spring tulips. The pain of losing him had slowly faded with time, and even more in the past weeks when she'd realized that shutting herself in a box by working all the time was no way to honor the tiny, beautiful baby who had been her son. Who should have had a chance to grow up into a boy and then a man. Seeing Rafael live his life on his own terms had opened her eyes to the realization that she wanted to live the same way. Without hiding, without fear of what others might think of her if they learned the truth.

But, oh, how wrong she'd been that could be possible. Her past mistake would always be there. Ben had blamed her, and she'd blamed herself. Now others did too, and she thought maybe they were right. Maybe she wasn't fit to be a midwife anymore. A woman who didn't listen to her own body probably shouldn't be listening to anyone else's.

So if she couldn't be a midwife anymore, where did she belong? What would she do with her life? God, she just didn't know. But she did know one thing. She could never be a wife and mother, because there was no way she could go through that kind of heartache all over again. She'd gone back into hiding from that, at least, and this time she was never coming out.

Staring down at the small stone carved with her baby's name, she became aware of a movement next to her and turned her head, only to have her heart completely stop in shock.

Ben.

For a moment she could barely process it. She opened her mouth to speak, but nothing came out. He gave her

a twisted smile then knelt on the grass next to her. "Hi, Gabby. Rough day, huh?"

He'd seen the news. "Yeah. Pretty rough."

"All that garbage on TV made me think about you and this little guy. Gave me a strangely strong need to come here, and now that I see you're here too, I figure that's the reason why."

"What do you mean?"

"Because the universe knows I need to make things right with you."

"Make what right?"

He stared at her a long moment, his hand gripping the back of his neck before he dropped it, placing it on top of hers. "Hell. I...I'd been thinking that maybe I'd call you after I stopped here today, but now that you're right in front of me, all the things I know I should say to you seem a lot harder than I thought they would."

Since she didn't have any idea what to say to him either, she kept quiet and just looked at him, waiting. Bracing herself for the worst.

"I know I treated you badly when our baby died inside of you," he finally said. "I was hurt at losing him and angry at the world about it. I took that anger out on you."

"No, you didn't. You didn't say much about anything." And in some ways that terrible silence, his inability to talk about it, had been worse to take than if he'd ranted at her.

"Maybe not. But when you blamed yourself I didn't tell you it wasn't your fault. I felt the same horrible loss you did, and it pushed me to act in a way I'm not proud of. I let you believe I blamed you, but I never did. Not really."

Again, she didn't respond, having no idea how to process what he was saying. How to feel about it. She'd held his blame, along with her own, so close to her bruised and battered heart. Had let it live there, a sharp splinter that had

stabbed and festered, and she hadn't even tried to remove it because she'd believed she deserved the pain.

"There's more, and I want to tell you about it," he continued, still wearing that wry smile. "I'm married now. Have a baby on the way, and after what happened to us I admit I've been damned scared. I've asked her doctor lots of questions, and he's explained things to me. So even if there was a part of me that wasn't sure back then, I know now. You working late that day, assuming the pains you felt were nothing? That didn't have a damned thing to do with losing our baby. It was just one of those really bad outcomes that happen sometimes."

Gabby's throat closed, and tears burned the backs of her eyes as she looked at Ben. The man who two years ago she'd expected to share her life with. Who had in one second of hardship left.

This was proof he was the good person she'd thought he was. That he'd been perhaps as immature and unprepared as she'd been in trying to deal with their loss. "Thank you for telling me this. It's been…very hard to know how to feel about it."

"I know. But here's something else I want to tell you. We both had a bad time of it, but I've finally found happiness again. I love my wife and can't wait until our baby is born. I don't know what's going on with you and this prince guy in the news, but you know…?" His smile broadened to become a real one. "It's worth taking a risk. It is. And he'd be one lucky guy to have you."

Unable to say another word, stunned by all he'd said, Gabby just stared at him. He reached out to squeeze her shoulder before he stood, and after a lingering look at their baby's headstone he was gone.

Gabby sat for long minutes, processing it all. The knowledge that he didn't blame her seeped slowly into

the fog in her brain. Pushed out some of the guilt she'd carried for so long. And as that guilt eased from her chest it was replaced by cautious optimism.

Maybe she could put the past behind her, the way Ben had. Maybe she could be happy again, and maybe that happiness could come from being with Rafael. Hadn't she decided, before the shock of the media mess, that she needed to try to be more like her old self? That spending time with him to see where it might lead was worth the risk of future pain?

A gusty breeze moved her hair, and she had to smile. She could feel it. A shift in the wind, both literally and figuratively. No more guilt. No more hiding. No more self-protection. Time to move on, and what better way than to reach for the hand of a certain handsome prince who, from what he'd told her about his relationship with his parents, just might be experiencing a little shift in the wind himself?

She looked down at the small gravestone. She kissed her fingertips then slowly caressed the name and date etched there before standing tall. As she walked to her car she knew that part of this healing, part of moving forward would come from sharing everything with Rafael. Talking about it over the phone wouldn't be the way to do it, but with any luck his mother would improve and he'd be back soon.

Her chest filling with a buoyancy she hadn't felt in a long, long time, Gabby fished her keys from her purse and got into the car. Then her heart smacked into her ribs when she saw Rafael had called and left a message.

A giddy feeling of joy bubbled through her, and she quickly brought up her voice mail. His voice was odd, not warm like it usually was. Not even filled with its normal

confidence, and in seconds the bubble deflated and flattened completely.

Her ears rang as she listened to the classic brush-off. "It was great knowing you, and I wish you only the best for your life…" Then his final quiet words felt like a hard slap of reality. *"Adios, mi bella."*

Adios, mi bella.

She wasn't sure how long she sat in the car, hands still holding the phone limply in her lap. Her pants, damp from the grass, now chilled her to the bone, and somehow she finally managed to lift her hands to the steering wheel to get the engine running and the heat on.

What a fool she was. Thinking Rafael, a man who'd stated more than once that he didn't believe in long-term relationships and forever-after, would want to be with her longer than a few days or weeks. But even as that knowledge felt like a huge hole in her heart she straightened her spine. Looked into the rearview mirror, swiped away the tears leaking from her eyes, and saw the new Gabby. A stronger Gabby. A woman who was moving on from the past to a new future. A person who deserved someone who loved her—hadn't Ben said any man would be lucky to have her? She'd thought maybe Rafael was that man, but that had been a pipe dream. A fairy tale.

Her cold hands gripped the steering wheel. Once she found a new job she'd find a way to balance work with finding a life that included other things. Maybe she'd even get lucky like Ben and find someone to love who'd love her back.

The hardest thing she'd ever done had been dealing with the loss of her baby. The next hardest thing?

Forgetting all about Rafael Moreno.

CHAPTER THIRTEEN

"So you agree that your mother looks good? That she's recovering well?"

Rafael looked at the anxiety in his father's eyes as they walked to his mother's room, surprised all over again at the intensity of it. Though he supposed he shouldn't be. Even if his parents didn't have a particularly close relationship, they'd still been married for over thirty-five years, so that had to mean something.

"The angioplasty went well, and every test so far shows she's doing very well. I'm sure they told you they're planning to release her tomorrow for some T.L.C. back at the palace."

"Yes. But I wanted to make sure you agreed with that."

Just yesterday, his father's words would have pleased him. At that moment, though, he didn't seem able to feel much more than a heavy emptiness. "I agree with it. I'm guessing you've scheduled more nursing care than she wants, and she'll be chafing at the bit about everyone fussing around her."

His father chuckled. "She's already chafing. You know your mother."

They entered the room, and his mother promptly frowned at him. "You're giving me that disapproving

look," he said. "Never thought I'd miss it, but at least it shows you're feeling pretty good."

"I'm wondering what's happened with your latest scandal. Really, Rafael, it's unbelievable."

"Why do you always pick the wrong women, son?" his father chimed in. "It's like you do it on purpose."

He stared at his father. Maybe he did. Maybe he'd always chosen women he knew were "inappropriate" as part of keeping his distance from them. But Gabriella? He hadn't really chosen her.

He'd been irresistibly drawn to her.

"Maybe I've done that in the past, Father, but Gabriella Cain is different from any woman I've ever known." He might not be able to be with her again, but he wasn't about to tolerate anyone saying nasty things about her. "She's not only beautiful, she's smart and good at her job and beyond caring to her patients. I don't know the whole story the media's been throwing out there, but I do know it has to be sensationalized and maybe even totally wrong. If you met Gabriella, you'd love her."

His mother's frown lifted into raised eyebrows, and she cocked her head. "Sounds like maybe *you* love her."

He stilled. Pictured Gabriella's sweet face and fiery hair and the tenderness in her eyes, and knowing he'd never see any of that again physically hurt.

Love her? Maybe he did. What he felt for her was unlike anything he'd felt before. But love was fleeting, he knew.

Both his parents were looking at him expectantly, but he didn't want to talk about Gabriella unless he had to, and changed the subject. "How does the surgical entry wound feel, Mother? Has the pain lessened?"

"Yes. It's not too bad."

"I've seen them change the bandages, and it looks bad to me," his father said. "Your mother's just tough. Always

has been." As he looked at his wife the man's eyes were filled with a warmth and softness Rafael had rarely seen.

"Is that a compliment or something else?" His mother reached for his father's hand and smiled at him.

"A compliment. As though I'd give anything else to my very special wife." He held her hand tight, leaning to give her forehead a lingering kiss.

Rafael stared at the way his parents looked at one another. At the...the *love* in his father's eyes as he gently stroked her skin, bruised from the needle sticks and IV.

His parents *did* love each other? Even though their marriage had been arranged and the time they spent together seemed to be far less than the time they spent apart? All Rafael had ever noticed had been cordial respect between them, but maybe because they were his own parents he hadn't really been looking.

All those questions and revelations jumbled around in his head until everything settled into a new order and a clear focus. And with that focus came another vision of Gabriella.

Until this very second, once his mother was completely well, he'd planned to keep living his life the way he always had, moving from place to place and from woman to woman and from job to job. Never dipping his toe deeper than the shallow end of the pool for fear of becoming trapped and emotionally entangled, ending up in a long-term loveless situation like his parents and brother.

Except, apparently, he'd been wrong about that. And could that mean he might be wrong about his sibling's marriage too?

It didn't really matter. What mattered was that he'd closed his mind and heart to any possibility of real love. Had shut it tight, not even realizing he'd been doing it. But wanting to see inside Gabriella's heart and mind for the

time he was with her had cracked his heart and brain open instead, just enough to let in a sliver of light. Instead of learning her secrets, she'd gently but directly gotten him to spill his own. To explain that he was the black sheep and always would be. Instead of judging him, she'd believed in him. Believed his parents must, too.

And he was damned if she hadn't been absolutely right.

He watched his father cup his mother's cheek in his palm, and their stunning love and deep connection struck him all over again.

At that moment he knew he looked at Gabriella exactly the same way. Looked at her in a way he'd never before looked at a woman, and if he was as lucky as hell, she just might look back at him the same way. He didn't have to worry about protecting her from him, because she'd turned him into a different man. He didn't have to worry about exposing her to media rumors, because he was ready to make a commitment to her he'd never dreamed possible until now.

"I'm in love with her." He actually said the words out loud he was so shocked. And rocked back onto his heels yet again.

"What did you say?"

He blinked to see both his parents looking at him quizzically. "I said I'm in love with her. Gabriella Cain. I'm in love with her, and I'd like to talk to you about it."

Normally, on a long flight Rafael could get some sleep in the comfortable bed on his family's jet. But that had proved impossible. He'd read medical journals he needed to catch up on, checked the stock market, and even worked on some crossword puzzles, which he hadn't done in years. But no matter what he did, his mind was only partly there. Gabriella occupied most of his thoughts, and all of his heart,

and every hour that passed before he could tell her how she'd changed him and ask her to be his wife felt like extended torture.

Finally, the early evening lights of L.A. stretched across the horizon and he found himself wondering which golden light, of the millions of lights switching on at that moment in the city, was the one lighting her cozy living room.

The jet's wheels had barely touched the runway when he switched on his cellphone to call her. He saw that he had a voice-mail message from James, and, much as he was desperate to talk to Gabriella, figured he should find out what James wanted, in case it had something to do with her. When he pulled it up to listen to it, he stopped smiling and stopped breathing at the same time.

Then listened to it again.

"Rafael, it's James. Do you happen to know where Gabby went? Give me a call."

What the hell? What did James mean?

He quickly punched in her number, and a cold dread began to seep through his veins when a recorded message said the number was no longer in service. He stared hard at the phone as if, somehow, he could reach inside to conjure Gabriella straight out of it.

What had he said in his voice-mail message to her? He couldn't remember exactly, but he didn't think it was anything that would have made her take off. Was it? Which probably meant, if she'd left L.A., it was because the horrible media story had driven her away.

If she was hurting and gone, the blame lay squarely at his feet and, damn it, he was going to make it right.

As the jet taxied down the runway, Rafael called James, cursing when he didn't answer. It seemed forever before the jet had parked and he could leave it to run to his car, which he'd arranged to have dropped off there for him. If

Gabriella had been nervous about the speed he'd driven in the mountains, she'd have closed her eyes for sure if she'd been in the car with him now, taking curves like the devil was on his heels. And he could practically feel it nipping, because a deep sense of foreboding had filled his chest. A feeling that this wasn't going to be as simple as showing up at her door, sweeping her into his arms and telling her that her past didn't matter and that he would always be there for her.

He skidded to a stop in front of her apartment and banged on her door. But of course there was no answer. Was she in there, or had she gone? He should have called James to see if he'd come here looking for her. He banged some more, until her neighbor's door opened.

"What's all the racket out here?" the man asked.

"Do you know if Gabriella Cain is home?"

"Saw her leave yesterday. Had a few suitcases with her."

Damn it! "Thanks." Rafael spun on his heel and pushed his car even harder to get to the clinic, parking it practically sideways before he ran inside.

Desperately hoping that somehow she'd shown back up after James had left his message, he checked her office first but it was quiet and empty. Now it was just a room, with all the life and energy gone from it. He put his hands on her desk and leaned on it, needing that support when he saw that her usual tidy stacks of papers were gone, and so were the few personal items he'd noticed there before.

"She handed in her resignation."

Rafael swung around at the sound of James's voice. His friend stood there looking grim and angry, rubbing the back of his neck with his palm.

"When?"

"Yesterday. That's why I'm here so late, trying to find a replacement. Not that it'll be easy to replace someone

like Gabby. I've been trying like hell to figure out where she went so I could talk her into coming back, but no luck so far."

"Why did she leave?"

"Because the damned news outlets were splashing photos of the two of you everywhere, and along with that some people were running their mouths about her past making her unfit to work here as a midwife. I'm tempted to call the news outlets who've run this damned story, but since they're always looking for a way to throw the media spotlight on me, too, I'm afraid it would just make it worse. Did you warn her this could happen if the two of you spent time together?"

"Not enough, obviously." Damn it, this was what he'd wanted to avoid all along, and he should have told her about the grainy photos from that first night together, when she'd fallen asleep at his house. Maybe she'd have been more prepared for this if she'd known they'd been dogging both of them from the start.

But things were different now. She wasn't just another fling, she was the woman he loved. He'd be more than happy to have that be headline news, if she loved him back.

The thought that she might not made it hard to breathe.

"I'm going to get with some of my people from the palace. See if they can find out where she's from, where her family is, or who her old friends are. I'll start there."

"All I know is that she's from Seattle. I'll keep working on it and let you know. I want her back too. Good luck."

James gave Rafael a quick, hard hug, then left and Rafael sat in Gabriella's chair to get started on the most important hunt of his life.

Gabby sat on the dock near her childhood home and stared out at the Pacific Ocean, pulling her jacket closer around

her to keep away the penetrating evening chill. Always, whenever she'd had problems in her life, she'd felt soothed by the sound of the surf. By watching the rhythmic waves slide up and down the sand. By seeing the orange sun gleaming lower in the sky to finally dip below the horizon. All of it usually left her feeling like she was ready to take on whatever challenge she had to face.

Her current challenge, forgetting about Rafael Moreno, felt pretty impossible. Taking the positive step to begin sending out applications for jobs had helped a little. Maybe once she moved somewhere to start afresh, met new people and didn't hide away like she had the two years she'd been at The Hollywood Hills Clinic, it would get better. Maybe forgetting him would be easier than she expected.

And maybe the seagulls would start swimming and fish would fly across the sky.

A sigh filled her chest. Surprised by a movement next to her, she looked up, and her heart ground to a complete halt.

"So, *querida*, you are here." Rafael dropped down next to her, and in his quiet voice was a note she hadn't heard before. "Should you ever become a felon, be glad to know you're very hard to find."

"Rafael. How…? Why…? Is your mother okay?" Her heart started up again in lurching thuds against her ribs, and she just stared in disbelief that he was actually there. And why, when he'd given her the brush-off and basically said goodbye, have a nice life?

"My mother is fine. Tell me why you left L.A." He reached for her hand, but she pulled it away. Somehow he couldn't have seen what was on TV.

She licked her lips, and her gut churned with dread, but she had to tell him. "The media ran a story. About me, and…and how I gave birth to my stillborn son. Talked about how I should have done things differently. Why I

shouldn't be a midwife and…it's all true. Except that it wasn't my fault. I realize that now, and I know I'm still good at what I do."

"I know. I heard the story." He reached for her again, and this time she let his warm hand engulf her frozen one. "Of course you're still good at what you do. Better than good. I'm so sorry this difficult part of your life has been thrown out there for all the world to see. It's all my fault, and I feel very badly about that."

So that was why he was here. To apologize for the media, which wasn't really his fault at all.

She stared back at the horizon because she couldn't bear to look at his face. "I don't think it's your fault any more than my losing the baby was mine. Don't worry, I'll cope."

"I know that too. You're a strong woman, not to mention talented and caring and so beautiful you make me ache." He took her face in his hands, the green eyes meeting hers filled with tenderness as he turned her toward him. "Tell me about your baby. Tell me what happened."

God, she didn't want to talk about it. But maybe telling the story would be part of the process to continue to heal. To truly put it in the past. "I was working late. Had finished a long shift, and my patient had been in labor a long time. She was very upset and exhausted, and even though I'd been feeling odd pains all evening I really felt I should stay with her, be there for her until her baby was born. She developed complications and ended up having surgery, and I couldn't just leave her with an OB she'd never met before. So I stayed, and her baby was born healthy."

She closed her eyes, not wanting to remember the rest of it. Rafael's hands slipped to her shoulders as he rested his cheek against hers. "And then what happened?"

"By then I was feeling really bad. I went to my office, and the pain was so overwhelming I collapsed. By the time

someone found me I was in premature labor." She pulled her cheek from his and opened her eyes, barely able to squeeze out the rest of the story. "I'll never forget the moment when they listened for his heartbeat, but there wasn't one. They attached the monitor to be sure, but nothing. My baby was dead. I had to deliver him, knowing he was gone. And never, as long as I live, will I forget how it felt to hold his small, motionless body in my arms, eyes closed, an incredibly peaceful look on his tiny, perfect face. The face of an angel."

Her voice broke as the memories flooded her. Rafael had said she was strong. Now he knew otherwise.

"I'm so sorry," he said, folding her close against him. She let herself cling to him for a long moment. Pressed her face to his neck. Let herself soak in his warmth one last time. "I've delivered stillborn babies, and I've seen the parents' pain. I can't imagine it. But I'm glad to hear you know it wasn't your fault. That probably your baby wasn't growing normally. Most likely, your pains came after he had passed away inside you, and whether or not you'd gone to see someone earlier about it wouldn't have made any difference."

His hand stroking slowly up and down her back felt even more soothing than watching the ocean. "I know. I do. But it's hard not to feel like somehow, if I'd done things differently, he'd be here now."

She could feel his face move against her hair in what she took to be a nod before he pulled back. "Thank you for sharing this with me. Now I'd like to share with you the second reason I'm here."

His face was so serious she readied herself for some other thing even worse than the first media blitz, though surely that wasn't possible. "What is it?"

"I'd decided I should stay at home for a while. Figured

I'd been running from there for too long and hurting others in the process." His wide palms cupped her face again. "Hurting you, both with the media focus and because I knew I couldn't give you the kind of love you deserve."

Oh, God. And here he was, hurting her now by stating the obvious. She tried to turn away from him, but he held her gaze.

"Then I found I was wrong. Again. I've been wrong about so damn many things, but the biggest was believing that there's no such thing as real love. Lasting love. I know I was wrong because I'm very much in love with you, Gabriella. And I know that I'll love you forever."

"Rafael." Her heart thundered in her ears so loudly it drowned out the sound of the ocean waves. What was he saying, exactly?

"I love you. Like I've never loved anyone before." This time he whispered the words. "And I hope and pray that, even though I sure as hell don't deserve it, you might love me back."

Tears stung her eyes and spilled over, and his thumbs slowly slid across her cheeks to wipe them away.

"I do love you. But it's me who doesn't deserve you. And someday you'll want children. Will need an heir for your country. I don't think I can go through losing a baby again."

"I don't need to produce an heir. My brother's wife is expecting as we speak, and since I know she wants a big brood, there will be more than enough Morenos running around the palace to satisfy the entire kingdom."

That vision managed to make her smile a little, even through her tears, because she could just see green-eyed, dark-haired Morenos who looked like Rafael, loudly tearing up and down marble hallways and breaking priceless

antiquities. And with that vision came the longing again to have a child, but hadn't she gone through enough pain already?

He must have seen something in her face, because his usual arrogant confidence seemed to be on shaky ground as he drew her closer. "The only thing I need in my life is you, Gabriella. I need you to help me see things I can't otherwise see on my own, except through your beautiful eyes. And because my parents are happy that I'm crazily in love with a wonderful woman, and thrilled at the thought of me never again embarrassing them, they gave me something to give to you. If you'll accept it."

The tenderness and intensity and even a shocking vulnerability in his eyes stole her breath, and it took her two attempts to find her voice. "Accept what?"

"This thing in my pocket that's digging into my ribs, and I hope you'll help me relieve my pain." His fingers stroked her cheeks once more before leaving them to pull a surprisingly worn-looking box from his jacket.

"That looks about a hundred years old," she said through sniffles she knew had to be awfully unattractive, but she couldn't seem to do a thing about the tears that kept leaking from her eyes.

"Four hundred, actually. My great-great…some big number of greats-grandmother was given this ring by some great-great-grandfather." He surprised her by folding his fingers back around the box, and she nearly begged him to let her at least look inside. His other fingers tipped her chin up to meet his eyes. "Will you marry me, Gabriella? Be my wife? My princess? Please say yes."

Gabby stared, unable to fully process his words, unable to speak, and he pressed his lips softly to hers before pull-

ing back again. "You're scaring me here, Gabriella. Will it help to see the ring?"

He flipped open the box, and she gasped at the huge, square-cut emerald surrounded by diamonds. An emerald that dazzled almost as much as Rafael's eyes. As Rafael himself. But not quite.

"It's beautiful," she whispered, "but I didn't need to see it to say yes. Yes, I love you and, yes, I'll marry you."

"Thank God," he whispered back. He pulled her close, and she could feel his body relax as he pressed his cheek to hers. "I promise you won't regret it. I'll do everything I can to make you happy."

Long seconds ticked by as they just held one another, and she knew he was feeling the same unbelievable connection radiating between them without another spoken word. When they slowly parted, he pulled the ring from the box and slipped it onto her finger. As she looked down at it, a bubble of happiness ballooned in her chest so big she thought she might just float away. At the same time she realized there was one important thing they hadn't talked about.

"I assume you want to go back to your country to live? Would I…if we're married…be able to work?"

"I'm not going to lie," he said, his lips twisting. "Being my wife will require helping with some charitable work I'd like to start in the kingdom, and public appearances. But we can live anywhere you want, and you can do whatever you want, including be a midwife. We can work together, if you like, or not. It's up to you."

"I don't know. You can be awfully overbearing and bossy."

"Another reason I need feisty and amazing Gabriella to keep me in my place." He gave her another lingering kiss then stood, holding out his hand to help her to her

feet. "What do you say we go back to L.A. for now, until we make a plan?"

"Yes." She twined her fingers with his, hardly able to believe this was really happening. "I think I'm finally ready to move on to wherever life takes me next. With you."

CHAPTER FOURTEEN

"HERE'S SOME NEWS I think you'll want to read with your breakfast, Gabriella," Rafael said, sliding several newspapers in front of her on the table.

"I'm enjoying being pampered by you in this beautiful house." She scowled and took a fortifying swig of the delicious coffee Rafael had made. "Why would you want to ruin that for me by making me read the news?"

"I don't think this news will ruin your morning." He refilled her cup and she looked up to see his lips were curved and his eyes were dancing.

Moving on from her past didn't mean she wanted to read the awful stuff that had continued to be plastered in all the media but she had to admit his expression made her curious. She glanced at the headline and her heart stumbled.

"What…is this?" She slowly picked up the paper, staring.

"The world is defending you, *querida*," Rafael said. "Shall I read a few of the quotes? *'Gabriella Cain is the best thing to ever happen to The Hollywood Hills Clinic.'* I like that one, since she's definitely the best thing to ever happen to me." He dropped a kiss on her head. "And how about this? *'Anyone who knows midwife Gabriella Cain knows this trash being said about her can't possibly be true.'*"

"Oh, my gosh." She stared up at him, her heart somehow squeezing and swelling at the same time. "This is incredible!"

"And my favorite, from Cameron Fontaine," Rafael continued, flicking through another paper. *"If Gabriella Cain isn't hired back by The Hollywood Hills Clinic there will be a boycott. And if there isn't an immediate retraction from the media, taking back all those ridiculous and inflammatory statements, influential actresses and studio directors like me are going to sue the hell out of every single one of them.'"*

Gabby put her hands to her cheeks and laughed. "Oh, my gosh, that's so Cameron. I guess she liked me after all."

"Loved you. As I do." He leaned down to kiss her cheek, moving on to her mouth, and just as Gabby was clutching his shirt and sinking into another delicious kiss, the doorbell rang.

"Well, who could that be? Maybe it's the media come to apologize."

"Like that would ever happen." There was something odd, secretive even, about the smile playing on his lips, and Gabby had to wonder why.

"You never know, when a woman like you has so much clout behind her." He winked and headed for the door, and when he returned a moment later a familiar voice came with him.

"Gabby. You've got to help me out," James said. "There's a near-riot at the clinic!"

"A near-riot? What are you talking about?"

"Several of your pregnant patients are refusing to see anyone else, and they're threatening a sit-in if you don't come back. They're mad as hell that you're gone and they're blaming me." James threw his arms wide, and she nearly laughed at the look of alarm on his normally cool,

impassive face. "Will you come back? Please? Tell me what it would take and I'll make it happen."

The swelling of her heart grew so much she could barely hold in all her joy. Then remembered she wasn't living her life alone anymore. That there were two of them now. Someday, maybe, she might even be ready to add a few more to the wonderful life she and Rafael would share.

She turned to him, and her face must have told him exactly what she was thinking because he stepped close, pulled her into his arms and kissed her forehead.

"The clinic is a pretty great place to work, isn't it?" He tipped her chin and his beautiful eyes smiled into hers.

"Yes. It is." She pressed her palms against his chest and smiled back. "How would you feel about us both working there?"

"You already know, Gabriella Cain," he said, his warm gaze a steady promise, "that wherever it is you want to be, I'm right there by your side."

* * * * *

HER PLAYBOY'S
SECRET

TINA BECKETT

To those who dare to chase their dreams

PROLOGUE

One week ago

IT WAS A curse heard around the world. Or at least around the ward of the Melbourne Maternity Unit.

Everyone on the ward went silent and several heads cranked around to see what the normally easygoing Lucas Elliot could possibly be upset about.

Darcie Green already knew—had braced herself for this very moment, wondering what his reaction would be.

Now she knew.

Still facing the rotation roster hanging on the far wall, Lucas didn't move for several seconds. Then, as if he couldn't quite believe what his eyes were telling him, one finger went to the chart, dragging across it to follow the line that matched dates with names.

She cringed as he muttered yet again, slightly lower this time. A few sympathetic glances came her way as people went back to their jobs. Isla Delamere, her former flatmate—now heavily pregnant—mouthed, "Sorry," as she tiptoed out of firing range.

A perfect beginning to a stellar day. She rolled her eyes.

Nine months in Australia and Darcie was just beginning to feel a part of the team. Except for Lucas's very vocal reaction at having the rota that matched hers, that was. He'd evidently not seen the list until just now.

Did he even know she was standing not seven meters behind him at the nurses' station? Probably not.

Then again, it was doubtful he would even care.

It wasn't as if she felt any better about having to spend an entire rotation with the handsome senior midwife. She just hadn't been quite as "loud" in expressing her displeasure.

Yes, she'd given him an earful about his periods of tardiness a few months back. But that had been no reason to call her an uptight, snooty, English…

Her eyes closed before the word formed, a flash of hurt working through her yet again.

Was the thought of being paired with her so hideous that he had to make sure everyone on the ward knew what he thought of her?

Evidently.

And why not? Her fiancé hadn't minded letting a whole chapel full of wedding guests know that he'd fallen in love with her best friend, who just so happened to be her maid of honor. Tabitha had promptly run over to him, squealing with delight, and thrown herself into his arms, leaving Darcie standing there in shock.

And, yes, Robert had called her uptight as well, right before he'd dropped the bomb that had ended their engagement.

Lucas's left hand went to the back of his neck, head bending forward as he massaged his muscles for a moment. When he finally turned around his eyes swept

the area, going right past her before retracing his steps and pausing.

On her.

Then his left brow quirked, a rueful smile curving his lips. "Sorry. Heard that, did you?"

Was he serious? "I imagine there were very few who didn't."

He moved forward, until he was standing in front of her—all six feet of him. "I bet you did some name-calling of your own when you saw the rotation." His smile faded. "Unless you requested we work this one together."

Sure. That's just what she would have done, left to her own devices.

She forced her chin up. "No, I didn't request it, but it doesn't bother me, if that's what you mean. I've had worse assignments." Before she could congratulate herself on keeping her response cool and measured, even when her insides were squirming with embarrassment, he gave her a quick grin.

"Touché, Dr. Green. Although since you almost had me fired the last time we interacted, I assume your 'worse assignment' didn't fare quite as well."

Since the assignment she'd been referring to had had to do with returning hundreds of wedding gifts courtesy of her ex, it would appear that way. "I don't know about that. I think he feels *quite* lucky not to have to deal with my—how did you put it?—'uptight English ways' any more."

Lucas's gaze trailed over her face, but instead of whipping off a sharp retort he leaned in closer. "Then maybe you should consider some behavior modification courses."

Although the words were made in jest—at least she thought they were—they still stung. Darcie pulled the edges of her cardigan around herself to combat the chill spreading from her heart to the rest of her body and then forced every muscle in her chin go utterly still, so he wouldn't see the wobble. "You're right. Maybe I should."

His head tilted, and he studied her for a minute longer. He reached out a hand as if to touch her, before lowering it again. "Hey. Sorry. I was teasing."

Maybe, but a part of what he'd said was true. Men did seem to find her "chilly and distant"—words her ex had also used to describe her during the last troubled weeks of their engagement. And he had been right. Compared to her, Tabitha was warm and bubbly and anything but distant.

Darcie couldn't help the way she was made, though, could she? She dragged her thoughts back to the man in front of her. She hadn't tried to be unreasonable during their confrontation a few months ago, whatever Lucas might have thought. Was asking someone to be prompt and to keep his mind on his job so unreasonable?

Well, she didn't really have her mind on the job right now either.

"Don't worry about it." She fastened the buttons on her cardigan to keep from having to hold onto it and drew herself upright. "I'm sure, if we both remain professional, we'll come off this rotation relatively unscathed."

He gave her a dubious-looking smile. "I'm sure we will."

As he strode away, his glance cutting back to the chart and giving a shake of his head that could only be

described as resigned, she realized that was the problem. Neither of them seemed able to maintain a calm professionalism around the other.

Two fortnights. That's all it was. Just because her rota corresponded with his, it didn't mean she had to stick to his side like glue. She could do this.

Doubt, like a whisper of smoke that curled round and round until it encased its victim, made her wonder if her ex-fiancé's cutting words were the hardest things she would ever face. She'd thought so at one time.

But as Lucas ducked around a corner and out of sight, she had a terrible suspicion she could be facing something much worse.

CHAPTER ONE

Present day

"CORA? WHAT'S WRONG, sweetheart?"

Lucas leaned a shoulder against the wall outside the birthing suite as his niece's voice came over the phone, dread making his blood pressure rise in steady increments. Every time he thought his brother was through the worst of his grief, he'd go on yet another binge and undo all the work he'd accomplished during therapy.

He took a quick glance down the hall. The coast was clear.

Lucas had worked hard over the last week to make sure his personal life didn't interfere with his job. As angry as he'd been at Darcie for giving him a public flogging over being late for work a couple of months ago, she'd been right. It was why he'd hired a childminder to help with Cora's care. Burning the candle at both ends was not only unwise, it could also be dangerous for his patients.

Had his parents still been alive, they would have been happy to help. But it had been almost ten years since the car accident that had taken their lives.

His niece's voice came through. "Nothing's wrong. I just called to tell you what Pete the Geek did today."

Cora's Belgian sheepdog. Muscles he hadn't been aware he'd contracted released all at once. "Can you tell me later, gorgeous? I'm working right now."

"Oh, okay. Sorry, Uncle Luke. Are you coming for dinner tonight?"

"I wouldn't miss it, sweetheart." He smiled, unable to resist the pleading note in her voice. "What are we having?"

"Prawns!"

Cora's birth was what had propelled him to change his career path from plastic surgery to midwifery. The lure of a glamorous life filled with beautiful women had faded away in a moment when Felix's wife had gone into labor unexpectedly. Lucas had delivered his own niece in the living room of his brother's home. As he'd stared down at the tiny creature nestled in his hands, Cora had blinked against the light and given a sharp wail of protest that had melted his heart. Seven years later, she still had the power to turn him into a soppy puddle of goo, especially since he and Felix were now the only family she had left.

He needed to get off the phone, but the ward was quiet—none of his patients were laboring at the moment. He cradled the device closer to his ear. "Prawns, eh? What's the occasion?"

She giggled. "Just because."

"You're going to spoil me." His chest tightened at how happy she sounded. He'd take this over those *other* phone calls any day.

"Oh," his niece said, "make sure you bring some briquettes for the barbie. Daddy forgot them at the store."

Felix had forgotten quite a few things lately. But at least he seemed to be pulling out of his current well of depression.

Footsteps sounded somewhere behind him, so he moved to end the conversation.

"Okay, Cora, I will. Looking forward to tonight."

"Me too. Love you bunches."

"Love you even more, sweetheart. Bye." He ended the call, only to have the very person he'd been hoping not to encounter stalk past him, throwing an icy glare his way.

Lucas sighed. The woman did seem to pop up at just the wrong time. He slid the phone into his pocket and decided to go after her. He had no idea why, but he liked trying to get a rise out of her. Within five steps he'd caught up with her. Matching her pace, he glanced to the side.

Not good. The obstetrician's lips were pressed together into a thin line, her expression stony.

He pushed forward anyway, throwing her what he hoped was a charming smile. "Were you looking for me?"

Her expression didn't budge. "I was, but I can see you're busy."

"Just taking a short breather between patients. What was it you wanted?"

She glanced at him, her eyes meeting his for a mere second. "Is Isla scheduled to see you this week?"

Isla Delamere was one of his colleagues as well as a friend.

"Yes, did you want to be there for her appointment?"

Her chin edged up in a way he was coming to recognize. "I'd planned to be. She's my patient as well."

Okay, he'd gotten a rise out of her, but not quite the kind he'd been hoping for.

He moved ahead of her and planted himself in her path before she could reach the door to the staff lounge. Why he was bothering he had no idea, but something in him wanted to knock down a block or two of that icy wall she surrounded herself with. "Listen, Dr. Green—Darcie—I know we got off on the wrong foot somehow, but can we hit the reset button? We have three weeks of our rotation left. I'd like to make them pleasant ones, if at all possible. What do you say?"

The tight lines in her face held firm for another moment, and he wondered if she was going to strike him dead for daring to use her first name. Then her eyes closed, and she took a deep breath. "I think I might be able to manage that." The corners of her mouth edged up, creating cute little crinkles at the outer edges of her eyes. "If we both try very hard."

Something in Lucas's chest shifted, and a tightening sensation speared through his gut. Had he ever seen the woman smile? Not that he could remember, and certainly never at him. The transformation in her face was…

Incredible.

He swallowed. That was something he was better off not thinking about.

Three weeks. He just had to get through the rest of this rotation. From what he understood, Dr. Green had only been seconded to MMU for a year, then she'd head back to England. He did some quick calculations. She had, what…three months left? Once their rotation was over she'd be down to two, which meant it was doubtful they'd be paired together again. He gave an inter-

nal fist pump, trying to put his whole heart into it. It came off as less than enthusiastic.

Because you still have these three weeks to get through.

He gave her another smile. "I think I can manage it as well."

"Well, good. Now that that's settled, when is Isla's appointment?"

He checked his schedule. "Next Wednesday at two."

Darcie pulled her phone out and scrolled through a couple of screens before punching some buttons. "I don't have anyone scheduled at that time, so I'll be there." She gave him another smile—a bit wider this time—and the wobble in his chest returned. And this time he noticed the crinkles framed eyes that were green. A rich velvety color. Sparkling with life.

Her lips were softer too than they had been earlier. Pink, delicate, and with just a hint of shine.

The tightening sensation spread lower, edging beneath his waistband.

What the hell? Time to get out of here.

"Great. See you later." He turned and started back the way he had come, only to have her voice interrupt him.

"Don't forget to call for a consult if anything unusual comes up."

He stiffened at the prim tone. "Yes, I know the protocol, thank you."

When she didn't respond, he turned around and caught something...hurt?...in the depths of those green eyes, and maybe even a hint of uncertainty. In a flash, though, it winked out, taking with it any trace

of her earlier smile and, very possibly, their newborn peace accord.

While that bothered him on a professional level, it was what he'd seen in her expression in that unguarded moment that made him want to cross over to her and try to understand what was going on in her head. He didn't. Instead, he chose to reiterate his comment in a less defensive way. "I'll ring if I need you."

Then he walked away. Without looking back. Praying the next weeks sped by without him having to make that call.

That man should wear a lab coat. A long one.

Darcie tried not to stare at the taut backside encased in dark jeans as he made his way back down the hall, but it was hard. No matter how much she tried to look anywhere but there, her peripheral vision was still very much engaged, keeping track of him until he finally turned down a neighboring corridor.

The thread of hurt from his curt response still lingered, just waiting for her to tug on it and draw it tighter. Why had he acted so put out to have her assistance on a case?

Was it the professional rivalry that sometimes went on between midwives and obstetricians?

She sagged against the wall, pressing her fingers against her temples and rubbing in slow, careful circles to ward off the migraine that was beginning to chomp at the wall of her composure.

What was it about Lucas that put her on edge?

The fact that he was a man in a field dominated by women?

Or was it the fact that all the expectant mums who

came through the doors clamored to be put on his patient list? Despite the run-ins they'd had over the past nine months, Senior Midwife Lucas seemed quite capable of doing his job with an ease and efficiency that only enhanced his good looks.

And they were good.

She tried to dredge up an unflattering image, like the time he'd come in late for work, dragging his fingers through his wavy hair, his rumpled clothes the same ones he'd had on when he'd left the previous afternoon. Nope. He'd been just as attractive then as the first time she'd laid eyes on him.

Ugh. She disliked him for that most of all.

Or maybe it was all those secretive phone calls she'd caught him making when he'd thought he'd been alone. Oh, those were definitely over the top. So many of them, right in the middle of his shift.

And he wondered why she was outraged when he came in late or took little side breaks to indulge in whispered conversations.

Could she be jealous?

She straightened in a flash. *No!* Just because Robert had decided she wasn't enough "fun", it didn't mean she should go ballistic over any man who wanted to indulge in a bit of pillow talk on the phone.

Maybe it wouldn't bother her so much if he didn't use the same flirty tones when in conversation with the MMU staff and his patients. The tone he turned on this "Cora" person—a kind of I'm-not-willing-to-commit-but-I-still-want-you-at-my-beck-and-call attitude that grated on Darcie's nerves. Especially after the way her ex had led her down the rosy path, only to

dump her for her maid of honor—who, actually, *was* a lot of fun to be with.

She sighed and went into the lounge to get a strong cuppa that she hoped would relieve the steady ache in her head and keep it from blooming into something worse.

As soon as she moved into the space, she knew it was a mistake. Lucas, it seemed, was the main topic of conversation among the cluster of four nurses inside.

"I swear one of his patients this morning had on false eyelashes. While in labor!" Marison Daniels blinked rapidly, as if trying to imitate what the woman had done. They all laughed.

If Darcie had hoped to slide by them, grab her tea and tiptoe back out of the room unseen, that hope was dashed when the nurse next to Marison caught Darcie's eye and gave the jokester a quick poke in the ribs with her elbow. The laughter ceased instantly.

Oh, Lord. Her face burned hotter than the kettle she'd just switched on.

"Sorry. Didn't mean to interrupt."

"You didn't interrupt," Marison assured her. "I was just headed back to the ward."

The others all echoed the same thing.

With a scurry of feet and tossing of rubbish, the four headed out.

Just what she needed. To be reminded that she was still very much an outsider when it came to certain things—like being allowed to let her hair down with the rest of them.

No, the pattern had been set from the moment she'd got off the plane. Oh, she'd made friends and people

were nice enough, but to let her in on their little jokes? That didn't happen very often, except with Isla.

Worse, she'd even overheard Lucas making fun of her English accent while on one of his phone calls to Cora. It hadn't been in a mean way, he'd just repeated some of her colloquialisms with a chuckle, but it made her feel self-conscious any time she opened her mouth around him. So she made sure she spoke to him as little as possible. And now that they were sharing a rota, she was still struggling to maintain that silence.

Not that it was going to be possible forever.

She could still picture the confident way he strode through the hallways of the ward, his quick smile making itself known whenever he met a patient. She wrinkled her nose. More than one expectant mum would have probably given her left ovary to bat long sexy lashes and claim the child she was carrying was Lucas Elliot's.

Including his current paramour, Cora?

Probably, but not *her*. She was done with men like him.

Her fiancé had been handsome and attentive. Until he hadn't been. Until he'd grown more and more distracted as their engagement had progressed.

Now she knew why.

And Lucas had Cora. She was not about to smile and flirt with a man who was taken. She wasn't Tabitha.

She packed leaves into the tea ball and dropped it into a chunky mug—a gift from her dad to remind her that her favorite footballers resided in England and to not let herself get swept away by a handsome face, especially one who lived halfway round the world.

Lucas's quirked brow swam before her eyes, and

she let out an audible groan, even as she poured boiling water into her cup. No matter how good looking he was or how elated she'd been to see the momentary confusion cross his expression when she'd smiled at him, she did not need to become like False-Eyelash Lady—the one Marison had carried on about.

There'd be a real corker of a reaction if someone caught her mooning after him. Or staring after him, like she'd done earlier.

She bounced her tea ball in the water and watched as the brew grew darker and darker, just like her thoughts. What she needed was to stay clearheaded. Like he'd said, they had three more weeks together.

He wanted them to be pleasant ones. She finished adding milk and sugar to her cup and then discarded the used tea leaves, rinsing the ball and leaving it on a towel for the next person who needed it.

"Pleasant" she could do, but that had to be the extent of it. Maybe she should be grateful for all those calls to Cora…maybe she should even hope the relationship stayed the course. At least for the next few weeks.

Which meant she would not go out of her way to put him at ease or cut him any slack if he came in late again. Neither would she give the man any reason to look at her with anything other than the casual curiosity his eyes normally held.

And once those three weeks were up?

Life would go back to the way it had been before they'd found themselves joined at the hip.

Joined at the hip. She gave a quick grin. That was one place she and Lucas would never be joined, even if the idea did create a layer of warmth in her belly. But it was not going to happen. Not in this lifetime.

With that in mind, she took a few more sips of the sweet milky brew, then, feeling fortified and ready to face whatever was out there, she headed off to see her next patient in what was proving to be a very interesting morning.

CHAPTER TWO

Felix wasn't at home.

Arms loaded with items for their dinner, Lucas set everything down in the kitchen. "Where is he?"

Chessa, the childminder, shrugged and said in a quiet voice, "He went out an hour ago, saying he needed to buy prawns, and hasn't come back yet."

Damn. "And where's Cora?"

"Outside with Pete." The young woman's brow creased. "Should I be worried? He's been good for the last few weeks, but he did put some bottles of ale in the fridge. I haven't seen him drink anything, though."

"It's okay. It's not your job to watch him. If he ever fails to come home before you're supposed to leave, though, call me so I can make sure Cora is taken care of."

"I would never leave her by herself, Mr. Elliot." The twenty-five-year-old looked horrified.

"I know you wouldn't. I just don't want you to feel you have to stay past your normal time."

The sliding door opened and in bounded Pete the Geek in a flash of brown and white fur, followed closely by Cora, whose red face said they'd been

involved in some sort of running game. The dog came over and sat in front of him, giving a quick woof.

Lucas laughed and reached in his pocket for a treat. "Well, you're learning."

He and Cora had been working on teaching Pete not to leap on people who walked through the door. By training him to sit quietly in front of visitors, they forestalled any muddy paw prints or getting knocked down and held prisoner by an overactive tongue. The trick seemed to be working, although if the tail swishing madly across the tile floor was any indication, Pete was holding himself in check with all his might.

Kind of like *him* when Darcie had smiled at him as he'd left the hospital?

Good thing he had more impulse control than Cora's dog.

Or maybe Darcie was training him as adeptly as Cora seemed to be training Pete.

"He wants his treat, Uncle Luke."

Realizing he'd been standing there like an idiot, he tossed the bacon-flavored bit to Pete and then bent down to pet him. "I think he's gained ten kilos in the last week."

He squatted and put an arm around both his niece and her dog.

Cora kissed him on the cheek, her thin arms squeezing his neck. "That's just silly. He doesn't weigh that much."

"No?" He gave her a quick peck on the forehead, grimacing when Pete gave his own version of a kiss, swiping across his eyebrow and half his eye in the process. "Okay, enough already."

He couldn't hold back his smile, however, despite

the niggle of worry that was still rolling around inside him.

Where the hell was his brother?

Standing, he kept one hand on Pete's head and smiled at the minder. "Would you try ringing his mobile phone and seeing how long he'll be while I fire up the barbie and get it ready? I don't know about everyone else but I'm starving."

His voice was light, but his heart weighed more than the dog at his feet.

"Of course," Chessa said. "I'll bring you some lemonade in a few minutes."

As he was preparing the grill, she came out with a glass and an apologetic shake of her head. "There was no answer, but I left a voice mail."

"Thank you. Luckily I brought some prawns with me, just in case. Feel free to stay and eat with us, if you'd like."

She smiled. "Thanks, but if it's all the same to you, I think I'll head back to my flat. Do you need anything else?"

"No, I think we're good."

Twenty minutes later he had the briquettes going while Cora and Pete—worn out from a rough-and-tumble game of tug of war—lounged in a hammock strung between two gum trees, the dog's chin propped on his niece's shoulder. Both looked utterly content. Rescuing Pete had been the best thing his brother had ever done for his daughter, unlike a lot of other things since his wife's tragic death. In fact, the last four years had been a roller coaster consisting of more lows than highs—with the plunges occurring at lightning speed.

He went in and grabbed the package of prawns

and some veggies to roast. Just as he started rinsing the shellfish, the front door opened and in came his brother. Bleary, red-rimmed eyes gave him away.

Perfect. Lucas already knew this routine by heart.

"Was our cookout tonight?" his brother asked, hands as empty as Lucas's stomach. "I forgot."

His molars ground against each other as he struggled with his anger and frustration. Was this what love and marriage ultimately led to? Forgetting that anyone else existed outside your own emotional state? Felix had a daughter who needed him, for God's sake. What was it going to take to make him look at someone besides himself? "Cora didn't forget."

His brother groaned out loud then mumbled, "Sorry."

"I'm just getting ready to throw it all on the barbie, so why don't you get yourself cleaned up before you go out there to see?"

The first two steps looked steady enough, but the next one swayed a bit to the left before Felix caught himself.

"Tell me you're not drunk."

"I'm not."

"Can you make it to your bedroom on your own?" The last thing Lucas wanted was for Cora to come in and see her father like this, not that she hadn't in the past. Many times.

Felix scowled. "Of course I can." He proceeded to weave his way down the hallway, before disappearing into one of the rooms—the bathroom.

Looks like you're spending the night on your brother's couch once again, mate.

Lucas had impressed on Cora the need to call him

if her father ever seemed "not himself." The pattern was bizarre with periods of complete normalcy followed by bouts of depression, sometimes mixed with drinking. Not a good combination for someone taking anti-depressant medication.

He made a mental note to ask Felix if he was still taking his pills, and another note to make sure he arrived at work…on time! As he'd found out, it was tricky getting Cora off to school and then making the trek to the hospital, but if the traffic co-operated it could be done.

Otherwise that hard-won peace treaty would be shredded between pale English fingers.

Strangely, he didn't want that. Didn't want to disappoint her after he'd worked so hard to turn things around between them. Didn't want to lose those rare smiles in the process. So yes. He would do his damnedest to get to the hospital on time.

And between now and then he'd have to figure out what to do about his brother. Threaten him with another stint in rehab? Take away his car keys?

He cast his eyes up to the ceiling, trying not to blame Melody for allowing his brother to twine his life so completely around hers that he had trouble functioning now that she was gone.

Lucas never wanted to be in a position like that. And so far he hadn't. He'd played the field far and wide, but he still lived by two hard and fast rules: no married women and no long-term relationships. As long as he could untangle himself with ease the next day, he was happy. And he stuck to women who felt the same way. No hurt feelings. And definitely no burning need to hang around and buy a house with a garden.

Finishing up the veggies, he faintly caught the sound of the shower switching on, the *poof* from the on-demand water heater confirming his thoughts. Good. At least Felix was doing something productive. He opened the refrigerator, pulled out the ale in the door and popped the top on every single bottle. Then he took a long gulp of the one in his hand, before proceeding to pour the rest of the contents down the drain, doing the same with every other bottle and then placing the lot in the recycle bin. If the beer wasn't here, Felix couldn't drink it, right?

Not that that stopped him from going out to the nearest pub, but at least that took some effort, which he hoped Felix didn't have in him tonight.

Lucas went outside and loaded the prawns into a cooking basket and set it over the fire, then arranged the vegetables next to them on the grate. Cora's empty glass of lemonade was next to his full one. She was still sprawled on the hammock and it looked like both she and Pete were out for the count. If only he could brush off his cares that easily, he might actually get a full night's sleep.

But maybe tonight would be different. He'd learned from experience that the fold-out cot in the spare room was supremely uncomfortable. He was better off just throwing a quilt over Melody's prized couch and set-tling in for the night there.

And he would wake up on time. He absolutely would.

And he'd arrive at work chipper and ready to face the day.

He hoped.

* * *

Something was wrong with Lucas.

He'd come through the doors of the MMU with a frown that could have swallowed most of Melbourne. She'd arrived at work armed with a smile, only to have him look right past her as if she didn't exist.

Ha! Evidently she'd been wrong about his reaction. Because there was nothing remotely resembling attraction in the man's eyes today. In fact, his whole frame oozed exhaustion, as did the two nicks on the left side of his strong jaw. He'd muttered something that might have been "G'day." Or it might just as easily have been "Go to hell."

She was tempted to chase him down and ask about his evening, but when she turned to do so, she noticed that the back of his shirt was wrinkled as if he'd... Her gaze skimmed down and caught the same dark jeans he'd worn yesterday.

Her stomach rolled to the side. The staff all had lockers, and the last time he'd come in like this he'd used the hospital's shower and changed into clean clothes. That's probably what he was headed to do right now.

The evidence pointed to one thing. That he'd spent the night with "Cora" or some other woman.

The trickle of attraction froze in her veins.

None of your business, Darcie.

Just leave the man alone. If she made an issue of this, they would be back where they'd started: fighting a cold war that neither one of them would win.

But why the hell couldn't he drag himself out of his lover's bed in time to go home and shower before coming to work?

Unless he just couldn't manage to tear himself away from her.

An image emerged from the haze that she did her best to block. Too late. There it was, and there was no way to send it back again—the one of Lucas swinging his feet over the side of the mattress, only to have some faceless woman graze long, ruby fingernails down his arm and whisper something that made him change his mind.

She shook her head to remove the picture and forced herself to get back to work.

Just as she did so she spied one of her patients leaning against the wall, her hands gripping her swollen belly. Margie Terrington, an English transplant like herself, had just come in yesterday for a quick check to make sure things were on track. They had been.

At least until now. From the concentration on her face and the grey cast to her skin, something wasn't right. Darcie glanced around for a nurse, but they were still tending to the morning's patients. Darcie hurried over.

"Margie? Are you all right?"

Her eyes came up. "My stomach. It's cramping. I think it's the baby."

"Let's get you into a room."

Alarm filled her. No time to check her in or do any of the preliminaries. This was the young woman's second pregnancy. She'd miscarried her first a little over a year ago, and she was only seven months along with this one. Too soon. The human body didn't just go into labor this early unless there was a problem.

Her apprehension grew, and she sent up a quick prayer.

Propping her shoulder beneath Margie's arm, they headed to the nearest exam room. One of the nurses came out of a room across the hall, and Darcie called out to her. "Tessa, could you come here?"

The nurse hurried over and got on the other side of their patient.

"Once I get her settled, can you see if you can find Lucas? He arrived a few minutes ago, so he might be in the lounge or the locker area. Let him know I might need his help."

"Of course."

The patient was sweating profusely—Darcie could feel the moisture through the woman's light maternity top. Another strike against her. If she had some kind of systemic infection, could it have crossed the placenta and affected the baby? A thousand possibilities ran through her mind.

Pushing into the exam area, the trio paused when Margie groaned and doubled over even more. "Oh, God. Hurts."

"Do they feel like contractions? Are they regular?" They finally got her to the bed and helped her up on it.

"I don't know."

Tessa scurried around, getting her vitals, while Darcie tried to get some more information. What she learned wasn't good. Margie had got up and showered like normal and had felt fine. Forty minutes later she'd got a painful cramp in her side—like the kind you got while running, she'd said. The pain had grown worse and had spread in a band across her abdomen. Now she was feeling nauseous, whether from the pain or something else, she wasn't sure. "And my joints hurt, as if I'm getting the flu."

Could she be?

As soon as Tessa called out the readings, the nurse went out to get the patient's chart and to hunt down Lucas.

"Let's get you into a robe and see what's going on."

"Wait." Margie groaned again. "I think I'm going to be sick."

Grabbing a basin, she held it under her patient's mouth as she heaved. Nothing came up, though.

"Did you eat breakfast?" Darcie started to reach for a paper towel, only to have Lucas arrive, chart in hand. He took one look at the scene and anticipated what she was doing. Ripping a couple of towels from the dispenser, he glanced at her in question. "What've you got?"

"This is Margie Terrington from Southbank. She's cramping. Pain in the joints. Nausea."

"Contractions?"

"I'm not sure. I'm just getting ready to hook her up to the monitor."

He tilted his head. "Theories?"

"None." She laid a hand on the young woman's shoulder. "Are you up to telling Lucas what you told me?"

Even as she asked it, Margie's face tightened up in a pained grimace, and she gave a couple of sustained breaths, dragging air in through her nose and letting it out through her mouth. A second or two later she nodded. "Like I told you, I took a shower this morning. Then I started getting these weird sensations in my side."

"What kind of weird?"

"Like a pulled muscle or something." She stiffened

once again. She gritted out, "But now my whole stomach hurts."

"Where's the father?" Lucas asked.

"He's at work. I—I didn't want to worry him if it's nothing."

Lucas frowned. "I think he should be here." He glanced at Darcie. "Can you get her hooked up while I ring him?"

If anything, Margie looked even more frightened. "Am I going to lose this baby too?"

Darcie's heart ached for the woman, even as her brain still whirled, trying to figure out what was going on. "Let us do the worrying, love, can you do that?"

"I think so." She wrote her husband's phone number on a sheet of paper and handed it to Lucas.

While he was gone, Darcie got Margie into a hospital gown and snapped on a pair of gloves. Then she wrapped the monitor around her patient's abdomen. Wow, she was really perspiring. So much so that it had already soaked through the robe on her right side.

And her abdominal muscles were tight to the touch. "Are you having a contraction right now?"

Margie moaned. "I don't know."

She started up the machine and the first thing she heard was the quick *woompa-woompa-woompa-woompa* of the baby's heart. Thank God. Even as that thought hit, a hundred more swept past it. A heartbeat didn't mean Margie's baby wasn't in distress, just that he was alive.

She stared at the line below the heart rate that should be showing the marked rise and fall of the uterus as it contracted and released. It was a steady line.

Placing her hand on Margie's abdomen again, she

noted the strange tightness she'd felt before. But it seemed more like surface muscles to Darcie. Not the deep, purposeful contraction of a woman's uterus.

Lucas came back and glanced at the monitor. "Your husband's on his way."

"Thank you." Another moan, and her hands went back to her stomach.

Lucas sat next to the bed and held the patient's hand, helping guide her through the deep breathing.

"She's not contracting." Darcie's eyes were locked on the monitor where a series of little squiggles indicated that something was happening, but it was more like a series of muscle fasciculations than the steady rise and fall she would expect to see. Could she have flu, like Margie suspected?

"When did you start sweating like this?"

Lucas's voice drew her attention back. He eased Margie's robe to the side and stared at the area where moisture was already beading up despite just having been exposed to the chilly air of the ward. Strange. Although Margie was perspiring everywhere—Darcie gave a quick glance at her face and chest above the gown—there was a marked difference between her moist upper lip and her right side, where a rivulet of liquid peaked and then ran down the woman's swollen belly.

"I don't know. An hour after my shower? Right about the time I started to hurt."

He peered at her closer. "You said you took a shower. Did you feel anything before or after it? A sting…or a prick maybe?"

A prick? Darcie stared at him, trying to figure out where he was going with this.

"No."

"Where did the pain start exactly?"

Margie pressed her fingers right over the area that was wet from perspiration.

He muttered something under his breath then glanced up at Darcie. "I need to make a quick phone call."

"What?" Outrage gathered in her chest and built into a froth that threatened to explode. Surely he was not going to make a personal call right now.

As if he saw something in her face, he reached out and encircled her wrist. "I want her husband to check on something at the house before he comes here," he said in a low voice.

The anger flooding her system disappeared in a whoosh as she stared back at him.

Margie's panicked voice broke between them. "What's wrong?"

"I'm not sure yet. But I don't think you're in labor."

"Then what?"

"I think you may have been bitten by a redback," Lucas said.

"A what?" Margie asked.

"It's one of our most famous residents," he said. "It's a spider. A nasty one at that."

A redback! Darcie had heard of them but had never encountered one, and since she wasn't from Australia, it had never dawned on her that Margie could have been envenomed by something. Her patient was also from England. She'd probably never thought of that possibility either.

She glanced at Lucas. "Are they that common?"

"Quite." He patted Margie's hand. "If that's the case we have antivenin we can give you, which should help."

"If it is a bite, will it hurt the baby?" She gritted her teeth and pulled in another deep breath.

"I think we've caught it at an early stage." His gaze went back to the monitor, which Darcie noted still held steady. "I want to have your husband check the towel and your bathroom."

The patient's eyes widened. "I used the walk-in shower in the guest bathroom this morning. I almost never use that one because it's quite a long way from the bedroom. But my mother is due to fly in to help with the house and baby in a few weeks, and I thought I could tidy things and scrub the shower stall down as I was bathing."

"I'm just going to pull Dr. Green into the hallway for a moment. I'll send the nurse in to sit with you."

Once they were outside the room, and Lucas had rung the husband, asking him to shake out the towel and examine the bathroom, she spun toward him. "A redback. Are you sure?"

"Pretty sure. Most Australians know what to look for, but no one else would. I've seen this once before. A redback bite that comes in looking like preterm labor."

She sagged against the wall. "God. I would have never checked for that. I didn't see a bite. Didn't even think to ask."

"You wouldn't have. And as for the bite mark..." He shrugged. "Small fangs, but they pack quite a wallop."

He gave a smile that looked as tired as she suddenly felt.

"Can we give antivenin to her during pregnancy?"

"We've given it before. I can't recall anyone hav-

ing a bad reaction, unless the patient is allergic to the equine immunoglobulin in the serum." He sighed. "There've been some conflicting reports recently about whether or not the antivenin actually works, but I've seen enough evidence to tell me it's worth a shot. Especially since she's miscarried once already."

Lucas's mobile phone buzzed, and he glanced at the screen. "It's him. Let's hope this is the answer we're looking for."

He punched a button asking a few questions before assuring the man that she should do well with the antivenin and telling him they'd be awaiting his arrival.

"He found the redback. It was still in the towel. A big one, from the sound of it." He dragged his fingers through his hair. "I'll need you to sign off on the medication. We'll go the intravenous route rather than administering the antivenin intramuscularly, since that's more favored at the moment."

"Of course." She closed her eyes with a relieved laugh. "God, I could kiss you right now. I never in a million years would have got that diagnosis right."

A few seconds of silence met her comment.

Hell. Had she really just said that? About kissing him?

Evidently, because when she dared to look at him again a thread of confused amusement seemed to play across his face. "I don't think now would be appropriate, do you, Dr. Green? But later…" He let his voice trail off in a way that gave her no question that he was definitely open to whatever later meant.

What? Hadn't he just come to work this morning all rumpled and sexed up?

Sexed up? Was that even a real expression?

Whether it was or not wasn't the point. It was unbelievable that he would roll out of one woman's bed and be ready and willing to kiss a second one. A perfect stranger, actually, since they barely knew each other.

Not likely, you jerk.

She gave the haughtiest toss of her chin she could manage and fixed him with a cold glare. "It's a figure of speech, Lucas, in case you haven't heard. I was just happy to know that Margie's symptoms have an explanation and a treatment. But get this straight. As grateful as I am for your help, I had no intention of *really* kissing you. Now…or ever. I have no interest in being part of a love triangle. Been there. Done that."

Before she could scurry away in horror over that last blooper, he murmured, "I stand corrected on the kissing, although you totally had me for a moment or two. But I'm intrigued by this supposed love triangle you envision us in. Care to enlighten me as to who the third party might be, or do I have no say in the matter?"

Was he serious?

She wanted to hurl Cora's name at him. Instead, by some superhuman force of will, she clamped her jaws shut before they had a chance to issue any other crazy statements. Then, without another word, she swung back into their patient's room to give her the news about the redback.

At least he hadn't asked her about the been-there-done-that part of her rant, because no one needed to hear her sad tale about the wedding that almost had been. Or the woman who'd stolen her fiancé's heart when he was supposed to be madly in love with her.

Since when had she become so reckless with her words?

Just like the ruby stripe on the infamous redback that warned of dire consequences to those who came in contact with it, the answer to her last question was inscribed with words that were just as lethal: Lucas Elliot.

He made her forget about everything but his presence.

The thing was, she had no idea how to go about scrubbing him—or the image of their lips locking in a frenzy of need—from her mind and finishing out the rest of her time in Australia in relative peace.

But she'd better figure out an antivenin that would work against his charm and inject herself with it. As soon as she possibly could.

CHAPTER THREE

"How's Cora?"

Isla settled herself on the paper-lined exam table like a pro, despite the burgeoning evidence of her pregnancy.

A week after they'd successfully treated the redback spider victim, Darcie had somehow managed to keep her tongue to herself.

Ugh. Now, why did that thought sound so raunchy?

And why was it that every time she was around Lucas her mind hadn't quite stopped doing mental gymnastics over every word the man uttered, turning them over and over and looking for hidden meanings?

There weren't any, and he hadn't brought up the subjects of kissing, love triangles, or anything else of a personal nature, for which she was extremely grateful.

Here Isla was, though, bringing up the one person she had no desire to hear about.

Lucas's supposed lover.

As if hearing her thoughts, he glanced at her before looking back at their patient. "She's great. Wants me to buy her a sports car."

Darcie's eyebrows shot up, even though she tried to keep her facial features frozen into place. The woman

had actually asked him to buy her a car? A pool of distaste gathered in the pit of her stomach. Just what kind of women did the man hang out with?

Isla, though, instead of castigating Lucas and telling him to kick the tramp to the curb, laughed as if she found that idea hilarious.

"Did you tell her she has to be tall enough to reach the pedals first?"

Her brain hit the rewind button and played those words over twice. Either he was dating a very short woman or…

"Yep. I also told her she has to be old enough to have her driving permit. So I'm safe for a few years."

Darcie couldn't help it. The words just came out. "Cora's not of legal age?"

"He hasn't talked your ear off about her yet? Wow." Her former flatmate blew out a breath. "She's his niece. And she gives him quite a bit of grief. Isn't that right, Lucas?"

The man in question studied Darcie as if he couldn't quite grasp something. "That's right, and…" The pupils in his eyes grew larger. "Oh, Darcie, I'm almost afraid to ask. Who did you think she was?"

"I—I…" She stammered around for a second then finally gave up.

He made a tutting sound then his lips curved. "I think I see. A love triangle, wasn't it? I don't know if I should be insulted or flattered."

"I just thought, she was—"

"My girlfriend?"

Isla's voice cut in. "Would someone like to clue me in on what you two are going on about? What's this about a love triangle?"

"It's nothing."

Lucas spoke at the exact same time she did. He then laughed, while Darcie's face flamed.

Their patient looked from one to the other of them. "Oh, this is definitely *not* nothing. But…" she patted her belly "…someone is starting to use my bladder as his own personal football. So unless you want to take a break while I visit the loo, maybe we should get on with this."

"Of course." Lucas pulled out his measuring tape and stretched it over the bulge of Isla's belly, writing the results on her chart. "Right on schedule. At this rate I think the baby will weigh in at a little over seven pounds. The perfect size for a first baby."

"Thank goodness, because right now my stomach looks to be the size of a football." She gave a light laugh. "I guess that's why this little guy feels like he's training for the World Cup."

"Anything out of the ordinary? Contractions?"

"No. Nothing. I feel great." She glanced at Darcie. "Except I have to break our date for the beach this afternoon. Someone called off sick, and they've asked me to fill in."

"Don't worry about it. Some other time."

"I know, but I promised to take you to see some sights, and with everything with Alessi and the baby, time has just slipped away." Isla slid a look at Lucas. "Aren't you two on the same rota?"

A pit lodged in her stomach. "Yes, why?"

"Well, because…" She gave the midwife a wide smile. "Would you mind going in my place? Darcie and I were going to make a list of things for her to see

and do. If she puts it off too much longer, she'll go back to England without having visited anything."

Her unease morphed into horror. "Isla, I'm sure he has other things to do with his off time than go to the beach."

"Actually, I'm free once our shift is over." The smile he gave her was much slower than Isla's and held a touch of challenge that made her shiver. "I'll be happy to help her make her list. And maybe even tick an item or two off of it. Since we *do* have the same rota. Unless she doesn't trust me, for some reason."

Isla skimmed her hands over her belly and gave a sigh that sounded relieved. "Of course she trusts you. That would be brilliant, Lucas. At this point, I would only slow her down."

They were making plans that she hadn't even agreed to. And go to the beach with Lucas? See those long legs stretched out on the sand beside hers? A dull roar sounded in her ears as panic set in.

"I'll be fine—"

A quick knock sounded before she could blurt out the rest of her sentence, that she would be fine on her own, that she didn't need company.

Sean Anderson, one of the other obstetricians, poked his head into the room. "Sorry, guys, they told me Isla was here." He looked at the patient, his expression unreadable. "One of your teen mums-to-be projects is at the nurses' station, asking for you. And after that your father wants to speak with you about your sister. I have a few questions about her myself."

Poor Isla. Not exactly the kind of thing one wanted to deal with when heavily pregnant.

Charles Delamere—Isla's father and the head of the

Melbourne Victoria Hospital—had given her friend nothing but grief over her older sister's mad dash to England and the reasons behind it. Sean hadn't been far behind in the question department. But according to Isla, she'd promised Isabel that she would never reveal her secret to anyone. Especially not to Sean, since his coming to the hospital nine months ago had been what had sent Isabel running for the door in the first place.

She tried to avoid the other man's gaze as much as possible, until Isla sat up and grabbed her hand. "Would you come with me, since you wanted to know more about the teen mums program?"

Her eyes said it all. She didn't want to be alone with Sean in case he grilled her again about Isabel. Darcie wouldn't have known about any of this except that Isabel's sudden departure had left an opening at both the MMU and in the Delameres' luxurious penthouse flat, which she'd shared with Isla until her friend's marriage to Alessandro.

Darcie had been all too happy to take Isabel's place, since she knew what it was like to run from something. In Darcie's case, it had been the right decision. In Isabel's, she wasn't so sure.

Isla hadn't told her much, but she knew Isabel was keeping something big from Sean. Maybe it was time for her to tell him the truth and see what happened.

But that wasn't her decision to make.

"Of course I'll come with you. It'll give me a chance to meet someone who's in the program."

As Isla threw her a grateful look and slid off the bed, Lucas, who'd been listening to their conversation without a word, wrapped his fingers around Darcie's wrist.

"I'll meet you by the entrance after work. This'll give us a chance to discuss some things as well."

Like how she'd somehow managed to leap to the conclusion that his niece was some floozy that kept him out late at night and caused him to have a flippant attitude about work? Heavens, she'd misjudged the man, and she wasn't exactly sure how to make it right. But going to the beach with him was the last venue she would have chosen. For the life of her, though, she couldn't think of a way to get out of it. "If you're sure."

"More than sure." His thumb glided across the inside of her wrist, the touch so light she was almost positive she'd imagined it, if not for the cheeky grin that followed. Then he released her. "Give me a ring when you're done."

"'Kay."

Once out the door, she went with Sean and Isla to the waiting area, her shaking legs and thumping heart threatening to send her to the floor. It took several deep breaths to get hold of herself.

It turned out the expectant mum was there to introduce Isla to a friend of hers—also a teen, also pregnant—who wanted to be included in the teen mums program. Darcie's heart ached over these young women who found themselves facing the unthinkable alone. She glanced at her friend, who greeted the newcomer with a smile, handing her a brochure that explained the enrolment process for TMTB. Darcie might not be able to understand what they went through, but Isla and Isabel understood all too well. Her chest grew tighter as she noticed Sean still standing behind them.

Oh, the tangled webs.

Once the girls were off on their way, Sean stepped

forward. Holding up a hand, Isla stopped him in his tracks. "Don't ask, Sean. I can't tell you." She hesitated, and her mouth opened as if she was going to say something else then stopped.

All the heartache with Robert came rushing back, and Darcie realized how much simpler it would have been if he'd told her the truth when he'd first realized he loved someone else, rather than dragging out the process. If he hadn't kept his feelings for Tabitha a secret, maybe things would have been easier on all involved.

That thought propelled her next words.

"Maybe you should call Isabel and ask her yourself," she suggested, grabbing Isla's hand and giving it a quick squeeze of reassurance. She was half-afraid Isla would smack her for sticking her nose where it didn't belong.

Sean's blue eyes swung toward her. "I tried when I heard she was leaving, but she wouldn't take my calls."

Instead of cutting her off, Isla nodded, wrapping her arm around Darcie's as if needing to hold onto something. "Maybe, Sean…maybe you should just go there. If you're standing in front of her, she can't ignore you."

"Go to England?" he asked.

That was a fantastic idea.

Lucas had planted himself in Darcie's path a couple of weeks ago, and she'd been forced to stand there while he'd had his say. Maybe Sean should do the same. Once everything was out in the open, they could decide what to do with the truth. Or at least Isabel would be forced to tell him to his face that she wanted nothing to do with him. Somehow Darcie didn't think that's what the other woman would say when it came down to it.

But, whatever happened, it was up to the two of them to hash things out. It wasn't Isla's responsibility, and she shouldn't have to act as intermediary, especially with a baby on the way. The last thing she needed was any added stress.

"I can give you her address, if you promise not to tell her where you got it," Isla added.

"My contract at the hospital *is* almost up." He dragged a hand through his hair, tousling the messy strands even more. "I'll have to think about it."

Isla's chin angled up a fraction of an inch. "I guess it comes down to whether or not you really want to know why she left, or how much you might come to regret it if you never take the chance and ask."

"I'll let you know if I need that address." With that, he strode down the hallway as if the very hounds of hell were hot on his heels.

Darcie sighed. "Do you think he will?"

"I don't know. Maybe the better question would be… if he *should*."

Why had he agreed to take her to the beach?

Lucas paused at the entrance to the car park to roll down the long sleeves of his shirt and button the cuffs against the cool air—or maybe he was gearing up for battle.

Having seen Darcie's face go pink when she'd realized Cora was his niece and not his lover had made something come to life inside him…as had her comment about a love triangle. The fact that she'd envisioned herself with him in that way was so at odds with how she'd always treated him that her flippant words had intrigued him. As had the thought of seeing her

outside her own environment. Would the woman he'd come to view as an English rose—beautiful skin, green eyes, and a set of thorns that would pierce the toughest hide—turn into someone different once she stepped off hospital property?

That was why he'd agreed. If she was going to make any kind of transformation, he wanted to be there to see it.

He glanced back inside the hospital as he waited. It was spring in Melbourne, and the air definitely bore a hint of that as it had been warmer than usual. Hence Isla's suggestion of going to one of the beaches hadn't seemed too crazy. In fact, the temperature was still holding at almost nineteen degrees, and the sun was just starting to ease toward the horizon, so they wouldn't need jackets. Although in Melbourne that could change at any time.

"Hi, sorry I'm late," Darcie said in a breathless voice as the automatic doors closed behind her. "I wanted to grab a cardigan."

She'd done more than that. She'd changed from her dark trousers and white blouse into a long gauzy white skirt and a knit turquoise top that crossed over her chest in a way that drew attention to her full curves. Curves that made his mouth go dry.

The transformation begins.

He swallowed, trying to rid himself of the sensation. He'd expected her to let her hair down in a figurative sense. He hadn't expected to see those soft silky strands grazing the upper edges of her breasts.

That he was still staring at.

Forcing his eyes back to her face, where the color of her shirt made her eyes almost glow, he blinked back

to reality. "Don't worry about it. Do you want to take the car or ride the tram?"

"Oh, the tram, please. I haven't ridden it to the beach yet, and it sounds like fun."

When he'd called the house, Chessa had said Felix was home and was grilling burgers on the barbie. When he'd tensely asked the childminder if he seemed "okay" she'd answered yes. For once he appeared clearheaded.

Thank God. The last thing he wanted to do was skip out on his date with Darcie and ruin his reputation with her all over again.

Nope. This was not a date. Something he needed to remember.

"How do you usually get to the beach, then? Taxi?"

She glanced at him as they headed for the nearest tram station. "I haven't actually been yet. I hear they're beautiful."

"You haven't been to any of them?" Shock made him stop and look at her. Isla had mentioned taking her to see some sights, but surely she'd at least visited some of Melbourne's famed beaches.

"Nope. No time. That's why Isla suggested starting there and making a list of some other things."

They started walking again. Hell, she'd been here how long? Nine months? "Well, I'm glad she mentioned it, then. We can get a snack at one of the kiosks if you want. The beaches are prettier in the morning, though."

Maybe he should take her to see the sun rise over the ocean. Those first rays of light spilling onto the water and sand made them flash and glitter as if waking from a deep slumber.

Like him?

Of course not. He wasn't asleep. He was purpose-

ful. Conscious of every move he made and careful to keep his heart far from anything that smacked of affection...or worse. He'd seen firsthand what had happened with Felix and Cora when Melody had died. He never wanted anyone to have to explain to a child of his the things he'd had to explain to his niece. That her father was very sad that her mother had gone away.

You mean she died.

Cora had said the words in her no-nonsense, too-adult-for-her-age manner that made his heart contract.

His niece needed him for who knew how long. He wouldn't do anything that would jeopardize his ability to be there for her.

Especially not for love.

That wasn't true. "Love" was exactly why he'd decided to remain single. He needed to expend all his emotional energy on a little girl who desperately needed a dependable, stable adult. Something that Felix couldn't be. At least not yet.

Buying their tickets, he eased them over to the queue, where a few people waited for the next tram to arrive.

Darcie's soft voice came through above the sound of nearby traffic. "I owe you an apology."

He glanced over in surprise to see her hands clasped in front of her, her eyes staring straight ahead. "For what?"

"For chastising you for being late all those months ago. I thought you were...that Cora was..." She shrugged.

The tram, with its bright splashes of color, pulled to a halt as he processed her words. They both got on and grabbed an overhead strap, since all the seats were full.

As they did so, he suddenly saw the whole situation through Darcie's eyes. If she truly had thought his niece was a woman, then all those times he'd come rushing into work after sleeping on his brother's couch had to look pretty damning when viewed through that lens.

He stepped closer to prevent anyone from hearing and leaned down. "I should have explained, but I thought it was—"

"None of my business. And it wasn't. If I had questions, I should have asked you directly."

Whether the reasons had been valid or not, she'd been right in expecting him to be prompt and ready to work when it was time for his assigned shift. "I should have tried harder."

Except that sometimes there'd been no way to do that. He'd had to take Cora to school on mornings that Felix had been recovering from a bender or, worse, when he hadn't come home for the night. There'd been that worry on top of having to care for his niece. There had been days he probably shouldn't have come in to work at all. Except his sense of duty had forced him to march in there—late or not—and do what he'd promised to do.

After a while, though, all those promises had begun to bump into one another and fight for supremacy. His niece had to come first. And he would make no apologies for that.

The tram started up and Darcie lurched into him for a second. He reached out with his free hand to steady her, but she recovered, pulling away quickly and clearing her throat. "Does your niece live with you?"

His grip tightened slightly on the handhold, but he

forced his voice to remain light. "She lives with my brother, but I help out with her every once in a while."

That was the understatement of the year. But he loved Cora. He'd give his life for her if he had to.

Sensing she was going to ask another question, he added. "Her mom died of cancer a few years ago."

She glanced up at him. "I'm so sorry, Lucas."

So was he. But that didn't change anything. "Thank you." He braced himself to go around a curve, and Darcie—not anticipating the shift—bumped into him once again. This time the contact sent a jolt of awareness through him. He just prevented himself from anchoring her against him, and instead changed the subject. "So how is it that you haven't seen any of our beaches? As busy as you are, surely you could have managed one side trip."

"It's no fun on my own." She gestured at the sights outside the tram, which were racing by with occasional stops to pick up or let off passengers.

With Isla busy building her own life, Lucas had never stopped to wonder how Darcie was faring now that she had the Delamere flat all to herself. That made him feel even worse. "You should have asked someone at the hospital to go with you."

"It's okay. I understand how busy everyone is."

Their bodies connected once more, and this time he couldn't help but reach out to make sure she didn't stumble or hit the passenger on her other side. She didn't object, instead seeming to lean in to brace her shoulder against his chest. Or that could just be his damned imagination since the contact seemed to be burning a hole through his shirt. Whatever it was, he was in no hurry to let her go again. Except they were

nearing the Port Melbourne Beach, which was one of the best locales for a newbie tourist. "Let's get off at this one."

When the tram stopped, he reached for her hand and guided her to the nearest door. Stepping down and waiting for her to do the same, he glanced around. "I want to get a notebook."

"What for?" she asked, brushing her skirt down her hips.

"To make that list Isla mentioned."

She reached into her bag and pulled out a small spiral-bound pad. "I have this if that would work."

"Perfect. We can sit down and put our heads together."

She paused then said, "Oh, um…sure, that would be great. But you really don't have to go with me to see the city."

It was said with such a lack of enthusiasm that he smiled. "I told Isla I would. Besides, I want to. It'll be one way for me make amends."

"Are you sure? If anyone needs to make amends, it's me."

He allowed his smile to grow as he took the notepad from her and headed toward the paved footpath that led to the beach. "You were just trying to avoid that love triangle you mentioned."

Darcie laughed, a low throaty sound that went straight to his groin and lodged there. "For all I knew, it could have been a love hexagon…or octagon."

"Hmm, that might be a little ambitious even for someone like me."

"Someone who jumps from woman to woman?"

He shook his head. "Nope. I don't jump. I just don't

stick around long enough to make any kind of angles—triangular or otherwise."

And if that didn't make him sound like a first-class jerk, he didn't know what did. "That didn't come out exactly right."

"It's okay. I understand. You're just not interested in serious relationships. Same here."

"Really? No serious relationships back in England?"

"Not at the moment."

"So there was someone?" The pull in his groin eased, but a few other muscles tensed in its place. Why did the idea of her being with someone else put him on edge?

"I was engaged. I'm not any more."

Those seven words were somehow more terrible than if she'd gone through a long convoluted explanation about why she and her fiancé had come to their senses and realized they weren't meant to be together. They spoke of heartbreak. And pain.

All the more reason for him to stay out of the dating pool.

"I'm sorry it didn't work out."

"Me too."

So she still loved the guy? She must. What the hell had her fiancé done to her?

He reached down and squeezed her hand, and instead of letting go he held on as they reached the wide footpath that ran along the far edge of the beach where other people strolled, jogged or rolled by on skates or bicycles.

"Wow, it's busy for so late in the afternoon," she said.

"It's a nice day. Do you want to walk in the sand or stick to the path?"

"Definitely the sand. Let me take my shoes off."
Stepping to the side and grasping his hand more tightly,
she kicked off one sandal and then the other, reaching
down to pick them up and tuck them into the colorful
tote bag she carried. "Your turn."

He let go of her hand long enough to remove his
loafers and peel off his socks, shoving them into his
shoes. He then tucked the notebook under his right arm
so he could hold his shoes with the same hand.

Once their feet hit the sand their fingers laced back
together as if by magic, and Darcie made no move to
pull away.

She was a visitor. Alone, essentially, and dealing
with a broken engagement. He was offering friendship. Nothing more.

And if she offered to drown her sorrows in his arms?

All the things that had gone soft suddenly headed
back in the other direction.

Hell, Lucas, you've got to get a grip.

It might have been better if she'd never shown him
her human side. Because it was doing a number on him.
Okay, so he could show her some things. Maybe he'd
invite Cora along for the ride. He could make sure his
niece was being cared for and have a built-in chaperone
should his libido decide to put in more appearances.

Darcie stopped halfway to the shoreline, her arm
brushing his as she took in the sights around her.

"What's that ship?" She motioned to where the
Spirit was docked, waiting on its next round of travel-
ers, its large sleek shape a normal part of the landscape
here at the beach.

"It carries passengers and vehicles across to Tasmania. Maybe that's first thing we should put on your list."

"Maybe."

Darcie's hair flicked around her face in the breeze from the surf, the long strands looking warm and inviting in the fading rays of the sun. His fingers tightened around his shoes, trying to resist the urge to catch one of the locks to see if it was as silky as it appeared. Good thing both of his hands were occupied at the moment.

"It's lovely here," she murmured.

It was. And he wasn't even looking at the water. Why had he never noticed the way her nose tilted up at the end, or the way her chin had the slightest hint of an indentation? And the scent the wind tossed his way was feminine and mysterious, causing a pulling sensation that grew stronger by the second.

"I agree." He forced his eyes back to the shoreline and started walking again. "Are you hungry? We could grab something and sit on the sand. Then we could start on that list while we eat."

She reached up and pushed her hair off her face with her free hand. "That sounds good. I should have brought an elastic for my hair."

"I like it down."

Green eyes swung to meet his. She blinked a couple of times. "It's not very practical."

"Neither are a lot of things." Why was he suddenly spewing such nonsense? He motioned to a nearby vendor. "How about here?"

They bought some ice-cream bars and ate them as they strolled a little further down the beach. By the time they'd finished they'd come across an area that wasn't packed with people. "Can we stop?" she asked.

"I didn't think to bring a blanket."

"It's fine." Dropping her shoes and bag onto the

soft sand, she sat cross-legged, covering her legs with her skirt. Then she propped her hands behind her hips and lifted her face to the sky. She released a quiet exhalation, a sound that spoke of letting go of tension… along with a hint of contentment.

She was still transforming—losing some of those hard, brittle edges she had at the hospital. Maybe they were simply a result of working long hours with little or no downtime. Because right now she was all soft and mellow, her billowing skirt and bare feet giving her a bohemian, artsy flare he'd never have equated with Dr. Darcie Green. And he liked it. The hair, the pale skin, the casual way she'd settled onto the sand, curved fingers burrowing into it. That firm behind that had bumped against him repeatedly as they'd ridden the tram.

The list! Think about something else. Anything else.

He opened the notebook and riffled through pages of notes from what must have been a medical seminar until he came to a blank sheet. He drew a pen from his shirt pocket. "So what would you like to see or do while in Australia?"

Her eyes blinked open but she didn't look at him. Instead, she stared out at Port Phillip Bay instead. "Mmm. Travel to Tasmania on that ship we saw?"

His pen poised over the paper as she paused for a second.

"Do some shopping. Visit a museum." Her brows knitted together as she thought. "See some of the parks. Go to a zoo."

She glanced his way, maybe noticing he wasn't writing. Because he was still too damn busy looking at her.

He shook himself. "Those are all safe things—

things every tourist does. You should have at least one or two things that are a little more dangerous."

"Dangerous?" Her eyes widened just a touch.

"Not dangerous as in getting bitten by a redback but dangerous as in fun. Something you never would have done had you remained in England. Something outrageous and wild." He leaned a little closer. "Something you'll probably never get a chance to do again."

There was silence for a few seconds then her gaze skimmed across his lips and then back up, her cheeks turning a luscious shade of pink.

Oh, hell. He was in deep trouble. Because if the most outrageous thing she could picture doing was pressing her mouth to his... Well, he could top that and add a few things that would knock her socks—and the rest of her clothes—right off.

"What are you thinking?"

She shook her head. "Nothing."

"Darcie." His voice came out low and gruff. "Look at me."

Her face slowly turned back toward him.

"If I write, 'Kiss a non-triangular Aussie' on this list, would you consider that wild and dangerous?"

There was a long pause.

"Yes," she whispered.

His gut spun sideways. He hoped to God he'd heard what he thought he'd heard, because he was not backing away from this. His brain might have come to a standstill, but his body was racing forward at the speed of light.

He set the notebook on the sand, one hand coming up to cup her nape. "Do you want to tick at least one thing off that list before we leave this beach? Because

you have a willing member of the male Aussie contingent sitting right next to you."

"You?"

"Me."

He reeled her in a little closer, his senses coming to life when her eyes slowly fluttered shut.

He would take that as a yes.

His body humming with anticipation, Lucas slowly moved in to seal the deal.

CHAPTER FOUR

HE TASTED LIKE ice cream.

Darcie wasn't quite sure how it happened, but that tram ride must have messed with her head, muddled her thinking, because somehow Lucas was kissing her, his mouth sliding over hers in light little passes that never quite went away.

That was good, because once the contact stopped the kiss would be over.

And that was the last thing she wanted.

There were people walking on the path not ten meters behind them, but it was as if she and Lucas were all alone with just the beach and the sound of the surf to keep them company.

His lips left hers, and she despaired, but he was back in less than a second, the angle changing, the pressure increasing just a fraction. Her arms started trembling from holding herself upright, and as if sensing her struggle he eased her down, hand beneath her head until she touched the sand.

The flavor of the kiss changed, going from what she feared might be a quick peck—the thing of friends or family members—to a full-on assault on her senses... a *kiss*.

If he was out to prove that Aussie men were hot-blooded, he'd done that. He'd more than done that. There was a raw quality to Lucas that she didn't understand but which she found she liked. As if he were a man on the edge—struggling to keep things casual but wanting, oh, so much more.

So did she.

Darcie opened her mouth.

The kiss stilled, and she wondered if she'd gone too far or if he was trying to process what to do at this point.

You said wild and dangerous. I'm laying myself open to it so, please, don't make me sorry.

He didn't. His tongue dipped just past her lips, sliding across the edge of her upper teeth before venturing further in. Her nerve endings all came to life at once, nipples tightening, gooseflesh rising on her arms.

Maybe she could tick that item off her list multiple times…right here, right now.

She wound her arms around his neck, reveling in the sense of urgency she now felt in his kiss. His free hand went to her waist and tightened on it, his thumb brushing across her ribs in a long slow stroke.

Then he withdrew, pulling back until he was an inch from her mouth.

"Damn." His curse brushed across her lips, but he didn't sound angry. Not like he had when he'd seen the rotation schedule. More like surprised.

He sat up, using the hand behind her head to help her up as well. "We'd better start actually making that list or it's never going to get done."

Who cared about some stupid list?

His jotting things down, though, gave her a chance

to compose herself. Well, a little. Because nothing could have prepared her for that kiss. Not her relationship with Robert or any of her past dating experiences.

Lucas was… She wasn't sure what he was. But he was good.

She glanced over at the sheet of paper where he'd made a list of about ten things. "Kiss an Aussie" was first on the list, but the tick mark he'd made beside it was now scratched through.

"I thought we were going to cross that off."

The look he gave her was completely serious. "We can't tick something off a list that didn't exist at the time it happened."

"We can't?"

"No." His eyes went dark with intent. "Because if you want to experience a real Aussie kiss, it has to be behind closed doors—with no audience to distract you."

Distracted? Who'd been distracted? Certainly not her.

But if he wanted to kiss her again—like that—she was more than willing to play along.

He scrawled a couple more words.

"Hey, wait a minute. I never said I wanted to bungee jump."

"Dangerous, remember?"

"But—"

"I have a friend who used to have a bungee-jumping business. He closed it last year but still lets friends take a dive from time to time. And I promised Cora—my niece," he reminded her with a smile, "that she could come out and watch me do a jump."

It was her turn to be surprised. "You bungee jump?"

"I have to get my adrenaline pumping somehow, since I don't have any love triangles to keep me busy."

That was something she didn't even want to think about, because she might end up volunteering if she wasn't careful.

She wouldn't mind meeting his niece, though. And it wasn't like *she* had to jump.

"Okay, I'll go. But I don't promise I'm going to do anything but watch."

"Oh, no, gorgeous, you're going to do a whole lot more than that. I promise."

Why had he invited her on his and Cora's day out?

Because he'd been too strung out on kissing her two days ago to think clearly when he'd written that item on her so-called list. She and Cora had been chatting the whole trip, with Darcie twisted around in her seat in order to talk to her. Why couldn't Cora have hated her on sight?

But she hadn't. And her "Are you Uncle Luke's girl-friend?" had turned Darcie's face the color of pink fairy floss. She hadn't freaked out, though. She'd simply shaken her head and said that she was just a friend.

Huh. He couldn't remember any friends kissing him the way she had.

And it had shocked the hell out of him. Prim and proper Darcie Green had something burning just beneath the surface of those cool English features. He had the singe marks on his brain to prove it.

As they stood on the edge of the tower suspended over a deep pool of water, Cora bounced up and down with excitement but Darcie looked nervous. "You don't have to do this, you know," he murmured.

"Are you sure it's safe? What if...?" She nodded toward Cora.

He understood. What if something happened in front of his niece? And maybe it hadn't been the smartest thing to bring her up here to watch. But she'd been begging to watch him do one of his jumps for a while now.

"Max Laurel is an engineer and a friend." He glanced over at where a stick-straight figure was adjusting some fittings. "He has his PhD in physics. I trust him. And at a hundred feet the tower isn't very high. Even if the bungee-cord snaps, there's a safety line. If that fails as well, I'll just go into the water."

He gave her a quick smile. "Like I told you earlier, he only does it for friends, he's not open to the public any more."

"What happens when you finish the jump?"

"Max will lower me the rest of the way into the water, and I'll undo the cables and swim to the side." He understood her nerves, but compared to what had happened between them back at the beach this felt pretty tame. No way was he about to admit that to her, though.

Neither was he planning on being the Aussie she checked off her list, despite his words to that effect.

Strung out on kisses.

Yep, there was no better way to put it than that. But it had to stop now. Because he had a feeling things could get out of hand really quickly with Darcie for some reason. And not just for him. She'd just come out of a bad relationship and he didn't want her to get the idea that anything serious could come of them being tossed together at work and for a few outside excur-

sions. He had enough on his plate with Felix and Cora to risk complicating his life any further.

"You ready, Luke?" his friend asked.

"I am. Can you hold on just a minute?"

Going down on his haunches in front of his niece, he put his hands on her shoulders. "Are you sure you're okay with this? I don't want you to be scared."

"No way! As soon as I'm old enough, I'm going to do it too."

Lucas had told her she had to wait until she was eighteen before attempting it. He wanted to make sure her bones and joints were strong enough to take the combination of her weight and the additional force that came from the jump. He smiled at her bravado, though. "Then let's get this show on the road."

"Darcie is going to jump too, isn't she?"

He glanced up at the woman in question. "Depends on how brave she's feeling."

"I'm only feeling half-brave. Is that enough?"

The fact that she was here, at the top of the tower, said she was more than that. She could have backed out of the trip altogether and he wouldn't have stopped her. But here she was. "More than enough."

"I'll cheer you on," promised Cora. "I wish Daddy had come, though."

Lucas hadn't told Darcie why he helped so much with his niece, and he was glad to keep it that way. For Felix's sake.

His brother was supposed to be seeing his counsellor today. Lucas could only hope he was keeping his word. His behavior the other day seemed to have snapped him back to awareness. Then again, they'd been down that same road a couple of times.

So he settled for a half-truth. "I'm sure he'll come next time. He had some things he needed to do today."

When he glanced at Darcie a slight pucker formed between her brows before it smoothed away again.

Did she suspect things weren't quite right in the Elliot household? Time to shift her attention.

"Okay, Max, are you ready for me?"

"Just about."

The next several minutes were spent attaching a thick cable to his ankles and an additional safety line to a harness that went around his torso. If something happened to the first elastic band the second one was meant to catch him. He'd done this at least twenty times with no ill-effects. Then again, he'd never had his niece and a woman watching him go over the side. Something inside him poked at him to show off for Darcie— do a spectacular swan dive or something, but that was out of the question. Safety had to come first when it came to Cora.

He moved into position, and Max checked everything once again and then gave him the thumbs-up sign. Lucas counted to three in his head and then…

Over!

He catapulted out into the air, gravity pulling him into a smooth arc as he began his downward trajectory.

The wind whistled in his ears, and he thought he might have heard Cora shout, but it was all lost in the exhilaration of the jump. Although, as the elastic began to grab and slow his descent, he wondered if even this could top that kiss he'd shared with Darcie.

Damn.

The bungee yanked him halfway back up before letting him fall again. But the closer he got to the end

of his jump, the more irritated he became. This had once filled his senses like nothing else ever could. And where he'd been happy to share it with her a couple of days ago, he was now not so sure that he'd done the right thing.

His bouncing halted, but unfortunately his wavering thoughts kept right on careening up and down, the whine of the motor as Max slowly lowered him down to the water failing to drown them out for once. Then he hit the pool and let his buoyancy carry him back to the surface, where he unhooked himself from the bungees and ankle straps, and did a slow side crawl to the edge of the pool.

He looked up and saw two faces looking down at him. One filled with an elation he recognized from years of seeing that same expression. One filled with uncertainty, as if the woman he'd known for less than a year had sensed what had been in his head as he'd done the dive.

This was not her fault. It was his own damn exhaustion and worry about Felix catching up with him. It had to be that. It couldn't be that Darcie had somehow struck a chord inside him that was still reverberating two days later.

If it was…then somehow he had to figure out a way to silence whatever she'd started.

Lucas was in the water at the far side of the pool. Waiting for her to jump so he could help her unfasten the bungees. Max told her he'd set the tension so that she wouldn't drop as far as Lucas had before it caught her up. Then the winch would let out the line until she slid into the water. Piece of cake.

Easy for him to say. Lucas hadn't come up to give her a pep talk or anything. He'd remained at the bottom, radioing up from a walkie-talkie on the side of the pool that he'd stay down and help Darcie.

Maybe it was just as well that he hadn't come back up because everything on her body was trembling. Even her hair follicles seemed to be vibrating in terror. She wasn't afraid of heights, but something about jumping and hoping an elastic cord would somehow stop her from hurtling headfirst into the water was a scary prospect.

"You can do it, Darcie." Cora's cheerful voice broke into her thoughts.

Not willing to let the girl see how scared she was, she pasted on a smile she hoped looked halfway real. "You'll be okay up here?"

"Oh, yeah. I'm going to take pictures of you as you go over."

Perfect. Just what she needed. For this moment to be recorded for all to see. She would have to find a discreet way to ask Max not to put it up on his wall of fame. Where Lucas's image appeared in several different sets of swim trunks his face was always filled with that same look of exultation, eyes closed as if taking in every second of the jump.

Speaking of jumps, she'd better go before someone got tired of waiting and pushed her over. "Okay, Cora. Count to three, and I'll jump."

"Woo-hoo!" The child yelled down to Lucas. "Get ready, here she comes. One…two…*three*!"

Darcie held her arms out from her sides and jumped as far away from the tower as she could, just as Max had instructed her. The fabric buckles of the ankle har-

ness were where her every thought was centered right now, and she squeezed her eyes shut tight. She fell… and fell. Suddenly, she felt a firm tug that turned her so she was facing the water—at least she assumed so since she still couldn't bring herself to look. A squeal left her throat before she could stop it as she bounced several times, still with her head pointed straight down. Then she came to a halt.

Hanging. Upside down. In midair. Just like a bat.

She chanced a glance down and saw that Lucas was there, right below her. The sight of him made her pounding heart calm slightly as a mechanical hum sounded from the tower above her. Slowly, she started moving downward at a steady rate. Coming closer and closer to those familiar features.

His arms stretched up as she came within reach and he put a hand around her shoulders, keeping her from plunging headlong into the water. Her body made a curve before his other arm wrapped around her hips. He went under, still holding her. That's when she realized he was treading water and her weight was sending him down. She struggled to free herself, kicking with her legs to keep from drowning the man.

But he didn't come back up. Instead, she felt his hands on one of her ankles, and she stopped paddling to let him undo the carabiner that attached the bungee cord to her legs. She sank beneath the surface and opened her eyes. There he was, fingers undoing the shank that held her ankles together, before moving further up to unclasp the static safety line at her waist.

His eyes were open as well, and they looked into hers. He reached out to finger a strand of her hair that floated between them, making her exhale a stream of

bubbles. Then he leaned forward and gave her a quick kiss before grabbing her hands and dragging her upward. A good thing, because suddenly she'd forgotten that she needed to breathe.

Once at the surface she dragged in a couple of ragged breaths while Lucas kept his arm around her waist and waited while she composed herself and prayed for her nerves to settle down just a bit.

"You did it."

"I can hardly believe I jumped." The elation was slow to kick in, but it was there now that she knew she was safely at ground level again.

"I can hardly believe it either." Lucas smiled and leaned in close to her ear. "Well, it looks like you got your first tick mark, Dr. Green. Congratulations."

Since she'd just jumped off a tower into the water, she assumed he was talking about the bungee-jumping item on the list they'd made together.

Which meant he wasn't counting that quick kiss in the water as having completed that other item on her list.

Because he was still waiting on the behind-closed-doors part to happen?

Oh, Lord. And she'd thought bungee-jumping was dangerous. It was tame compared to what her head conjured up.

The prospect of being with Lucas in a quiet, non-public place had to qualify as wild and outrageous, right? Because right now she couldn't imagine a scarier prospect than finding herself back in his arms.

CHAPTER FIVE

CORA WAS ASLEEP.

Glancing in the rearview mirror on the way back to the house, a shard of concern worked its way through his chest. He hadn't realized until after he'd helped Darcie from the pool that his niece had been taking pictures of their jumps. He wasn't quite sure what she'd been able to see from the tower, but he hoped that impulsive peck on the lips had been safely hidden beneath the water.

Why had he done that anyway? Kissed her. Again.

Because as he'd seen her sail toward him at the end of that bungee cord she had been so different from the person he'd imagined Darcie Green to be for the last nine and a half months. She'd seemed as free as a bird, tethered only by those safety cords. He'd halfway thought she'd back out of it once the time came. She hadn't.

He was happy for her in a way that was alien to him. And unsettling.

Maybe he should get some things straight with her. Only he didn't want to do that in front of his niece in case she wasn't really asleep.

"Do you mind if we drop Cora off first?"

"Of course not. But I can take a taxi if you want to just drop me off at the hospital."

"Your flat is on the way back, so it's not a problem. You're still at the Delamere place, right?" He'd been to the luxurious penthouse flat for a few parties thrown by Isla and Isabel.

"Yes, I'm there. Are you sure you don't mind?"

"Not at all." He glanced over at her, noting she'd gone back to her prim way of sitting with her hands clasped in her lap. "Did you have fun today?"

After he'd done a couple more jumps—Darcie demurring that once had been more than enough—they'd put on some dry clothes and had then had lunch with Max. That's when Cora had mentioned getting dozens of pictures and that she couldn't wait to show them to him and Darcie.

Showing them to him was one thing. But Darcie?

He was going to preview them first before that happened.

"I did, actually." Her eyes flicked to his and then back to the road in front of them. "I'll probably never get a chance to do anything like that again. Please, tell your friend thank you."

Darcie had already told him multiple times. In fact, she'd seemed to hang on his friend's every word during lunch. He'd been glad in a way, but watching her laugh over something Max had said had also caused a dark squirming of his innards he wouldn't quite call jealousy but it was something he didn't recognize. And didn't like.

"I noticed you exchanged social media information so you can do that."

She frowned and threw him a sharp glance. "Should I not have? He was the one who initiated it."

Yes, he had. And the last thing he wanted was to risk Max's friendship over a woman who would be gone in a couple of months.

He settled for saying the first thing that came to mind. "Max's a nice guy. He doesn't have a lot of experience with women."

Oh, and that sounded awful. Darcie evidently agreed because a dark flush came to her cheeks. "I think it would be better to let me off at the hospital, if you don't mind."

Prim. Uptight. Formal. All things he associated with the Darcie of three months ago. Not the warm, open woman who'd accompanied him today.

He took his hand off the wheel and covered her twined fingers. "I didn't mean that as a cut, Darce. I know you wouldn't do anything to lead him on." Why he'd felt the need to shorten her name all of a sudden he had no idea. But he liked it. Liked the way it rolled off his tongue with ease.

Another reason it would be good to talk to her. Because she was a nice girl. Just like he'd talked about Max being a nice guy. He didn't want to do anything to lead *her* on. And those two kisses they'd shared could have definitely made her think things were headed down the wrong path.

Weren't they?

Absolutely not.

"You're right. I wouldn't lead him—or anyone else—on, or make them think things that weren't true."

The words were said with such conviction that Lucas

glanced at her again and made an educated guess. "Your ex?"

"Yes." She paused for a moment. "Let's just say it's made me careful about how I interact with men."

Wow. Had that been part of those angry sparks that had lit up the maternity ward whenever he'd had dealings with her? He wasn't sure. But one thing he did know, he didn't want to go back to those days.

So maybe he should just cool the warning-her-off speech he'd planned. Wasn't he assuming a lot in thinking she was going to fall all over him because of his two lapses in judgment? Wasn't he being an egotistical jerk to think he was that irresistible?

Good thing the drive over to Felix's house gave him time to think before he did something else stupid.

Speaking of his brother's house… They were nearing the street. He put his hand back on the gear lever and downshifted as he turned at the corner. Five houses went by and they'd arrived.

Once in the driveway, he motioned for Darcie to wait while he got Cora out of the backseat. Unbuckling his niece and easing her from the car, he swung her up into his arms. She peered out of one eye then flicked it shut again.

"Cora, have you been pretending to sleep this whole time?"

"No." The word was mumbled, but there were guilty overtones to it.

Perfect. Good thing he'd decided not to tackle heavier subjects while driving.

And his comment about Max, and practically holding her hand a few minutes ago? Hopefully Cora's eyes had been pasted shut and had missed that.

But knowing his niece…

He gave an inner groan, his mind going back to the camera dangling on a cord around her neck.

Nothing he could do about that at the moment except take her inside and hope she forgot all about it by tomorrow morning.

The first thing he heard when he opened the door was a loud belch from somewhere inside.

Oh, hell. Not now.

He turned to Darcie. "Do you mind waiting here for a minute? I'll be right out."

Proving his point about his niece feigning sleep, her eyes popped open. "Oh, no. She has to come in. I want to take her back to see my room." She held up her camera. "We can look at the pictures I took on my computer."

"Luke? Is that you?" His brother's voice came from the living room, keeping him from commenting on Cora's suggestion. "I've been wondering when you were going to get home."

Felix *sounded* sober. Whether he was or not was another matter. "Yes, it's us."

Stepping in front of Darcie so he could enter first had nothing to do with being rude and everything to do with scoping out the situation. Cora was used to it—in fact, his niece had turned into a mother figure for her broken parent. But it was getting to the point where Lucas was going to have to intervene and take drastic action.

Again.

He set Cora on her feet but held her hand as they made their way to the living room, Darcie just behind him. There his brother sat in a recliner, staring at the

television. Lucas glanced at the floor beside the chair. There was no sign of beer…or any other alcoholic beverage, for that matter. Could he have heard them come home and got rid of it? That burp had sounded pretty damning.

"Hey, girlie, come over here and give Daddy a hug."

Cora rushed over to her father and threw herself into his arms. That's when Lucas noticed the picture. The one of Felix, Cora and Melody taken in this very living room shortly after their daughter's birth. It was on the end table next to Felix and not in its normal spot on the fireplace mantel.

And when his brother's eyes met his they were red-rimmed.

He was drunk…maybe not from alcohol but from the deep grief that he refused to let go of. He held onto it as tightly as he did his liquor.

Damn. Don't do this now, Felix.

Unaware of what was going on, Darcie shifted next to him. His brain hummed as he tried to figure out a way to get her out of there without her realizing something was very wrong. Cora slid from her father's arms and hurried back to Darcie with a smile. "Come see my room."

Darcie's gaze took in Felix and then Lucas, as he stood there, jaw tight, fingers itching to curl into fists at his sides. He forced them to stay still instead. "Sure," she said to the little girl. "Let's go."

The pair trailed off down the hallway, while Lucas stared at his brother. "Have you been drinking?"

"Only one." He reached behind his back and pulled out an empty beer bottle. At least, Lucas hoped it had

been empty before he'd secreted it behind him. "Something happened to the rest of them."

Lucas thought he'd dumped all the bottles. Evidently not. "Did you hide this one?"

"Yep." His brother waggled his head. "Good thing, too. Someone must have drunk all the rest of them. I think Chessa might have a drinking problem. Maybe we should fire her."

The childminder wasn't the one with a problem. It was his brother, in all his bitter glory.

"I dumped them. She didn't drink them."

"What?" His brother got to his feet, gripping the bottle in his fist. "You've got no right, Luke."

His voice went up ominously, causing Lucas to glance down the hall where Cora's door was wide open.

"Don't do this, Felix." He kept his own tone low and measured, hoping to lead by example.

"Don't *you* do this." Felix bit out the words. "You have no idea what it's like to lose someone important to you."

Yes, he did. He was watching it happen right before his eyes. Felix was a shell of the man he'd once been. A sad, drunken shell.

He decided to divert the subject if he could. He didn't want Cora or Darcie to hear his brother at his worst—or listen to the tears that would inevitably follow one of his tirades. "Are you taking your medication? You're not supposed to drink with it."

"I'm not."

Lucas wasn't sure if he meant he wasn't taking his medication or if he wasn't drinking. But since he was now shifting that bottle from one hand to the other, he

would have to assume it was the latter. That he was off his antidepressants.

He took another quick look down the hallway then held his hand out for the beer bottle.

His brother surprisingly handed it over without an argument, probably because it was empty. He went over to the recycling bin and tossed it inside, hearing the clink as it landed on other bottles—hopefully the ones Lucas had emptied the other day.

When he went back he knew what he was going to say. "I love you, Felix, and I was hoping I'd never have to say this, but if you can't get your act together, Cora's going to have to come live with me for a while."

His brother shook his head, eyes wide. "You wouldn't take her from me. She's all I have left."

"I don't want to. But I can't leave her here to watch you spiral back down, not when you've worked so hard over the last several months."

Felix sank into his chair. "I know. I need to pull it together, but…" He glanced at the picture of his wife.

With a sigh, Lucas took the picture and put it back in its spot on the mantelpiece just as Cora and Darcie came back into the room.

Darcie's face was pink and her glance went from him to Felix. Her hair was a riot of curls from their day at Max's and the sea air. It framed her face in a way that made his breath catch in his lungs. Lucas glanced at the group of pictures on the ledge over the fireplace.

Was this how his brother had started down that dark road? An initial attraction that had turned into an obsession that refused to let go, even after Melody's death?

Hell if he knew, but if that's the way it worked, he didn't even want to stop and glance at that road.

Hadn't he already? With both those kisses?

His jaw tightened and he glared at his brother. "Are you going to be okay tonight?"

"Yeah." Except Felix wouldn't quite meet his eyes. "Cora and I are going to be just fine. I've got big plans for us. Pizza and a movie. That one with all the singing and ice and snowmen."

His niece squealed. "I love that movie. You have to sing with me this time, Dad!"

"Yep, we're going to sing." He threw Lucas a defiant glare that dared him to argue with him.

He wouldn't, and his brother knew it. Not right now. But he would soon if Felix couldn't get back on track.

And if he had to take Cora away? What then for Felix?

That was one thing he didn't even want to think about. All he knew was that there came a time when the needs of his niece had to take precedence. And that time was drawing closer every day.

Darcie hadn't slept well. She wasn't sure if it was from looking at those pictures of her and Lucas frolicking in the pool or from the memories of him helping her take her restraints off.

That had to be it, because she certainly hadn't had a lot of restraint when it came to the man. And she needed some. Desperately. At least Cora hadn't captured that kiss they'd shared in the water.

She breathed a prayer of thanks.

Dressing quickly, she scowled at the dark circles beneath her eyes that told a tale of a long, hard night.

There'd been those pictures, yes. But there'd also been something about Lucas's brother. He'd seemed just a little "off."

Not that she could pinpoint what made her think that. Cora had seemed happy enough when she'd interacted with him.

Maybe it was her coworker's behavior that had set her on edge and not Felix's.

Lucas had been tight-lipped the whole time he'd talked to his brother, and when she'd been in Cora's room, staring at those damning images, she'd thought she'd heard one of them raise his voice. She wasn't sure who it had been, though.

And it completely obliterated her view of Lucas as a self-indulgent playboy. His face had been deadly serious as he'd faced off with his brother. Were there hard feelings between the pair?

If so, he'd said nothing about it on the way back to her flat. And when she'd invited him up, he'd refused, saying he had an early morning. Well, so did she.

Another thing that had skewed her image of him. What man in his right mind would give up an opportunity to get into a woman's flat and into her pants?

Certainly not the Lucas she thought she knew.

Then again, she'd thought Cora was a full-grown woman back then. She didn't remember hearing Lucas talk about any other women over the months she'd known him. If anything, it was the other way around. Women talked about him. Wore false eyelashes for him. Threw themselves at him.

He hadn't taken the bait once that she knew of.

Maybe he's just not interested in you, dummy. He could have an unspoken rule about dating co-workers.

And kissing them? Did he have a rule against that too?

Not that she could tell. And she knew of at least a couple of the female species who would kill to have been in her shoes on either of those occasions.

Dwelling on this would get her nowhere. She tossed down the last of her tea with a sigh and went to finish dressing. At this rate, it was going to be one very long, depressing day.

Darcie made it to the maternity ward and signed in with just minutes to spare. Her eyes automatically tracked to the sign-in sheet, looking for Lucas's name. The space was blank. Strange. He wasn't here yet.

After all that blubbering about having an early day today? Irritation marched into her belly and kicked at its sides a couple of times. Maybe she'd been wrong after all. Maybe he did take the bait from time to time…just not when she was the one dangling it.

Fine. She wasn't going to wait around for him to check in.

Even as she thought it, she stood there and brooded some more, while the clock crept to three minutes past the hour, and the second hand began its downward arc, reminding her of Lucas's bungee jump yesterday. And, like yesterday, he was headed straight for the bottom… of her respect.

He was officially late. Again.

What was with the man? He never seemed irresponsible when you talked to him. But his actions? Another story.

Even as she thought it, Lucas came skidding around the corner, hair in glorious disarray, face sporting a dark layer of stubble. He took one glance at her and then took the pen and signed in. Five minutes late. Not enough to throw a fit about but he'd obviously not been home.

"Where were you?"

He flicked a glance her way then one brow went up in that familiar nonchalant manner that made her molars grind. "Keeping tabs on me, are you?"

She wanted to hurl at him, "You're late, and I want an explanation!" She wanted something other than his normal flippant response—the one that went along with the MMU's view of him: a charming playboy who took nothing seriously.

He'd diagnosed Margie Terrington, though, when she hadn't.

Because everyone in Victoria knew what redback bite symptoms were.

Except her.

"No, of course not. I just…" For some reason she couldn't get the words out of her mouth, not while tears hovered around the periphery of her heart.

She would not beg him for an explanation. Or ask him to reassure her that he wasn't this rumpled couldn't-care-less man who stood before her, as delicious as he looked.

He stepped closer. "I know I'm late. And I'm going to be later still once I go back and shower. But I'll make it quick." His jaw tightened. "All I can do, Darcie, is say I'm sorry."

Still not an answer. But at least all that glib cheekiness was gone.

She glanced at the patient board. "It's still quiet. I'll let Isla know you're here and that she can go home."

"Thanks." Warm fingers slid across her cheek and his glance dipped to her mouth before coming back up to her face.

Heat flashed up her spine. He wouldn't. Not here at work.

Before she could pull back—or remain locked in place, which was what her body wanted her to do—he withdrew his hand and took a step back.

"It would help me a lot if you didn't go all pink every time you saw me—peace treaty or not, a man's only got so much willpower."

"I don't go pink!" Even as she said it, heat flamed up her neck and pooled in her cheeks, proving her a liar. It also broke the bubble of anger that had gathered around her.

Lucas laughed and tapped her nose. "Like I said…" He let the sentence trail away and then headed for the locker area, dragging both hands through his hair and whistling as he went.

Whistling!

Passing him in the hallway, Isla turned to glance at his retreating back before her eyes came to meet hers. Warmth again flooded her face as her friend drew near. "Well, I see he got here." She looked closer. "Why are you so red?"

"I—I…" What could she say, except deny it again?

"Oh, God. You two aren't…" Isla lowered her voice "…doing it, are you? I know I suggested he take you to the beach, but—"

Darcie reared back. "Of course not," she said in a loud whisper.

"Then why does the man look like he just rolled out of someone's bed? And why are we whispering? There's no one around."

Darcie cleared her throat and walked to the nurses' station. "We're whispering because I don't want any ugly rumors floating around about my personal life."

"Personal life?" Isla rubbed her belly. "You actually have one?"

The words might have stung had they not come from her friend. But Isla was right. "No. Can you blame me?"

Tessa came from a room with a chart in hand. She'd evidently overheard the last part of Darcie's declaration because she said, "You need to get out there and live it up a bit. Melbourne has some awesome nightclubs. Maybe we could make it a group outing."

"I don't know…"

Isla took up the cry. "Yes! You have to go at least once. I can't believe I didn't take you."

"You were kind of busy, remember?" An understatement if there ever was one.

Her friend laughed, hand still on her burgeoning stomach. "Maybe just a little. But, seriously, you can't leave Australia without seeing at least a little of the nightlife."

The three of them were still joking about it when Lucas appeared less than ten minutes later. Wow, the man was fast, she'd give him that. His hair was damp from his shower and he'd changed into fresh clothes.

"What are we talking about, ladies?"

"Oh…nothing." Even as she said it the slow flush rose in her face like clockwork. One side of his mouth lifted but, thank God, he said nothing about it this time.

Isla nudged her. "Darcie hasn't been to any of the nightspots. None. Zip. Can you believe it?"

"It seems there's quite a lot she hasn't experienced yet."

Lucas said it with a totally straight face, but she glanced sharply at him.

Tessa cocked her head, drumming her short fingernails on the counter. "Maybe I can get a group together to go to the Night Owl tonight. They have brilliant music and dancing. How does that sound, Darcie?"

"Well, I…" She didn't dance if she could help it. Another thing that had worn thin with Robert, who had loved it.

"If Darcie's going to make a checklist of things to do while in Australia, that should definitely go on it."

Great, just what she needed, to have him remind her of his challenge—that she pick things that were outside her comfort zone. Clubbing was definitely one of those. Not that any of them had suggested making the rounds and getting drunk.

She tried one last time. "I have to work tomorrow."

Lucas parried with, "We'll watch our step and make sure you're not arrested."

"Arrested!"

Isla put a hand on her arm. "He's kidding. You should go, Darcie. Especially since Lucas seems to be offering his services as a bouncer. You know, in case a thousand guys start hitting on you. I, unfortunately, am not allowed to have any fun for another month or so, even if Alessi would agree to let me go."

Darcie snuck a glance at Lucas, who didn't look at all put out with the idea of tagging along.

The nurse picked up a chart with a grin. "I have

to go back to work now, unlike some of you. I'll ask around and whoever wants to come can meet up at the entrance of the hospital at eight, okay? Wear something sparkly."

And with that, Tessa and Lucas both walked away without giving her a chance to refuse. And the hunky midwife had left without actually confirming that he would be there—protecting her from unwanted advances.

Unfortunately, if he did come, Darcie had no idea who was going to save her from him—or from herself.

CHAPTER SIX

SHE'D WORN SOMETHING SPARKLY. And green. And clingy as hell.

That dress was probably banned in ten countries. There was nothing vulgar about it, but the neckline scooped far enough down that a hint of creamy curves peeked over the top of it. And it was snug around her hips and the sweet curve of her backside, exposing an endless length of bare leg. He'd been trying not to stare as the group of them had taken off from the hospital and headed toward the railway station. But, holy hell, it was hard.

"Did you go shopping?" Because he just couldn't see Darcie pulling something like this out of her wardrobe. Not that he was complaining. No, he was salivating. And thinking about all the men at that club who were going to see her in this dress was doing a number on his gut.

"No. Isla loaned it to me. I didn't bring anything suitable for a night on the town."

Suitable. That was one word for it. What it was suitable for was the question. Because in his mind he could see himself peeling the thing down her shoulders and

right past all those sexy curves. They might just get arrested after all.

Why had he agreed to come again?

Oh, yes. To ward off any unwanted advances. If that was the case, he was going to have his hands full. Because he might end up having to fight off his own advances if he couldn't get his damned libido under control. Right now it was raging and growling and doing all it could to edge closer to this woman.

Thank God, the train ride was a short one. And there were seats this time, instead of having to stand and have her bump against him repeatedly. Within another few minutes they arrived at the Night Owl, a club frequented by young professionals looking to let their hair down.

The second the doors opened the music hit him between the eyes. Loud, with a driving beat, blast after blast of sound pumped out into the night air. Despite his cocky words earlier in the day, Lucas had not gone to a club since his early days at medical school. Life had been too hectic, and after Melody had died he just hadn't had much else on his mind except his brother and Cora.

Ten people in all had come with them. The rest of the group went in, but when Darcie started to pass through the door she backed up as if changing her mind, only to crash into his chest. Her backside nestled against him for a split second before she jerked away again.

His internal systems immediately went haywire.

That decided it. He wanted to be here. With her. For whatever reason.

Maybe it was just to escape the highs and lows that

had become a normal part of life these last years. He'd enjoyed the bungee-jumping trip far too much. He was ready to repeat the energetic day. But in all-adult company this time. The club would do that and more.

Strangely, the noise would insulate them, keep their words from being overheard by those around them.

When she again hesitated he leaned down. "It's okay, Darce. I'm right here with you."

There was that short version of her name again, sliding right past his lips like it belonged there. He didn't know why that kept happening, but it did the trick. She stepped through the door. And as if he'd fallen down the rabbit hole in that old children's book, the inside of the club morphed into something from another place and time.

Darkness bathed the occupants, except for brief snatches of light that flooded his pupils. The extremes made it hard to focus on anything for more than a second at a time so bodies became puppets, moving in jolts and jerks as if controlled by outside forces. The sensation was surreal. Anything that happened in the club tonight would take on a dreamlike quality: had it happened, or hadn't it? Maybe that was for the best.

Tessa came back and grabbed Darcie by the arm, dragging her away and making a drinking motion with her hand, since it was probably impossible for her to yell above the noise.

When had it become noise? At one time in his life he would have been yelling for the DJ to turn the sound up. Not any more. He squinted, trying to see where the group from the hospital had gone. When he trained his eyes to capture the second-long flashes emitted by the strobe he could just make out the dim overhead lights

of the bar at the far side of the room. At least those weren't blinking on and off.

A few minutes later he was there, squeezed between Darcie and some guy on her left—who shot him a look that could only be described as a glare. The man picked up his drink and moved on to another woman a few seats away. Tessa laughed and saluted him with her drink, while the glass in front of Darcie contained something that looked fruity and cold, with plenty of crushed ice—and probably a shot of something strong. The bartender came over with a quizzical lift of his brows.

"Just a lemonade," he yelled above the music.

Darcie threw him a wide-eyed glance. "I thought we were supposed to be living dangerously."

"I still have to get you home in one piece, so it's better for me to play it safe. At least for tonight." Lucas had had enough of Felix's drinking problems to last a lifetime. Except for that swig of beer he'd taken in his brother's kitchen, he hadn't touched the stuff in almost two years.

Some of their party had broken off into pairs and were already out on the dance floor—he squinted again—if that could be called dancing. The body parts moved, but they were disjointed…staccato. Although maybe that had to do with the lights blinking on and off.

Darcie put her straw to her mouth and took a sip of her drink then stirred the concoction while glancing around at the nightclub. The Night Owl was living up to its name, although it seemed a little early for the die-hard crowd. How much more packed could the place get?

"Are these kinds of things big in Australia?" she shouted.

This was ridiculous. They were both going to be hoarse by the time they got to work tomorrow if they kept this up. He drew her closer and leaned down to her ear. "I'm not a big nightclub person."

She tilted back to look at him then moved back in. "You bungee jump, but you don't go out drinking with the guys?"

Her warm breath washed across his ear, carrying the scent of her drink. Strawberries. Or mangoes. Okay, so maybe this wasn't going to be the disaster he was imagining because he liked having her close like this.

The guy from the seat next to him had evidently struck out with woman number two, because he was back. Bodily inserting himself between the two of them and turning his back to Lucas.

"Dance?"

He couldn't blame the guy. Darcie was beautiful. But if anyone was going to dance with her, it was going to be him.

Standing, he poked the intruder in the shoulder to get his attention. The man—a body-builder type with bulges and lumps that bordered on unnatural—didn't budge. So Lucas moved out and around until he was facing the competition.

Darcie was already shaking her head to the offer. Instead of taking the hint, the jerk held out his hand.

Lucas stared him straight in the eye. "She's with me, mate. So try somewhere else." Taking her hand, he said, "Come on, gorgeous. Bring your drink."

She grabbed her glass and went along with him,

throwing the other man an apologetic look. What the hell? Had she wanted to dance with him?

This time it was Lucas who hesitated. He stopped and glanced down at her.

"Here, try some," she said, holding her beverage up to him. "It's really good."

As much as he did not want to try some girly-girl drink, he noted the creep from the bar was still glowering their way. Probably hoping to corner her alone. To send another message, he took the glass from her and sipped from the straw...and made a face. He couldn't help it. That wasn't a drink. That was some kind of smoothie or something. But the act of putting his mouth where her lips had been—where they had applied suction and...

He took another sip. A bigger one this time and let it wash down his throat. Not so bad the second time around.

Handing it back to her, he towed her further out onto the floor, where dark forms kicked and flapped and buckled, only to come up for more. It reminded him more of a fight scene from a movie than actual dancing.

Flashes of green from her eyes met his. "I'm not much of a dancer."

There was something about the way she said it. As if she expected him to be upset. Hardly.

She couldn't be any worse than what was going on around him. "Let's pretend the music is slow and not worry about what everyone else is doing." He'd had to swoop in again to be heard. "Can you dance with your glass in your hand?"

"No. Help me finish it." She took another drink, the

contents of the large goblet dropping a quarter of an inch, then held it out to him again.

He was going to pay for this later, when the memories came back to haunt him in his sleep. But he drank anyway. Relished the slight taste of her on the straw.

When the glass was empty he motioned for her to wait and then deposited it on the nearest table, ignoring the surprised looks from its occupants. Then he strode back to Darcie and took her right hand in his, his other arm settling across her hips and pulling her close. When his attention swept the bar for the man who'd hit on her, he didn't see him. Good. Because tonight there would be no cutting in.

Darcie was all his. At least for a few hours.

If Cora didn't call.

Closing his eyes and settling her against him, he allowed his senses to absorb the feel of her curves, the scent of her hair and the way it slid like fine silk beneath his chin.

He tuned out the music…and tuned in Darcie instead. Only then did he allow his feet to sway, taking quarter-inch steps and allowing his inner rhythm to take over. Her arm crept up, her hand splaying across the skin on the back of his neck, fingers pushing into the hair at his nape.

Decadent.

Isla was right. There were some things that just shouldn't be missed. And dancing with Darcie was one of them.

She shifted against him with a sigh. "This is much better than what they're doing."

"Who?" His eyes cracked open, letting the chaotic scene back into his head.

"Everyone. I don't normally like to dance. But this feels okay."

"Yes, it does."

The song ended and the room paused for three or four seconds, while Lucas cursed silently. Then, as if the universe had read his mind, another song came on. This was slow and soothing and not quite as loud. The atmosphere shifted. The strobe went off in favor of dim, steady lighting.

Arms twined together and single dancers edged off the floor to let the couples have a turn.

"Is this better?" he murmured into her ear.

"Mmm, yes."

Lucas's hand tightened on her back, thumb skimming up her spine and drawing his palm along with it until it was between her shoulder blades, before gliding back down to her waist.

Hell, this was nice. Maybe a little too nice.

Darcie must have sensed it too because the fingertips that were against the lower part of his scalp brushed back and forth, sending a frisson of raw sensation arrowing down to his groin.

He willed away the rush of need that followed, trying to think about anything else but the pulsing that was beginning to make itself known in not-so-subtle ways.

Football. Kayaking. Hiking.

He dragged various activities through his head and forced his brain to come up with five important items about each one, before moving on to the next. Anything to keep from having to step back a pace or two in order to hide her effect on him.

Because he didn't want to go. Not until this song was over and done. And maybe not even then.

There. Things were subsiding. Slowly. But as long as she didn't...

Her fingertips dragged downward, emerging from his hair and sliding sideways across the bare skin of his neck.

"Darce, are you trying to make me crazy?" Because if he didn't say something, she was going to end up with one hell of a surprise.

Her cheek moved away from his chest and she glanced up at him. "I wasn't trying to. Why, am I succeeding?"

Something about the way she'd said that. As if surprised. Or curious. Or a whole lot of things. None of them good because it just stirred him to say more stupid things. They'd all agreed to leave separately, so they could each decide when they'd had enough. But no way was he letting Darcie leave there on her own.

"Yes." He let that one word speak for him, because it was true.

"So I can cross this off my list, right?"

"Driving me crazy?"

"No." She gave a soft laugh. "I was talking about coming to a nightclub."

His brows went up, and he realized without that godawful strobe light he could finally see her without the additional shock on his senses. Being this close to her was as heady as laying her down on the sand at the beach had been. "I thought you might be angling to finally cross something else off your list."

Her tongue came out, moistening that full lower lip. "What's that?"

She was going to make him say it, wasn't she? "Kissing an Aussie."

"But I thought you said that had to be behind closed doors in order to count." The breathiness of her response made him smile.

"It does. But that can be arranged."

Her fingers at the back of his neck tightened, and her eyes closed for a second.

Was she going to turn him down? His body started to groan and swear at him for screwing this up. Maybe he should limit it to just the kiss. But, hell, he didn't want just a kiss. He wanted to carry her down some dark hallway and toss her on a bed...expose every luscious inch of her. And *then* kiss her.

When her eyelids parted again she gave a nod. "Then yes. But only if it's a wild and outrageous kiss."

He couldn't resist. He leaned down and nipped the jawline next to her ear. "Trust me. I can make that happen."

The song ended, and Lucas realized he and Darcie were no longer dancing. In fact, they were just standing there in each other's arms, staring at each other.

"Let's go back to Isla's flat."

"What?" He pulled back, thinking he'd surely misunderstood. He wanted to be alone with her, not visit Isla and Alessandro.

She laughed, unwinding her arm from around his neck and grabbing his hand as she made her way off the dance floor. "I mean the Delamere flat, where I'm staying. Alone."

That was more like it. Besides, that end of town was closer than his own place. And his barely furnished flat

left little to be desired as far as what she was probably used to. "That sounds like a plan. Lead on."

Darcie was somehow able to find her keys in the tiny glittery purse that she'd slung over her shoulder as they'd left the Night Owl and arrived at the large opulent building Charles Delamere owned. She punched the code into the box by the front door and heard the click as it unlocked. She'd seen it so many times the place didn't even register any more, but with Lucas standing there behind her she suddenly felt self-conscious as they made their way across the marble foyer.

"You've been here before, right?" She didn't want him to get the idea that she was rich or anything. But she'd never thought anything less of Isla for living here, so why would she think Lucas was any different?

Maybe because it mattered what he thought, and she wasn't quite sure why.

"I have. Isla liked to entertain, so I've been here several times."

Entertain. As in a group? Or just Lucas? "Oh, um…"

"We were never involved," he murmured, as if sensing her thoughts.

"Oh, I didn't think—"

"Didn't you? You thought I might be involved with a whole horde of females at one time."

She had. And when had she moved so far away from that initial opinion she'd held of him? Maybe when she'd met Cora and seen how much he cared about his niece. And maybe—when she put all those phone calls into context—they'd become sweet. Whatever it

was, she no longer believed many of the things she'd once thought.

"People change," she murmured.

His hand tightened on hers for a second and his footsteps faltered.

Had she said something wrong?

"Yes, they do."

They stopped in front of the lift and Darcie punched the button to call it. Lucas leaned a shoulder against the wall next to her and studied her face, a slight frown between his brows. Right on cue, heat surged into her cheeks.

His mood seemed to clear and he smiled. "I don't think I've ever seen a woman blush as much as you do."

"I can't help it. It's just the way I'm made."

His eyes skimmed down the rest of her, pausing at the neckline of Isla's slinky dress. "I'm kind of partial to the way you're made."

Her face grew even hotter and he chuckled. Then the lift arrived, saving her from having to respond to his comment.

They both got on, and Darcie nodded at the camera tucked into the corner of the lift, hoping he'd understand her meaning.

He did, because he leaned down, his warm breath washing over her cheek. "Don't worry, gorgeous. I don't want an audience this time. Although later…"

When her eyes widened, his hand went to her lower back, fingertips skimming up her spine until he reached her nape. One finger made tiny circles there beneath the curtain of her hair. Pure need spiraled through her as he added a second finger, the pair trailing down and around the back of her dress, which was scooped

like the front of it was. To the camera, it would appear as if they were both just standing quietly, but inside her chest her heart was jumping and things were heating up.

A fine layer of perspiration broke out on her upper lip as she struggled not to close her eyes or utter the soft sounds that were bubbling up in her throat. Was there a microphone connected to that camera?

Up, up they went, racing toward the penthouse while Darcie's legs turned to jelly, and the need to touch him back began growing in her chest. In her belly. In her hands.

She curled her fingers into her palms to keep them from reaching for him.

"Do you like that?" he whispered.

Was he joking? Couldn't he tell? She glanced at their reflection in the mirror across from them and noted her nipples were puckered, showing even through the fabric of her strapless bra and her dress, although both were thin.

Ping.

The lift slowed, and Lucas stopped stroking her neck, his warm hand wrapping around her nape instead. When the doors opened, she practically fell out onto the dark glossy floor of the entrance to the flat. Hands shaking, she tried to hit the lock with her key and missed the first time, only to have Lucas's fingers cover hers and guide them to the keyhole, unlocking and opening the door in one smooth movement.

They went inside. "D-do you want a tour?"

"Mmm…yes, but not of the flat." He took the keys from her hand and the purse from her shoulder and put them both on the slate surface of the entry table.

Her teeth dug into her lower lip as Lucas came back and put his hands on her shoulders, thumbs edging just beneath the fabric covering them. This was a man who bungee-jumped and practically made love to her on an open beach. Who teased and tormented her senses on the dance floor and again in the lift. He didn't want a feeble tour or a half-hearted response from whatever woman he was with.

Robert's face as Tabitha had thrown herself into his arms was branded in her mind. That was what her ex-fiancé had wanted. Not a mild-mannered woman who was far too "safe."

Was Lucas going to find her wanting as well? Would he regret having put all this effort into getting her into bed?

That brought up another question. Was that why he'd done everything he had…the trip to the beach, the list, the nightclub? To sleep with her? Her insecurities grew.

She had no illusions that this was anything but a one-night stand. She'd made it clear that she didn't want anything more than that either. But maybe she should make it clear that she probably wasn't as wildly experienced as some of the women he'd been with.

"I—I'm not…" She licked her lips as Lucas went still. "I'm probably not very good at…" Her voice died away a second time, so she had to use her hand to made swirly motions in the air and hope he got the gist of her meaning.

He tightened his grip on her shoulders slightly. "Please, tell me you're not a virgin."

"No!" The denial came out as a squeak, so she

cleared her throat. "My fiancé just found me a bit… dull in that respect."

Lucas didn't move for several seconds, but a muscle pulsing in his cheek made her squirm. Was he wondering how to get out of the flat without hurting her feelings?

"You don't have to stay if you don't want to." There. She'd given him a way to escape.

He shook his head. "I'm not planning on going anywhere, unless you decide to throw me out." He then gave a smile that could only be described as rueful. "My experience with you has been anything but dull."

She remembered his curse when he'd seen her name on that rotation list. Actually, she had been more outspoken with him than she was with most people. But only because he'd irritated her with his attitude and his tardiness. Okay, so maybe she wasn't dull at work. But here? "I'm not very adventurous."

He leaned down and gave her a slow kiss. One that started off soft and easy and gradually built…his hand sliding into her hair and gathering the strands in his fist. When he pulled back again she was breathless and right back to where she'd been in the lift—melting with desire and wanting nothing more than for him to drag her down those three steps to the living area and take her right there on the couch.

"Then you won't mind if I'm adventurous enough for both of us."

The pressure of being someone she wasn't lifted. She could do that. She could let Lucas call the shots and introduce her to things she'd never tried before—

just like he had standing on that high tower, and again after she'd landed in the pool.

This man lit her senses up like no one ever had. "No. I won't mind."

"Well, then." He began bunching her dress in his fists, gathering more and more material in them until the hemline was at the very tops of her thighs. "We won't need this." Up and over her head went the dress, which had no zipper, the stretchy material allowing him to strip it off her body with ease. He turned and carried the garment across the space, going lightly down the steps and placing it over one of the leather chairs in the living room.

When she started to follow him, he held up his hand to signal her to wait. He slowly made his way back up, his eyes on her the whole time. "You're beautiful, Darce. I don't know what your ex told you, but 'dull' is not a word I would ever use to describe you."

He reached for her hands as a warm flush crept up her body. It only increased when he carried her hands behind her back and moved in to kiss her again. This one slow and lingering, his lips brushing across hers, the friction driving her crazy. "Where's your bedroom, sweetheart?"

"Down the hall. First door to the right."

"Down the hall we go, then." Before she could move he released her hands and swept her into his arms as if she weighed nothing.

He arrived at her room and edged her through the door, stopping for a second as if to take in the space. Although she was sleeping in Isabel's old room, she'd boxed up the other woman's mementos and substituted

a few things she'd brought with her. But other than that the space was devoid of a lot of personal items other than the bed and dresser. There were built-ins that were still almost empty.

Walking over to the queen-size bed that had her wondering if it would hold Lucas's frame, he glanced down at her, eyes unreadable. "You never planned on sticking around, did you?"

She was surprised by the question. Everyone at the hospital knew she was only here for a year. After that she'd be leaving. Had he expected her to fill the room with stuff, only to have to get rid of it all a few short months later? And that's what it was looking like at this point: a few short months. Her time in Australia had flown by. Much quicker than she'd thought it would. But it had done what she'd intended it to do—erased the pain of Robert and Tabitha's betrayal. "You knew I was only here for a year."

His muscles relaxed, as if she'd given the correct response. Except she didn't know what the real question was. That he didn't want her to stick around, because of the conflict that had flared between them periodically? Or that he was making sure she wasn't going to place any more importance on tonight than he planned to? He didn't have to worry on that account. She'd already bought her return ticket months ago, right after their first big blow-up.

She blinked up at him. "Are you sure you want to stay?"

"You keep asking me that as if you hope I'll change my mind." He dropped her on the bed and then followed her down. "I won't."

She wound her arms around his neck. "Well, okay, then. As long as we're both clear on what happens on the other side, we should be good."

"Let's worry about right now. And then we can deal with the other stuff tomorrow." With that, his mouth came down, blotting out everything except for the fact that this was exactly where Darcie wanted to be. In this man's arms.

CHAPTER SEVEN

He was going to make this a night she would remember.

Not because he was that good but because her words had picked at a sore spot within him. No, he didn't want any permanent relationships, but he was stung by how easy she seemed to think it would be to walk away from him. An idiotic response, considering his own attitude, but he'd never been a rational man when it came to Darcie.

Her bra had no straps to peel down so he settled for following the course of an imaginary strap with his fingers, making sure his short nails kept light contact with her skin as they made their way across her shoulders.

Her reaction was to arch a few centimeters off the silk duvet cover. His flesh reacted in kind. Arching up and away from his body, only to be stopped by the fabric of his dress trousers. That would soon be remedied. But not quite yet.

He continued down her arms, going past the crook of her elbows and only stopping when he reached her wrists, which he caught up in both of his hands. He carried them over her head and rested them there, catching sight of bright green eyes as they stared at his face. He wanted her hands out of the way for what he did next.

Her lips were parted and glossy from his kisses, so he leaned in for another quick taste, glorying in the way they clung to his and followed him up an inch or two as he moved away. He gave a pained laugh.

Dull? Hell, her ex was an idiot. This woman was responsive, giving, and sexy as they came. She hadn't put any limits on their time together. When he'd said he was going to be adventurous enough for both of them, her glance had heated instantly.

Which brought him back to his point. He wanted to make this good. Wanted to leave her with no doubt that she was exciting and desirable. Not just to him but to plenty of other men. He'd caught Max's glances at her during the bungee jump. And the guy at the bar? Oh, he'd been interested all right. The thought made his blood pressure shoot up, just as it had at the Night Owl.

Hooking one of his legs between hers, he edged her thighs apart, keeping his foot just behind her ankle in case she was tempted to squeeze them shut again. She didn't even try. That in itself made Lucas's flesh surge, putting up some new demands. He was willing to oblige some of them…but others would have to wait.

He let his fingers slide over the sweet curves peeking just above her bra. Her skin was smooth and incredibly soft. He wanted more. Keeping his leg between hers, he reached beneath her body and searched for the clasp. Found it. Flicked it open.

He then dropped the garment over the side of the bed, and drank in the view before him.

Heavenly. In every way.

Her nipples were drawn up tight—pink and perfect. Darcie's eyes were open now. She made no move to

cover herself with her hands, although her breathing ratcheted up a notch.

That was as far as he got before he could stand it no longer. He leaned down and tasted her, drawing one peak into his mouth and letting his tongue wander over it.

She moaned and arched higher, pushing herself into his touch.

Yes. This was what he needed. He applied more pressure, using her response as a gauge for how much friction she wanted from him.

Hell if she didn't ask him to up the ante even more. When his teeth scraped over her, her hands came down on his head, but instead of pulling him away her fingers buried themselves in his hair and she pushed hard against him.

He came up panting, body raging, wanting to end it all right here, right now. Instead, he let his mouth cover hers, tongue plunging inside again and again, while she maintained her grip on his hair.

Pulling away in a rush, he ripped her undies down and found her hot and wet and ready. He kissed her once again, letting his index finger sink deep into her. Just like he was about to. He got off the bed.

"Do. Not. Move." He growled the words, stripping in record time, letting the sight of her flushed body drive him to action—to find the condom and rip into it, sheathing himself.

Then he was back with her, over her. Finding her. Sliding home to a place where pleasure and madness fought for supremacy.

He set up a slow, easy rhythm that was all for her, ignoring his own wants and needs.

"Lucas." His name was whispered. Shaky. A silent plea he couldn't ignore.

"I'm here, gorgeous." He edged out and then pushed deep.

Darcie responded with a long drawn-out moan, lifting her hips, her hands going to his shoulders and holding on.

Kissing and licking the length of her neck, he allowed her tight heat to wash over him in a wave, careful to hang onto whatever control he still had. He wanted this to last.

And that surprised him.

He usually saw to his partner's pleasure first and then concentrated on his own. He had it down to a science almost. But here he was, breaking his own rules. She hadn't climaxed. And he didn't want her to. Not yet. He wanted to lose himself when she did—wanted to watch the exact second she came apart. He could only do that if he knew when...

He rolled over, carrying her with him until she was on top, straddling his hips. Her eyes jerked open, and she looked at him uncertainly.

"You set the pace, Darcie. Do what feels good to you."

While I watch.

She hesitated for a second then her instincts seemed to take over. She braced her hands on his thighs, just behind her butt and lifted up and came back down as if seeing how it felt. Then her eyes fluttered shut, teeth digging into her bottom lip as she moved over him a second time. Then a third. Again and again, she lowered herself onto him and rose back up. His

own personal angel, set on propelling them both toward paradise.

Until Lucas began to ache from holding back.

It was time.

Pressing his palm against her lower belly, he allowed his thumb to find that sensitive place between her thighs. Her head went back, little whimpers coming from her throat and spilling into the air around him. Sexy sounds. Earthy and full of need.

Her movements grew jerky, hands tightening on his thighs.

"Yes, sweetheart, that's it," he gritted. "Let it all go."

With that, Darcie's whole body stiffened, her insides flaring for a split second before clamping down hard on his erection and exploding into a series of spasms that rocked his world, that made him grab her hips and pump wildly, washing her orgasm down with his own. He poured every emotion he had into the act, until there was nothing left.

And yet he was still full. Full of Darcie. Full of those luscious aftershocks that had him pulling her down hard onto him, eyes closed as he absorbed all of it and more.

When he looked up again her eyes were open. Looking at him. A trembling question in those bright green depths.

She had doubts?

He drew her down until she was lying across his chest, her face nestled against his neck. "You okay?"

"Mmm-hmm." A hesitation. "You?"

"Perfect. Absolutely perfect." He leaned down and kissed the top of her head. "And you're about to cross one thing off your list."

"The kiss?"

He should say yes. End it once and for all. It would be on a good note. One they could both smile about years from now. But he didn't want to. Not with his body already beginning to reset itself. So he said instead, "Not yet. I'll tell you when."

With that he rolled her back beneath him and pressed his mouth to hers.

Darcie had been walking around in a daze.

Beginning with the moment she'd woken up in an empty bed. For some reason, she'd thought Lucas would wake her to say goodbye if he decided to leave. He hadn't. But after the second lovemaking session she'd been exhausted. And replete. And something about going to sleep with his arm anchoring her close to his body had given her a sense of comfort she hadn't felt in a long time.

How long had he stayed once she'd drifted off? A few minutes? An hour?

The only thing that had made her smile—since she'd been squirming with embarrassment over some of her actions—had been that Lucas had ticked the "kiss a non-triangular Aussie" box and drawn an arrow out to a smiley face. *A smiley face.* She'd never known a man to use one before.

And the fact that he'd rolled out of her bed and actually felt like smiling made a lump come to her throat. She'd assumed with Robert it had been her problem... that he'd been rejecting her. Maybe he'd been rejecting them as a couple. Because although Lucas had used the word "uptight" when he'd grumbled about that roster,

he hadn't given any indication last night that he still found her that way.

Instead, he'd smiled.

She kept twisting that fact round and round in her head. It had to have meant he was as satisfied as she was, right?

Grabbing the clipboard for her next patient, she glanced at the name. Margie Terrington, their redback bite patient. She glanced at her mobile phone, wondering if she should call Lucas in to join her for the consultation, but she was leery. She hadn't actually spoken to him yet today. Why ruin her mood before she had to?

She pushed through the door, only to stop short. Lucas was already in the room. But, then, why was the chart…?

He glanced at her with an undecipherable expression. "I thought you might eventually make it to work today."

Eventually make it? She'd been twenty minutes early, just like most days. Which meant he'd been…

Even earlier.

The very corners of his mouth went up, making her heart lift along with them, but she was careful not to let on to her patient that Lucas was teasing her. "I did indeed." She greeted Margie and flipped through her chart, asking a few questions.

Lucas sat and listened to the back and forth for a minute or two before asking his own question. "Any problems from the antivenin?"

"None." The expectant mum rubbed her belly. "I can't thank you both enough for figuring out what was wrong."

"Thank Lucas, he was the one who realized you'd been bitten."

The young woman shuddered. "My husband tore the rest of the house apart to make sure there weren't any more of them."

They finished checking her over, letting her listen to the baby's heartbeat to reassure her that all was indeed well after the scare the previous week. "Did your mum come to Australia? With your husband working, I know it'll be a great help to have her here. We could all use a little support." As Darcie well knew from her parents' support after what Robert had done.

They'd been thrilled that she'd been able to go to Australia to get away from everything that had happened. She'd barely prevented her dad from punching her ex-fiancé right in the nose. But she'd grabbed his arm at the last moment. Everyone had parted semi-amicably. And the only heart that had been broken that day had been hers. She'd been left in the wedding chapel all alone after everyone had left—her mum seeing to all the last-minute explanations and canceling the venue for the honeymoon.

"Yes, she arrived just a few days ago," Margie said. "She already loves it here. And, yes, we could all use the support of family. After our other…loss…I wondered if I would ever be happy again. I thought I'd never get over it."

Lucas stood with a suddenness that made both women look at him. He glanced at Darcie and then away, muttering that he needed to check on another patient.

She frowned.

That look wasn't anything that resembled a smi-

ley face. And she had no idea who that "other patient" could be because there wasn't anyone listed on the schedule board for another hour. There were a couple of patients in rooms, and she'd noticed one poor woman was curled on her side, sucking down nitrous oxide with a rather desperate air, but they all had other midwives attending them. After saying goodbye to Margie, she went into the hallway and glanced down the corridor, but there was no sign of him. Darcie had hoped to talk to him about how they were going to treat last night.

Already one of the other nurses had cornered her and asked why she'd left the nightclub so early. She'd feigned a headache and said she'd caught the train back to her flat. Not a total lie. But she certainly wasn't going to tell anyone she'd dragged Lucas home with her. She couldn't even bring herself to admit all they'd done together, much less admit it to anyone else. It would be much better if they had some kind of joint cover story to hand out to anyone who asked. Present a united front, as it were.

Even if they weren't united.

Oh, well. Stepping outside the hospital to get a breath of fresh air, she heard her name being called. Not by Lucas but by a child. Darcie swung round in time to see Cora and her dad coming toward them on the footpath. Cora broke into a run and gave her a fierce hug as soon as she reached her, Felix trailing along behind. When he finally caught up he looked a bit shamefaced and maybe even a little shaken up. "Do you know where my brother is?"

"I don't. We just finished up with a patient, though, so he's here somewhere." Darcie didn't want to admit

that she had no idea where he'd gone or why. Her stomach was beginning to do a slow dive to the bottom of her abdominal cavity, though.

"I can stay here with Darcie, Dad. She won't mind, will you?"

Felix scratched the back of his neck. "I don't know, Cora. I think we should just go home."

"But you can't! You promised me, and you promised Uncle Luke." Cora's voice came across shrill and upset.

If anything, her father looked even more unsure. "I know, but Chessa is sick and I'm not leaving you home alone."

Darcie didn't have any idea what was going on, but whatever it was sounded important, judging from Cora's overly bright eyes. Tears? Looking to defuse the situation, she said, "Why don't I try to reach his mobile and see where he is?"

But when she tried to do that, the phone went right to voicemail. Strange. Unless he had it off so he wouldn't have to talk to her. His behavior in Margie's room had set her alarm bells ringing earlier. And now this. Her stomach dropped even further. She settled for leaving a message. "Hello, Lucas, it's Darcie." Why she felt compelled to explain who she was when he would know from the caller ID was beyond her. She went on, "Felix and Cora are here at the south entrance. Would you mind stopping round if you get this within the next few minutes?"

She pressed the disconnect button, only to have Cora tell her, "We tried to ring him too, but he didn't answer."

That didn't sound like Lucas. He doted on his niece.

"I could keep her here with me for a while. I have an office where she could hang out until Lucas turns up."

A look of profound gratitude went through Felix's eyes. "Are you sure it's no trouble? I have an appointment and our childminder is ill."

"It's fine. Leave it to me." She took Cora by the hand. "We'll get on famously until then."

Felix looked uncertain for all of five seconds then he nodded. "Okay, I appreciate it."

"Bye, Daddy," Cora said. "Maybe Uncle Luke can drive me home and get me an ice lolly on the way."

Darcie's heart twisted. So much for hoping he might want to come home with her. Again.

What? Are you insane?

Evidently, because her mind had, in fact, already traveled down that path and was trying to figure out a way to make it come true.

Giving Felix her mobile number and waving him off with what she hoped was a cheerful toss of her head, she made her way back inside the hospital, Cora following close behind.

Once in her office, the little girl found a pull-apart model of a baby in a pregnant belly that Darcie kept to show her patients. She'd forgotten it was on her desk when she'd offered to bring Cora here. "I'm not sure your dad would want you looking at that."

"Oh, I know all about how babies are born. Uncle Luke's a midwife. I have to know."

Darcie couldn't stop the smile. "You do, do you? And why is that?"

"Because I'm going to be a midwife too. Did you know that Uncle Luke helped my mum have me? She couldn't make it to a hospital."

No, she hadn't known, because Lucas hadn't talked about anything personal, she realized. In fact, he knew some pretty intimate stuff about her, while she knew almost nothing about him. Like whether or not his parents were still alive. Or why he'd gone into midwifery in the first place.

Because it was none of her business.

Careful not to pump the girl for information, she settled for a noncommittal response that she hoped would end the conversation.

It didn't. "Mummy died of cancer."

That she *did* know. "I'm sorry, Cora."

"I don't remember much about her. But I do remember she always smelled nice…like chocolate biscuits."

Darcie swallowed hard, forcing down the growing lump in her throat. What would it be like to lose your mother at such a tender age? Her own mum was still her very best friend and confidante. She decided to change the subject once and for all, since neither Felix nor Lucas would appreciate knowing her and Cora's chat had revealed old heartaches. "Speaking of biscuits, Cora, would you like to go down to the café and see if they have something good to eat? I'll just let the nurses know where I'll be."

"Yay!" Cora grabbed her hand and tugged her toward the door. "Does the coffee shop have espresso, do you think?"

She gave the little girl a sharp glance, not sure if she was joking or not. "How about we both stick with hot chocolate?"

"Even better. Daddy sometimes forgets to buy the chocolate powder."

"Then hot chocolate we shall have."

Fifteen minutes later they were in the cafeteria at a table, with Cora imitating the way Darcie drank her chocolate. It made Darcie smile. She could see why Lucas was so very fond of her. The girl was exuberant and full of life, despite the tragedy she'd suffered at such a young age. Then again, children were resilient, a characteristic she often wished was carried into adulthood.

The buzzer on her phone went off and when she looked at the screen her eyes widened. Lucas. He must have got her message. She answered, forcing herself to speak cheerfully, even though her heart was cranking out signals of panic. "Hi."

"May I ask where you are, and why my niece is with you? You're not in your office."

"I...uh..." Oh, God, it hadn't been her imagination in Margie's room. He *was* upset with her for some reason. Only she had no idea why or what she could have done. "We're in the cafeteria. Felix said he tried to ring you, but you didn't answer."

That was really the crux of the matter. Why Lucas had failed to answer anyone's calls.

"I forgot to charge my battery after..." He paused, then forged ahead, "I got home. I had to get the extra charger from my vehicle in the car park."

Oh, well, that answered the question about where he'd gone and why he hadn't picked up his mobile. It didn't answer why he was acting the way he was. "Okay. Well, Felix said the childminder is ill and he had an appointment to keep. He asked if I could watch Cora for a few minutes."

Had Felix not left him a message, like she had?

"I'll be right down to get her."

She tried to smooth things over. "Why don't you join us instead? We're drinking hot chocolate and eating biscuits."

He mumbled something under his breath that she couldn't hear before he came back with, "One of us should stay on the ward."

It was a slow morning and there were several other midwives on duty. Surely he didn't mind sharing her break time?

She simply said, though, "Whatever you think is best. I'll see you when you get here." Then she disconnected before he could say anything else. The last thing she wanted to do was get into an argument with him just when she thought they'd turned a corner.

Turned a corner? Sleeping with him was so much more than that.

Was that what this was all about? Did he suddenly regret what they'd done? Or was he just afraid she was going to become clingy and expect something from him he wasn't willing to give?

She suddenly felt like a fool. Played with and then discarded, like she would have expected him to do with other women. And why *not* her? She was no better than anyone else. Certainly not in Lucas's eyes.

"Darcie, are you okay?" Cora's worried voice broke into her thoughts.

She forced a smile, picking up her hot chocolate and taking a sip of the now-tepid liquid. "Fine. Your uncle is on his way down to have tea with you."

"Shall we order him something, do you think?"

"Oh, I think he can manage that on his own." Another quick smile that made her feel like a total fraud.

"And once he gets here I need to get back to work. I have patients that need attending to."

"Can't you stay a little while longer? I know Uncle Luke would want you to."

No, actually he wouldn't. But there was no way she was going to say that to a little girl. "Sorry, love, I wish I could."

The second Lucas arrived Darcie popped up from the table. "See, here she is all safe and sound."

His eyes searched hers for a moment, and she thought she caught a hint of regret in their depths. "I had no doubt she was safe with you."

His hand came out as if to catch her wrist, but Darcie took a step back, going over to Cora and leaning down to kiss the top of her head. "I'm off. Have fun with your uncle."

Then, without a backward glance, she made her way out of the café, wishing she could grind the last fortnight of their rotation into dust and sweep it into the nearest bin.

CHAPTER EIGHT

LUCAS FOUND HER just outside the Teen Mums-to-Be room.

Isla had the door to the tiny conference room open, and she and Darcie were discussing ways to promote the program and give it more visibility. When Isla's eyes settled on him, however, they widened slightly. "I think someone wants to talk to you."

Darcie glanced back, and then her chin popped up, eyes sparkling. "May I help you with something, Mr. Elliot?"

Her sudden formality struck him right between the eyes. He wasn't the only who noticed. Isla looked from one to the other then murmured that she would see Darcie later and left, quietly closing the door behind her.

He'd cursed himself up one side and down the other for the way he'd spoken to Darcie on the phone yesterday. Margie talking about her miscarriage and wondering if she'd ever be happy again had scrubbed at a raw spot inside him that just wouldn't go away. Because he'd wondered the same thing about his brother time and time again—whether he'd ever be happy again, or if he'd simply wander the same worn paths for the rest of his life or, worse, destroy himself and damage

Cora in the process. Love and loss seemed to go hand in hand.

But that had been no reason to take it out on Darcie.

Better make this good, mate.

"I wanted to apologize for being short with you yesterday."

"No need. I should have simply asked your brother to take Cora home when he couldn't reach you, appointment or no appointment. I didn't realize you were so against me spending time with her." Her lips pressed together in a straight line.

She was angry.

And gorgeous. Especially now.

He'd settled Cora in his office yesterday while Felix had gone to his therapy session, and between him and the nurses they'd taken turns keeping her occupied. Every time he'd checked in on her she'd chattered non-stop about Darcie. She'd loaded the pictures from their time at Max's bungee-jumping tower onto his computer. One of those shots had taken his breath away. It had been taken just after he'd unhooked her carabiners, just after he'd kissed her. She'd broken through the surface of the water at the same time as he had, brown hair streaming down her back, fingers clutching his.

And their eyes had been locked on each other. He could only hope none of the nurses had seen the picture.

But in that moment he'd realized why he was so against Darcie and Cora spending time together. Because Darcie was too easy to love. Much like Melody had been.

Cora had already grown attached to the obstetrician. That fact made his chest ache. She'd lost her mother,

and very possibly her father. This was one little girl who didn't deserve to experience any more hurt. And she would if he wasn't careful. Because Darcie would be leaving the country. Soon.

He'd tried to apologize to her yesterday, but by the time his brother had come to pick Cora up, Darcie had been flooded with patients and unable to stop and talk. At least, that's what she said. And when their shift had ended, she'd left immediately.

"No, you did the right thing," he said. "I was upset with myself for not getting those calls and leaving you to deal with the whole mess." A partial truth. But if his mobile phone had been charged, he could have avoided all of this.

"Mess?"

Damn, he wasn't explaining himself very well. "Things with my brother are complicated at the moment, and I was worried."

Darcie's brows puckered, but she didn't ask what the complications were. "It was no problem. Cora and I get on quite well."

"Yes, I've noticed."

If he were smart he'd have let things continue the way they had yesterday—with Darcie put out with him—until their rotation ended. But the note of hurt in her voice, when he'd demanded to know where Cora was, had punctured something deep inside. He'd found he just couldn't let her think the worst of him.

Which was why he was here.

She glanced at the door Isla had closed, probably planning her escape. So Lucas blurted out, "Which thing on your list were you thinking of tackling next?"

He'd made a promise. He couldn't very well renege

on it, could he? Yes, he damn well could. He was just choosing not to.

"I hadn't given it much thought today."

He should have said goodbye when he'd woken up in her bed, but he'd been too damned shocked to do anything but throw his clothes on and get out of there. He rarely spent the night at a woman's flat, most of the time leaving soon after the physical act was completed. Because the aftermath always felt uncomfortable. Intimate. And holding a woman for hours after having sex with her? Well, that was something a husband or boyfriend did. Lucas didn't want either of those titles attached to his name.

But he didn't want to hurt anyone unnecessarily either. Especially one who'd already been treated badly by someone else. One he'd promised wouldn't have to accomplish her to-do-while-in-Australia list on her own.

Besides, he'd promised Isla as well.

"How about the pier? We could walk along it tonight, see the moon shining on the water." It had been on the tip of his tongue to suggest a trip to the dock where his sailboat was moored, but he had the same internal rule about that as he did about spending the whole night with a woman. He didn't do it.

"That wasn't on my list."

He offered her a smile. "Maybe lists were made to be changed—added to."

She stared up at him for a long second. "Maybe they were. Okay, Lucas. The pier. Tonight."

Relief swept over him, not only because he wasn't breaking his promise to show her the sights—and the pier at night was one of his favorites—but that she

was back to calling him by his first name. He liked the sound of it on her lips.

Especially in that breathy little voice that—

Back to business, Lucas.

"Okay, then, do you want to meet after our shift?"

"Sounds perfect."

Just as Darcie reached for the door handle of the teen mums' room, Tristan Hamilton, MMU's neonatal cardiothoracic surgeon, came sprinting down the hallway. "Flick's in labor."

Isla pushed the door from the other side, making it known that the rooms were not soundproof. "Are you sure?"

Tristan dragged shaky fingers through his hair. "I'm sure. So is she. She knows the signs."

"It's still early." Lucas said what everyone was probably thinking. Heavily pregnant, Tristan's wife had already been through a lot. So had Tristan. The baby had inherited his father's heart defect—a defect that had required Tristan to undergo a heart transplant when he'd been younger. Thankfully, a specialized team had done surgery on the baby in utero a few weeks ago, repairing the faulty organ and inserting a stent, but the baby was still recovering. The fact that Flick had gone into labor wasn't a good sign. It could mean the baby was in distress. A complication from surgery?

He glanced at Darcie, who nodded. "We're on our way."

Isla, the worry evident on her face, said, "I'll come too."

"No." Darcie moved closer and squeezed the other woman's hand. "You're needed here. We'll keep you up to date on what's happening."

"Promise?" Lucas noted Isla's hand had gone to the bulge of her own stomach in a protective gesture he recognized.

"I promise."

Then the trio was off, Tristan leading the pack, while Darcie and Lucas followed behind. Once back on the ward, it was obvious which room Flick was in by the bevy of nurses rushing in and out.

The second they entered the space, Flick—already in a hospital gown—cast a terrified glance their way. "They're coming faster, Tristan. Every two minutes now."

While her husband went to hold her hand, Lucas and Darcie hurriedly washed their hands and snapped on gloves. Lucas nodded at Darcie to do the initial exam while he hooked up the monitor.

Without a word being said, she moved into position. "Tell me if you start contracting, Flick, and I'll stop."

Lucas watched the woman's expression, even as he positioned the wide elastic band of the monitor around her waist. Once he switched it on the sound of the baby's heart filled the room, along with a palpable sense of relief. No arrhythmias. No dangerous slowing of the heart rate. Just a blessedly normal *chunga-chunga-chunga-chunga* that came from a healthy fetus.

Darcie's face was a study in concentration as she felt the cervix to judge its state. If Flick was still in the early stages of labor, it might be possible to halt it with medication.

Grim little lines appeared around her mouth as she straightened. "Have you noticed any leakage?"

"The baby's been pressing hard on my bladder so..." Her eyes went to her husband. "The amniotic sac?"

Darcie nodded. "It's trickling. And you're at five centimeters and almost fully effaced. There's no stopping it at this point, Flick. Your baby is coming."

"But his heart…"

Tristan, standing beside his wife, looked stunned. "You'd better get Alessandro down here."

The neonatal specialist was in charge of the hospital's NICU. Once the baby was born, Alessandro would make sure everything was working as it should and that the child's tiny heart was okay.

Darcie asked one of the nurses to put in a call, and then she moved up to stroke Flick's head. "It's going to be all right. You're only a few weeks early."

"Mmm…" Flick's blue eyes closed as she pulled air in through her nose and blew out through her mouth. Tristan leaned closer to help her, while Lucas glanced at the monitor. Contraction. Building.

The baby's heart rate slowed as the uterus clamped down further, squeezing the umbilical cord. Everyone held their breath, but the blips on the screen picked up the pace once the contraction crested and the pressure began to ease.

Lucas came over and said in a low voice, "She's going fast for her first."

A few seconds later Alessandro appeared in the room, along with a few more nurses. He studied Flick's chart and then watched the monitor beside the bed for a minute or two. "Let me know when she's getting close. I'll have everything ready."

He shook Tristan's hand. "Congratulations. It looks like you're going to be a daddy today. Have you got a name picked out for her?"

The baby's sex wasn't a secret any more. Tristan and Flick were having a girl.

"We're still having heated discussions about that," Flick said with a shaky smile. "I hoped we'd have a few more weeks to talk it over."

Her husband laid a hand on her cheek. "Let's go with Laura. I know how much you love that name."

"Are you sure?" Tears appeared in her eyes, but then another contraction hit and her thoughts turned to controlling the pain.

Alessandro's attention turned to the monitor to watch the progression. "Everything looks good so far. Call me when the baby crowns, or if you need me before that." He gave Flick's shoulder a gentle squeeze and then nodded at the rest of them and left the room.

Once labor was in full swing, the room grew crowded with healthcare workers. Flick refused the offer of nitrous oxide, afraid that anything she put into her body at this point would affect the baby, even though the gas was well tolerated and often used to manage labor pain.

"I need to push." Flick's announcement had Darcie at her side in a flash.

She checked the baby's position once again then nodded. "You're all set. Are you ready, Mum?"

"Yes."

They waited for a second as Flick found a comfortable position.

Tension gathered in the back of Lucas's head as he assisted Darcie, while Tristan remained closer to his wife's head, murmuring encouragement.

Lucas saw the climb begin on the monitor. "Okay, Flick, here it comes, take a deep breath and push."

The woman grabbed a lungful of air, closed her eyes and bore down, helping her contracting uterus do its job. Tristan counted to ten in a slow, steady voice and told her to take another breath and push again.

The pushing phase went as quickly as the rest of the labor had gone. Ten pushes, and Darcie signaled that the baby had crowned. "Someone ring Alessandro."

He must have been close by because he entered the room within a minute and stood at the far wall.

"Here we go, Flick."

Another group of pushes as Darcie guided the baby's shoulders. Then the baby was there, cradled in Darcie's hands. She passed the baby to Lucas, and then worked on suctioning the newborn's mouth and nose, the red scar from surgery still very evident on her tiny chest.

A sharp cry split the air, and Lucas smiled as bleary, irritated eyes blinked up at him. Laura cried again, waving clenched fists at him and probably everyone else in the room. "Welcome to the world, baby girl," he murmured.

Tristan cut the cord, and then Alessandro took over, carrying the baby over to a nearby table and belting out orders as he listened to the baby's heart and lungs for several long minutes. There was no time for Lucas to worry about that, because they still had the afterbirth to deliver.

A few minutes later baby Laura was placed on Flick's chest with a clean bill of health.

"I don't foresee any problems." Alessandro smiled down at the new parents. "Her heart sounds strong so the surgery was obviously a success."

Flick grabbed her husband's hand, her eyes on his. "See? Don't you start worrying, Tristan. She's fine."

Lucas knew the man had agonized over the baby's health the entire time, but the problem had been caught and corrected early enough to prevent any major damage to her heart. She would need additional surgery as she grew and her veins and arteries matured but, other than that, she had a great prognosis.

Isla stuck her head into the room. "How are they?"

Flick heard her and motioned her in. "See for yourself."

The head midwife crept closer to where Flick was rubbing her baby's back in slow, soothing circles.

"Good on you. She's beautiful, sweetheart. Congratulations."

Alessandro put his arm around his wife's waist, his hand resting on her pregnant belly. "And now we need to let them get to know one another."

As soon as the room had cleared of most of the nurses, and the baby had successfully latched onto Flick's breast, Tristan leaned down and whispered something in his wife's ear that made her smile, although her face bore evidence of her exhaustion.

Lucas's chest tightened. What if all hadn't gone well in here today? What if something had happened to Flick? It was obvious Tristan was deeply in love with her.

His brother's face swam before him. The times he'd drunk himself into a stupor or lain in bed, unwilling to get up and take care of himself or Cora. On days like that it had been left to Lucas to care for them both.

He glanced over at Darcie and found her looking back at him, although her eyes swung away almost immediately. What would it be like to love a woman

and not fear she might one day disappear off the face of the planet?

It was better not to even entertain thoughts like that.

Haven't you already?

No.

He and Darcie had been on a few outings. Spent one night together. That did not a relationship make. And if he kept telling himself that, he could make sure it stayed that way.

He glanced at his watch and realized the end of their shift had come and gone. They should have been off duty an hour ago. A deep tiredness lodged in his bones and suddenly all he wanted to do was sit on that pier with Darcie and stare out over the water.

Just for companionship. Just to have someone to share today's victory with.

He walked over to the happy couple. "Do you need anything else? Something to help you sleep?"

"I don't think any of us are going to have trouble in that area." She kissed the top of her baby's head. "Thank you so much for everything."

Tristan echoed that. "I'm going to stay here with them tonight to make sure everything is okay."

And that was their cue to leave. Darcie must have realized it too because she smiled then walked over and kissed Flick on the cheek. "Take care, young lady. Ring if you need anything. You have my mobile number?"

"Yes. Right now, though, all I want to do is watch her sleep."

Lucas followed Darcie out the door and to the nurses' station. "Are we still on for tonight?"

She pushed a lock of hair behind her ear, glancing at the clock. "Do you still want to? It's after nine."

"If you're not too tired. We can get something to eat on the way."

"I'm fine." She hesitated. "As long as you're sure."

Right now, Lucas had never been more sure of anything in his life.

The moon was huge.

Seated on the side of the pier with her legs dangling over the side, Darcie stared out at the light reflected over the water. "I've never seen anything quite like this."

"I know. It's why I enjoy coming out here from time to time."

She cocked her head in his direction. "I should have made time to do things like this right after I came to Australia. But I wasn't in the mood to do anything besides work."

"Your ex?"

"Yes." This was probably the last thing Lucas wanted to hear while he sat here: her tale of woe. But somehow she found the whole story pouring into the night air. And it felt good. Freeing to actually tell someone besides Isla.

Lucas was silent until she'd finished then said, "Your ex was a bastard. And your maid of honor... well, she wasn't much of a friend, was she?"

She shrugged. Nine and half months had given her enough distance to see the situation more objectively. Yes, Tabitha and Robert could have handled things differently, but it had been better to learn the truth this side of the wedding vows than to have faced the possibility of cheating and a divorce further on down the line. "I think it was hard for both of them. And I

don't think they meant to hurt me. That's probably why our engagement continued for as long as it did. But it would have been easier if they'd been honest with themselves…and with me."

"Being honest with yourself doesn't mean you have to act on your impulses."

She frowned. "So you think it would have been better for Robert to go ahead and marry me?"

"No. Maybe it would have been better for him not to become engaged in the first place."

Interesting. She was seeing a new side to Lucas. "Is that comment speaking to my situation? Or do you simply not believe in marriage?"

"It's not so much that I don't believe in it, I'm just apathetic about the whole institution." He leaned back on his hands and stared at the night sky before looking her way again. "But I didn't bring you here to talk about my philosophies on marriage or anything else. I came to enjoy the view."

"I am enjoying it." She took a deep breath, the salty tang that clung to the air filling her senses and rinsing away the stress of the last two days. "It's lovely. You're a very lucky man to be able to come down here whenever you want and take it all in."

"I am a lucky man."

When she turned to glance at him, he was watching her.

"What?" She pulled her cardigan around herself, unsure whether it was because of the slight chill in the air or because he was making her feel nervous.

His brows went up. "Nothing. I'm just taking it all in."

Her? He was taking her in?

A shot of courage appeared from nowhere. "The view's quite good from where I'm sitting as well."

The breeze picked up a bit, and a gust of air flipped her hair across her cheek and into her eyes. She went to push it back, only to find he'd beaten her to it, his hand teasing the errant locks behind her ear. The light touch sent a shiver through her.

His fingers moved to her nape, threading through the strands there and lifting them so the air currents could pick them up.

Why did everything the man said or did make her insides coil in anticipation? And how could he go from cool and distant to so…here? Present. Insinuating himself into her life and heart in subtle ways that took down all her defenses.

Her mind swept through the events of the day and replayed them. How he'd deferred to her in the delivery room today, letting her take the lead in Flick's delivery while not losing that raw, masculine edge that made him so attractive to her.

And to a thousand other women like her.

Just when she started to thump back to earth his fingers—which were still at the back of her neck—suddenly tangled in her hair, using his light grip to turn her head.

"Your fiancé missed out."

His brown eyes roved over her face, touching on her lips then coming back up. "You're the whole package, Darce. A beauty. Inside and out. And I…"

He let go of her so quickly she had to catch her balance even as he finished his thought, his tone darkening. "And I shouldn't have brought you here."

Where had that come from? One minute he was

going on about her hair and how he found her beautiful. The next he was saying he regretted having brought her to the pier.

Hurt—a jagged spear of pain that slashed and tore at everything it came in contact with—caused her voice to wobble. "Then why did you?"

"Because I wanted you to see what I do when I come out to the bay. But all I see right now…is you. And I want to do more than just look."

Everything inside her went numb for a second. Then a swish of realization blew through her, soothing the hurt.

He wanted her. Wanted to touch her. Just like the other night at her flat.

"You can. You can do more."

Before she had time to think or breathe he moved. Fast. His mouth covered hers in a rush of need that was echoed in her. She wanted him. Now. Here. On this pier.

His hand went behind her head as his tongue sought entry. She gave it to him, opening her mouth and letting him sweep inside. He groaned, and the sound was like a balm and a stimulant all at once, although she didn't know how that was possible. Maybe just because of who he was.

Darcie's mouth wasn't the only thing that opened. Her heart did as well, letting him in. Just a crack at first, but then growing wider and wider until he filled her. Surrounded her. Inside and out.

She allowed herself to revel in it, at least for now. Soon she'd have to come back to the real world, but for the moment she would inhabit the land of wish lists and

wishful thinking—a place where anything was possible. Where anything could happen.

And, God, she hoped it happened. Soon. Because the need inside her was already too big to be contained.

She pulled back, even though everything was screaming at her to keep going. "Lucas."

"I know." Both hands sank into her hair and he held her still as he ran a line of kisses down her cheekbone, over her jaw, until he reached her ear. "If I don't stop now, I won't."

What? Stop? That's not what she'd meant at all.

"I don't want you to."

A flash of teeth came, followed by, "I don't think you want me to rip your clothes off on a public pier, do you?" A brow lifted. "Unless you're into exhibitionism. Although the thought of having you pressed naked against that bank of windows at your flat—with me inside you—is pretty damned tempting."

Something in her belly went liquid with heat. Not at the thought of exposing herself to thousands of people but at Lucas—inside her.

"My flat is too far away."

He paused for a moment and then stood and held out his hand. "I know the perfect place."

CHAPTER NINE

"I DIDN'T KNOW you had a boat."

No one did. This was the one place Lucas could come that was totally private. Totally his. Where he could get away from the stresses of the day or—when Felix had been in a particularly bad state—the horrors of his own thoughts. The small sailboat had cost him several months' salary, but it had been money well spent. He would live on it were it not for the fact that he needed to be close to the hospital…and to Cora and Felix.

And he'd never brought anyone here…especially not a woman.

So why Darcie?

He stood with her on the deck as the boat swayed at its mooring. Why was this the first place that had come to mind when he'd realized what she wanted?

It was close. And they both wanted sex. It was the obvious choice. Even as he thought it, he knew that wasn't the reason at all.

She was waiting for an answer, though, so he said, "I like the water, and it's nice to have a place where I can enjoy it."

She smiled, leaning against the railing on the far side of the vessel. "I thought that's what the pier was for."

"Sometimes I want a little more privacy." His lips curled, and knowing she'd probably take the words the wrong way he went on, "For myself. Not for any love triangles."

She eased over to him and ran her fingers from the waistband of his jeans up to his shoulders. "I thought we'd already established you don't do any angles at all."

He didn't do a lot of things. But he liked the feel of her hands on him.

Gripping her waist, he dragged her to him, making the boat rock slightly. "So…do you want to stay topside? Or go down below?"

Her brows went up and a choked laugh sounded. "I assume you're not referring to parts of the body."

"No. Because in that I'm definitely an all-inclusive kind of guy." He leaned down and brushed his cheek against hers. "I meant do you want to stay here on deck or go to the cabin?"

"Okay, that makes more sense."

More than once he'd slept beneath the stars on the boat, letting the sounds and movements of the water lull him to sleep. As cool as it was right now, there was no need for air-conditioning.

Darcie glanced at the dock. "Does anyone ever come out here?"

Rows of other boats surrounded them. The small marina was the place of weekend sailors. But in the middle of a workweek? It was always deserted.

"Just me." He smiled, playing on his earlier theme. "Sorry, no one to watch us but the seagulls."

Even in the dark her face flamed. "That's not what I meant."

"Wasn't it?" His hand slid up her side until it covered her breast. The nipple was already tight and ready. "How brave are you feeling, Darcie?"

He tweaked the bud, glorying in the gasp it drove from her throat.

"Right now? Braver than I was during that bungee jump."

"Let's stay out here, then, where we can see the moon."

His hands went to the hem of her cardigan and shirt and swept them over her head, letting the garments drop onto the plank deck. When he touched her arms they were covered in goose bumps, although her skin felt warm. "Are you cold?"

"No." As if in answer, she undid the buttons of his shirt and yanked it from his jeans, helping him tug free from the long sleeves. She tossed it on top of her clothes. The sight stopped him for a second. But just one. Then he was curving his hands behind her back and finding the clasp on her black silk bra. "Last chance to back out, Darcie."

She leaned up and nipped his shoulder. "Just take it off, will you?"

"My pleasure." He unsnapped the bra, and on impulse dangled it over the railing beside them.

Yes, he liked seeing it there, the inky color contrasting with the sleek chrome. It was his declaration to the universe that she was his for tonight. And he knew something else that would look perfect beside it.

He allowed his fingers to trail over the curves he'd exposed. Just for a second, then he released the snap

on his jeans and pushed them down his legs, kicking them to the growing pile of clothes beside him. Then he did the same for her. Much slower, kneeling down, so he could savor every inch of her along the way.

Black silk met his eyes. The same color as her bra. He allowed his palms to trail over her hips as he stood, until the slick fabric met the perfect mounds of her ass. He squeezed, pulling her against him and allowing his stiff flesh to imagine that silk sliding over his bare skin.

He had to know. He pulled away, only to have her reach for him. "Just a second, gorgeous. I'm coming right back."

Reaching down to scoop up his jeans, he retrieved a packet from his wallet and set it on the rail next to her bra. Then off came his boxers. His flesh jerked as he drew her back to him.

He closed his eyes as his naked arousal met the silk of her undies. And it was everything he'd imagined. Slick. Arousing. His hands went to her behind and kneaded as he pumped himself against her, slowly, reveling at the contrast between the silky fabric and the warm skin of her belly.

When he felt hands on his own ass, his lids flew apart. "Hell."

He pushed beneath the elastic, and then, unable to wait any longer, he slid her last remaining item of clothing down her hips, waiting until she stepped free before draping it next to her bra.

Mmm…yes. Just like he'd thought. He liked seeing her displayed there. Liked having her on his boat.

Grabbing the condom, he swept a hand beneath her thighs and her shoulders and hauled her into his arms,

where he kissed her for what seemed like forever. This time she gave a little shiver, and he noticed the breeze was a bit cooler than it had been on the pier. Still kissing her, he eased to his knees and then lowered her to the deck, her pale skin looking glorious against the shiny teak planks. The raised edges around the deck provided a windscreen, and, balling up their clothing, he lifted her head so she'd have something to cushion it. "Better?"

"It's all good, Lucas. Nothing could be better."

He grinned down at her. "Wanna bet?"

Kneeling between her legs, he sheathed himself, then let his hands move in light, brushing strokes up her inner thighs, until he reached the heart of her. She was already moist and his fingers wanted to linger and explore, but he knew once he let them he was there to stay. And there were other places he needed to visit.

He lowered himself onto her, supporting his weight with his elbows, then murmured against her lips, "Too heavy?"

"Mmm…no. Too perfect."

That made him smile. He didn't think he'd ever heard a woman refer to him that way before. He liked it.

He'd told her the truth earlier. She was gorgeous, inside and out, sporting an inner glow of health and life that made him wonder how he could have ever thought of her as cold.

She didn't feel cold. She felt warm and vital and he itched to lose himself in her all over again.

But first…

He nuzzled the underside of her breast, savoring the taste of her skin as he came up the rounded side and across until he found her nipple. Drawing it into his

mouth, he let his tongue play over the peak, hoping to coax the first of those little sounds he knew she made.

And, yes, it was heady being out here in the open, even though he knew no one could see them unless they climbed aboard and walked to the port side of the boat. But the thought that someone could…and that Darcie was letting him love her beneath the stars…was testament to her trust. One he wasn't sure he deserved.

But he liked it.

He applied more suction, and there it was. A low moan that pulled at his flesh and slid along the surface of his mind like a lazy day in the sun. Or maybe it was more like being in the eye of a storm. A fleeting moment of calm, when you sensed chaos lingering nearby…knew you'd soon be swept up in an unstoppable deluge.

And when that happened, he knew right where he wanted to be. And it wasn't pinning her to the deck where he couldn't see or touch.

He pulled back and climbed to his feet, holding his hand out to her.

"Wh-what?"

"Trust me." He picked up his shirt and helped her slide her arms into it, leaving it open in the front and allowing his fingers to dance over her breasts and then move lower. Touching her and relishing the way her eyes closed when he hit that one certain spot.

Putting his forehead to hers, he stopped to catch his breath for a second. "I want you on the railing."

It was the perfect height. She'd be right on a level with that core part of him. And Darcie's silhouette on the water? There was nothing he'd rather see…experience.

She glanced behind her, where her bra and undies were still draped, and backed up until she was against the chrome, her hands resting on the gleaming surface. "Help me up, then."

Gripping her waist, he lifted her onto the rail, his blue shirttail hanging over the other side, giving them a modicum of privacy, although they didn't need it. Her arms twined around his neck and her legs parted in obvious invitation. He moved in, his chest pressing against the lush fullness of her breasts, his flesh aching to thrust home.

"Hang onto me, Darce." Letting go of her waist, he allowed a couple of inches of space to come between them so he could touch her. Her face. Her breasts. Her belly. And finally that warm, moist spot between her legs that was calling out to him.

"Ahhh…" The sound came when he slid a finger inside her, her feet hooking around the backs of his thighs as if she was afraid he was going to move away. Not damn likely. He was there to stay.

His mind skimmed over that last thought. Discarding it as he added another finger. Went deeper. Used his thumb to find that pleasure center just a few millimeters to the front.

Darcie leaned further back over the side of the boat, her hands going to his shoulders, her legs parting more. This time Lucas was the one who groaned. Splayed out like this, he could see every inch of her, watch the way her breasts moved in time to his fingers as he pressed home and then pulled back.

"Want you. Inside…" The words were separated by short, quick breaths. She was getting close. So very close.

And he didn't want her to go off without him.

There it was. The same sense of need he'd had the last time they'd been together. He moved into position and guided himself home. Paused. Then he thrust hard. Sank deep. His breath shuddered out then air flooded back into his lungs.

Tight. Wet. Hot.

All the things he knew she'd be.

And it was all for him.

He held himself still as she whimpered and strained against him. It wouldn't take much to send him over the edge. He counted. Prayed. Closed his eyes. Until he could take a mental step back.

Only then did he wrap his arms beneath the curve of her butt to hold her close. He eased back, pulling almost free. Remained there for an agonizing second or two before his hips lunged forward and absorbed the sensations all over again. Over and over he drove himself inside her and then retreated.

He leaned forward. Bit her lower lip. Made her squirm against him.

"Please, Lucas. Please, now."

He knew exactly what she was asking for. "Make it happen, gorgeous."

Changing the angle, he reconnected with her, then pushed deep and held firm as she ground her pelvis against him, letting her choose her own speed, her own pressure, all the while cursing in his head as his eyes reopened to watch her face—taking in the tiny, almost desperate bumping of her hips.

His hands tightened on her, barely aware that the vibrations from their movements had sent her undies over the rail and into the water, and that her bra wasn't

far behind. He didn't care. Didn't want to stop for anything.

Legs wrapped tight around him, Darcie's movements became frantic, nails digging into his shoulders…for all of five seconds—he knew because he was busy counting—then her head tilted toward the sky, hair streaming down her back, and she cried out in the darkness.

That was it. All it took. Lucas pumped furiously as the tsunami he'd been holding at bay crashed down on top of him. He lost himself in her, legs barely supporting his weight as he rode out his climax, knowing a tidal wave of another kind was not far behind. Coming on him fast.

He stared straight ahead so he wouldn't have to see it, wouldn't have to acknowledge its existence, and found her watching him, her gaze soft and warm.

Accepting.

At that moment the second realization hit him, splashing over his head and making it impossible to breathe. To think.

He loved her.

In spite of everything he'd been through with his brother. In spite of the dangers of letting himself get too close—too emotionally involved—the unthinkable had just become reality. He'd fallen for a woman. And now that he had, there wasn't a damned thing he could do about it.

She could only avoid him for so long.

Two days had passed, and she was still reeling from what they'd done on Lucas's boat. How he'd buttoned her into her cardigan and slacks—her undergarments

nowhere to be found—probably resting on the bottom of the boat slip, waiting on some unsuspecting soul to find them when it was daytime. Mortified, she made Lucas promise he'd go back and see if he could locate them—hoping her argument against pollution had been convincing enough.

They'd been in her locker the next day—how he'd known the combination she had no idea, but she was thankful no one had to see him handing her the plastic bag that contained her errant underwear.

If anything, though, it made her feel even more embarrassed. How had he found them? A net? A gaff from his boat? Or had they just been floating on the surface of the water, trapped between his boat and the dock?

That thought made heat rush into her face. She picked up her pace as she went down the hallway toward the double glass doors of the waiting room, which swished open soon as she got close. She was supposed to meet Isla for lunch.

But when she arrived she saw her friend deep in conversation with Sean Anderson. Oh, no. Surely he wasn't giving her a hard time again about Isabel. She sped up even more and arrived in time to hear her ask if he'd heard from her sister. The opposite of what Darcie had expected to hear.

"No. And I'm not sure I want to, at this point."

"Really?" her friend asked, giving Darcie a quick glance. "After all that, you're just giving up?"

"I don't know. But I do want some answers. And I don't think I'm going to get them here."

"I'm sorry, Sean. I wish I could help."

Darcie decided to speak up. "Maybe you should consider going to the source."

"Funny you should say that," Sean said. "I decided to take Isla's advice. My contract runs out at the end of the week. I'm flying out as soon as it does."

The two women looked at each other, and Darcie's heart began to thump. Maybe she couldn't fix her own growing problems with Lucas, but maybe Sean could solve his. "So you're going…"

Sean nodded. "To England."

Isla clasped her hands over her belly, knuckles white. "Don't hurt her. Please. You have no idea what she's been through."

"I have no intention of hurting anyone. All I want is the truth about why she left."

Her friend studied him then reached out and touched his arm. "Good luck, Sean. I really mean that."

"Thanks." And with a stiff frame and tight jaw he strode down the hallway toward an uncertain future.

Well, join the club. Who really knew what the future held. Certainly not Darcie, who was busy hiding out and praying that Lucas gave her some time to recover. She needed to figure out what it was she wanted from him before he suggested tackling the next thing on her list.

Because that list had begun to revolve around a common theme, one that was getting her in deeper with each item ticked: Sit on a beach and kiss an Aussie. Bungee jump from a tower and kiss an Aussie. Dance at a club, and make love to an Aussie. Climb on a boat…and open her heart to an Aussie.

Darcie didn't know how much more she could take. Because her heart was now in real danger, and she was more afraid than she'd ever been in her life…even dur-

ing that moment when she'd realized Robert didn't love her. He loved someone else.

Because if that happened with Lucas, she didn't want to stick around to see it. The result would be a gaping wound no amount of surgery or medical expertise could repair. It involved who she was at an elemental level. And in opening her heart she feared she'd set herself up for the biggest hurt of her life.

Isla said something, and Darcie swung her attention back to her friend. "I'm sorry. I missed that."

The midwife smiled. A quick curving of lips that looked all too knowing and crafty. "I said, don't look now, but trouble is headed your way."

That was the understatement of the year. Then she realized Isla's eyes were on something behind her.

Darcie turned to look, thinking one of her patients was coming to see her, only to catch sight of the same glass doors she'd just come through swishing open to let in the last person she wanted to see today.

Lucas.

He looked devastating in a dress shirt and black slacks. Her glance went back to the shirt. Blue button-down.

Oh, no. Surely that wasn't the shirt he'd draped around her while they'd...

Warmth splashed into her face and ran down her neck, spreading exponentially the closer he got.

"Hello, ladies."

Instead of sweeping past and continuing on his way, he stopped in front of them.

Isla's smile grew wider. "Darcie, I think I'm going to have to back out of our lunch date. I need to see Alessi about...tires for his car."

Tires? For his car?

Before she could call her friend on the obvious fib, Isla had retreated back through the doors, leaving her with Lucas and a few folks in the waiting room, who seemed quite interested in the various dramas unfolding in the MMU.

As if he'd noticed as well, he pulled her over to the far wall, well out of earshot. "Felix and Cora are on their way to the park with a picnic lunch. It's not far from the hospital, so I thought you might like to tag along. It's something you should see before you leave the country."

Leave the country. Why did that have an ominous ring to it?

Lucas went on, "From what Isla said, I take it you haven't eaten yet."

Rats. That would have been her first excuse if he approached her. It was why she'd practically begged Isla to have lunch with her for the last two days. And now her friend had turned traitor and abandoned her.

Her eyes met Lucas's face. He seemed softer all of a sudden. As if the weight of the world had been lifted from his shoulders. But what weight? Maybe he was just happy to be having lunch with his niece and his brother. It was obvious he loved that little girl and that she adored him back.

As if sensing her hesitation, he added, "Cora would love to see you. She's been asking about you for days."

Well, that was a change. Before, he hadn't seemed keen on her spending time with his niece.

Her heart settled back in place. The comment about leaving Australia hadn't meant anything. "I guess it would be all right."

"I'm glad." One finger came out and hooked around hers and the side of his mouth turned up in way that made her stomach flip. "Did you get my little package?"

He was definitely in a cheerful mood today. Did she dare hope it was because of the time they'd spent together over the last three weeks? How strange that something she'd dreaded with every fiber of her being could have turned around so completely.

She decided to add some playfulness of her own. "Little? I thought the package was a decent size. But, then again, I don't have much to compare it to."

"Witch," he murmured. "Maybe you need a refresher. It has been a couple of days after all."

A refresher? He wanted to be with her again?

Maybe she wouldn't wind up on the hurting side of the fence after all. As long as she was careful. And took things slowly. She'd been thinking about seeing if the Victoria had any permanent positions available, but she'd been putting it off because of Lucas. She didn't want to stick around if they were going to end up fighting each other further on down the line.

But right now she didn't see that happening.

"Maybe I've just forgotten." She threw him a saucy smile.

"Mmm...I need to work harder next time, then, to make sure that doesn't happen." The finger around hers gave a light squeeze. "Meet you in the car park in fifteen minutes? I have one more patient to schedule, and then I'll be free."

"Okay," she said. Her spirits soared to heights that were dizzyingly high. A fall from up here could...

She wasn't going to fall. For the first time in a long

time she caught a glimpse of something she hadn't expected to feel.

Hope.

Pete the Geek was on a rampage.

Reclining on the blanket that Darcie had somehow scrounged up, Lucas lay on his back, hands behind his head as he watched his niece chasing the dog around their little area of the park. Pete never went far, but seemed intent on having his little bit of fun on this outing, since the cold packed lunch hadn't been on the menu for him.

Darcie sat next to Lucas's shoulder and laughed as Cora just touched Pete's collar, only to have him leap out of reach once again. "He has his timing down to a science, doesn't he?"

"He does at that." He couldn't resist taking one of his hands from behind his head and resting it just behind Darcie's bottom. No one could see. But he just needed to touch her. Not in a sexual sense, although that always hovered in the background where this woman was concerned. But he found he wanted that closeness in more areas. Just for now. In a very little while she would be gone, and while there might be pain in letting her go, at least she would be alive. It wouldn't be like losing someone to death. He could accept loving her within those parameters.

He'd warred with himself for the last two days but had come up with a compromise he hoped he could live with. He would let himself go with the flow. For the next couple of months.

She sent him a smile in response.

Warm contentment washed through him. Maybe this

was why Felix had gone so far off the rails after losing Melody. Lucas had never felt like this about a woman. He loved her. He no longer even tried to deny it. And after staying away from her for two days he'd found he was miserable—and he'd had to find her. Be with her.

For the next two months.

He found himself sending his subconscious little memos. Just so it wouldn't forget. This was a temporary arrangement.

Felix seemed better. His therapy was evidently kicking in. He was fully engaged in what Cora was doing with Pete, really laughing for the first time in years. "Maybe if you tempt him with the ball?"

Cora spun back toward them, while Darcie held out the ball that had landed near her hip a while ago. Leaning down, the little girl flung her arms around Darcie's neck and popped a kiss on her cheek. "I'm so glad you came!"

"I'm glad I did too."

Lucas tensed for a second then forced himself to relax. Darcie and Cora could still keep in contact, even after she flew back to England. There was email and all kinds of social networks. It wouldn't be a drastic break. Just one that would fade away with time.

His niece rushed off with the ball in hand and threw it hard toward Pete, who loped off after the offering with a bark of happiness, scooping it up in his jaws and trotting back toward the blanket.

Lucas smiled and shook his head, his attention going back to Felix.

Only his brother wasn't watching Cora any more. His gaze was on Lucas, his eyes seeming to follow the

line of his arm to where it disappeared behind Darcie's back.

Swallowing, he returned his hand to behind his head, and then as an afterthought sat up completely. Darcie glanced at him, head tilted as if she was asking a question. Swamped by a weird premonition, he got to his feet and slapped his brother's shoulder, urging him to come with him to help Cora round up the dog and bring him back to the picnic area.

He watched Felix as they worked, but whatever he thought he'd seen in his brother's face was no longer there. Felix smiled and joked and was finally the one to grab hold of Pete the Geek's collar and snap the leash onto it. Once they were all back at the picnic area he saw that Darcie had packed everything up and was on her feet. "I probably need to get back to the hospital."

That uncertainty he'd caught in her expression from time to time was back.

Because of him.

This was ridiculous. He was imagining demons where none existed. Probably excuses created in the depths of his own mind. There was no reason history had to repeat itself. "I do too. I'll walk you." On impulse, he leaned down and kissed her cheek, watching as they turned that delicious shade of pink he loved so much.

He turned back to say goodbye to Cora, noting his brother's eyes were on him again. He returned the look this time. "Everything okay?"

"Yep. I need to get Cora home so Chessa doesn't worry. Besides, I have some drawings I need to get to."

Felix had once been a respected architect. When he'd married Melody he kept on working, even though

she'd been wealthy enough that he hadn't had to. He'd inherited a fortune after she'd died, but it had meant nothing to him. He'd withdrawn from work and every other area of his life, including Cora. It made Lucas's heart a little bit lighter to see him showing an interest in something he'd once been so passionate about.

"Anything interesting?"

"I don't know yet. I'll have to wait and see what it looks like before I decide."

Kind of like Lucas himself? Waiting to see what things with his brother looked like before going on with his life?

Maybe. He wasn't sure. He still hadn't sorted it all out in his head, but he knew he wanted to spend more time with Darcie. Both during their rotation and after it was over.

For how long? Until she left for England?

He slung an arm around her waist, no longer certain of that, despite his earlier lecture. That drawing hadn't been completed yet. Maybe, like Felix, he should wait to see how things shaped up before deciding things like that.

Felix's eyes were on them again, although a smile stretched his lips. "I'll see you tomorrow, then, right?"

"Definitely." He walked over and kissed the top of Cora's head then ruffled the fur behind Pete's ears. "Be good, you guys."

"We will, won't we, Pete?"

Lucas gave his brother a half-hug. "You'll be okay taking them home?"

"Of course. I wouldn't have brought them otherwise." His brother's voice was just a little sharper than he'd expected, and Lucas took the time to really look

at him. Felix's skin was drawn tight over his cheeks, but he still had that same smile on his face. Maybe he was just tired. He hadn't done outings like this in years. Lucas couldn't expect him to spring from point A to point B in the blink of an eye. It was better not to push for more until his brother was ready.

Just in case, he didn't put his arm back around Darcie's waist. That could wait until his brother and Cora were in the car and out of sight. Besides, he didn't want them to witness him kissing the living daylights out of her right there in the park. Which he intended on doing. Then they could go back to work and act like nothing had ever happened. And hopefully Darcie would be amenable to him driving her home afterward. Enough so that she'd ask him up for coffee?

His brother loaded everything in the car. Cora gave one last wave before she got in and they drove away.

Taking hold of Darcie's hips, he tugged her close.

She grinned up at him. "You know, I think *you* might be the one with exhibitionist tendencies, not me."

"Where you're concerned, anything's possible." With that, he proceeded to do what he'd said he was going to and slanted his mouth over hers, repeating the act until she was clinging to him, and until he was in danger of really showing the world what he felt for this woman. "Time to get back to work."

Her mouth was pink and moist, and her eyes held a delicious glazed sheen. He'd put that there. And he intended to keep it there for as long as possible all through the night.

And then he was going to invite her to come to dinner with him at Felix and Cora's house tomorrow eve-

ning. They wouldn't mind, especially since he was the one doing the grilling.

After that? He wrapped his arm around her waist and walked with her the rest of the way to the hospital.

He'd have to see what the drawing looked like further on down the road, but he could afford to give it a little more time to take shape. At least for now.

CHAPTER TEN

LUCAS WASN'T AT WORK.

Darcie did her rounds, trying not to think the worst. He'd been fine at the picnic yesterday. And he'd spent most of last night at her place, making love to her with an intensity and passion that had taken her breath away. After several different places and positions, he'd finally groaned and dragged himself from beneath her covers. "I need to get home so I can be at work on time tomorrow morning." He leaned over and rested his arms on either side of her shoulders, bracketing her in and swooping down for another long kiss. "My rotation partner is a slave driver. She gets all put out when I come in rumpled, wearing the same clothes I had on the day before."

"Maybe that's when she thought you were involved with all sorts of different women."

He'd laughed. "How disappointing it must be to find out what a square I actually am."

"Just the opposite. I was jealous of the way the patients in the MMU always seem to fawn over you. I just wouldn't admit it to myself."

With a laugh, he'd scooped her up and kissed her shoulder. "See you in the morning, gorgeous."

That had been the last she'd heard from him.

She'd walked on cloud nine as she'd got ready for work. Then, when she arrived, she eagerly waited for him to make an appearance and toss her one of those secretive smiles she was coming to love.

But there'd been nothing. No phone calls. No text messages. And nothing on the board to show his schedule had been changed.

Surely he'd made it home safely.

And even though he hadn't said the words, he had to care about her. The way he'd touched her at the park and put his arm around her in full view of his brother and niece had said he wasn't embarrassed to be seen with her.

She cringed at that thought. That was something the Darcie of old would have worried about. Her experience with Robert had shaken her confidence in herself as a woman to the very core. Lucas was slowly building it back up. Kiss by kiss. Touch by touch. He acted like he couldn't get enough of her.

Well, the feeling was mutual.

Today she was not going to let his tardiness get the better of her. She was going to simply enjoy what they'd done last night and not worry about anything else. He'd eventually turn up. He'd probably stopped in to see Cora or something. Or maybe he'd had to drive her to school, which he'd said he'd done on occasion.

He wasn't in bed with someone else. Of that she was sure. Because she was feeling the effects of his loving this morning. It was a delicious ache that reminded her that, no matter who fluttered their lashes at him, Lucas had chosen her.

She sighed and glanced at her watch again. An hour

and no word. There was nothing to do but go on with her day and not worry about it. She was tempted to ring his mobile, but was afraid that might seem desperate or needy. So she let it go.

The morning continued to race by at a frenetic pace. Then one o'clock came with no time to break for lunch. She'd just completed one delivery and was heading for the next laboring patient when she saw Isla at the nurses' station. She hurried over.

"Have you heard from Lucas? Or do you know if he's arrived at work yet? I haven't seen him all day."

Her friend blinked at her for a second and then her eyes filled with something akin to horror. "Oh, sweetheart, you haven't heard?"

Only then did she see that Lucas's name had been crossed off today's rota and Isla's name was written in instead. That had to have been done after she'd looked at it this morning.

Darcie's vision went dark for a second or two. "Heard what?"

"Oh…I'm so sorry. I got a call around an hour ago, asking me to step in." She reached out and gripped her hand. "Lucas is in the emergency department…"

Isla's voice faded out in a rush of white noise but the words "alcohol poisoning" and "gastric lavage" came through, before a nurse came out of the room of her next patient. "Mrs. Brandon is feeling the urge to push, and she's panicking. She isn't listening to instruction, Dr. Green."

Somehow, Darcie managed to stumble into the room, and despite her clanging heart she was able to coax the nitrous mouthpiece from between the woman's clamped jaws and get her to focus on pushing at

the appropriate times. The baby was a large one, and Darcie had to do some fancy maneuvering to get the baby's shoulders through the narrow space. Then he was out and wailing at the top of his lungs. Darcie wished she could drop onto the nearest chair and join him for a hearty cry. But she couldn't. And it was another hour of praying for a break before one finally came and she could make her way down to Emergency.

Her heart was in her throat. Lucas had alcohol poisoning? How could that be? She'd never seen him touch a drop of the stuff, except for the sips she'd talked him into taking of her drink. And he'd made the most godawful face once he had. She'd convinced herself he was a teetotaler, that he just didn't like alcohol. But maybe she'd got it all wrong. Maybe he was a recovering alcoholic. Or, worse, one who binge-drank for seemingly no reason.

But alcohol poisoning was more than just a couple of drinks. It was a life-threatening toxic buildup that came from downing one drink after another without giving the liver time to filter the stuff out of the blood.

Why hadn't Isla come back to find her as soon as she'd heard the news?

Maybe because she'd been just as swamped as Darcie had been—and just as exhausted. She saw on the patient board that the letters "TMTB" had been scrawled beside two of the names, so her friend had to have been run ragged with those girls—and with all the aftercare that went along with teen pregnancies.

She paused just outside the doors to the emergency department, unsure what she was going to find. Isla would have surely told her if Lucas was in danger of dying, wouldn't she? Maybe the stomach pumping had

done its job and he was already on the road to recovery. Maybe he was simply too ashamed to face her.

As well he should be.

Anger crawled through her veins, pushing aside the worry and fear. If he were an alcoholic, shouldn't he have told her? Refused that offer of a drink she'd given him?

A thought spun through her brain. What if that sip had sent him over the edge? An alcoholic shouldn't drink *any* type of liquor. Ever.

All those late mornings…the rumpled clothes. The surly demeanor when he finally arrived.

God.

She squared her shoulders and stepped on the mat that would open the glass doors and went through. Noise and shouting hit her. The place was just as busy as the MMU had been. Making her way over to the desk and hoping to find a nurse or someone who could provide her with information, she searched the patient board for a familiar name.

Out of the corner of her eye she caught sight of him.

Lucas.

He was on his feet, leaning against a wall. She'd recognize those broad shoulders and wavy hair anywhere. But he didn't look right. He was slumped, leaning against the flat surface as if he could barely hold himself up.

The waiting room was crowded, but surely he'd been seen already. Alcohol poisoning was normally run up to the top of the list. Could Isla have exaggerated or made a mistake?

At that moment his eyes met hers.

And what was in them tore apart any thought of

exaggeration. There was torment and pain in that red, bleary gaze.

So much pain.

Hurrying over, she stopped next to him.

"Lucas, what's wrong? Are you ill?" she asked.

He didn't answer, just shook his head. His hair was tousled, and two of the bottom buttons of his shirt were undone, as if he'd thrown himself together in a rush.

"I don't understand. Isla said something about alcohol poisoning. She wasn't talking about you?"

"No." Lucas's hands fisted at his sides. "Did you think she was?"

"I didn't know what to think." Confusion swirled around her head. Why did he seem so angry?

"It's not me. It's my brother."

"Felix?" The sound of a siren drowned out his response as an ambulance pulled up to the front entrance. The sound of slamming doors came and then a gurney rushed in with a patient who was obviously in bad shape from the number of healthcare staff heading toward him. When she could finally be heard again she asked, "What happened?"

Two seats opened up as a couple with a child were called back to one of the exam rooms.

She took his hand to lead him over to the chairs so he could sit down before he fell down. He tugged free of her grip but followed her over to the seats. A chill went through her that had nothing to do with Felix's condition as they both sat.

"What happened to Felix?"

He propped his elbows on his knees and stared at the ground. Without looking at her, he said, "He drank himself into a stupor."

"Oh, no." So it was alcohol poisoning. Isla had been right about that. "What about Cora?"

He gave a mirthless laugh. "She's the one who rang me this morning. Felix was out all night, and when he finally made it home he collapsed in the foyer. Chessa had to spend the night at the house because she couldn't reach me. And so here I am."

Her heart squeezed tight. They hadn't been able to reach him because he'd been at her house until almost three that morning, his mobile and car keys deposited on her entry table. "I'm so sorry, Lucas. Will he be okay?"

"I don't know. He may be too far gone this time."

This time?

Things fell into place in the blink of an eye. This was why Felix had seemed off when she'd met him those weeks ago—why he and Lucas had argued. He was the alcoholic, not Lucas.

"He seemed fine at the park."

"He was." Lucas lifted his head long enough to glance in her direction. "At least I thought he was."

That explained something else. Lucas had seemed light and happy. Happier than she'd ever known him to be. She'd assumed it had been because of their budding relationship. But maybe that hadn't been the case at all. Maybe it had been because his brother had been doing so well. Maybe all those affectionate touches and looks had been spillover from what had been going on with Felix.

And last night? Had that simply been an overflow of happiness as well?

Her brain processed another fragment. He hadn't rung her to tell her where he was this morning. Or

that his brother was in trouble. He—or someone—had notified Isla instead.

Maybe he hadn't wanted to worry her.

But surely he knew she'd be frantic when he didn't show up for work.

Her thoughts spiraled down from there. He hadn't bothered to tell her the truth about his brother's condition. Or what he'd been dealing with for who knew how long. He'd led her to believe things were fine. With Felix and Cora.

With her.

Just like Robert had done.

When trouble had come to visit, she'd been the last one to find out—and the result had been devastating.

You're jumping to conclusions, Darcie. Give the man a chance to explain.

Only he didn't. He just sat there. She'd had to drag every piece of information out of him the entire time she'd known him. Was this what she wanted? A lifetime full of secrets? Of wondering if things were okay between 'hem?

No.

Something inside her wouldn't let her give up quite so easily, though. Not without trying one last time to reach him.

"He'll be okay." She knew the reassurance was empty. She had no idea exactly how bad things were. Only Lucas and the doctors knew how much liquor he'd ingested or how much damage had been done to his liver and other organs.

"Will he?"

"What did the doctors say?" She had to keep pushing. To see if he was worth fighting for.

Because she loved him.

Oh, God, she loved him, and she didn't want to have to let him go, unless there was no other option.

"They pumped his stomach. Rehydrated him with fluids and electrolytes. I just have to wait for him to wake up."

She didn't understand. "Will they not let you back to see him?"

"I needed to think about some things. I'll go back in a little while."

"And Cora?"

"She's still with Chessa. We both thought it best not to have her here until we knew something definitive. She's already lost her mum. I don't want her to panic over what might happen to her dad. Unless it actually does."

"It might not come to that." She licked her lips and got up the nerve to slide her hand over his. This time he didn't shake her off. But he also didn't link his fingers through hers or make any effort to acknowledge the contact. "Is there anything I can do to help?"

"If he makes it, he'll have to go to rehab. A residential one this time. I can't trust him to care for Cora at this point."

Which was why he'd been late those other times. Another piece fell into place.

He'd had to take care of his niece when his brother had been too sick or too drunk. And what had she done? She'd yelled at him in front of a roomful of people on one of those days. Guilt washed over her, pummeling her again and again for assuming things that hadn't been true. For not asking him straight out if

something was wrong. Maybe she could have helped somehow.

Maybe she still could.

"If you need me to watch Cora, I—"

"No." The word was firm. Resolute. "We'll be fine."

Another chill went through her, and the premonition she'd had earlier came roaring back to haunt her.

He was still going to pretend that things were okay—shutting her out without a moment's hesitation. She removed her hand from his and curled it in her lap.

Lucas sat up, his mouth forming a grim line. "I think I'm going to take some personal time. I have Cora to think about, and I'll need to deal with Felix. I can't do that and work at the same time."

Her heart stalled. "How will you live?"

"I have some savings. And Cora's care comes from a trust fund her mother left for her."

"I see." She licked her lips. "How much time are we talking?"

"A couple of months at the very least. Maybe more." He didn't skip a beat. He'd obviously already thought this through.

She did the calculations and a ball of pain lodged in her chest. He'd be out until after she left Australia and headed back to England. Surely he couldn't mean to drop out of her life as quickly as he'd come into it. Not after everything that had happened between them.

"I could come by after work, help with the cooking."

"I think it would be better if you didn't, Darcie. Please. For everyone's sake."

For everyone's sake. Whose, exactly? His?

"I don't understand."

"Felix is here because he can't get over the death of

his wife, despite years of therapy. When he saw you and I together at the park…" He shrugged. "You knew there was never going to be anything permanent between us. At least I thought you did. And right now I have to think about what's best for my family."

His eyes were dull and lifeless. So much so that it made her wonder if he even knew how much he was hurting her with his words.

Then he looked at her, and she saw the truth. He knew. He just didn't care.

The ball grew into a boulder so big she could barely breathe past it. He was dumping her. His brother's illness provided the perfect excuse.

Only, like her ex-fiancé, he didn't have the decency to come to her and tell her until it was as obvious as the nose on her face.

Well, that was okay. She'd survived being jilted at the altar, so she could survive the breakup of something that amounted to a few nights of sex and adventure. He'd wanted to do some wild and outrageous stuff? Well, she'd done enough to last a lifetime. And she didn't have it in her to stick around and watch her world fall apart piece by piece.

One thing she *could* do was make this final break as easy as possible for the both of them. "I'm truly sorry about Felix, and I hope everything works out with him. But if your decision to leave the MMU has anything to do with me or the time we spent together, this should put your mind at ease. I've decided to go back to England early."

He eyed her for several long seconds before saying, "When did you decide this?"

Right now. Right this second. When I realized I'm

good enough to warm your bed at night but not good enough to take up permanent residence in your heart— to share your joys and heartaches.

But she couldn't say that. Not unless she wanted the remnants of her shattered pride to fall away completely and expose everything she'd hoped to hide.

Then the perfect response came to her in a flash, and she snatched at it, before taking a deep breath and looking him straight in the eye. "I decided last night."

CHAPTER ELEVEN

ISLA SLAMMED OPEN the door to his office, green eyes flashing. "What did you do to Darcie?"

Lucas hadn't seen her for the last two days, so he'd assumed she'd already flown home. In fact, that was why he was still at work, tying up loose ends, albeit with shorter hours. Chessa was staying with Cora during the day, and at night he went and slept on the couch.

Felix was still in the hospital, but he was slowly regaining his strength. His brother had admitted what Lucas knew in his heart to be true. That seeing him and Darcie together had reopened wounds that had scabbed over but never fully healed.

And what about Darcie?

He'd hurt her, but he hadn't known what else to do. His brother's life was at stake—because of something he'd done. He couldn't let that happen again.

Besides, hadn't he seen time and time again how love brought you to the brink of disaster and sometimes tossed you over the edge? Everything he'd seen lately had reinforced that. Margie's miscarriage. Tristan and Flick almost losing their baby. His brother almost losing his life.

Isla crossed her arms over her chest, clearly waiting for him to answer her.

"Thank you for knocking before you burst in." When the jibe earned him nothing but a stony stare he planted both his hands on his desk. "I didn't do anything to her, Isla. She said she decided to go back to England earlier than planned."

"Why? Did you sleep with her?"

Hell, if the woman wasn't direct. "I don't see that that's any of your business."

"Maybe not. But I think she was right about you. You're nothing but an arrogant, self-righteous bastard who thinks he can sit above all of us and not dirty his hands with real life and real love. I know…because my husband was once just like you."

"She said that about me?" He tried to ignore the hit to his gut that assessment caused. "As for Alessandro, I bet he didn't have a drunken brother to contend with. Or a niece who needed him."

"And that justifies you hurting Darcie?"

No. Nothing justified that. And he would be damned every moment of his life for what he'd done. But she'd said she was going to leave anyway.

It was a lie, you idiot. You'd practically hung a do-not-disturb sign on your heart and dared anyone to knock. And then once she did, you slammed the door in her face.

Because of Felix.

Really?

Was it because his brother had relapsed—which he'd done on several other occasions without any help from him—or was it because he was too afraid to "dirty his hands", as Isla claimed.

He'd once sat on a beach and dared Darcie to do something wild and outrageous. And she'd risen to the challenge and beyond. And yet here he sat, too afraid to make a list of his own because "loving Darcie" would be at the top of it.

He was terrified of holding his hand out to her for fear of losing her. And the thought of becoming like his brother—a shell of a man...

But what about what Isla had asked? Did any of that excuse what he'd done to Darcie? Because of his own selfish fear?

"No," he said. "It didn't justify it."

Isla seemed to lose her steam. "I didn't expect you to agree with me quite so quickly."

"I know what I did. And I'm not proud of it." If he had it to do all over again, would he? He'd made an impulsive decision while his brother had been fighting for his life—a huge mistake, according to the experts. He should have given himself a day or two before deciding something that would affect both of their lives.

The memory of her laughter, those pink-cheeked smiles...that raw sincerity when she'd offered to help with Cora's care. He'd thrown it all away. He hadn't given a thought to how she might have felt, or how right it seemed to be with her. He'd only thought of himself. And in that process he'd done to her what he'd been so afraid might happen to him. He'd abandoned her. Left her standing all alone.

"Isla, you're a genius. And I'm a fool." He got up and went around the desk and planted a kiss right on her forehead.

Her face cleared, and she laughed. "I won't tell

Alessi you did that. He might knock your teeth right out of your head."

"He knows you're crazy about him…and the whole world knows how he feels about you."

"True. So what are you doing to do about all this other stuff?" She rolled her hand around in the air.

What *was* he going to do? He'd run Darcie off and it wasn't like he could do anything about it. He was here. Having to make sure his brother made it in to rehab as soon as he was released from the hospital. He couldn't just hop on the first flight to England and leave Cora by herself. He was stuck.

"I don't know, actually. I have responsibilities here."

Her mouth curved into a half-smile. "Isn't it lucky, then, that Alessi loves me as much as you say he does?"

Lucas had no idea what that had to do with anything. "Yes, I guess it's lucky for you."

"And for you too. Because he happens to know someone high up at the airline Darcie was scheduled to fly on."

He only caught one word of that whole spiel. "Was?"

"It seems her flight was overbooked, and she was booted to one that leaves tomorrow afternoon."

Hope speared through him, causing him to drop back into his chair. "She's still in Melbourne?"

"For another day. Yes."

"Why the hell didn't you say something before now?"

"Because I wasn't sure you loved her enough to fight for her. And if you don't, she deserves better."

He swallowed. She deserved better anyway. Better than that bastard ex of hers. Better than *him*. "You're right. I'm not good enough for her."

"I might have agreed with you a few minutes ago but I saw your face when the enormity of what you'd done hit you. You were frantically trying to figure out a way to make it right…to get to her. Well, Alessi and I have just given it to you. Don't waste it, Lucas. Because by tomorrow afternoon she'll be gone, and it'll be too late."

He got to his feet. "If she's gone, it'll be because she doesn't want me. Because as of right now I'm going to fight for her with everything I have in me and hope to God she'll forgive me."

Darcie wandered through the empty flat, which was in much the same state as when she'd arrived. There were suitcases sitting neatly side by side, and in her purse was a one-way ticket. She'd come here looking to escape a painful past, only to end up fleeing a new situation that was even worse.

Her feelings for Lucas were light years beyond the ones she'd had for Robert, which maybe explained why he'd found her lacking that certain spark. She had. It had taken Lucas to put a match to it and bring it to life.

Only he'd evidently felt even less for her than her ex had. Because he'd made no pretense of loving her or even wanting a long-term relationship with her. Hadn't he told her that in plain English at the very beginning, when he'd first suggested putting pen to paper and making that list?

She gave a pained laugh. "He did, but you just couldn't accept that, could you? You had to fall in love with the man, didn't you?"

A knock sounded at the door and Darcie froze, wondering if someone had heard her. The doorman was

supposed to ring the interphone if she had a visitor. Her heart thumped back to normal. It was probably just the taxi. She'd asked the airport to send someone if they found her an earlier flight. The sooner she was out of Melbourne the better.

She felt like such a fool and every second she stayed in this flat—in this country—was a horrid reminder of how she'd practically groveled at the man's feet, only to have him knock her offer aside and ask her to leave him alone.

Which was what she was trying to do.

She scrubbed her palms under her eyes, irritated that she had turned into the weepy female she'd vowed never to be again.

Hauling her suitcases to the front door, she went back for her purse and opened the door. "Do you mind getting those? I…"

It took three or four blinks before she realized the man standing at the door wasn't a taxi driver. Or the doorman.

It was Lucas.

Oh, God, why was he here? To make sure she really, really, *really* understood that he didn't want her?

Well, Lucas, I might have been a little slow on the uptake, but once the message sank in it was there to stay.

"I thought you were the taxi driver. How did you get past the doorman?"

"I didn't. He recognized me." He paused. "From before." Said as if she might not remember their last encounter in this flat. Unfortunately it was burned into her brain with a flamethrower.

She strove for nonchalant. "How's your brother doing?"

"He's out of danger. Looking forward to getting the help he needs. I think being in hospital gave him the shock of a lifetime."

"I'm glad." She was. As hurt and angry as she was at Lucas, she hoped Cora would finally have her father back. "And Cora?"

"She misses you."

Pain sliced through her chest. "Don't. Please."

Lucas glanced to the side where her suitcases sat. "May I come in for a minute?"

"Why?" She didn't think she could take another blow. Not when she was struggling not to memorize every line and crag of that beloved face.

"Because Cora isn't the only one who misses you."

The words took a moment to penetrate her icy heart. Then she started to pick them apart. "You mean Isla and the rest of the staff?"

"Yes, but not just them."

She licked her lips. "Then who?"

Fear buzzed around in her stomach while she waited for him to say something. Anything.

His chest rose as he took a deep breath. "Me. *I* miss you. I don't want you to go."

"You practically offered to pack my bags."

"I was stupid. Scared. My brother is the way he is because he desperately loved his wife. When she died…well, he was never the same. I don't want to end up like that."

She worked through those words. "And you're afraid if you meet someone, you will."

He nodded.

A terrible, wonderful atom of hope split into two. Then three. "Come in."

She stepped aside as he moved into the room and glanced around. Waiting for him to finish and turn back toward her, her brain continued to analyze what it knew. Somehow he'd found out she hadn't left.

Isla.

Darcie had called to tell her that her flight had been delayed. But why would she tell Lucas?

"You say you miss me, that you don't want me to go, but I need something more than that." This time she wasn't willing to settle for less.

He came back and took her hands in his. "I know you do. Which is why I want you to come with me."

"Where?"

"It's a secret. But by the end of it I hope you'll have the answer you need."

The buzzing fear turned into a tornado that whipped through her system and made her doubt. Was he was going to lead her on a merry chase, only to get cold feet again and decide he was better off without her?

Maybe.

So why was that list they'd made a couple of weeks ago stuck in the front pocket of her purse…complete with the smiley face he'd drawn next to the kiss-a-non-triangular-Aussie entry? Because she didn't want to forget. But, like him, she was afraid.

He'd overcome his fear long enough to drive to the flat, though, without knowing what kind of reception he'd get. Didn't she owe it to herself to follow this through to the end? She could always catch that flight tomorrow if it didn't work out.

"Okay, I'll come."

He closed his eyes, the lines between his brows easing. When he opened them again, the brown irises seemed to have warmed to a hue she recognized and loved. A few more atoms split apart, some of them coalescing back together and forming a shape she could almost decipher. He glanced at her clothes. "Can you get those wet?"

"Wet?" Was he going to kill her and toss her lifeless body over the side of his boat? That made her smile. A few more particles merged together. "I think they'll survive."

Twenty minutes later they pulled up to a place she recognized. But it wasn't his boat. "Why are we here?"

"Trust me." He got out of the car and came around to her side and opened the door. She stood on the footpath, staring up at a familiar tower.

"We're going bungee jumping? Now?"

"You're not. I am."

She had no idea what was going on but he'd asked her to trust him. So she walked with him to meet Max, who stood waiting at the entrance. The man pushed his glasses higher on his nose, looking spectacularly pleased with himself for some reason. "Come in. Come in. Everything's ready." He disappeared through the wooden privacy gate.

Lucas murmured, "Remember when you jumped, I waited for you in the pool at the bottom?"

"Yes." She wasn't sure how she got the word out as her throat felt dry and parched.

"I want you to go to the side of the pool and wait for me this time." He gave a half-smile. "Don't ask me why until you've unhooked me."

They went through the gate, a million questions

swirling through her mind. Max led her down to the pool, while Lucas climbed the steps to the tower.

She gasped. The water was crystal clear, just as before...but the surface was littered with rose petals. Thousands of them in every color imaginable—red, purple, yellow, white, pink.

Max didn't explain, he just asked her to wait there. "Lucas knows how to unhook himself, but he wants you to go into the water and do it for him this time."

"I don't know how."

The engineer gave her a knowing smile. "He says you do. Just do what your heart tells you."

If she did that, Lucas wouldn't be diving head-first into a pool. They'd be hashing this whole thing out on the couch in her flat. Or in bed, depending on how well the discussion went.

But then Max was gone, joining Lucas in this crazy game of who knew what.

He appeared at the top. His shirt was off. He must have worn swimming trunks underneath his jeans because his tanned legs were on display. He looked strong and powerful. But from the words he'd said back at the flat, he'd hinted he was anything but.

But, then, neither was she. She had her own fears to struggle through. And if they couldn't do it together, then they needed to work on them as separate individuals.

Except those atoms were still dividing. Still joining. She peered, trying to make out what it was becoming. Then, just as Lucas dived far out into the air, arms spread apart, she saw it. It was his face, and the expression on it was similar to the one he had when he looked at Cora. When he looked at his brother.

Love. And fear.

A mixture of two emotions that were intertwined so tightly it was impossible to completely separate them. She knew, because the two were battling it out within her heart as well.

Lucas hurtled toward the pool before being jerked back at the last second, just as he'd been the previous time. The air displaced by his fall made the petals sift over the surface of the water, like ice skaters twirling in colorful costumes. Then the winch began to whine as it slowly lowered Lucas closer to the water. Time for her to get in.

She slipped into the pool, surprised to find some kind of footing where they'd had to tread water before. It felt like wood, but it was high enough that she didn't have to swim, she could simply walk toward him in chest-high water. When she looked up at him, she found his eyes on her. In their depths was a question. She swallowed, emotion bubbling up in her throat and threatening to escape as a sob. She loved this man. Loved him with all her heart. And she was willing to take him as he was, fears and all, if that's what he wanted.

God, she hoped that was what he wanted.

He didn't say anything, but when he was close enough to touch she gave him a quick kiss on the lips just before his head disappeared beneath the surface, followed by the rest of him. Soon he was hidden from view by the layer of flower petals. Momentary panic went through her. How was she supposed to unhook him? Max hadn't shown her, and Lucas hadn't said anything at all.

Just do what your heart tells you.

Darcie ducked beneath the surface and found him lying on the boards three feet below, the petals shading the area. He could just stand up if he wanted to… it was shallow. But he didn't. She pushed herself down and followed the cord that held his ankles. Unsnapped it. Then the one attached to the harness at his back. It stuck for a second and she wiggled it, suddenly scared he wouldn't come up if she couldn't get it off. There. The hook released.

He was free.

Lucas grabbed hold of her waist and hauled her to the surface, breaking through the layer of velvety petals.

The question he'd told her to ask once he'd completed the jump came out before she could stop it. "Why?"

He pushed damp strands of hair off her face. "Do you remember what it felt like to take that leap?"

She nodded.

"What did you feel?" he murmured, his arm now around her waist.

She thought for a moment, trying to gather her jumbled thoughts. "I was so scared. I didn't want to go through with it, and I felt like screaming the whole way down. But once I reached the pool, and you unhooked me, there was this sense of exhilaration…I can't even describe it."

He nodded. "I know. Because I felt the same things as I sat on the beach with you and started making that list. Terrified. Like I'd lost my stomach, my heart and my head all at once. I fell, and I haven't stopped falling. But I was too afraid to finish it. To let you come alongside me and undo those ropes."

Her eyes watered. She knew exactly what he was talking about. "I feel it too," she whispered. "The fear."

"I love you, Darcie. It took me a while to understand what I'd find once I reached the bottom of that jump—to get past my fear and open my eyes, to really look at what was waiting for me. It was you."

She threw herself into his arms and lifted her lips up for his kiss. It was long and slow and thorough. Once she could breathe again she laid her head on his shoulder. "I love you too, Lucas. You're right, it was scary and making the decision to go over the edge wasn't an easy one. But it was worth it. All of it."

"Yes, it was."

"Hey, Uncle Luke," a voice came from the top of the tower. "When is it my turn to jump?"

Cora stood peering over the edge at them, and even from this distance Darcie could see the little girl's infectious smile.

Laughing, she nipped the bottom of his jaw. "Good thing I didn't leave you there to drown. You were awfully sure of yourself."

"No. I wasn't sure at all. But I hoped."

She hugged him tight. "Aren't you going to answer her question? When can she jump?"

Lucas kissed her cheek, and then shouted back up, "Not for many, many years, sweetheart."

EPILOGUE

WELCOME HOME!

The words, scrawled in pink childish letters and flanked by a heart on either side, greeted them as they opened the door to Lucas's flat.

Three weeks on a beach, and Darcie was still as white as the paper banner. She didn't care. Besides, they hadn't actually spent all that much time sunbathing while in Tahiti. A fact that made her smile.

"Aw, I think I know who wrote that." Darcie twined her arms around her new husband's neck. "But at least we're all alone, because I have something I want to—"

The panicky sound of a throat clearing came from behind the black leather couch, followed by a yip. And then two. A child giggled.

"Oops." Darcie's face heated, as she whispered into his ear. "Not so alone after all."

Lucas made a face at her, just as people came pouring from seemingly every room of the place. The kitchen, the two bedrooms, the veranda. And finally, from behind the couch, appeared Cora, Pete the Geek, Chessa...and Felix.

Cora and Pete launched themselves at the newlyweds and her poor husband *oomphed* as the dog—apparently

forgetting everything he'd learned—careened into his side, nearly knocking him down. Darcie barely managed to keep from falling herself.

"Oh, my gosh!" Darcie knelt to hug Cora, peering at the mass of people around them. It looked like most of the MMU staff had turned up for their return—which begged the question: who was minding the maternity unit?

Isla came over and planted a kiss on her cheek as Darcie stood, keeping hold of Cora's hand.

"How was the honeymoon?" her friend asked.

She returned her friend's hug. "Spectacular. How's the baby?"

"Growing like a little weed." She motioned over at Alessandro, who was cradling their infant in his arms. "I barely get to hold him. Flick says Tristan is the same way."

It certainly appeared so, since Tristan had a baby carrier strapped to his chest with his daughter safely ensconced inside it. Flick waved at her.

Darcie gazed around at the people she'd come to know and love over the past year and her eyes threatened to well up, although she somehow forced back the tide. Lucas was still a little spooked by tears. He'd overcome a lot of his fears, but every once in a while he looked at her as if afraid she might disappear into the ether.

And she might. But that's not how she planned to live her life. And she certainly wasn't going to let her husband dwell on it either.

Then her eyes widened as her gaze skimmed the rest of the room.

There, still standing behind the couch, were Felix

and Chessa. And the childminder had a certain pink tinge to her cheeks that looked familiar. And— Oh... *Oh!* Felix's arm was slung casually around the woman's waist. It looked like she and Lucas hadn't been the only ones who'd been busy over the past couple of months.

Felix had completed his rehab program a few weeks before the wedding and had been on the straight and narrow ever since, according to the texts they'd got from Chessa. But she hadn't mentioned anything about a budding romance.

As if noticing her attention was elsewhere, Lucas glanced up from the group of people he was chatting with and caught her eye. She nodded in Felix's direction. She saw the moment he digested what he was seeing. His Adam's apple dipped. And then he was moving, catching his brother up in a fierce hug that was full of happiness.

And hope.

It was the best gift anyone could have given him— seeing his brother on the cusp of a bright new future. And little did Lucas know that another surprise awaited him. One she'd postponed telling him until just the right moment.

That moment was now. He could handle it. They both could.

When the tears came this time she didn't stop them, feeling Isla's arm come around her waist and squeeze. "It's wonderful, isn't it?"

"Yes."

Before she could say anything else he was back, grabbing her to him, his breathing rough and unsteady.

"Lucas." Her fingers buried themselves in the hair at the back of his head, praying she was doing the right

thing as she leaned up to whisper, "I know it's early, but our friends aren't the only ones having babies."

He leaned back and looked at her for a long second, a question in his eyes. She gave a single nod.

"I love you," was all he said, before he drew her back against him, burying his face in her neck.

And when she felt moisture against her skin, she knew it was going to be okay. Her big-hearted husband was finally ready to accept that the world could be a good place. It brought sadness at times, yes, but it was also full of kindness and laughter and contentment.

All because they'd dared to do something outrageous and wild and completely dangerous: they'd fallen in love.

* * * * *

VIRGIN MIDWIFE, PLAYBOY DOCTOR

MARGARET McDONAGH

With thanks to…

Joanne, Sheila and Jenny for inviting me
to be part of this exciting project and for
all their hard work and encouragement

Shelley of Web Crafters for designing me
such a great website!

And D, BB and B from T…
(you know who you are!)

Thanks for making this such a
moving experience!

CHAPTER ONE

'SOMETHING'S WRONG, isn't it?'

Midwife Chloe MacKinnon unwrapped the blood-pressure cuff from around Avril Harvey's arm and tried to offer the anxious woman a reassuring smile. 'Your blood pressure is rather high,' she admitted, masking her own growing concern as she re-checked the notes and previous readings.

'What about the other things?' Tears glistened in Avril's pale blue eyes, while her swollen fingers nervously shredded a paper tissue. 'I've always suspected things weren't right but the people at my previous practice in Birmingham told me not to worry. They said they were normal signs of pregnancy.'

Chloe took one trembling hand in hers and squeezed gently before returning to her chair. This was the first time she had seen Avril. The woman had moved to the small Cornish town of Penhally Bay in the last couple of weeks with her husband, Piers, both determined that their longed-for child would grow up in a better environment than the inner city. But this was Avril's first baby. And at thirty-nine, being short in stature, underweight and with a history of migraines, she had a few of the risk factors that warned Chloe to be on her guard. Add in the symptoms she had presented with that morning, and Chloe was worried about Avril's well-being as well as for that of her baby, suspecting that she had developed pre-eclampsia.

'I always saw my GP at my old practice as well as the midwife.' Avril paused and bit her lip. 'Could I see one of the doctors here today?'

'We're more midwife-led here…' Chloe hesitated as fresh tears spilled down the mother-to-be's cheeks.

'I don't want to be a nuisance, and I don't mean to doubt your expertise. It's just that I don't know anyone and I don't know what to think. I'm so scared.'

Chloe smiled, wanting to put her at ease. 'I understand, Avril, don't worry. I'll ask one of the doctors on duty to see you.'

The GPs left straightforward cases to Chloe and her colleague, Kate Althorp, but if it would set the distressed woman's mind at rest to have the second opinion, Chloe wasn't going to be awkward about it. Avril was alone in a strange place and feeling vulnerable, clearly on edge, her pale skin sallow, her short blonde hair lank. Time was of the essence. All that mattered was the safety of both mother and baby.

'Thank you, Chloe.' Avril gave a weary sigh, pressing the fingers of one hand to her temple. 'I wish my husband was with me.'

'Would you like me to call him for you?'

'No, it's all right. After dropping me here, Piers had to make the half-hour drive to St Piran for a meeting at the secondary school. He's an art teacher and he'll be working there when the new term begins,' she explained tearfully. 'We were looking forward to the summer to settle into our new home first and prepare for the baby. He won't be back for another couple of hours.'

Nodding, Chloe reached for the phone and keyed in the extension number for Reception. She watched as Avril turned her head to stare sightlessly out of the window of the room on the first floor of the expanding Penhally Bay Surgery. Chloe had tilted the blinds to keep out the full effects of the merciless July sunshine and was grateful for the coolness inside the building.

'Hello, Sue,' she said when her call was answered by the head receptionist. 'I'm with Avril Harvey for her antenatal appointment. Would you ask one of the doctors to pop upstairs for a few minutes? Thank you.'

The tone of Sue's reply assured Chloe that the woman had grasped the seriousness of the situation and would respond swiftly to the request. Hanging up, Chloe returned her attention to Avril.

'What made you choose to settle in Penhally Bay?' she asked, trying to distract the woman from her worries.

'We've been here several times for weekends and holidays—we even spent our honeymoon here ten years ago.' A reminiscent smile lightened Avril's expression. 'We both love the friendly, peaceful atmosphere, and Piers finds inspiration here for his painting.'

'Cornwall has always drawn artists. One of my friends, Lauren, is physiotherapist here, and she's an avid painter, too. Some of her work hangs on the wall in the waiting area downstairs.'

Interest momentarily chased the shadows from Avril's eyes. 'I noticed those. She's very good. Piers's paintings are more abstract. He's hoping to have time to develop and sell his work alongside the teaching.'

'So your move was both personal and professional?' Chloe encouraged.

'It seemed ideal when the job came up in St Piran. We never expected to have a child after such a long wait, but when we discovered I was pregnant, we both wanted a different kind of life for our family. I don't know what I'll do if anything happens to my baby.' A sob escaping, she rested one palm over her stomach.

Rising to her feet, Chloe pulled another tissue from the box she kept handy, then rounded the desk, squatting down to put a comforting arm around Avril's thin shoulders. 'Try not to

imagine the worst-case scenarios. Even if there is something amiss, it doesn't mean you won't have a perfectly healthy baby. We're going to do all we can to help you,' she said reassuringly, handing over the fresh tissue.

'Thank you.' Avril blew her nose and dabbed at her tear-stained cheeks. 'I'm sorry to be so silly.'

'You're not being silly. It's an emotional and worrying time.'

Before she could continue, a brief knock sounded and the door opened. Chloe glanced up, barely suppressing a groan as Dr Oliver Fawkner strode into the room with his customary swagger, exuding self-confidence and blatant sex appeal. Oh, no! Why did it have to be him? Dressed in dark grey chinos and a crisp white shirt, he looked cool and unruffled, the shirt's short sleeves showing off tanned, olive-toned skin and leanly muscled forearms dusted with dark hairs. Straightening, Chloe stepped round the far side of her desk, self-consciously putting a solid barrier between them.

Oliver had been working as an extra GP at the practice since mid-June as cover for the surgery's increasing workload, the busy holiday season and while Lucy Carter continued her maternity leave. No one could deny what an excellent doctor Oliver was. But for reasons she couldn't explain, he made her feel acutely nervous. He was just too…everything. Too masculine, too much the playboy, too outrageous, too sure of himself. And far too devastating in the looks and charm departments for any woman's peace of mind. Especially a woman like her. One who shied away from male attention and anything that made her feel uncomfortable.

Nothing and no one made her feel more uncomfortable than bad boy Oliver Fawkner.

'Chloe. I heard you wanted me.'

The rough-edged, smoky voice sent a shiver rippling down her spine. Despite being five feet seven, Chloe had a long way to look up Oliver's ruggedly athletic six-foot-three-inch frame

before she met the gleam of amused devilment in brown eyes as sinful and dangerous to the health as the finest chocolate. Chloe forced herself not to react when he sent her a cheeky wink. The man was a rogue. And he never missed an opportunity to tease her, flirt with her, disturb her, which only made her more tongue-tied and feeling like a gauche country bumpkin.

'Dr Fawkner, this is Avril Harvey,' she said, trying to hide her uneasiness and maintain her cool professionalism as she gave Oliver the personal details he needed about their patient's age and circumstances.

Stepping forward with his trade-mark smile, Oliver shook the woman's hand. 'Hello, Avril, it's good to meet you.'

'Th-thank you, Doctor.' Avril managed a teary smile in response. 'I'm sorry to be a bother, asking to see you.'

'You are not a bother. What seems to be the problem?' he asked, and Chloe tensed as that warm, molten gaze held her captive once more.

Clearing her throat, she dragged her gaze free and stared down at the notes. 'This is Avril's first appointment with us after moving to Penhally with her husband. She is in her thirty-second week, and until now has been attending her previous practice in Birmingham for her antenatal checks.'

'They said I was worrying for nothing,' Avril commented, continuing to shred the tissue, revealing her anxiety.

'Avril's been experiencing headaches, which are not uncommon for her with her history of migraines, but she has also had episodes with her vision, including floaters. Then there is the oedema—and lack of weight gain,' Chloe explained, meeting Oliver's gaze again, glad to see he was now in full doctor mode and all signs of teasing had vanished. 'I did the routine checks today and there is some protein in Avril's urine. Her blood pressure has spiked, too. The notes show it has been irregular in the past, but while the last reading re-

corded was 145 over 85, two weeks ago, today it was 190 over 110, the highest ever.'

Oliver frowned with concern, squatting down beside the mother-to-be, talking quietly to her as he examined her hands and assessed the level of swelling in her legs and ankles. Gently he rested a hand on her belly, and Chloe suspected that the smallness of the baby and Avril being underweight had not escaped his attention. He was very good with patients. Chloe just wished she felt as secure and untroubled when working with him as she did with the other male doctors in the practice, none of whom affected her the way Oliver did. Her awkward-ness around him disturbed her as it was not something she had ever experienced before.

'Avril, I don't want you to worry unduly,' Oliver told the woman, continuing to hold her hand. 'But I agree with Chloe that your symptoms are more serious than your previous practice believed.'

'Oh! I knew it. What's wrong with me, Doctor? Is it the stress of the move?'

Oliver glanced up and Chloe nodded for him to continue. She wasn't territorial about her role when a second opinion was beneficial, and she worked well in partnership with the GPs to deliver the best possible care to her patients. As Avril was new and nervous, and seemed to trust Oliver, Chloe was happy to take a back seat for now.

'We suspect you have a condition called pre-eclampsia,' Oliver explained, and Chloe, impressed again with his patient care, noticed how he was respectful to include her and not take over completely.

'That's dangerous, isn't it?' Avril's voice rose with alarm. 'Is my baby going to die?'

Oliver was swift to reassure her, without scaring her unduly, about the dangers to her own health, which Chloe knew was of concern at this point. 'Not if we can help it, Avril. Pre-

eclampsia affects about one in ten pregnancies and is caused by a defect in the placenta.' He glanced up and sent Chloe a quick smile, inviting her to participate.

'That's right. The baby receives nutrients and oxygen from the mother through the placenta,' she explained to Avril. 'That's why it is so important to have regular antenatal checks because the symptoms don't always show up in the early stages. Today we've seen signs that you could be affected. You have protein in your urine, your blood pressure is considerably elevated, and you have swelling in your hands, legs and feet, plus the headaches and visual problems. If we catch things straight away, there is every chance that both you and your baby will come through this without further ill-effects.'

Avril was clearly struggling to absorb all the information. She turned her anxious gaze back to Oliver. 'What will happen? Can you give me something to make it go away?'

'No, I'm sorry, Avril, but there isn't a medical cure as such.'

'But my baby!'

Chloe handed over another tissue, which the woman took in her free hand, the other one still clasped within Oliver's. 'I know it's distressing, but you need to keep as calm as you can. Chloe will refer you to the hospital in St Piran and—'

'Is that really necessary?' Avril interrupted.

'I'm afraid it is.' Oliver's tone was firm but gentle. 'They'll monitor your symptoms, keep a close eye on your blood pressure and the levels of protein in the urine. It may be that after a day or two you can go home on strict bed rest, but they will advise you what is best.'

'Once you are lying down, especially on your left side, it is possible that your blood pressure will come down. It's a question of how effectively they can keep you settled and stable,' Chloe added.

'And if they can't?' Avril fretted.

Oliver remained calm and persuasive. 'They'll do some

tests, check your blood, and they'll listen to your baby's heart with a foetal monitor. You'll also have an ultrasound to check on the condition of your baby. Depending on what they find, they may suggest you have a steroid injection to help the baby's lungs, and you may have some other drugs for your blood pressure, and maybe some magnesium. Ultimately, the best way to protect you both would be to carry out a Caesarean and deliver your baby straight away, but that is something your doctor and midwife at the hospital will discuss with you.'

'Oh, my goodness.' Tears trickled from Avril's eyes as she sat back on the chair. 'I'm only thirty-two weeks along.'

'Everything will be done in the best interests of your baby's health and your own,' Chloe reassured her.

Oliver released Avril's hand and rose to his feet. 'Can your husband come and collect you to drive you to the hospital?'

'He's already gone to St Piran. I don't know what to do,' Avril cried.

'I can take you.' Chloe glanced up from writing a note to the midwife and doctor at the hospital. 'I'm free until after lunch when I have a couple of house calls to make before my afternoon clinic. One of those calls is halfway between here and St Piran, so it won't be a problem. We can phone your husband, Avril, and have him meet you at the hospital.'

The woman sank back in relief. 'That is so kind of you. I wouldn't like to go on my own in a taxi or something. Are you sure you don't mind?'

'Not at all,' Chloe assured her with a smile.

Her nerves tingled as she felt Oliver watching her, and her gaze was drawn to his against her will. Dark eyes focused intently on her making her shift uneasily on her chair. How did he do that? What was it about this man that made her so edgy? Thick, lustrous, over-long dark hair brushed the collar of his shirt and framed a face that was far too handsome. The straight, well-proportioned nose, sensual mouth and chiselled, mascu-

line jaw, combined with those wicked chocolate eyes to
complete the playboy package…the wealthy, devil-may-care
doctor who, according to rumour, loved to surf and live the high
life. A life totally opposite from her own. Shaking her head to
rid herself of her unwanted thoughts about him, she mustered
her reserves and kept her voice controlled.

'Thank you for your assistance, Dr Fawkner.'

A knowing smile curved his mouth. 'Always a pleasure,
Chloe. I'll organise an outside line so Avril can contact her
husband while you write your notes for the hospital. Then I'll
help her downstairs.'

Chloe wanted to decline, to send him away, but she had to
place Avril's needs above her own. 'All right,' she conceded,
her evident reluctance widening Oliver's smile, a boyish
dimple appearing in his left cheek.

Focusing on her task, she tried to ignore the masculine
rumble of his voice, followed by Avril's tearful but brief conversation as she explained developments to her husband.

'He's going directly from the school to the hospital,' Avril
confirmed, once again holding Oliver's hand as he helped her
to her feet.

'That's good news. Chloe, I'll take Avril down in the lift and
meet you by your car.'

'Thanks.'

Chloe gathered up her things and hurried down the stairs,
stopping at Reception to explain what was happening and to
collect the notes for her home visits. She was ready to head
outside when the lift doors opened and Oliver gently guided
Avril towards the exit. Once Avril was settled in the car, her
seat belt in place, Chloe walked round to the driver's side, disconcerted when Oliver followed her. She opened the door, but
the light touch of his fingers on her bare arm made her jump,
and she paused, looking at him in confusion, alarmed at the
way her skin burned from his touch.

'Let me know how things turn out?' he asked, and his genuine concern warmed her.

'Of course. I can check in with you later.'

'I'll look forward to it.' He hesitated a moment and Chloe fought not to reveal her discomfort when he leaned across her, making her all too aware of him as he ducked his head through the open door to talk to their patient. His body brushed against hers, and she sucked in an unsteady breath, only to find herself inhaling his unfamiliar, earthy, male scent. 'Good luck, Avril. I wish you and your husband a healthy baby. Now I'll leave you in Chloe's capable hands. She's a terrific midwife—you can trust her to give you the very best care and advice.'

Chloe was still reeling from Oliver's praise when he straightened, held her gaze for an endless moment, then stroked one finger across the tip of her nose. 'Drive carefully, babe,' he instructed, his voice soft but husky, before he stepped back to let her slide behind the steering-wheel and close the door.

Fighting down a fresh welling up of confusion, trying to ignore the way her nose prickled and her arm still tingled from the caress of his fingers, Chloe strapped on her seat belt with shaky hands and started the car. She backed out of her parking space and eased onto Harbour Road. As she headed towards the curve of the seafront and the turning to Bridge Street in the centre of town, which would take her along the side of the river and out towards the St Piran road, she glanced back one last time in her rear view-mirror.

The image that stayed with her was of Oliver, hands thrust into his trouser pockets as he stood outside the surgery, watching her go.

Despite a busy surgery, the afternoon dragged by and Oliver had a tough time concentrating and putting invasive thoughts of Chloe MacKinnon from his mind.

'Keep off that leg as much as possible for the next few

days, Linda,' he advised the young tourist, having strapped up her sprained ankle.

'I will,' she promised with a rueful smile. 'No dancing for me for a while.'

Oliver handed a prescription for some painkillers and anti-inflammatories to the girl's companion, reminding them again of the best course of action. 'Rest, ice, compression and elevation. If you have any problems don't hesitate to phone or come back and see me.'

'Thanks, Doctor.' The young man grinned at him, appearing to relish his role of nursemaid to his pretty girlfriend, helping her out of the room as Oliver opened the door and followed them through Reception.

'The pharmacy is the next building along Harbour Road.' Oliver stood with them outside the surgery entrance and pointed them in the right direction. The late afternoon heat radiated off the tarmac and sunlight shimmered on the waters in the harbour opposite where fishing boats and assorted pleasure craft bobbed on the gentle swell. 'They'll sort out the medication while you wait.'

Oliver watched for a moment as his final patient of the day hobbled along beside her boyfriend, then he went back inside and, after exchanging a few words with the receptionists, he returned to his desk in the consulting room that had been made available for his use while he was there. The previous occupant, Lucy Carter, married to Ben, an A and E consultant at St Piran, and daughter of the surgery's senior partner, Nick Tremayne, was on maternity leave.

Sighing, he set about the task of updating his patient notes and dealing with the ever-present pile of paperwork, but his attention wandered in a predictable direction. To Chloe. Whose room was immediately above his own. His gaze lifted, as if somehow by staring at the ceiling he could see her, will her presence. She was all he seemed to think about these days. And

she scarcely appeared to know he was alive. It was a novel and not very pleasant experience.

He had only been in Penhally Bay a short time, but he had been drawn to Chloe from the moment they had met on his first day in his new job. And he meant what he had said earlier. Chloe was an excellent midwife…the best he had worked with. He admired her skill, her kindness, the way she always went that extra mile for the mums-to-be who meant so much to her. Like today, accepting Avril's need for another opinion and putting herself out to drive the obviously panicked woman to hospital. Perhaps he had been working too long in an impersonal big city practice. His time back in Cornwall had opened his eyes again to the true meaning and enjoyment of proper community medicine.

London had been a blast. At first. He'd had the brains to breeze through medical school, had enjoyed a successful career and an active social life since qualifying and, thanks to his family's success, he'd had the money to live life to the fullest. A cynical smile tugged his mouth. There had been good times, but his lifestyle had had its downsides, too. He was tired of those who were impressed by the family name, the bank balance, the exaggerated reputation. Tired of being used. He wanted to be seen for himself, the person he was, and not for the added trappings or as a prop to give someone else a good time. He had become mistrustful, dubious of people's—women's—motives.

He had grasped the opportunity to come back to Cornwall, his home county. His family was here, although thankfully far enough away from Penhally to allow him privacy. He loved them. They loved him. They had just never understood him. Never understood his need to make his own way and not be swallowed up in Fawkner Yachts like his grandfather, his parents, his brother and his sister. It had always been medicine that had drawn him, excited him, not the family business.

Being back in Cornwall had added benefits. He could indulge his passion for surfing and jet-skiing on an almost daily basis. And already he felt reconnected, enjoying his work in a way he had not done in the cut-and-thrust impersonal world London had become for him. Having made a conscious decision to change his life, the plan had been to settle in Penhally Bay and lie low while he established himself. He had no experience of long-term relationships, had never lived with a woman, but it was one of the things he most wanted…to find a nice girl, to settle down, to have a family. Eventually. What he had not anticipated had been meeting anyone who interested him so soon. And Chloe MacKinnon more than interested him.

She was unlike anyone he had ever known. He had never felt like this about a woman before and he was wary, unsure of venturing into the unknown. In the future, he wanted something different, some*one* different, and from all he had seen and heard so far, Chloe fitted the bill in every way. Just thinking about her made him smile and sent the blood pumping faster through his veins, a curl of heat flaming in his gut.

Chloe was the cutest thing he'd ever seen. Wholesome, in the nicest way, she had an earthy, natural beauty, something she seemed completely unaware of. She seldom wore make-up—she didn't need it. Her skin was smooth, almost translucent, while her eyes, a stunning moss green, shone between long, dusky lashes. Luscious, rosy lips begged to be kissed. At work she kept the luxuriant waves of her long ebony hair restrained in a braid, knot or ponytail, but he ached to see it loose in all its wild glory, to run his fingers through it, bury his face in it, to breathe in the lingering scent of fresh apples and sunshine that always clung to her.

Restrained was a word that could apply to Chloe in general. Serene and intelligent, she had a quiet humour that appealed to him and a sense of fun that came to the fore when she was relaxed with her friends. He had seen how she devoted all her

energies to her mums-to-be and to the newborns she appeared to love with passion. She would make an amazing mother. But it was her other passions that sparked his interest and made him curious. From what he had discovered, Chloe's life outside work was a closed book—aside from her loyalty to her female friends and the evenings out she spent with them, he had no idea where she went, what she did, or who she did it with.

No doubt about it, Chloe intrigued the hell out of him. She seemed so together, so content, but she was a very private person and he had found it an uphill struggle to get close to her. At first he had assumed she must have a husband or boyfriend, for sure, but he had been amazed to discover that Chloe had no one special in her life. Furthermore, she was content that way. Why? It didn't make sense that someone so lovely and smart would be alone. But it left the field open for him. Not that he was making any headway. Chloe kept her distance from him and his own uncertainties about the timing and his suitability for a relationship made him cautious about pushing too fast.

Completely without artifice, Chloe had an air of innocence about her, one that surprised him, yet soothed his jaded spirit. He was used to women flaunting themselves and making obvious advances—it came with the territory. The Fawkner name and money drew women like iron filings to a magnet. For a time he hadn't minded. Hell, he had been young and carefree, and he had made the most of the opportunities that had come his way. But he wanted something different now—he wanted Chloe MacKinnon. He just hadn't expected it to happen so soon and wasn't sure he was ready. Yet he wasn't able to keep away from her.

Not that it had got him very far. For the first few days Chloe had treated him with the same friendly professionalism she bestowed on all her colleagues, but when he had made his personal interest in her known, she had been endearingly and

puzzlingly shocked. He might have found her reaction amusing had it not led to her cooling noticeably, turning formal and businesslike, and clamming up more tightly than a bank vault.

Shaking his head, he ran his fingers through his hair, an image of Chloe vivid in his mind. She had a body to die for, but she had no notion how sexy she was. Even in the short-sleeved white tunic and loose navy blue trousers she wore to work, she turned him on as no other woman ever had. Her figure was stunning. A classic hourglass shape, with lush, full, feminine curves…soft and mouth-watering. His fingers itched to touch, his mouth to taste. But he could never get within a foot of the skittish Chloe and that was beginning to frustrate him no end.

It was a new experience for him to have to work so hard to gain a woman's attention, to get her to even speak to him outside work, let alone go out with him on a date. But despite her reserve and his own caution about getting involved with someone so soon, he wanted her more and more each day. The simmering desire nagged at him, refusing him respite, and he couldn't get her out of his head. Which meant that he somehow had to find a way past those prickly defences. Especially if he ever hoped to take her to bed. The very thought of having her naked, laid out for him, those long, inky-black tresses tumbled over his pillows, that voluptuous body arching under him as he loved her, was enough to make him harder than he'd ever been and so burning with frustration he thought he might go up in flames.

A knock on his door made him jump. For a moment he imagined it was Chloe—longed for it to be her—even if she had just come to tell him how things had gone with Avril at the hospital.

'Come in,' he called, his voice rough with desire, his heart racing in anticipation.

His gaze was fixed on the door as it slowly opened and he

almost couldn't breathe as he waited for Chloe to enter his room. When he saw, instead, that his visitor was senior partner Nick Tremayne, he struggled to swallow the wash of bitter disappointment.

'Oliver, do you have a few moments?'

'Of course, Nick.' He summoned up a smile. 'What can I do for you?'

In the short time he had been in Penhally, Oliver had come to admire the older man. He was an excellent doctor, knowledgeable if a bit aloof, but there were tensions he had yet to understand, especially between Nick and Kate Althorp, the former practice manager who had returned to her career in midwifery and now worked alongside Chloe in the practice. He suspected that Nick was a difficult man to get to know, one who felt deeply but who found it hard to share those feelings, a man who shut himself off and stuck stubbornly to a rigid point of view. Thankfully, Oliver had rubbed along well with his enigmatic boss…so far.

Exuding impatience, Nick strode across the room to gaze silently out of the window before he turned and moved back to the desk. Looking troubled, Nick folded his tall frame to sit in a chair opposite, his dark hair showing signs of grey, his gaze restless as it darted around the room.

'Is something wrong, Nick?' Oliver probed after a moment.

'What?' The older man looked up in surprise, as if disturbed from his private thoughts. 'Oh, no. No, just a lot on my mind. How are things with you? Settling in all right?'

Oliver leaned forward and folded his arms on the desk. 'Very much so. I'm enjoying my time here immensely.'

'Good. I'm glad,' he murmured, drifting again as if considering something.

Waiting patiently, Oliver reflected on the snippets of gossip he had heard. He didn't know the history between Nick and Kate, but it was clear that something had happened between

them recently as they were barely speaking. At least, Nick was barely speaking to Kate, Oliver amended. Kate looked stressed and unhappy, while the tension whenever the two were near each other was palpable.

'So, Oliver,' Nick said, apparently having come to a decision. He rubbed his palms together and shifted on the chair. 'I have a favour to ask of you.'

'I'll be pleased to do what I can to help.'

Nick nodded, sitting back, his expression serious. 'I noted from your CV that you've had a special responsibility for antenatal services in a previous practice.'

'That's right,' Oliver confirmed, wondering where this was going.

'I have some extra duties coming up in the next weeks, working with the town committee regarding the twinning of Penhally with a small town in Normandy. It would be of great assistance to me if you could take over my antenatal role. Just for the time being.'

Regarding his boss closely, Oliver wondered if the twinning committee thing was a ruse. He suspected Nick wanted an excuse to avoid Kate. Frowning, he considered the request. While he didn't want to become embroiled in practice politics or take sides in whatever dispute had occurred between Nick and Kate, he couldn't deny that taking on the extra duties had an appeal. Saying yes would mean more time working closely with Chloe. And the more time he could spend with her, getting to know her, easing past her defences and deciding if there was something worth pursuing, the better as far as he was concerned.

'No problem, Nick.' There was no way he was going to turn down an opportunity to be near Chloe. 'I'll be happy to cover for you.'

The older man's relief was evident. 'Excellent. Thank you, Oliver. I'll fill you in on things and if it's not too short notice,

perhaps you could start by attending the next meeting with the midwives?'

'Sure.' Oliver pulled his diary towards him and opened it. 'When is it?'

'Actually, it's in about half an hour. I, um, have to leave early,' he finished, having the grace to look uncomfortable at the lame explanation.

Hiding a smile, Oliver nodded. 'Don't worry about it.'

He listened and made notes as Nick went through the salient points he needed to know, a shiver of anticipation fluttering inside him at what lay ahead. The prospect of breaking the news to Chloe and Kate that he would be replacing Nick for the immediate future was an unappealing one. He imagined that each woman would have her own reasons to be unsettled by the change. But he wasn't going to shy away from the challenge. This unexpected turn of events could work in his favour. He was wary about the timing, unsure where any relationship might go, but instinct told him there could be something interesting between them. And desiring her as he did, he now had the perfect chance to try to woo Chloe MacKinnon.

CHAPTER TWO

CHLOE watched Kate check her watch for the tenth time in as many minutes. Kate was quite a few years her senior but they had always got on well together. The friendship had deepened further since Kate had returned to work alongside her as a midwife after giving up her job as practice manager and taking a refresher course so she could resume her previous career.

'Kate, are you all right?'

Uncharacteristically fidgety, her companion glanced up and attempted a half-hearted smile. 'Fine. Fine.'

'You realise you're holding that file upside down?' Chloe asked with calm concern.

'Oh!' Kate stared at the offending object in her hands and closed it, setting it on top of the pile in front of her. 'Sorry, Chloe, I'm as jumpy as anything.'

'Nick?'

'Who else?' Kate's wry laugh was brief and without humour.

Chloe smiled in sympathy. Having only very recently been privy to details of the latest turmoil between Kate and the senior partner at Penhally, she was worried about her friend and couldn't help but be annoyed at Nick's behaviour. True, it had to come as a shock to learn by chance that he was the father of Kate's nine-year-old-son, Jem, but to her mind his reaction

had been excessive and his treatment of Kate inexcusable. Given the tension that now existed between the two of them, it was unsurprising that Kate was nervous at the prospect of their weekly antenatal meeting. The previous meetings since Nick had learned of Jem's paternity had been fraught and awkward.

'Would you rather I took the meeting on my own and brought you up to date on Monday?' Chloe offered, wanting to spare her friend and colleague further distress.

Kate shook her head. 'No, my love, thank you. I have to face him and I'm not going to run away. I've known him a long time and he has his own way of dealing with things. He can be so stubborn,' she added with a sad, resigned smile.

'If there's anything I can do…'

'Actually…' Kate straightened, a frown of consideration creasing her brow. 'I hate to impose, but are you busy tonight?'

'No, I've nothing special planned.'

'You're not going out with the girls?'

Chloe shook her head. 'Not this Friday. I'm meeting Lauren at the farmers' market tomorrow morning before my lunchtime parents' class, then we're getting together with Vicky in the evening. What did you have in mind?'

'I think I should see Nick away from work, explain things from my point of view, and leave him to mull the situation over on his own.' Kate paused as if uncertain of her plan. 'It may not work, but I feel I have to try. If you don't mind me dropping Jem off at your place for an hour or so—he does so love seeing you and playing with your cats—then I could go and talk to Nick.'

'That would be fine,' Chloe agreed as they arranged a convenient time.

Chloe hoped Kate knew what she was doing. As the older woman had rightly said, Nick could be extremely stubborn and difficult. She didn't want to see Kate hurt even more. Before

she could express her concerns, the door swung open and Chloe saw that Kate's surprise matched her own when it was Oliver and not Nick who walked into the room. He was carrying a tray, and Kate hurried to clear a space on the desk so he could put it down.

'I brought refreshments,' he explained with a smile, handing around mugs of tea before passing Chloe the sugar bowl and a spoon, clearly having noted her sweet tooth. She wasn't sure what to make of that. Removing the tray, he replaced it with a biscuit tin. 'I snaffled the last of Hazel's Cornish fairings, too!'

Kate smiled at him, ever gracious and polite. 'Thank you, Oliver, this is very welcome.'

Hooking a spare chair towards him with one foot, Oliver sat and reached for his own mug. He was far too close. Her stomach tightening, her pulse racing alarmingly, Chloe drew in a ragged a breath and battled the urge to edge her own chair further away. What was he doing here? And why did he always make her feel so strange?

'Any news on Avril?' Oliver asked, opening the tin and taking out one of the delicious ginger spiced home-made biscuits.

'Yes. I was going to tell you but you were still with patients.' Chloe bit her lip cursing her defensiveness. Oliver's gaze met hers, a smile playing around his mouth, and she looked away, setting her mug down to mask her trembling fingers. 'They are monitoring Avril but it is looking increasingly likely that a Caesarean will be necessary. Probably on Monday…if she remains stable over the weekend. I'll let you know when I hear anything.'

'Thanks, I'd appreciate that. Let's hope mother and baby are both fine.'

Chloe nodded, noting how Kate sipped her tea and glanced anxiously towards the door. Her friend met her gaze and then

looked at Oliver. 'Nick's not coming, is he?' she asked, undis-guised hurt in her brown eyes.

'No, Kate, I'm afraid he isn't. I'm sorry.' Oliver sounded sincere and understanding. 'He's asked me to stand in for him with the antenatal work for the next couple of weeks because he has extra responsibilities on the town twinning committee.'

'I see.'

Kate's smile was strained and Chloe wasn't sure which she wanted to do more…hug her friend or give Nick a piece of her mind. This was a public slap in the face for Kate but Chloe had to admit she had been surprised by and grateful for Oliver's sensitivity. It sounded as if he thought Nick's behaviour was wrong and the town twinning work an excuse, but he was polite enough not to say so. She met his warm gaze, a confused mix of emotions swirling inside her. At the moment, however, she was too worried about how Kate was feeling to concern herself with the prospect of having to work more closely with Oliver.

With evident effort and fierce determination, Kate raised her chin. 'Shall we get on, then? We have quite a bit to cover and I don't want to be late home for Jem. I have plans this evening,' she added, meeting Chloe's gaze.

'Of course,' Chloe agreed after a moment of hesitation, still concerned at the thought of Kate going to confront Nick. 'If you're sure.'

'Positive,' Kate insisted firmly.

Oliver put his mug on her desk and took out a notebook, seemingly unaware of the undercurrents. 'OK, ladies. Be gentle with me!' His cheeky wink made Kate smile, and for that Chloe was grateful. If only she herself didn't feel so awkward around him.

'We've covered Avril Harvey, one of our new patients. There's nothing more we can do there until we hear from the hospital,' Chloe began, opening the file and making her own

notes. 'All being well, mother and baby will come home safely in the days ahead.'

'We'll keep an eye on them for a few weeks before handing them over to the health visitors,' Kate agreed.

Oliver concurred. 'Fine. Who's next?'

For a while they discussed their ongoing cases, including local vet, Melinda, married to GP Dragan Lovak, who was five months pregnant and maintaining excellent health.

Kate selected the next file and filled them in on one of her cases. 'I'm regularly seeing Stephanie Richards. All is going well with her pregnancy but she's twenty-two and nervous about having this baby on her own. Her boyfriend left her and isn't interested in being a father. Stephanie's in a rented flat in Bridge Street, and there's not much help from her own family so she needs extra support from us. Her baby is also due at the end of October—the same as Melinda's.'

'As far as potential problems are concerned, I have one mother showing signs of possible placental abruption,' Chloe informed them, waiting while Oliver made a note of the name and details. 'Angela Daniels had some discomfort and spotting. She was checked out at St Piran where they did an ultrasound and full blood count, plus a Kliejaur test to detect the presence of foetal red cells in maternal circulation. It was determined that the problem was mild and Angela was sent home on bed rest once the bleeding had stopped. She's in her twenty-ninth week now.'

'So we keep a close eye on her,' Oliver commented, busy with his notebook.

'Absolutely. She's on my list and she has my pager and mobile numbers in case of an emergency.' Chloe informed him. 'Angela's also having more regular checks with the consultant at the hospital. Likewise Susan Fiddick. Didn't you see her yesterday, Kate? What is the update on her?'

Her concern for the young woman evident, Kate referred to

her file. 'The breech was spotted at her thirty-six-week appointment and they tried to turn the baby at the hospital this week, the thirty-eighth. It wasn't successful and the procedure was abandoned. St Piran is predicting difficulties and have offered Susan an elective Caesarean next week. However, Susan and her husband want her to have the baby at home by vaginal delivery. While we're all for keeping things natural whenever possible, I've advised them to reconsider…there could be problems in the next week or two,' Kate warned them.

'We'll give you any help you need,' Chloe promised.

Kate smiled. 'Thanks. Let's hope they make the decision for themselves. Now, what about our new babies?'

'I understand there's a detailed newborn screening programme in operation throughout the region.' Oliver glanced up at Kate, his gaze moving to linger on Chloe until she shifted uneasily. 'Nick mentioned it now covers cystic fibrosis?'

Chloe nodded. 'Yes, CF is now included in the screen along with sickle cell disease, phenylketonuria and congenital hypothyroidism. We do a heel-prick test on the babies when they are between five and eight days old and the samples are sent to the Newborn Screening Laboratory Service in Bristol. They test the blood for immunoreactive trypsinogen. In babies with CF, this is increased in the first few weeks of life. If IRT is found, they do DNA tests. Sometimes they require a second sample when the baby is three or four weeks old.'

'So far our babies have been clear, thank goodness,' Kate added, 'but an early diagnosis means early treatment and the prospect of a longer, healthier life.'

'I've just sent samples in for three babies, including little Timmy Morrison.' Chloe paused and gave an affectionate smile. 'Beth and Jason have been waiting years for their first child.'

'Is he the baby you delivered at their home in the early hours last Friday?' Oliver asked, returning her smile.

'Yes. They were over the moon, it was very emotional.' Embarrassed, knowing how involved she became with her mums-to-be and their babies, she dragged her gaze from Oliver's warmly knowing one and focused her attention back on the files in front of her. 'Kate, what about the Trevellyans?'

'They are having a break from IVF for a month or two, but we're keeping in regular contact while they decide what to do. I want to follow this journey through with them but…'

'What's wrong?' Oliver frowned when Kate paused.

Kate sighed, wrestling with her thoughts. 'Fran and Mike are Nick's patients. So are Susan and Darren Fiddick. I'm not sure what to tell them about the new arrangements. No offence, Oliver, but some patients are going to want to stay with Nick.'

'None taken, I assure you.' Chloe couldn't doubt the sincerity in his voice. 'The patients' needs are the most important thing and somehow we'll sort this out so that they don't have to lose either you or Nick. Don't worry, Kate. I'll have a word with Nick on Monday. I'm sure that me taking over his duties is only a short-term measure.'

Kate looked hopeful, but Chloe felt less reassured that Nick would see sense. She was grateful to Oliver for trying, however. Smiling to convey her thanks, she was confused by the flare of something hot and intense in his eyes. Her alarm increased as he shifted closer. Reaching out for another ginger biscuit, his arm brushed against hers and caused an inexplicable prickle of sensation to shoot along her nerve endings. Disconcerted, she leaned away to fuss with the files again, wondering why it was suddenly hard to breathe and uncomfortably warm in the room.

'Other than the new couples booked in for preliminary appointments next week, and anything unforeseen that comes up, I think that's it for now,' she said, her voice less steady than normal.

The others agreed, and Chloe was relieved when Oliver

gathered up the tea things and biscuit tin, putting them all back on the tray and leaving the room. She immediately felt calmer and more settled with him gone.

'I'll see you later, then, Chloe,' Kate murmured, stacking her files.

'OK.' She bit her lip. 'You still think this is a good idea?'

A mix of inner pain and fierce determination shone in the older woman's eyes. 'I think this meeting proved what needs to be done. I can't let patients suffer because of Nick's displeasure with me personally. Not that Oliver isn't a great doctor, he is, but people like the Trevellyans and the Fiddicks deserve better from Nick. They trust him to come through for them. He can't abandon them because of me.'

'Just be careful.'

'I will.' Smiling, Kate patted her arm. 'Thank you for caring. Now, I'm going to put these files away and collect my things from the staffroom.'

Chloe watched her go, sighing as she rose to her feet and made her own preparations to leave. With luck, she'd have time to go home, feed the cats, shower, change and have a snack before Kate dropped Jem off. It had been another long, busy week and she was tired. She loved her job but it could be very demanding on her time and energy, and she never knew when she could be called out by one of her mothers during the night or at a weekend. Babies didn't follow a nine-to-five, five-day-a-week schedule! Smiling to herself, she gave her room a final check and then turned to leave, shocked to find Oliver blocking her doorway.

Oliver leaned against the doorframe and watched as Chloe finished tidying her desk, a smile on her face as she turned towards him. He regretted the way that smile faded, to be replaced by wary uncertainty as her footsteps faltered and she

hesitated just out of his reach. Knowing faint heart never won fair lady, he pressed ahead with his plan to ask her out.

'Hi.'

'Hello.' She looked puzzled as her gaze met his then flicked away again. 'Is something wrong?'

As nervous as a teenager, he summoned a smile and tried to look more confident than he felt. 'No, not at all. I was just wondering… Would you like to come out for a drink or something tonight?'

'Me?' Amazement shone in her green eyes before she ducked her head.

'Yes, you!' He couldn't help but laugh, shaking his head at her total lack of self-awareness. Surely guys asked her out all the time? 'Why not you?'

She regarded him in silence, apparently devoid of an answer. Closing the distance between them, he couldn't resist brushing a few wayward strands of hair that had escaped her ponytail back behind her ear. This close to her, he saw the tiny network of faint scars that crisscrossed the side of her neck and dipped to her left shoulder. He'd not noticed them before. As his fingertips trailed over the series of narrow white lines, he felt the shiver that rippled through her at his touch before she froze as if in shock.

Concerned at the thought of her being hurt in any way, his voice dropped to a husky whisper. 'What happened, babe?'

'Nothing.' Beneath his fingers he detected the rapid and irregular beat of her pulse. 'An old childhood mishap.'

Oliver didn't believe her. He could tell from her evasive tone, not to mention the shadow of remembered pain clouding her eyes, that there was much more to the event that had left these marks on her satin soft-skin than she had divulged. He was alarmed because he had never felt this intensely about a woman before. Why Chloe? What was it about her that drew

him? He was impatient to know all about her, but he sensed her skittishness and knew he needed to take his time with her.

'So,' he said, getting them back on track and reluctantly removing his hand from her skin, 'about tonight…'

'I'm sorry, I can't.' Her voice sounded less steady and assured than before. 'We can talk more about any patient queries you have next week.'

She thought he was asking her out to talk about patients? Frowning, he shook his head. 'No, that's not it.' Frustrated that she didn't seem to understand his intentions, he thrust his hands in his pockets to stop himself reaching for her again. 'Chloe.'

She shifted uneasily, looking ready to flee. 'I already have plans, Oliver. I need to go.'

'Sure.' He was still puzzled by her reaction but he let it go…for now. Knowing she often met up with physiotherapist Lauren Nightingale and some of their other friends, he smiled again. 'Girls' night out?'

'No. Not this time.'

'You have a date?' Bitter disappointment and a wave of jealousy coursed through him. Had his caution meant he had missed his chance? Had some other man beaten him to Chloe?

She edged around him towards the door, her movements jerky. 'Excuse me. I'll, um, be late.'

'Of course.' Swallowing a curse, he reluctantly stood aside to let her by. 'Maybe another time.'

Scowling, unsure of himself, wondering what the hell he was doing chasing after the woman when he wasn't sure he was ready to get involved, he watched Chloe hurry to the stairs and disappear from view. He had been positive she wasn't seeing anyone. Her rejection left a sour taste in his mouth and an ache inside him. Not to mention the fact she had seemed so surprised that he would ask her out at all. Why was the idea so strange

to her? What was wrong with him? Did Chloe just see him as some feckless playboy, like so many other people did?

Why was he even torturing himself over her? There had always been women who wanted to be with him, but he hadn't been interested in any of them. All he could think about, all he wanted, was Chloe. Something about her drew him in. In some inexplicable way, just being around her centred him, calmed him, made him feel real. There was so much about her he had yet to discover and he sensed there was something mysterious she held inside. He wanted to know her. Wanted Chloe to trust him, to open up to him. The prospect of an evening alone wondering where she was, what she was doing…and, dammit, who she was doing it with…was distinctly unappealing.

'Oliver?'

Glancing round in surprise, he saw Kate hovering at the staffroom door. He moved to join her, thankful to discover they were alone.

'How are you doing, Kate?' he asked, concerned that she had looked pale and stressed since the upset with Nick.

'I'm fine.'

He wasn't taken in by the brave smile she sent him. 'You can talk to me. If you ever need to.'

'Thanks.' He saw her knuckles whiten as she gripped her hands tightly together.

'I'm sorry about today. About Nick ducking out of the antenatal meeting.'

'It's not your fault.' She tried another smile, no more successful than the last. 'Nick and I have to work this out between us, Oliver.'

'OK.' He'd back off…for now. But he'd be keeping his eye on her just the same.

Kate's expression lightened as she watched him. 'How about you?'

'Me?'

'I've noticed you seem smitten with our Chloe.'

'Yeah.' That was one way of putting it. Oliver sent Kate a rueful smile. 'Not that I'm getting very far. Chloe treated me with the same friendliness she does everyone else for the first few days I was here but now she's cooled and it's almost impossible to get close to her.'

Now Kate's smile was genuine. 'I think it dawned on her that you were seeing her in a way that the other doctors don't.'

'I was interested from the first moment I met her.'

'Chloe wouldn't have realised that,' Kate commented, surprising him.

'Why not? She's a beautiful woman. Men must beat a path to her door.'

Kate shook her head. 'Hardly.'

'What are you trying to tell me?'

'Just that Chloe really is as unaware and innocent as she seems.' Kate paused and rested a hand on his arm. 'Tread carefully with her, Oliver.'

He was sure there was more here than Kate was saying. 'Tell me about Chloe.'

The older woman's expression contained a mixture of amusement and caution. 'What do you want to know?'

'Everything. Anything.' He ran a hand through his hair, his frustration showing. 'I just asked her out. She turned me down flat. She seemed to think I wanted to discuss work, but…I don't know. I gather she has a date tonight, anyway.'

'Actually, she's watching my son for me while I run an errand.'

'She is? Why didn't she say so?' Oliver stared at her in bemusement. 'I know you're friends, Kate. What do you think I should do? I didn't plan on getting involved with anyone when I came here,' he admitted, sitting down and resting his elbows on his knees. 'But…well, I hadn't counted on meeting Chloe.'

Kate frowned, taking a chair next to his. 'Chloe is…'

'What?' he prompted after she paused and the silence lengthened.

'She's not like the kind of women you're probably used to mixing with.'

He raised an eyebrow at that, irritated by the way so few people saw beyond the image. Sure, he enjoyed life, he liked to have a good time, indulge in the things he could afford and which gave him pleasure and relaxation away from the pressures and responsibilities of his work, things like surfing and jet-skiing. That didn't mean he was a jerk.

'I wanted time to settle, for the community to accept *me*, not judge on rumour and gossip or the family name.' He paused, reining in his disgruntlement. It wasn't Kate's fault. He needed to earn a new reputation, a true one. 'I've noticed you and Lauren are very protective of Chloe.'

Kate's expression softened. 'Chloe is special. Be patient, Oliver. Go slowly. Don't scare her.'

'She's frightened of me?' Shocked, he stared at Kate in disbelief. He respected women, would never cause anyone harm. 'I don't understand. I'd never hurt her.'

'Not intentionally, maybe.'

'But—'

'Chloe puts up a lot of barriers and not many people get to know the real woman,' Kate explained. 'Her work is her life and that has always suited her.'

'She doesn't date?'

'No.'

Confused, Oliver studied Kate's face. 'But why? She's intelligent, beautiful, funny.'

'I know.' The older woman's smile was filled with affection and a hint of sadness. 'You'll have your work cut out to persuade Chloe. It won't be easy. But I think you'd be good for her.' She hesitated a moment, biting her lip as she considered him. 'I can't break a confidence, Oliver, and Chloe is one

of my best friends. I don't know everything, but I do know that she has issues.'

'Issues?'

'I can't say more. I would if I could—and I encourage you to persevere.'

He mulled over the information. 'Issues from her past? With men?' Was that why Chloe was so skittish?

'Only Chloe can explain…if she trusts you enough.'

So, if he really wanted to take things further, he had to keep working hard to earn Chloe's trust. Patience wasn't his strong suit, not when he wanted something badly enough…and he did want Chloe. To her friends she was special. Hadn't he sensed that, too? There was something different about her. Wasn't that why he was still interested when a relationship so soon had never been on his agenda? For some reason he couldn't yet fathom, Kate saw something in him, and was encouraging him not to give up on Chloe. He had no idea where the journey would end, but for now he was along for the ride.

'Oliver, I think you should talk to Lauren. She knows much more than I do about Chloe's past…not that she'll divulge any secrets. But she might have some better advice on how to gain Chloe's confidence.' Kate hesitated, her gaze assessing. 'If you're serious about this. Chloe's not a temporary kind of girl.'

'I know that.' Oliver frowned, seeking a way to explain feelings he scarcely understood himself. 'I came here to begin a different life, Kate, to settle down. This is new to me, but I'd like the chance to get to know Chloe, to see what develops. She affects me in ways I've never experienced before.'

'Then I think you'll find Lauren and I will do all we can to help.'

A slow smile curved Oliver's mouth as hope flared inside him. He didn't imagine wooing Chloe was going to be easy, not from the subtle, mysterious hints Kate had given him. He

wasn't even sure of himself, of what he was getting into. But giving up on Chloe was not an option.

Kate stood outside Nick's imposing stone built house, situated at the opposite end of the village to her own whitewashed cottage. Was she doing the right thing? She had managed to sound confident when she had told Chloe of her plans, but much of that bravado had evaporated. It was impossible to explain how hurt she was. Nick had genuine cause to be angry at the way he had found out about Jem—overhearing her confidential confession to Eloise that day at the surgery must have been a shock—but she didn't feel it excused his behaviour towards her since. Today he had taken the easy way out in his eagerness to avoid her, but in doing so he had drawn Chloe, Oliver and a host of patients into their personal disagreement, and that wouldn't do.

Having worked up a fresh head of indignation, she walked along the path to the single-storey extension where the top half of the yellow-painted stable door stood open. Inside the expensively fitted kitchen, all wood and granite and steel, Nick stood at the island unit, his back to her. Before she lost her nerve, she rapped on the door. Nick swung round in surprise, his face creasing in a scowl of displeasure, the expression in his eyes cooling, leaving her in little doubt that she was not welcome. Tough.

'What do you want?' he demanded, voice harsh.

'We need to talk, Nick.'

He folded his arms across his chest, withdrawing into himself. 'We have nothing to talk about.'

'You're wrong.' As he turned and left the room without another word, she reached over the lip of the door and opened the bottom half, swinging it open and following him into the main part of the house, finding him in the airy sitting room. 'Don't walk away from me!'

'You're trespassing.'

'For goodness' sake!' Usually slow to ire, Kate wanted to shake the man. 'How long are you going to keep this up? It isn't going to go away by ignoring it.'

Nick faced her, his scowl deepening. 'I've told you, I don't want to talk about it. I feel betrayed, I—'

'*You* feel betrayed? That's rich. For once in your life stop and think how other people might feel. How *I* might feel.' Her hands clenched to fists at her sides. 'What we did, Nick, we did together. It was a terrible time, we needed each other. Then we both admitted it was wrong and we never spoke of it again. I had the guilt of betraying James while he was out there, dying, his body never found. How do you think it was for me, coming to terms with losing my husband, discovering I was pregnant from my one night of comfort with you? What was I supposed to do? Come and tell you and Annabel about it? Or would you rather I had sprung it on you a few years later while you were going through your own desperate grief at losing your wife? When would have been the "right time", Nick?'

He looked surprised at her outburst but no more approachable. 'I don't know. I don't have any answers. What do you expect of me?'

'Nothing. Nothing at all,' she shot back, knowing she had long ago given up expecting anything from the man she had always loved but who had chosen another woman over her, a woman for whom he was still grieving.

'What about Lucy, Jack and Edward?' he demanded, naming his grown-up children. 'What do you think this will do to them?'

'I have no idea. All I do know is that they are adults, exceptional people who have their own lives and responsibilities. You can tell them or not, as you think fit. What really worries you? That they'll think less of you?'

Shoving his hands in his pockets, Nick turned away to stare

out of the window. 'My relationships with all three of them haven't been easy.'

'No.' Kate resisted pointing out that he was largely to blame for that. It wouldn't help the current situation. 'The person who most concerns me is Jeremiah. He's only a child. I don't want him hurt.'

'I repeat, what *do* you want?' he challenged, swinging back to face her, his expression fierce.

Kate held her ground. 'I have no intention of making demands on you, or of publicly outing you as Jem's father. If you would like to spend more time getting to know him until you decide what you want to do, that's fine with me, but I won't have him hurt, used or tossed aside if it gets too much.' Taking advantage of Nick's continued silence, she pressed on. 'At work, I want you to at least be civil. It isn't fair on the other staff, or the patients, that you treat me like a pariah. Today was embarrassing for everyone, especially Chloe and Oliver. And it isn't right for people like the Trevellyans and the Fiddicks that you put our personal business before their medical needs. They are *your* patients, Nick. We have to see their journeys through with them, even if you cut back some of your other antenatal work for patients not on your list. We're adults. We made adult decisions, adult choices, adult mistakes. We have to bear the consequences like adults,' she finished, the fight draining out of her.

A muscle pulsed along Nick's jaw and he evaded her gaze. They stood in tense silence for several moments until Kate could bear it no longer. Her shoulders slumped. She knew him well enough of old to know he wasn't about to unbend, not until he had time to think things over for himself. If only she didn't still care for him, if she didn't still love him, despite all their ups and downs and all that had happened in their years of friendship.

'Think about it, Nick,' she advised quietly. 'I'll see myself out.'

She was shaking, her pulse racing from the fraught encounter, as she walked back towards the centre of the village. Finally she was passing the library and approaching the cluster of six cottages known as Fisherman's Row, which occupied the last of the space before the harbour bridge and the turning to Bridge Street. Forcing back the threat of tears, she stopped outside one of the colourful old cottages and rang Chloe's doorbell.

With Jem safely occupied, kicking a ball around the small enclosed garden at the rear of her cottage, Chloe dried her hands and went to answer the front door.

'Hi,' she greeted, stepping back to let Kate enter, noticing the glisten of unshed tears in her brown eyes and the paleness of her face, presumably evidence of her recent encounter with Nick. 'Come on in. I've just made some fresh lemonade.'

'OK.'

'Jem's out at the back. He's been fine. He wore Pirate and Cyclops out in no time,' Chloe chattered on, gesturing to the two cats curled up asleep side by side in an armchair.

Kate managed a smile. 'Thanks, Chloe. For everything.'

'No problem.' Returning the smile, she poured two glasses of the ice-cold, tangy drink and handed one to her friend. 'Would you like to sit a while?'

'That would be good.'

They chose chairs by the open doors, watching Jem play outside. Chloe curbed her nosiness but couldn't help wondering what had happened when Kate had visited Nick. It seemed clear that Kate didn't want to talk about it, however. Nick was a wonderful doctor, but he could be difficult, and he was known to be rigid in his opinions. Chloe ached for her friend and the predicament she now found herself in.

Kate had recently taken her into her confidence about Nick being Jem's father and, whilst she didn't know the circumstances of how it had all come about, she knew how much her friend fretted over it and felt guilty. Chloe could understand how Nick felt at not being told before, but she could also understand Kate's point of view. Although Kate had always been staunch in her friendship and support, Nick often appeared to take her for granted and not appreciate all she did, for the practice and for him. If both of them had felt guilty for their aberration all those years ago, and then both had needed to deal with bereavement at different times, it couldn't have been easy for Kate to know what to do for the best.

'Chloe?'

'Hmm?' Feeling relaxed, she leaned back in the chair and sipped her drink.

'Why did you let Oliver think you had a date tonight?'

Surprised at Kate's question, Chloe faced her. 'I'd made arrangements with you.'

'I could easily have changed my plans.'

'But why?' She frowned in confusion. 'Oliver probably just wanted to talk about work after our meeting. I told him we'd discuss it next week.'

Kate laughed. 'That's not at all what he wanted, Chloe!'

'It isn't?'

'No, my love!' Shaking her head, Kate reached out and patted her arm with amused tolerance. 'Oliver's interested in you.'

A prickle of breathless apprehension rippled through Chloe. 'Excuse me?'

'As a woman. Chloe…' She sighed, her smile reflecting both affection and a hint of exasperation. 'I know you don't think of yourself that way, but you *are* a woman. A beautiful woman. And Oliver has noticed.'

'He can't have!'

Laughing again but kindly, Kate finished her lemonade. 'Oliver reminds me of my late husband, James, when he was that age. The whole sexy surfer image and the warm charm, but with that underlying kindness and honesty.'

'But what am I going to do?' Chloe fretted, with increasing alarm.

'It's a new experience for you, I know, but why not try it?' Surprisingly calm in comparison to her own raging emotions, Kate's voice was gentle with understanding. 'Spend time with Oliver. Get to know him. You might find you enjoy being with him.'

With the heavy weight of her past preying on her mind, holding her in chains, Chloe stared at her friend, speechless with shock. How could Kate even suggest such a thing?

'Oh, Chloe, my love!' Chuckling, Kate set down her empty glass. 'You should see your face!' Sobering, the older woman reached out and took her hand. 'I know a little about your past, but maybe this is the perfect time for you to finally put it behind you. I hate to see you missing out on such a big part of life. Outward images can be deceptive. There's so much more to Oliver. Don't judge him on rumour. He could be the perfect man to teach you to be a woman in the fullest sense of the word—the real woman you are inside—if only you would let him.'

CHAPTER THREE

'HELLO, Oliver.'

At the sound of the female voice behind him, Oliver turned from scanning the crowds at Penhally's Saturday morning farmers' market and met Lauren Nightingale's slate-grey gaze. Tall, athletic and curvy, she was attractive, with an engaging smile, her long, light brown hair glowing lighter under the summer sunshine. Excellent at her job, the thirty year old was renowned for building rapport with her patients—and, he had discovered, affectionately teased for her inherent clumsiness. Oliver had only heard good things about her, and following the interactions he had already had with her through work, he liked her immensely.

'Hi, Lauren.'

Unable to help himself, his gaze strayed past her, eager for a glimpse of Chloe, whom Kate had hinted would be here with her friend today. He felt deflated when he could find no sign of her.

'Kate was right, you do have it bad!'

'Sorry?' The teasing in Lauren's tone had him switching his attention back to her. A frown creased his brow. 'What did you say?'

Grey eyes sparkling with mischief, Lauren linked her arm through his and led him towards a haphazard collection of

tables and chairs. 'Sit for a few minutes. We'll have something to drink and discuss a strategy.'

'A strategy?' Feeling he had stepped into some kind of twilight zone, Oliver's frown deepened, but he did as instructed and sat down.

'About Chloe.' A dimpled smile appeared as Lauren faced him. 'I assume she is the reason you are here?'

'You assume correctly,' he admitted, returning the smile.

Accepting a chilled fruit smoothie, he began to relax as it dawned on him that Kate must have told Lauren about their talk, and that the younger woman was possibly not averse to the idea of him dating Chloe. At least, he hoped that was what Lauren meant by planning a strategy. Again his gaze strayed around the shifting crowds of tourists and locals examining the stallholders' wares.

'I'm afraid Chloe won't be joining us,' Lauren told him, correctly reading the direction of his thoughts. 'She was paged this morning to attend a pregnant tourist staying at the Anchor Hotel.'

Trying to mask his disappointment, Oliver nodded and decided to get straight to the point. 'So Kate's spoken of my interest in Chloe?'

'She has. And however daft it sounds, I feel as protective of Chloe as some old Victorian aunt.' The warning was softened by the smile and the laughter in her eyes, but was there nonetheless.

'That's OK. I'm glad Chloe has such good friends looking out for her,' he answered calmly, hoping to allay any fears Lauren might have. 'This isn't a game for me, Lauren. I don't know what you might have heard about my past, but—'

She raised a hand and forestalled his words. 'I'm not much of a one for heeding rumour and gossip, Oliver. I take people as I find them. And I'm a pretty good judge of character. You may not have been with us long, but I like you, so does Kate,

and we both think you could be just what Chloe needs. But things are not going to be straightforward,' she finished, and this time her warning sounded more serious.

'Kate mentioned there were issues, but I don't know what they are.' He met Lauren's gaze, his own sincere. 'You and Kate both say I should keep trying. What is it you think Chloe needs? And why me?' he asked, his uncertainty showing, unsure himself whether he, who had never had a steady relationship, was able to deliver what her friends believed he could. 'What can you tell me that I need to know if I'm to begin to win Chloe's trust?'

Lauren took a sip of her tangy drink, her expression thoughtful. 'First of all, Chloe doesn't date.'

'You mean she isn't dating anyone right now?' Oliver clarified, but Lauren was shaking her head.

'No, I mean she doesn't date. Full stop.'

'Ever?' For a moment he was sure he had misunderstood but then remembered Kate had said something similar the night before. 'Chloe never dates at all?'

'That's right.'

'But why?'

Lauren's grey gaze was sombre as she faced him. 'It's a long story, Oliver, and it isn't mine to tell. I won't break Chloe's confidence, no matter how much I support what you are trying to do.'

'I wouldn't expect you to. So where do I go from here?' he persisted, puzzled.

'You'll have your work cut out for you.' Lauren's words again echoed Kate's and her smile was just as sad. 'Be Chloe's friend, don't take away her choices, don't push too hard too soon.'

A heavy knot of suspicion tightened his gut. 'Someone hurt her in the past? Physically? Emotionally? Or both?' Lauren didn't reply but, then, she didn't have to. The shadows clouding

her eyes as she withdrew her gaze answered his questions more effectively than words.

They were answers he found hard to come to terms with. At some time in the past someone had abused Chloe. Pain lanced through him at the unpalatable knowledge. And anger at the unknown person who'd hurt her. Various scenarios, each more disturbing than the last, played through his mind. The new knowledge explained why Chloe devoted herself to her work, ignoring her beauty and her sexuality, friendly and warm, yet always trying to remain professional, keeping up some invisible barrier. No wonder her close friends were so protective of her.

He wanted to protect her, too, but he also felt daunted. It was a big responsibility to shoulder. Was he the right man to gentle Chloe back to life? Wary and anxious, he sat back and finished his drink, a succession of thoughts running through his mind. He doubted himself, yet Chloe's closest friends had chosen to believe in him, to trust him. After his experiences in the past, it was a heady feeling, and the start of what he had come here to find…being recognised and accepted for himself.

Everything led back to Chloe, the woman who had filled his waking moments and fired his sleeping ones with erotic dreams since the moment he had met her. The idea of any other man claiming her was unthinkable. His mind was made up. He would do all he could to earn Chloe's trust and learn her secrets. To awaken her sensuality. To show her what it was like to be loved and cherished. A step at a time.

'I'll be seeing Chloe tonight,' Lauren told him, drawing him from his thoughts. 'Kate and I will do our best to encourage her to give you a chance, but the hard work will be up to you.'

'Thanks, Lauren. I'll do all I can to live up to your faith in

me, to not let Chloe down.' He hoped he was up to the task, that he wouldn't fail her.

Smiling, Lauren drained her drink. 'I believe you. So, what are you doing this weekend?' she asked, and Oliver assumed the talk of strategies for wooing Chloe was over.

'Luckily I'm off duty. Today it's surfing if the waves are right, otherwise jet-skiing. Tomorrow I thought I might take the bike out and explore. I don't know this part of Cornwall very well.'

Lauren's gaze sharpened. 'You have a motorbike?'

'Yeah. My main indulgence…along with my surfboard and jet-ski,' he admitted with a rueful smile.

'I've never ridden myself, but I know a couple of popular places where riders meet up. You might want to check them out early tomorrow morning, get some tips. It would be worth your while.'

'Great. Thank you.' Surprised at Lauren's insistence, Oliver jotted down the names of the hangouts she mentioned, marking one in particular that she recommended. 'I'll take a run out there.'

'I hope you meet up with a kindred spirit tomorrow.' For a moment, her eyes gleamed with something Oliver couldn't interpret, then she was turning away and gathering her things. Rising to her feet, she brought their chat to an end. 'See you, Oliver. Good luck.'

'Bye, Lauren. Thanks again.'

Oliver watched Lauren walk away, his mind full of thoughts and fledgling plans to win Chloe round and prove to her that he could be her friend…and more, in time.

'How did things go today? Everything OK with the mother and baby at the hotel?'

In her kitchen, opening a bottle of red wine, Chloe looked up at Lauren's question and smiled. 'Thankfully both are doing

fine. They're staying in St Piran Hospital overnight as a precaution as there was some postpartum bleeding. Nothing major. The baby boy is fit and healthy. Eight pounds two ounces. There is also one very scared, very confused but very proud father.'

'Did the woman really not know she was near term?' her friend asked, an incredulous expression on her face.

'No. She didn't keep her antenatal appointments or scans because her mother told her she'd done well enough in her day and she didn't believe in a lot of interference.' Chloe grimaced, pouring the wine and handing Lauren a glass.

'Thanks.' They walked out to the tiny patio at the back of Chloe's cottage and sat to enjoy the warmth of the evening. 'All's well that ends well. I'm sure she'll be more careful with antenatal care if she has another baby.'

'I hope so. She did have a bit of a shock. So did the staff and residents of the Anchor Hotel!' Chloe chuckled, then took a sip of her wine. 'Do you want any nibbles before Vicky gets here with the pizzas?'

'No, I'm fine. Thanks.'

Chloe enjoyed meeting up with her friends. Often, like tonight, they got together at each other's houses, or they went out for a meal or to the cinema, or sometimes went dancing at one of the nightclubs in nearby Rock. With Lucy, Melinda and Eloise all wrapped up with their new husbands and, in some cases, babies or pregnancies, it was Lauren, Vicky Clements and herself who most regularly met up now. Vicky, an old school friend of Lauren's, worked at her mother's hair and beauty salon in Penhally. Chloe was three years younger than both of them, and although they hadn't been close during their school days, they had known each other all their lives in the village. Their friendships had grown in adulthood. Vicky was good fun, but she was also a terrible gossip, and Chloe was careful to guard her secrets around her. Apart

from Kate at work, Chloe was closest to Lauren. And Lauren and Kate were the only people who had any inkling about her past…and the way that past impacted on her present and her future.

'There must have been something in the Penhally water this last year or so,' Lauren commented after a short silence, reclaiming Chloe's attention.

'How do you mean?'

'So many people falling in love, getting married, having babies…' Lauren looked at her and laughed. 'And not necessarily in that order!'

It had certainly been a busy time for the village and its residents. Among the many happy events to take place had been the marriage of vet Melinda Fortesque to GP Dragan Lovak. Chloe and Lauren had been bridesmaids at the wedding. Former neighbours in Fisherman's Row, Dragan and Melinda had recently moved into their dream home on the outskirts of the village and were awaiting the arrival of their first baby in October.

However, it hadn't all been people getting together and living happily ever after. Lauren herself had broken up with Martin Bennett, her long-term boyfriend. Not that she seemed upset about the split, far from it. Lauren had been more contented and freer these last weeks. Which surely lent weight to Chloe's view that you should be responsible for your own happiness and you didn't need a man. She said as much to Lauren now.

'It's true that things didn't work out with Martin. We were drifting for a long time and we never would have worked, but that doesn't mean I don't want another relationship. I'm certainly not going to be celibate for ever. I'm just taking a breather because I was with Martin so long, on and off, and I want to be sure where I am and where I am going before I meet someone else…hopefully in the months ahead. I enjoy sex, Chloe. Most people do. I know you had a terrible experience

and example with your parents, but it isn't always like that. Far from it.'

Chloe bit her lip. 'I know you and Kate think I'm missing out, but how can I miss what I've never known? I'm happy with my life. What more do I need?'

Her thoughts automatically turned to Oliver. She couldn't believe he had asked her out. Not that it meant anything to him. Kate had to be wrong about that. Rumour had it that he could have his pick of women—beautiful, available, experienced women. Women who were the antithesis of her. Why on earth would Oliver be interested? And why did she find him so unsettling, so challenging? She had never reacted to any other man the way she did to him.

'I saw Oliver today.' Lauren's words, echoing her own thoughts, had Chloe's gaze jerking up in surprise. 'He really likes you, Chloe. I think you should give him a chance to show you how good a relationship can be.'

Chloe shook her head. 'I'm not designed or destined to be with anyone.'

'Nonsense.'

'But Oliver…?' Confused, Chloe took a hasty gulp of her wine, a swirl of unknown and frightening emotions rampaging inside her. Her voice was mocking when she spoke again. 'The virgin midwife and the playboy doctor? I don't think so, Lauren. I'm not the sort of person to hold Oliver's interest for a second, not if he knew about me. He'd either laugh or be bored in five minutes.'

'You're underestimating him.'

'I—'

'Why not let Oliver decide for himself?' Lauren's smile was understanding, even as her words challenged all Chloe's preconceived notions. 'He might surprise you.'

Chloe remained silent for several moments, wrestling with

uncertainty. 'I'm scared, Lauren,' she finally admitted, her voice shaky.

'I know.' Her friend leaned over and gave her a gentle hug. 'But I agree with Kate. I hate to see you only living half a life. There is so much out there for you…if you would just allow yourself to take a chance. If you don't, you're allowing your father to win, to control your life from the grave just as surely as he did before.'

Chloe sat back, lost in thought, trying to convince herself that Lauren and Kate were wrong. Her life was fine the way it was—she had a career she loved, good friends, hobbies she enjoyed. How could she need more? Need something she had never known and never wanted? She had never felt sexual desire and she had no conception of missing anything. All desire and sex and love meant to her was what she had seen her father do to her mother…along with the way he had also controlled her from a young age. In her experience, giving herself to a man meant pain and domination and humiliation, just as she and her mother had endured for years.

No one knew the full horror of it. Lauren knew part of her story. She had been there to help her all those years ago when she had needed someone. Chloe would never forget the debt she owed her friend. As for Kate, Chloe had confided the basic details, but she suspected the older woman had read more between the lines. But asking her to step outside her comfort zone, to consider something she had always rejected, to awaken a part of her she didn't even know she had…? Racked with indecision, she met Lauren's gentle grey gaze.

'I don't know what to do, Lauren.'

'Take things slowly. Get to know Oliver better. Spend time with him,' her friend advised. 'How do you feel when you are with him at work?'

'He makes me confused, jumpy, on edge. I don't understand it,' she admitted.

Lauren smiled. 'That's good.'

'It is?'

'Sure. It means you're aware of him, connecting.' Lauren paused a moment, her voice serious when she spoke again. 'Nothing can change what happened in the past, Chloe, but you can change the hold that past has on your future. Think about it. You have tomorrow to yourself. Get out in the country, like you planned.' She reached out and took her hand. 'Knowing what I do about you and your past, do you think I would encourage you to let Oliver close if I didn't trust him to take care of you? He's a good man, Chloe. Nothing like your father. Let him prove it.'

Before Chloe had the chance to reply, the sound of Vicky's shrill call reached them. 'Yoo-hoo! Anyone home?'

'We're out here,' Lauren called back, giving Chloe a moment to compose herself.

Chloe watched as Lauren moved to place her empty glass on the table, but she misjudged the distance and the glass hit the edge before toppling to the ground.

'Damn!' Lauren exclaimed as the glass shattered. 'I'm sorry, Chloe.'

'Don't worry about it. I'll clear it up. Mind you don't cut yourself.'

Tutting, irrepressible Vicky Clements, short and thin and sporting a different hair colour every week—today it was bright red—stepped outside. 'Well done, Lauren, as clumsy as ever, I see!'

Chloe shared a sympathetic smile with Lauren, infamous for her mishaps, and went to fetch the dustpan and brush. Part of her was relieved Vicky had arrived, curtailing further uncomfortable discussion, but another part of her knew it was not going to be anywhere near so easy to banish the welter of thoughts churning in her mind—all of which featured the disturbing presence of wickedly attractive Oliver Fawkner.

* * *

Early on Sunday morning, Oliver rode out of Penhally Bay, past the headland, where the church and lighthouse sat, and up Mevagissey Road to the cliffs above the beach where he had surfed the day before. He always felt an intense freedom and peace when he was out alone on his bike, and this early there were few people about to intrude on his solitude.

He had scarcely thought of anything but Chloe in the last hours, turning over all Lauren had said, worrying about what she *hadn't* said but had implied about Chloe's troubled past. Preoccupied by trying to formulate a plan to gain Chloe's confidence, he followed the directions Lauren had given him as he passed the Smugglers' Inn, then turned into the country. A short while later he was surprised to find a motorbike hire and repair place called Addison's Yard in a secluded wooded setting, then it was behind him and he rode on to the hidden beauty spot Lauren had recommended. It was beautiful. A high point on a rocky promontory, it overlooked the surrounding coast and countryside.

From Lauren's description, he had expected to find a group of bikers gathering here before heading out for a day's ride, but as he pulled off the road, he could only see one other bike. The powerful Yamaha engine idled beneath him as he pondered whether to approach the rider, who sat astride an impressive-looking red Ducati, apparently enjoying her privacy.

There was no doubt that the rider was female, given the way she filled out the lightweight black and red leathers. Oliver slowly approached, wondering why the woman had her helmet on and her visor down. Surely both must hinder her enjoyment of the view and the weather. Cruising up beside her, he switched off his bike and took off his own helmet and gloves.

'It's fantastic up here,' he commented, but his opening gambit earned him only a brief nod of the head. Anxious to ensure that

the woman didn't feel uncomfortable alone with him, he decided to focus on their shared interest. 'That's a great bike.'

'Mmm.' A noncommittal grunt sounded from behind the visor.

OK. Shaking his head, wondering if Lauren was wrong about the helpfulness of fellow enthusiasts, Oliver tried again. 'I'm new to the district. I was told this was the place to come to learn of some good places to ride.' His frown deepened as his companion grunted some unintelligible reply. 'Sorry, I missed that.'

The woman shrugged. Oliver looked her over, admiring her lush curves. She almost looked like... He snapped off the ridiculous thought. Of course not. His mind was playing tricks on him. But as he studied her more closely, he noted the way a curl of dark hair had escaped from under her helmet. And then he saw the tiny feather of scars on her neck below her ear, visible above the collar of her leathers. He leaned closer and a faint hint of fresh apples teased him on the breeze. No way! He rocked back, unable to believe it. Lauren had to have known! She had sent him here to find his kindred spirit, he remembered. Hot damn!

'Chloe!' He heard a muffled yelp from inside her helmet and laughed aloud. 'I know it's you, babe. Your secret is out.'

She flipped up her visor, familiar green eyes sparking with indignation and annoyance. 'How did you know it was me?'

'I'm coming to know you—and several things gave the game away.' Reaching out, he traced the web of scars on her neck with one fingertip, feeling the tremble of her flesh beneath his touch. Pausing a moment to leisurely peruse her stunning body, his gaze rose and caught the blush that stained her cheeks before teasing, 'You look fantastic. I never would have pegged you as a biker chick, though.'

Green eyes clouded before she glanced away. 'You may believe you know me, Oliver, but I'm not at all what you think.'

And from the sound of her voice she imagined he wouldn't want to know her if he learned the truth. She couldn't be more wrong. Anger at whoever had stripped her of her confidence in herself as a woman rose inside him like an unstoppable tide. He took one of her hands in both of his. Her skin was so soft, her hand strong but gentle, fitting perfectly into his larger ones. He meant the touch to be reassuring, but even this simple contact fired his blood and sent desire fizzing through his body, reminding him he had to keep a tight rein on his self-control…at least for the time being.

'Chloe?' He waited until she drew in a ragged breath and allowed her wary gaze to return to his. Then he laid his cards on the table, honestly and sincerely. The only thing he kept back was how badly he wanted to take her to bed, knowing she was nowhere near ready to hear that yet. 'I want to know you, all of you, and to be your friend. Nothing you can tell me will make me care any less about you, or not want to know you.'

She gave a shaky laugh, her anxiety obvious. 'I don't know.'

'I'm not running away, Chloe. This isn't some passing fad to me. But I'm happy to go slowly, for us to take our time getting to know each other until you feel comfortable.' Raising her hand, he pressed a brief kiss to her palm and released her, putting some space between them so she wouldn't feel crowded. 'So, how about today? Can we take a ride together?' He cursed himself for the phraseology. The double entendre hung between them but she seemed refreshingly and innocently unaware of the kind of ride he really wanted to share with her. Banishing his erotic thoughts, he kept his voice soft and cajoling. 'I'd love to see your favourite parts of Cornwall. Will you show me?'

She debated for an inordinate amount of time, indecision evident in those expressive green eyes. Tense, she finally nodded, her smile nervous. 'All right.'

It was such a minor victory, and yet Oliver felt as elated at

this one small achievement as he would winning the World Rip Curl Super Series surfing title or the Isle of Man TT bike race. Silently thanking Lauren for pointing him in the right direction, he pulled his gloves and helmet back on, waiting for Chloe to be ready. He was still overwhelmed and delighted to discover her unexpected adventurous spirit and love of bikes. It proved that they had more than work in common—and that the fledgling feelings he'd had for Chloe from the first were worth exploring. There was so much he wanted to share with her but he had to move cautiously, both to gain her trust and to work through his insecurities about his own past. Today he had the chance to begin that process. He couldn't wait.

Far too conscious of Oliver beside her, Chloe readied herself for their ride, silently cursing Lauren whom she imagined had been the traitor who had tipped Oliver off about where to find her that morning. Her friend had been clever, she'd give her that. Oliver had been surprised when he had recognised her. She was still amazed he had done. Hell's bells, she'd nearly fainted in shock when he'd rolled in on his impressive-looking black Yamaha and taken off his helmet!

After a fun evening with Lauren and Vicky, she had gone to bed, her rescued cats, Pirate and Cyclops, curled up near her feet, but all her dreams had been filled with images of the playboy doctor who had knocked her life out of kilter in a few short weeks. Not to mention Lauren's and Kate's combined advice to give Oliver a chance.

Sunday had dawned promising another hot, sunny day, and she had left early for Addison's Yard. With little space and no offroad parking at her cottage in Fisherman's Row, she garaged her Ducati with the enthusiastic couple who owned the bike business. After a cup of coffee with early birds Roger and Jean Addison, she'd embraced the freedom her bike afforded her and had ridden the short distance to one of her favourite

secluded places to think and plan her day. To discover she shared her secret passion for motorbikes with Oliver brought another rush of confused emotions.

Feeling that sinful dark gaze focused on her, she glanced up. The way he looked at her was like a caress...not that she knew what the caress of a man felt like. But Oliver always made her feel unsettled yet strangely alive. Her palm still tingled from the kiss he had so unexpectedly and shockingly placed there. She felt gauche, out of her league. There had to be any number of experienced women keen to be with him—she wasn't so blind or stupid that she didn't realise Oliver was incredibly good-looking—so why was he interested in someone like her? Maybe if he found out about her past his interest would cease, no matter what he said to the contrary.

A smile curved his mouth and she had the unnerving feeling he knew what she was thinking. 'One step at a time, babe. Let's enjoy our day. OK?'

'OK.' Chloe heard the doubt in her own voice and knew he'd heard it, too.

She flipped down her visor, cutting off his view of her face so he couldn't read her expressions any more. Filled with nervous anticipation, she started her bike and led the way into what, for her, was the unknown...spending time with a sexy, attractive man who made his interest in her abundantly and frighteningly clear. Quite what she was going to do about that, if anything, remained to be seen.

Chloe couldn't believe how quickly the day sped by, or how disappointed she was that her time with Oliver was nearly over. They'd ridden miles along the coast and inland, spending time on Bodmin Moor with its wild landscape, granite tors, standing stones and unique history. She had imagined Oliver as a typical beach boy, interested only in surfing and women,

but he'd proved to be a fascinating companion, keen to learn things, sharing unexpected bits of information and, most surprisingly of all, keeping her laughing all day. They had shared a picnic lunch on the moor, spent the afternoon exploring on both bike and foot, then had enjoyed an early fish-and-chip supper along the coast before making their way home. By evening they were back in Penhally, Oliver having followed her home after she had left her bike in its secure garage at Addison's Yard.

As she opened her front door, conscious of Oliver behind her, Chloe couldn't remember when she had last enjoyed herself so much. Usually, getting out on the bike was her escape and she liked to be alone to relax and unwind, but sharing things with Oliver today had made everything even better...special. Which was a bit scary in itself. She hadn't expected to relax with him, to enjoy being with him, for him to be so thoughtful and smart and funny. But she had—and he was.

He hadn't pressed her for details about her own life but he'd been open in telling her about himself, his childhood, the pluses and minuses of growing up in a well-known and wealthy family. The self-deprecating humour with which he had related tales of his scrapes and mishaps had brought tears of laughter to her eyes. All the while, though, she'd felt sad that she had nothing similar to offer about her own time growing up. A time dominated by her father's anger, his fists, his vicious tongue.

'What are you thinking?'

Oliver's husky voice broke through her reverie. Manufacturing a smile, she shook her head. 'Nothing.'

'You look sad.' His voice gentle, he crossed the living room, closing the gap between them.

'No.' Her memories were sad but she didn't want the past

spoiling this magical day, one she had never expected to have.
'I'm fine.'

But the thoughts, having intruded, were not so easy to
banish. Was Lauren right? Was she allowing her father to
control her life now as much as he had when he'd been alive?
Not for the first time, she wondered what Oliver would think
if she was ever able to confide in him about her father's
mental, verbal and physical abuse. No matter what he had said
about accepting anything she told him, she felt ashamed and
embarrassed about her past. And she was sure he would laugh
when he found out about her complete lack of experience
with men.

She knew that her years of conditioning at home with her
father had caused her to shut down one whole side of herself,
but she hadn't felt she had been missing anything, had genuinely never felt interest in or desire for a man. It was Oliver
who was awakening those kinds of feelings within her. And she
was scared. Scared to open herself up to hurt, scared Oliver
would either despise her or ridicule her for her past.

She was startled from her introspection when Oliver took
both her hands in his. Uncertain, she looked up and met his
dark, intense gaze, aware of the way her pulse raced and her
skin tingled from his touch as his fingers stroked the sensitive
insides of her wrists.

'Thank you for today, Chloe.'

His smoky voice increased the feeling of intimacy and made
her skittish. 'I had a good time,' she admitted truthfully, earning
herself a boyish smile.

'I'm glad. I really enjoy being with you, and I'd like us to
spend much more time together.'

'Why?' She couldn't hide her confusion. 'You could have
anyone.'

A chuckle rumbled from his chest. 'I don't want *anyone*. I
want *you*.'

'I'm no good at this.'

'You mean letting a man get close to you?' he asked, no hint of judgement in his tone.

'I don't know how to be what you want me to be.'

For a moment his fingers tightened on hers, then he released them, but only so he could cup her face, drawing her gaze to his. Dark brown eyes looked deeply into hers. His touch was warm, sure but gentle, making her quiver from head to toe. Her chest felt tight and she wasn't sure she could remember how to breathe.

'Chloe, I never want you to be anything or anyone but yourself.' He was serious, intent, sincere. 'I like you just the way you are.'

'But—' Her words were silenced as he brushed the pad of his thumb across her lips.

'I'm not going to hurt you. We'll take things as slowly as you want,' he promised, and despite her wariness and doubt she felt warm deep inside, her heart thudding against her ribs. 'Give me a chance, babe…give us a chance. I want you to feel comfortable, to know you can trust me with anything.'

She finally managed to draw in a ragged breath. 'Oliver…'

'Shh. One step at a time. OK?'

'OK,' she finally agreed, not at all sure she knew what she was doing, but when he smiled at her like that she took leave of her senses, and the thought of more days like today was too tempting to resist.

'Thank you.' She saw him take a deep breath of his own, as if he was relieved or something. His thumbs stroked softly across her cheekbones, his eyes darkening as he stared at her mouth. 'May I kiss you goodnight?'

Chloe's eyes widened. 'You want to kiss me?'

'I do. Very much.' The chuckle rumbled out again, his smile deepening, bringing the dimple to his cheek. 'Is that so bad?'

he teased, eyes twinkling with amusement. 'Or such a surprise? You look like you've never been kissed before!'

'I haven't.'

He laughed, clearly disbelieving her, then his expression sobered as he continued to study her face. 'Damn,' he groaned, his body tensing. 'You're serious.'

Oliver's shock was only what she had expected. She had known he wouldn't understand. How could he think she was anything but an oddity? Chloe ducked her head as an astonished silence stretched between them. At least he knew part of the truth about her now, even though it was bound to drive him away and cool his interest in a single moment. She tried to step back but his hold tightened. He tilted her head up, but she resolutely closed her eyes so she wouldn't see the mocking derision she was sure must be in his.

'Chloe…look at me.'

'No,' she murmured, hands clenched to fists at her sides.

Oliver's hands slid along her neck to burrow into her hair, his thumbs grazing the line of her jaw, tipping her chin up further. 'Open your eyes, babe,' he insisted softly, his voice persuasive, a husky whisper that seemed to reach all her nerve endings.

Biting her lip, she mustered some bravado and forced herself to meet his gaze, surprised to find nothing but kindness and caring and honesty.

'Did you think I was going to make fun of you, or walk away?'

'I don't know.' Chloe shrugged. 'Maybe. Yes.' Frowning, she searched his gaze. 'I'm not like the kind of women you must have dated.'

'No, you're not,' he agreed, and for a moment her heart sank and a surprising wave of disappointment washed through her. 'But they're in the past. They don't interest me. You're different, Chloe. In a good way. And I'm *not* walking away.' Her

heart started thudding again. She opened her mouth to protest, but the fingers of one hand brushed across her lips, silencing her. 'I'm serious when I say I don't want anyone but you. I meant it when I told you we'd take things at your pace. When you feel ready to talk, to tell me about your past and why it has held you back from experiencing your full potential as a desirable woman, I'm here to listen. Until then we'll spend more time together, get to know each other, whatever you want.'

She had no idea why, but she believed him. And she felt a crazy sense of nervous excitement she had never experienced before. Trying to block out the warnings of her past, she thought of Lauren's and Kate's advice, and especially of Oliver, this day they had shared, and took a tentative step out on a limb. 'Yes.'

'Yes?'

Oliver looked puzzled and she smiled. 'Yes, you may kiss me goodnight,' she whispered, her nervousness bringing a tremble to her voice.

Chocolate eyes turned dark and fiery as her words sank in. Again his hands moved to cup her face and her own hands rose to his chest, resting there uncertainly. Even through the soft leather she could feel the rapid beat of his heart, and when she breathed in, she inhaled the subtle masculine fragrance of him. She liked it. Her whole being shook as his head lowered and her eyes fluttered shut, the breath leaving her in a rush as his mouth met hers, his lips moving gently…warm, sure and seductive. Unable to help herself, she leaned into him. The kiss lasted no more than ten seconds. It wasn't enough. Already she wanted more, wanted to do it again, wanted it to go on for ever, and she barely suppressed a whimper of protest when he slowly pulled back.

Confused, she opened her eyes, saw Oliver's smile. Then he was letting her go, and she swayed, leaning against the sofa

for support as she watched him walk away. Speechless, she pressed a hand to her mouth where the imprint of his still lingered. She licked her lips, tasting a teasing hint of the unfamiliar flavour of him. At the door, Oliver stopped and looked back at her, his eyes dark and unfathomable, his voice smoky with promise.

'Goodnight, Chloe. I'll see you tomorrow. Sweet dreams, babe.'

CHAPTER FOUR

OLIVER spent a couple of moments between patients updating his notes and preparing a referral letter to the cardiac consultant at St Piran. He was troubled by the worsening angina of the woman he had just seen, who smoked, had high blood pressure, high cholesterol and a family history of heart problems. Frowning, he concisely explained his concerns and requested the consultant's opinion.

It was Wednesday afternoon, and he was still shocked by the discoveries he had made on Sunday…the amazing day he had spent with Chloe. She was everything he had imagined and so much more. But absorbing the reality that she was twenty-seven-years old and had never even been kissed was taking some time.

Knowing she was in the room above, taking an antenatal clinic, his gaze strayed upwards. So near and yet so far. She was beyond innocent. How? Why? He had told her he would give her the time she needed to trust him, and he meant it, but that didn't mean he wasn't eager to understand why someone so beautiful and together had absolutely no idea about her own body, about need and pleasure and sexual fulfilment. Chloe wasn't being coy or shy or playing a game. She was genuine— and for some reason she had never had or explored sexual feelings.

At first, from the things Lauren and Kate had implied, he had assumed Chloe had been hurt by a previous boyfriend. But that was clearly not the case. Something much more fundamental must have happened in her earlier years to have caused her to shut off a whole part of herself. She had feared on Sunday that learning the truth of her inexperience would drive him away, make him lose interest. The opposite was the case.

Far from putting him off, Chloe's innocence brought a wave of affection and a rush of possessive satisfaction that no other man had touched her. *He* wanted to be the one to awaken her desires and teach her about the pleasures of her body, to show her how beautiful and sexy she was. But he couldn't banish the flickers of doubt that nagged at him. Was Chloe right for him? Was *he* the right man for *her*? Lauren and Kate appeared to believe so and claimed to see beyond the playboy stereotype he sought to escape. Did Chloe?

Nothing in his past had prepared him for a woman like her. Yes, he was wary, but he couldn't now imagine not having her in his life. With Chloe it would be all or nothing. He needed to go on seeing her, to win her trust and friendship, but he would have to be very sure of himself and his plans for the future before he took things beyond a few simple kisses. He was getting too far ahead of himself. For now he would spend as much time as he could with her outside work…which wasn't as easy as it sounded.

As well as being on call to her expectant mothers, Chloe had several out-of-hours ante- and postnatal groups, plus a parenting class for new mothers and fathers, in which she gave general support and advice on anything from care of the newborn to breast-feeding problems. Then there was the well-woman clinic where she helped with a range of issues, including family planning and pre-conception advice. Aside from a few snatched work-related conversations at the practice, including news of the safe delivery by C-section of Avril

Harvey's baby daughter on Monday, there had been little chance to see her at all.

But tonight, all being well, Chloe was his…for a few hours, at least. And he planned on making the most of them, talking, learning more about each other, just being together so she would feel more at ease and begin to trust him. He frowned, realising how involved his emotions were becoming with this woman. Perhaps it was time to stop doubting himself, to stop worrying that this was all happening sooner than he had planned and just see where the road ahead might lead…for them both.

Oliver glanced at his watch. He loved his job, gave one hundred per cent to his patients at all times, but he was longing to be alone with Chloe and he had another half an hour to go before both their clinics ended and he could take her home. With a resigned sigh, he pressed the buzzer and prepared to welcome his next patient.

'Let me take him for you,' Oliver offered with a smile, rising to his feet to help the harassed-looking young woman who struggled to manoeuvre a double buggy into the consulting room, one child aged about two strapped in and complaining noisily, a baby of a few months held in her free arm.

'Thanks so much.' The woman gratefully handed over the baby to Oliver's care, her answering smile rueful. 'Whoever said having the two so close together was a good idea wants their head examined.'

Chuckling, Oliver balanced the baby against his chest. 'Take your time,' he advised, waiting while she parked the buggy, sat down and endeavoured to quiet the fractious two-year-old.

'Sorry about that.' She brushed a few strands of mousy hair back from her overheated face.

'No problem.' Oliver glanced at the notes, familiarising himself with the Anker family's names. 'What can I do for you today, Juliet?'

'It's Leo,' she informed him, referring to the baby he was still holding. 'He has a cold—in this weather, can you imagine!—and he seems to have trouble breathing sometimes.'

'Let me have a look at him. How long have you noticed the problem?'

Juliet bared Leo's chest so Oliver could listen to his lungs. 'Just a couple of days. I'm probably worrying about nothing, but…'

'It's always better to be safe than sorry.' Oliver gave her a reassuring smile before resuming his thorough examination. 'His lungs are clear,' he told her a short while later, looping his stethoscope round his neck. 'Everything sounds fine. And his temperature is normal. When is Leo's breathing worse?'

'Mostly when he's trying to feed.'

Oliver checked the notes once more. 'And are you still breast-feeding?'

'Yes. I really wanted to. I had trouble managing it with William, but Chloe was wonderful, helping me through both pregnancies and supporting me afterwards. I had no problems at all feeding Leo,' she explained proudly, dressing the baby again.

'Chloe's an excellent midwife.' Oliver was all too aware of how his heart had leapt at hearing Chloe's name. With an effort he forced his mind back to the matter at hand. 'The best thing to do with Leo is to put a couple of saline drops in each nostril before feeding. That will help to thin and disperse any congestion, and he should find feeding much easier. You can also try holding him in a more upright position until he is over the cold.'

A relieved smile stripped the worry from Juliet's rosy face as she strapped Leo into place beside his now silent, watchful brother. 'That's great. Thank you so much, Dr Fawkner.'

'No trouble. You have two fine sons.' He held the door open and helped Juliet guide the buggy out of the room. 'Let me

know if Leo's cold doesn't clear in another couple of days, or if you have any other concerns.'

His next patient was a middle-aged man with recurrent muscular pain in his back. After prescribing some analgesia, he recommended that the man see Lauren Nightingale for some gentle physiotherapy to help strengthen his back.

'I'm willing to try anything, Doctor,' he agreed with a wan smile.

Smiling in sympathy, Oliver made a couple of notes. 'I'll see to the referral and Lauren will contact you directly. Any problems, come back and talk to me.'

As the man made his uncomfortable departure, Oliver reflected on another mixed afternoon surgery while he waited for his final patient of the day to come through. The summer influx of tourists and surfers brought an upsurge in minor injuries and illnesses. He had been taken on at the practice to assist his new colleagues in covering the additional cases on top of the usual workload of local families, farmers and fishermen. In the weeks he had been in Penhally, he had seen everything from surfboard collisions to scrapes on the rocks, weaver and jellyfish stings, fractures, sprains, cuts that needed stitching, and had given what seemed a never-ending series of tetanus injections.

Oliver looked up and smiled as a knock on the door announced the arrival of Rachel Kenner. He had seen from the notes that the local vicar's daughter seldom visited the surgery, but one look at her frightened blue eyes told him that something serious and troubling had brought her there today. Gently he sat her down and tried to put her at ease. Slender and shy, with short blonde curls and a nervous manner, she looked younger than her seventeen years and very vulnerable.

'Hello, Rachel. Take your time and make yourself comfortable,' he said encouragingly as she shifted restlessly on the chair. 'What can I do to help you today?'

Clasping shaking hands together in her lap, she stared at him in silence for several long moments and then burst into tears.

Chloe had just shown her last mum-to-be of the afternoon out of the room when the phone rang. She returned to her desk, grimacing at the sight of the pile of paperwork awaiting her, and picked up the receiver.

'Sorry, Chloe, am I interrupting?' Sue, the head reception-ist apologised.

'No, Sue, it's fine. Mrs George has just left. Is there a problem?'

'Oliver asks if you could pop down to his consulting room as soon as you are free,' Sue continued and Chloe's heart skit-tered at the sound of his name and at the request. She was still gathering her wits as Sue continued. 'He has Rachel Kenner with him.'

Surprise jolted Chloe from her wayward thoughts about the man whose all-too-brief kiss three days ago still left her jittery, ridiculously excited and confused. 'Rachel? OK, I'm on my way down.'

Wondering why Reverend Kenner's shy, studious daughter might need her, Chloe hurried down the stairs to the suite of consulting rooms, frowning as she knocked on the door of what had been Lucy's room but which Oliver was now using.

'Come in.'

Stepping inside, Chloe felt another burst of nervous antici-pation, then she met Oliver's darkly sinful gaze. Warmth stole through her whole being. For just a moment something intense and deeply personal burned in his eyes, and a small smile played at his mouth, then he was back in professional mode, as if the private connection had never happened.

'Thanks for coming down, Chloe.'

'No problem.' She dragged her attention away from the man who had hijacked all her thoughts of late and focused on

the girl who sat by the desk, tear tracks marking her pale cheeks, a pile of soggy tissues clutched in her shaking hands. Chloe's heart went out to her, and she moved to her side, slipping an arm around her slim shoulders. 'Hello, Rachel, my love. Whatever has happened?'

Her question set off another burst of sobbing. Chloe held Rachel while she cried, raising a querying gaze to Oliver who looked on with sympathetic concern.

'Rachel's come to see us because she has a problem she's not sure how to handle,' he explained after a moment, choosing his words with care. 'I said we'd do all we can to help.'

'Of course we will,' Chloe agreed robustly, giving Rachel an encouraging smile.

Oliver hunkered down on the other side of the distraught girl and offered her a fresh tissue. His kindness touched Chloe's heart. 'Rachel, do you want to explain to Chloe, or would you like me to tell her?'

'You d-do it. P-please.' Sniffing, Rachel wiped her face and blew her nose.

'OK.' Oliver moved back, giving the teenager some space. His voice was matter-of-fact and without judgement or drama. 'Rachel had a short relationship with a boy whom she thought cared about her. Now she fears she's pregnant and she's worried about telling her father.'

Chloe couldn't have been more surprised. Rachel was the very last person she would ever have imagined being in this difficult situation. Not just because she was the vicar's daughter, or even because she was shy, but because she had been so focused on her education and her dream to be a teacher. As for Rachel's father, Chloe knew how close he and Rachel were, especially since her mother had died some years ago, leaving them alone. Reverend Kenner was a kind-hearted, generous and understanding person, and Chloe knew he would stand by Rachel no matter what. Those were bridges that could

be crossed after they had determined whether the teenager *was* pregnant.

'First things first, then,' Chloe decided, following Oliver's no-nonsense approach. 'We'll do some checks to make sure, but what makes you believe you are pregnant? Have you done a home test, my love, or are you guessing because you've missed some periods?'

'Both,' Rachel admitted. The crying had stopped for now, but her voice sounded thick with tears.

Chloe gave her shoulders a reassuring squeeze. 'And how far along do you think you are, Rachel?'

'F-four months.' She hiccuped, smiling gratefully when Oliver crossed the room, returning with a cool glass of water for her. 'Thank you,' she whispered, taking a few sips. 'It only happened the once. He s-said it would be all right.'

Oliver looked resigned and Chloe smothered a sigh. How many times had they heard a tale like this one? Once was all it took. 'You don't think the father of the baby will stand by you?'

'I know he won't,' she scoffed, full of hurt and scorn.

'Can you tell us what happened?'

Rachel raised her head. Her blue eyes were red-rimmed and her lower lip trembled. 'I couldn't believe he had even noticed me. I should have known better. But he told me he cared, and he was nice to me when we went out a few times. I was stupidly flattered. I'd never had a boyfriend before. They tend not to notice me because I am shy and bookish, not to mention being the vicar's daughter,' she added with a touch of cynicism.

'But this boy did notice you?' Oliver encouraged.

'So I thought…at the time.' Rachel took another drink of water and drew in a ragged breath, fresh tears spilling from between her lashes and trickling down her pale cheeks. 'But it was all lies, just to get what he wanted. He didn't force me to have sex, I wanted to by then, but it wasn't what I expected.

I didn't enjoy it.' More tears slipped free. 'He wasn't caring at all. It really hurt.'

Chloe gave her another hug and waited until the girl calmed again. 'Who was it, Rachel?'

'G-Gary Lovelace.'

Somehow Chloe bit back a retort. Damn those Lovelaces. They were a well-known problem family in Penhally, the father in prison, not for the first time, and the mother left alone with several difficult children. Gary, the eldest at seventeen, was good-looking but lazy and always in trouble. Thrown out of school, he was now unemployed and following in his father's unsavoury footsteps. That Rachel had become one of Gary's targets was more than upsetting. Judging by Oliver's expression, he hadn't yet come into contact with the Lovelace family during his first weeks at the practice. Checking that Rachel wasn't watching, Chloe shook her head and mouthed to Oliver that she would explain later. His brief nod confirmed his understanding.

'Gary never came near me again,' Rachel continued, her shoulders shaking as she sobbed. 'I tried to talk to him, to tell him about the b-baby, and he just laughed. He said being with me had been a joke, payback to my father for his do-gooding ways.'

'Oh, Rachel,' Chloe soothed, seeing the murderous look on Oliver's face, knowing he would like a few minutes alone with wretched Gary Lovelace, just as she would.

They took some time to gentle Rachel through the necessary tests and health check, confirming the pregnancy.

'Have you given any thought to what you want to do?' Oliver asked gently as he sat back down at his desk.

'Not really.' Rachel bit her lip. 'For a while I tried to pretend none of it was happening. I have so many plans for my life. I desperately want to be a teacher. But how am I going to manage

with a baby? I do know that I can't get rid of it, no matter what the circumstances or why it's here.'

Drawing up another chair, Chloe sat beside her. 'We'll do everything we can to support you, Rachel, but I honestly think you need to tell your father.'

'Oh, but I can't!' the teenager all but wailed.

'Rachel, I agree with Chloe,' Oliver announced in support. 'I know it must be scary to face these things, but your father is a good man and he'll stand by you.'

Rachel ducked her head, her shoulders shaking. 'He'll be so disappointed in me. He's so wrapped up in his community work, I hardly see him any more.'

'He loves you dearly. And you love him.' Chloe rested a reassuring hand on Rachel's arm. Her thoughts strayed for a moment and she wondered what it must be like to have a good, caring father, as Rachel did, a man so different from her own. Suppressing a shiver, she pushed her memories away. 'You're going to need his support, Rachel. This isn't something you can hide from him.'

'I just don't know how to tell him.'

Chloe opened her mouth to make a promise, then closed it again and glanced at Oliver. He smiled, a glint in his eye, as if he knew what she had been about to say.

'Would you like Chloe and me to come home with you and help explain things to your father?' Oliver offered, and Chloe smiled at him in gratitude, knowing he had somehow been in tune with her train of thought.

'You'd do that?' Rachel looked from her to Oliver and back again. 'Really?'

'Of course. If you think it would make things easier for you.'

Looking young and scared, Rachel nodded. 'Yes, please.'

'All right.' Glancing at Oliver, Chloe rose to her feet. 'I'll just pop upstairs and fetch my things, then I'll be ready to go.'

Rachel clutched her hand before she could leave. 'Thank you. Thank you both, so much.'

'Do you think Rachel will be all right?'

Hearing the worry in Chloe's voice, Oliver reached for her hand and linked his fingers with hers. So much for his plans to have her to himself for the evening, he thought wryly, given the hour or more they had spent at the vicarage after driving Rachel home. Not that he begrudged helping the teenager smooth things over with her father, or answering their endless questions. He didn't. He was just impatient to have Chloe to himself as their time alone together was precious.

'Your judgement was perfect,' he reassured her now. 'Yes, Rachel's father was shocked and upset, but he's devoted to his daughter and it's obvious he's going to stand by her. The plan to involve the aunt and uncle who live in Plymouth, and who are experienced and regular foster-parents, sounds an excellent one.'

'It would be wonderful if they agree to help Rachel care for the baby when the time comes, while she continues her A levels and does her teacher training at Plymouth university,' she agreed, sounding more hopeful.

'Exactly. And in the meantime, Rachel has her father…and us.'

The smile Chloe bestowed on him turned his heart over and sucked the air out of his lungs. 'Yes. She does. Thank you for being so good with her.'

'It wasn't me, it was you.' It was no good. He couldn't wait another moment. Coming to a halt, he drew her to face him, his free hand cupping her cheek. Slowly, carefully, he placed an all-too-brief, all-too-chaste kiss on her lips. 'You're pretty special, Chloe MacKinnon.'

A becoming blush pinkened her cheeks. 'I am not.'

'Now, we could argue about that for the rest of the

night…and I'd most definitely win,' he teased, starting them walking again.

Back at her car, Chloe opened the doors. 'Do you want me to drop you at the surgery so you can collect your own car?'

'No, it's OK. I'm not on call tonight and I can easily walk to work in the morning.' He didn't intend to waste another second of time with Chloe. 'How about we pick up something to eat?'

'That sounds nice. But I have some chicken and things for a salad in the fridge. It won't take me long to put something together. If you'd like that?' she finished doubtfully.

Did she believe such a plan might be too homely for a supposed playboy like him? He'd soon disabuse her of that worry, but that she might think it brought a sting of disappointment. The shallowness and false impressions were things he had come to Penhally Bay to escape. It mattered to him that Chloe saw the real man.

'Perfect.' He stroked one finger along her bare forearm, feeling her shiver in reaction, seeing confusion and awareness darken her eyes. He smiled and withdrew his touch. 'Thank you for asking me. I'd love to spend some quiet time at home with you.'

As she turned away and started the engine, he noticed that her hand wasn't entirely steady and she sounded more than a touch breathless. 'OK.'

Back at her cottage in Fisherman's Row, Oliver insisted on helping her put the impromptu meal together. 'Tell me about Gary Lovelace,' he requested, smiling at Chloe's unladylike exclamation.

His smile faded, however, when he learned about the reputation of the family and the endless problems they seemed to cause.

'Eve Dwyer knows more about them than I do. She's a practice nurse who lives in the village, but she's currently on

an agency placement in Newquay until a vacancy becomes available back here,' Chloe explained, taking some tomatoes from the fridge and beginning to chop them. 'According to Eve, Tassie, the ten-year-old girl, is the only decent one in the Lovelace family. I don't know the whole story, but the mother, Amanda, just can't cope, and Eve is involved doing what she can to help Tassie. Gary is the main troublemaker and is leading his younger brothers astray. It sounds as if he played poor Rachel ruthlessly in one of his games. I can just imagine his sick thrill at getting the vicar's daughter in trouble.' The knife sliced through the juicy tomatoes with vigour and Oliver winced at the symbolism. 'I'd like a few moments to have my say to that boy.'

'Join the queue.'

Chloe made a murmur of agreement. 'I think most in Penhally feel the same way. Oh, blast,' she finished, setting down the knife and raising her finger to her mouth.

'Have you cut yourself?'

'It's nothing.'

Concerned, he took her hand, holding it under the cold tap for a few moments. 'Have you got any plasters?'

'In that drawer.' She pointed across the other side of the kitchen and he soon found what he needed. 'I'm getting as bad as Lauren in the clumsy stakes!'

'What is it with her?' he asked, moving back and carefully drying Chloe's cut finger on some clean absorbent kitchen roll, applying pressure to stem a fresh welling of blood.

'Lauren's always been accident-prone. Why?'

Oliver shrugged. 'I just noticed she doesn't judge distances well when she's reaching for something, and she trips over or walks into things that are in shadow.'

'You think there's something wrong?'

'Probably not if she's always been like it,' he soothed, regretting having caused Chloe any concern about her friend. But

something nagged at him about Lauren's clumsiness. Pushing the thought from his mind, he gently applied the plaster over Chloe's cut. As he finished, she went to pull her hand away, but he held on. 'Wait. I haven't kissed it better yet.'

'Oh!'

Cradling her left hand, pale and delicate-looking against his darker skin, he slowly raised it, enjoying the feel of her soft skin. He placed a feather-light kiss over the injured spot, lingering a moment, his gaze holding hers, before he released her.

'There we go, babe.'

'Right. Thanks.' She looked adorably flustered. Swallowing, she turned back to the counter. 'Um, did I tell you Avril Harvey might be well enough to bring her baby home on Friday?'

Oliver hid a smile at her unsubtle change of subject. 'You did. It's good news that mother and daughter are doing well. Her husband must be relieved.'

'Yes, he is.' Placing the cold chicken on plates, Chloe drizzled dressing over the fresh salad. 'And I gather you spoke with Nick.'

'He's agreed to take back his own cases, including the Trevellyans and the Fiddicks, but I'll handle any other antenatal work not on his list for the time being,' he clarified, taking the cutlery and a jug of iced water to the table.

'Thank you. Kate will be pleased. At least Nick is being civil to her at work again—if not friendly.'

Oliver would have liked to ask what the issue was about but he didn't want to intrude on a private matter between Kate and Nick, and he also didn't want to spend this time with Chloe talking about work. He steered the conversation back to more personal things and they discussed books and music, films and motorbikes while they ate their chicken salads with soft granary rolls warmed in the oven.

'That was great,' Oliver praised when they had finished.

'Would you like some ice cream?'

Carrying the plates back to the kitchen to wash them, Oliver smiled. Chloe and her sweet tooth! 'Please.'

After drying up, he leaned against the counter, watching as she spooned out two bowls of hazelnut meringue ice cream. The uniform she still wore failed to mask her womanly curves. She was so beautiful, with her clear skin, luxuriant dark hair and those stunning green eyes. His body tightened with desire. To resist reaching for her and spoiling all his good intentions to take things slowly and let Chloe set the pace, he walked into the cosy living room. Sitting on the sofa, he familiarised himself with her two rescue cats. He knew the ginger one who had lost an eye was called Cyclops, while the all-white cat with a black patch over one eye was called Pirate.

'How did you do that?' Chloe asked a few moments later, eyes wide with surprise as she watched him stroke the cats.

'Do what?'

'Make friends with Pirate. He's very wary of trusting people, especially men. He didn't have a very happy start in life.' Her words ended abruptly and shadows clouded her eyes, as if she realised that she could have been talking about her own past. Looking uncertain, she handed him a bowl and spoon. 'Here.'

'Thanks, babe.'

Before she could move away, Oliver caught her free hand and encouraged her to sit beside him on the sofa. Sensing her unease, he kept things light, giving her time to relax again. The ice cream was excellent and he said so.

'It's from the Trevellyans' herd of pedigree Guernseys,' Chloe told him, savouring every spoonful of her treat in a way that tightened his gut more by the second. Smiling, she set her empty bowl aside. 'Mike and Fran, along with Mike's brother and sister-in-law, Joe and Sarah, produce some wonderful

things. I love their blue cheese. They have a great farm shop and also sell at the weekly farmers' market.'

Oliver turned to face her, using the pad of one thumb to brush across her lips and the corner of her mouth. 'Stray ice cream,' he murmured, raising the thumb to his own mouth and sucking it.

'Oliver…'

He heard the uncertainty in her voice, but also the edge of arousal, which was matched by the darkening of her eyes. As much as he needed his next breath in order to survive, he *had* to kiss her, but he didn't want to rush her or push her too far too soon. Slowly, he leaned closer, giving her every opportunity to stop him, to move away, to say it was not what she wanted. Needing to touch her, but careful not to scare her by pulling her against him and wrapping his arms around her as he so longed to do, he closed one hand loosely around her wrist. He could feel the rapid beat of her pulse, and he loved the feel of her soft skin beneath the light caress of his fingertips. His gaze fixed on the lushness of her lips. Chloe swayed towards him. He closed the last of the distance, brushing his mouth lightly across hers, feeling and hearing her gasp as he used the tip of his tongue to clean any remaining ice cream from her skin. She was so sweet, so pure. Being with her felt so right. He longed for the day he could kiss and lick her all over.

'You taste delicious, Chloe.'

With a soft moan, she pressed her lips to his, unskilled but enthusiastic…not that he was complaining. Far from it. Used to obvious women who knew what they wanted and how to play the game, Chloe was a refreshing change. He felt protective of her. Everything about her was different. He had never felt for another woman as he did for Chloe. Had never been prepared to spend so long wooing a woman. And it had never been so important to gain someone's trust and friendship.

Oliver pulled back. Raising his free hand, his fingers traced the shape of her face. Moss-green eyes opened, fringed by sooty lashes, and she surprised him by following suit, her own fingers exploring the contours and textures of his face. Just that simple touch from her set him on fire. Catching her exploring hand, he brought it to his mouth, focusing his gaze on hers, watching her reactions as he teased her palm with his lips and tongue tip, nibbling the mound by her thumb with his teeth, making her moan.

'Oliver?'

'Mmm?' Feeling the tremor run through her, hearing the huskiness in her voice, he licked tiny circles in the centre of her palm with his tongue tip. 'You like that?'

'Yes. But…'

Responding to her nervousness, he stilled, seeing her flush and glance away. 'But?' he encouraged, his heart in his mouth as he waited to hear what she was going to say, hoping it wasn't to ask him to stop.

Chloe sucked in a ragged breath. She had never known feelings of desire and need before, and she found it hard to understand what was happening to her body. When Oliver touched her and kissed her, even looked at her with that melting dark gaze, she felt strange. Tingly and warm. Excited but nervous. Needy. He brushed his fingers over her skin and her flesh burned. He kissed her, lightly, briefly, and her body quivered in a way she had never experienced before. Deep inside she felt a knot of tension, a restlessness, an ache she wasn't sure how to assuage.

Oliver had never laughed at her or made her feel stupid. Amazingly, he still seemed to want her. And he was so patient, so gentle…undeniably sexy. Her past may have caused her to shut down that part of herself, but she didn't get to be a twenty-seven-year old midwife in the twenty-first century without understanding the mechanics of sex. She talked about it every

day without embarrassment. Doing anything in practice was another matter entirely, and now she had Oliver here, had discovered how much she was enjoying being with him, she didn't have a clue what to do. A self-deprecating smile curved her lips.

'Chloe?'

His husky voice drew her from her thoughts and she realised he was still waiting for her to answer his question. His fingers stroked the sensitive flesh along the inside of her forearm and she couldn't halt the quiver that rippled through her. Could she ask? Would he mind?

'I want—' Again her words halted and she cursed herself for being so nervous.

'Tell me what you want, Chloe.' He rested his hand along the side of her neck, his thumb caressing her skin, and she leaned into his touch, seeking more. 'Never be scared to say what you need. You can always ask me anything, tell me anything. OK?'

She nodded, then sucked in a deep breath. 'I like you kissing me,' she finally admitted, bringing a dimpled smile to his handsome face.

'It's going to get even better.'

'I don't know what to do. I want…' She bit her lip, seeing his gaze drop back to her mouth. She remembered how his had felt moving teasingly over hers. It wasn't enough. 'Will you show me how to kiss properly?'

'You can count on it, babe,' he promised roughly, something hot and primal flaring in his eyes, filling her with excited anticipation and a new burst of wariness as she couldn't entirely let go of the memories of her past.

Edging closer, she tentatively rested a hand on his shoulder. 'What would lesson one be?' She was surprised at her own boldness. Surprised, too, by the inner realisation that she was coming to trust Oliver to be careful with her, to not harm her.

'Chloe…' He tensed, and for a horrible moment she thought she had misread the situation and made a fool of herself. She went to pull back, but he stopped her. 'Wait.' His eyes were impossibly dark and she discovered with amazement that his hand was unsteady as he moved to brush some wayward strands of hair back from her face. 'Are you sure?'

'Yes.' Her answer was a bare whisper, a curious mix of certainty and uncertainty churning inside her.

'Slow and easy,' Oliver murmured, almost to himself, she thought. His tongue tip peeped out as he moistened his lips, and her stomach jolted in response, but he paused again, holding her gaze. 'Any time you want to stop, we stop. OK?'

Chloe nodded, sure she was going to burst with impatience if she didn't feel his mouth against hers again…now. And then he was moving, his hand slipping round to the back of her head, his fingers sinking into her hair, his head lowering to hers. She tried to breathe and found it was almost impossible. Her heart pounded in her chest. She felt his warmth, scented his enticing masculine aroma. Then his mouth met hers, firmer this time as it moved rhythmically, knowing and arousing.

She gasped as he nibbled her lower lip, then he gently sucked on it, and she thought she was going to melt. Her hand tightened on his shoulder as she tried to balance herself. The urge to draw him closer, to press herself against him was overwhelming, but he deftly took charge, retreating when she impatiently wanted to move on, keeping her on the edge, desire spiralling more and more, leaving her feeling heady and out of control.

When his tongue teased the seam of her lips, they instinctively parted for him. She momentarily froze as she tasted him, sweet but rawly male, for the first time. Clinging to him, a whimper escaped as he changed the angle, deepening the slow, thorough, strength-sapping kiss. The tip of his tongue stroked around the insides of her lips, teasing her, before dipping

inside, making her want more. But when her own tongue ventured forward to meet his, he retreated, denying her quest. Far, far too soon, the kiss was over. Chloe moaned a protest when she felt Oliver withdrawing from her, breaking contact, pulling back.

Confused, dazed, she finally managed to force her eyes open and focus on his face. His small smile was pure wickedness and gave another kick to her fluttering stomach, but she was gratified to hear that his own breathing was ragged. Realising how she was clutching him, one hand gripping the fabric of his shirt on his shoulder, the other having become entangled with his, their fingers locked together, she forced herself to relax her hold. She had no idea what to say. All she wanted to know was when they could do it again. It had been amazing.

Oliver's hand slid free of her hair, grazing across her cheek before his fingertips traced her mouth which felt swollen and sensitised from their kiss. His eyes were even darker than before, heated, watchful. She wondered what he was thinking, whether the kiss had meant anything at all to him…a kiss that had completely blown her away.

Before either of them could speak, the sound of her pager intruded on the intimate, electrically charged silence. To her regret, Oliver set her further away and released her. She felt bereft without his touch. Pulling herself together, knowing someone needed her, she fumbled for her pager with unsteady hands, anxiety gripping her when she saw who the urgent plea was from.

'What's wrong?' Oliver asked, as if reading her sudden tension.

'It's Angela Daniels. My mother-to-be on bed rest with placental abruption.' She met Oliver's dark, concerned gaze. 'She's haemorrhaging.'

CHAPTER FIVE

THE THREE hours since the call to Angela Daniels's emergency had passed in a blur. Chloe sat huddled in the passenger seat of the car and glanced across at Oliver, absorbing his strong, handsome profile in the shadows of the night. He had been a tower of strength. Having insisted on accompanying her, they had arrived at the house to find Angela's husband, Will, in a state of shock and panic, while Angela herself had collapsed on the bedroom floor and was in a bad way. Chloe had focused all her attention on Angela. Oliver had summoned the air ambulance, and then had taken charge of calming Will before coming to assist her in trying to stabilise Angela's deteriorating condition.

Seeing the woman on the floor and all that blood had brought back a terrible nightmare and for a moment Chloe had frozen, fearing that the outcome of this event would be the same as the one years ago. She had been scared that she wouldn't be good enough, competent enough. But thanks to Oliver, and the rapid dash by air ambulance to St Piran in the gathering dusk, both Angela and her baby were alive. For now. Chloe doubted whether either would have survived had they been forced to make the half-hour journey to hospital by road. As it was, the helicopter had delivered them there in minutes. Whether Angela would pull through after the amount of blood

she had lost, as well as crashing twice in Resus before her baby was delivered by Caesarean, remained to be seen. Having gone along in the helicopter, Chloe now felt exhausted after the drama of the evening, drained both physically and emotionally.

Walking out to the hospital waiting area, covered in blood and battered by distressing memories, she had been amazed, relieved and more grateful than she could say to find that Oliver had followed by car to St Piran and was waiting to collect her. He had taken one look at her face and said nothing at all. He'd just been there, which was what she had needed, the look in his dark eyes one of concern and compassionate understanding. When he had slipped an arm around her, she had stiffened momentarily, but then she'd remembered that this was Oliver, and for reasons she couldn't explain, she felt safe with him. Again, he had seemed to instinctively judge her reaction, and he'd kept her close as he'd led her to the car, without ever making her feel threatened or restrained.

They were nearly back in Penhally Bay now. All she wanted was to get home. Have a shower. Face her demons. After parking the car, Oliver locked up and followed her to her front door. It was nearly midnight and the street was almost deserted, just a few tourists walking along the seafront. At the end of the eastern wall of the harbour, on the promontory beyond the church, stood the lighthouse. In the darkness of night, its beam arced out across the water, warning of the dangerous rocks where the wreck of the *Corazon del Oro* lay, the infamous seventeenth-century Spanish treasure ship which still drew tourists and divers to Penhally. Turning their backs on the village, Oliver took the keys from her shaky fingers and guided her inside her cottage. Resting his hands on her shoulders, he ushered her towards the stairs.

'Up for a bath or shower, then into bed, babe,' he instructed, his voice soft but brooking no argument. 'I'll make you a drink.'

She felt she had to attempt a token protest. 'You don't have to do that.'

'I know. But I want to. Now go,' he finished, dropping a kiss on the top of her head.

Too tired and shaken to manage further disagreement, she walked slowly up the stairs, feeling Oliver's gaze on her all the way.

Oliver watched Chloe head upstairs, a frown of concern creasing his brow. He wasn't sure what but something had happened. Something other than the emergency with Angela Daniels. Chloe had been amazing with the terrified mother-to-be—calm, professional, reassuring and skilfully efficient—but there had been a shadow in her eyes, such inner pain it had rocked him. No way was he leaving her until he knew she was all right. And, hopefully, he could encourage her to talk it out, to share whatever burden she had carried tonight.

He headed for the kitchen and hunted out the necessary ingredients for hot chocolate. It wasn't the weather for it as the night was sultry after another sweltering July day, but Chloe needed something comforting. And as he couldn't take her to bed and love her into a state of pleasured oblivion, the hot chocolate would have to do for now. Waiting for the drink to heat, hearing the shower running upstairs, he leaned against the counter and thought back over the evening.

Chloe's innocent eagerness to experiment, her shy boldness in asking for what she wanted, had both delighted and encouraged him. And it had been increasingly difficult to keep a rein on his desire as he had kissed her—less chastely than before. She had been nervous but she had enjoyed it, and he had been careful to call a halt before she had been ready to stop, leaving her disappointed and wanting more. He couldn't wait for the day he could kiss her freely, letting loose all the passion and hunger he had for her. But it was too soon. That had been re-

inforced by the way Chloe had tensed when he had put his arm round her at the hospital. Apparently kissing was one thing, being held was something else entirely. Something he would have to work on gently now he knew of her anxiety. Now he had admitted to himself that, whatever his doubts, no way could he walk away from this woman. Chloe needed someone to coax her out of her inner prison. He wanted to be that man. To be good enough for her. He wanted to discover what it was that haunted her and to try to make it right.

Tonight wasn't the time to ask, but he did hope to learn what had affected her so deeply with Angela. By the time the hot chocolate was ready, the shower had stopped. He found a container of tiny marshmallows and dropped a couple into her mug to melt, then headed upstairs, unexpectedly meeting her emerging from the bathroom. He stopped, unable to move, scared he'd drop the drinks or go into meltdown like a marshmallow himself at the sight of her dressed only in a soft, figure-hugging, sleeveless vest top and a flimsy pair of cotton boxers that revealed the length of her legs.

Great legs. Not too slender, but shapely and well curved. He could imagine all too clearly how they would feel wrapped around him as he… No, he couldn't afford to think erotic thoughts right now. He dragged his gaze upwards, only to halt at the delectable view of her full, firm breasts. Oh, hell. To torment him even further, pebbled nipples pressed out the thin cotton fabric of her top. His mouth watered. His hands craved to be free to fill themselves with her tempting flesh. Instead, his fingers tightened round the mugs in desperation and he valiantly sought to ignore the clamour of his own body as it responded to the sight of hers.

He cleared his throat, his voice gruff. 'Bed.' For a moment he closed his eyes. If only he could join her there.

Chloe, apparently innocently unaware both of the image she presented and his reaction, complied without comment. He

followed her into her room, knowing he had to have taken leave of his senses…and that a cold shower was going to do little to stave off the state of his raging desire for Chloe tonight. Painfully aroused, he watched as she moved to the bed, sliding beneath the single light sheet that was her only covering for the heat of the summer night. Handing her the mugs, Oliver toed off his shoes. Propping himself next to her, on top of the sheet, he accepted his mug and then took her free hand in his, waiting for her to relax before even thinking of drawing her closer.

For a while they sipped their drinks in silence. He could feel her tension—it almost vibrated off her—and it was there in the tautness of her face reflected in the glow of the single lamp on the bedside chest next to her.

'You did a great job tonight, Chloe.'

Setting her empty mug aside, she shrugged. 'It was touch and go. I was grateful for your help. I know Angela wanted to be at home but, given the signs on her last scan, it may have been wiser had she stayed in hospital.'

'That was the consultant's call. Not yours.'

'Yes. I know.'

OK, so she wasn't blaming herself for the sudden deterioration in Angela's condition, which had been one of his fears. If that wasn't the issue, what was it that had upset her? Careful not to scare her by holding her down, he leaned across her to put his mug next to hers. Moving back into place, he slid an arm around her shoulders and drew her closer, cradling her head against his chest. With one hand he stroked the loose locks of her glossy, ebony hair.

Chloe held herself stiffly against him, but he didn't move, just waited, offering comfort, revelling in being able to hold her for the first time. The fact that she hadn't immediately pulled away was a major breakthrough. Even if she wasn't actively participating.

'Relax,' he murmured, keeping his voice low. His heart clenched when she drew in a ragged breath, only for it to shudder out of her. 'You're shaking. Don't you like being hugged?'

He thought she wasn't going to answer, but when she finally spoke, he had to strain to hear her whispered words. 'I'm not used to it.'

'I hope to be doing it a lot…if you'll let me,' he told her softly, careful to keep his hold loose so she didn't feel restrained.

He wanted answers but knew he had to be calm and patient, however frustrating it might be. Until he knew what had happened in her past, he didn't know what he was working against, what could alarm her or having her backing off. He felt like he was walking on eggshells.

'You are an incredible midwife, Chloe,' he praised, returning to their former conversation.

'Thank you.' He heard the surprise and pleasure in her voice at his compliment.

'I've worked with many people in different places who "do midwifery" but you are a proper midwife for all the right reasons and in all the right ways. I admire your desire to let things develop naturally for both mother and baby, using as little intervention as possible and putting the mother first. The care here is very patient-led and holistic. It's refreshing. And it's a real pleasure to work with you and Kate. You really believe in what you are doing. It's not just a job.'

'Not to me. I enjoy what I do.'

'It shows.' He continued stroking her hair. 'What made you choose midwifery as a career?' he asked, knowing when he felt her stiffen that he had touched something raw inside her. 'Chloe?'

A deep painful sigh escaped her but she didn't pull away.

He waited, hoping she was coming to trust him enough to confide in him about something important to her.

'I came home from school one day to find my mother lying on the floor, bleeding.'

The words cut through him and he smothered a groan as it dawned on him what seeing Angela must have meant to Chloe. 'Tonight made you remember.'

'Yes. For a moment I froze, and it was as if I was reliving it.' A tremor ran through her and he instinctively cuddled her closer. 'I was ten. My mother was six months pregnant.' Her voice was flat but the underlying emotion was obvious and Oliver ached for her. 'I called the ambulance but it seemed to take ages to come. The person on the phone told me what to do, and I tried…tried to keep calm and help. My mother survived, but it was hopeless for the baby.'

So she had become a midwife, needing to do all she could to help others as she hadn't been able to help her mother? 'It wasn't your fault, Chloe,' he reassured her, his voice rough.

'I couldn't do anything. I let my little brother die.' A sob of guilt was barely suppressed at her confession.

'Chloe, you were a child. You were not responsible, not to blame,' he insisted, wanting to ease the pain she had buried all this time and which had come back to haunt her after finding Angela in a similar situation. 'With the knowledge you now have, you know that even the best professional could not have saved your brother. Sometimes these things happen, a fluke of nature.'

'He killed him.'

Oliver hesitated, not sure if she knew what she was saying, or whether the trauma the ten-year-old child had endured had made her confused. 'Who did?' He moved his fingers under her hair to soothingly massage the back of her neck.

'My father.' She sucked in a ragged breath, still tense in his arms. 'He'd gone off on one of his rages. He hit her, she

fell…and he kicked her in the stomach. That's why she miscarried. He said he never wanted the baby anyway. He left her to bleed to death, wanted them both to die, and he went out fishing. If I hadn't come in and found her… Later he blamed me for saving her.'

'God, Chloe.'

This was the first real confidence she had ever shared with him. Instinctively he gathered her unprotesting form closer still, breathing in the fresh apple scent of her hair and skin. What she had told him was shocking enough, but the way she had recounted it, as if such violence at home had been nothing unusual, made him feel sick. What must it have been like to grow up in that kind of environment? And then it occurred to him that he may have unwittingly discovered the root of the problem. Was the dark spectre in Chloe's past her father? If so, it made sense that she never wanted to speak of her childhood. It seemed that every time he came closer to an answer, all he found were more questions.

Oliver couldn't bear the thought of Chloe being hurt in any way. Yet someone *had* hurt her. And the prime suspect was her father. It tore at him that she had been emotionally and physically dominated by someone who should have loved and cared for her. No wonder she didn't trust those emotions. Or men. Despite everything she had been through, she had survived and triumphed, at least in terms of her career, her friendships, her hobbies. But she had closed her mind and her heart to love, men and sex. He had yet to find out the full details of what had happened, but he desperately wanted to teach Chloe that she could trust him not to hurt her or control her, that it was safe to experience with him all the things she had banished from her life until now.

'I'm sorry,' she murmured, making him frown.

'There's nothing whatever for you to apologise for.'

She relaxed more against him. 'Thank you for being here this evening.'

'I'll always be here for you, babe.'

As he spoke the words, he knew how much he meant them. While part of him was scared of what he would be taking on by pursuing things with Chloe, he recognised that he was in too deep, his emotions and his desires ensnared, to back away and let her down. Lost in his own thoughts, he dropped a kiss on the top of her head, his free hand moving to whisper up and down her bare arm.

Something had happened to him the day he had met Chloe. Her friends said she was special and the more he came to know her the more he knew that was true. From the first moment he had been drawn to her. He thought back over the pleasant but meaningless relationships he had been involved in over the years. Most had been brief and temporarily satisfying, but had never filled a hidden void he had never allowed himself to acknowledge until recently, when the urge for a different and settled life had brought him back to Cornwall.

With Chloe, the smallest, most seemingly insignificant progress felt like the greatest victory of his life, and just being with her made him happy. Yes, he wanted to make love to her, but what he felt with Chloe, what he *needed* with her, was about so much more than sex. For the first time in his life he wanted a woman for more than a mutually enjoyable but short-lived affair. Chloe was more. So much more in every way. Yet the responsibility of all that meant weighed heavily on him. He didn't doubt his steadfastness. He wanted to settle down, to have a family of his own, and he knew that when he found the right woman, he would be loyal and faithful and loving, in for the long haul. *Was* Chloe the one? Could she see beyond the Fawkner name and the old reputation to the person he was inside?

With his mind occupied, Oliver held Chloe until she fell

asleep. Nothing would please him more than to slide under the sheet and stay with her all night, but he knew what small communities were like and he wasn't prepared to make her the subject of unwitting gossip. He wanted people here to see him for what he was now. If and when Chloe asked him to stay of her own free will…well, that was a different matter entirely. Regretfully, he eased away and slipped on his shoes. Making sure she was comfortable, he watched her sleep, his chest tight with longing and his growing feelings for her.

Turning away, he used the pad and pen Chloe kept on the bedside chest to write her a note. Leaving his message where she would find it when she woke up, he bent and kissed her lightly on the forehead before switching off the lamp and leaving her room. After checking that her cottage was secure, and that the two cats had fresh water, he took Chloe's spare keys, let himself out and locked the door after him.

He walked the short distance up Bridge Street to the flat Nick had arranged for him to rent until the end of July. Soon he would have to make more permanent plans. But even knowing he wasn't going to spend many of the few hours left of the night asleep, he couldn't think about anything now. His mind was too full of Chloe.

'I hear you had an eventful night,' Kate commented with a sympathetic smile when Chloe arrived at work the next morning.

'That's one way of putting it.' Yawning, Chloe sat down at her desk. 'Angela Daniels got out of bed to visit the bathroom, had a dizzy spell, fell to the floor and caused the already damaged placenta to rupture. It was only thanks to the air ambulance that we arrived at the hospital in time. I'm going to ring and see how she's doing.'

Kate gestured to the desk. 'Oliver left a message for you. He said he knew you would be worried, so he phoned St Piran

first thing. Angela had a stable night and she's doing well. The baby is fine. It's all in the note.'

'Thanks.'

Tears stung Chloe's eyes and she looked away from Kate's knowing gaze. Oliver had been wonderful the previous evening. She hadn't felt at all scared when he had held her. Far from it, actually. She had felt safe and secure, so much so that she had confided to him about her mother's miscarriage. Oliver had been so understanding and supportive. And then she had fallen asleep in his arms! She couldn't believe it. Despite only having a few hours of rest, she had awoken feeling relaxed...and strangely disappointed to find herself alone. Opening her eyes to the sun-filled room, her gaze had fallen at once on the note he had left for her.

I hope you slept well. I made sure all was safe and secure before I left—and both Cyclops and Pirate were fine. Thank you for sharing part of your past with me. I'm always here for you when you feel ready to tell me the rest. You are a terrific midwife and an amazing woman. I'll see you later, babe. Call me if you need anything. Love, Oliver x

It made her smile just thinking of him. He was nothing like she had first imagined him to be when he had joined the practice. Lauren and Kate were right. There was so much more to him than the sexy surfer image. He was smart and funny, kind and thoughtful...all qualities that came naturally to him. But always there was that underlying thread of intimacy, of warmth and caring, that made her feel both nervous and giddily excited.

Remembering how he had signed the note made her think of claiming the kiss he had left her. Which made her think of kissing in general. After her lesson the previous evening, when

he had shown her how magical and arousing it could be, how wonderful he tasted, how incredible he made her feel, she could kiss Oliver for ever. She felt hot and tingly just thinking about it and she couldn't wait to do it again. Funny that she had never been interested before, had never spent a second considering it, and now, thanks to a few hours and a couple of kisses with Oliver, she could think of little else.

Chloe worried that Oliver saw more than he should. He was frighteningly attuned to her, the only person who saw deeper than the surface veneer she had worn for more years than she could remember. She had a few close friends, including Kate, but it was Lauren who knew more about her than anyone. Yet even from her she kept back an awful lot. That Oliver saw the person inside both scared her witless and made her feel secure, cared for, warm.

Although Oliver was aware of her inexperience, and now knew about her mother losing the baby—and why—she was worried that if she did bring herself to confide more about the nature of her childhood, she would drive him away. He had said he wanted to know, that nothing would change how he felt, but she wasn't so sure. She was ashamed of her past, of her father and the legacy his brand of abuse had bestowed on her, and she wasn't sure she could handle the emotions that might flood out if she unlocked things she had kept hidden so deeply inside her for years.

'Oliver told me he'd sorted things out with Nick about the antenatal work.' Kate's comment drew her from her reverie. She looked up, saw her friend's brave smile, and knew the situation with Nick still hurt her. 'I think the compromise will suit everyone—and our Friday meetings should be more comfortable.'

'I hope so. Have you spoken to Nick?'

Kate averted her gaze. 'Only in passing—about work. That's an improvement, anyway.'

'Kate…'

'I know, my love. But Nick has to come round to things in his own time. He's not ready yet to consider letting Jem into his life.' She sighed, sipping her coffee. 'I know people see Nick as being aloof, and he can be, but I've know him a long time, known the losses and disappointments he has endured, the responsibilities he's shouldered. He finds it hard to address his feelings—to open himself up to more hurt and loss.'

Chloe nodded. It was true that there was much she didn't know about Nick, or his relationship with Kate. She just thought her friend deserved someone who would make her happy rather than bring her so much angst and uncertainty.

'How are things going with you and Oliver?' Kate asked, changing the subject.

Again Chloe fought a blush. 'OK.'

'You've been seeing him?'

'Yes.' Closing the file in front of her, Chloe folded her arms and leaned on the desk. 'He's been very patient, very kind. I've really enjoyed his company.'

'That's wonderful!' Kate smiled in delight, a twinkle in her eyes. 'He's a very genuine man. Not to mention an exceedingly handsome one!'

Chloe couldn't deny that, even if she did still wonder why he wanted to be with her when any number of women would be after him. She met Kate's gaze and felt warmth stain her cheeks. 'He kissed me.'

'And?'

'I liked it,' she admitted.

She had more than *liked* it. She was impatient to kiss him again. And, she realised, she was coming to more than *like* Oliver, too.

'I'm really pleased for you, Chloe. You deserve to find happiness.' Kate paused, her expression turning serious. 'If you feel something for Oliver, if he is awakening you to the things

you have missed and never known before, don't be too scared to go for it. He's a good man. He'll look after you.'

'That's what Lauren said. But what if he is just passing through? What if he leaves Penhally when his contract ends and I'm nothing but a diversion?' she asked, acknowledging and voicing her fears aloud for the first time.

'I believe Oliver is far more serious about you than that. Have you asked him why he came back to Cornwall?'

Chloe shook her head. 'No. We haven't discussed that.'

He had told her all about his childhood, funny tales from medical school, snippets about his London life, but he had never said if he was back in Cornwall for good. She was scared to ask, scared to be told he would be leaving soon.

'Don't lose this chance, my love. See Oliver for the man he is. Something special, some*one* special, doesn't come around very often.' Kate paused, a sadness and depth of experience in her eyes that made Chloe believe her friend was thinking about Nick. 'Ask yourself what you want most, how you feel when you are with him—and how you would feel if he *did* leave and you had never taken that risk.'

The phone rang then, announcing that her first patient had arrived, bringing an end to her conversation with her friend.

Kate gathered up her things. 'I'm off on my home visits. If I have time, I'll call in at the Trevellyans' farm. Fran was sounding down last time we spoke and I'd like to check up on her. My first visit is to Susan Fiddick.'

'I thought she went to the hospital yesterday.'

'She did…and the scan shows the baby is still breech. But she insisted on coming home, ignoring St Piran's advice for the Caesarean.' Kate looked concerned. 'I'm hoping to talk her round—and Nick said he would speak to her as well.'

Chloe offered a sympathetic smile. However natural they tried to keep the whole pregnancy and birthing process, sometimes it wasn't easy matching the woman's wishes with the

safest care. Not when nature intervened and things didn't go according to plan.

'Good luck. I hope everything works out.'

'Thanks.' Kate paused on her way to the door. 'I hope things work out for you, too. With Oliver. Think about what I said, my love.'

And think she did. Throughout a morning busy with appointments at the surgery, followed by an afternoon of home visits around the district, Oliver was never far from her mind. When she arrived back in Penhally, she was running late, with time only to sort out her paperwork and grab a quick snack before her evening duty at the well-woman clinic. Things were winding down in the surgery when she went in, but Sue was behind the reception desk and waved her across.

'Everything all right?' Chloe asked with a smile.

'It's been manic.' Looking stressed, Sue grimaced. 'Kate is in St Piran. She was called back out a couple of hours ago when Susan Fiddick went into labour. *Now* she's finally agreed to intervention.'

Chloe shook her head. Poor Kate. And poor Susan. 'What about Jem?'

'He's staying over with a school friend.' Sue shuffled her messages. 'Here we go. These are for you. And Oliver has asked you to see him before you head off for the clinic. He's finished his patient list.'

'OK.'

Chloe's stomach filled with butterflies and her heart skittered. Why did Oliver want to see her? Was it about work...or something else? Feeling breathless, she hurried up the stairs to drop off her things and put her patient files away, then headed back down to the consulting rooms. Oliver's door stood ajar and she paused a moment watching him, noting the uncharacteristic frown on his face as he studied some papers.

She tapped on the door. Their gazes met and she was sur-

prised at the serious expression in those devilish brown eyes. 'You wanted to see me?'

'Chloe, hi.' The smoky tones of Oliver's voice did curious things to her insides.

'Is there a problem?'

'Come in a minute.' He rose to his feet and crossed to meet her, closing the door before dropping a brief kiss on her lips. 'Take a seat.'

He perched on the edge of the desk near her and a very different fluttering, this time of unease, knotted her stomach. 'What's wrong?'

'It's about the Morrisons,' he told her.

'Baby Timmy?' She rubbed suddenly damp palms on her trousers. 'Oliver?'

A ragged sigh escaped. 'The results have come back from the heel-prick tests.'

'Already? And?'

'Chloe…the test for cystic fibrosis is positive.'

Her fingers clenched around the arms of the chair, her knuckles white as she battled away the unprofessional sting of tears. She knew she became too involved with her mums and their babies. She couldn't help it. Her job meant the world to her. Beth and Jason had tried so long for their baby and had suffered two miscarriages before little Timmy had come along this summer. There had been nothing in their history to suggest cystic fibrosis was a worry, no family incidence. But they must both be carriers and the one in four chance had hit them.

'Chloe?'

'Have you told them?' Somehow she forced the words out, pushing the image of Timmy from her mind.

'Not yet. And not without you. I didn't want you finding out alone, seeing the report left on your desk.' He paused, reaching out to take one of her hands in his. 'Maybe you would like it if we break the news to them together?'

His thoughtfulness touched her and she quelled a fresh threat of tears, unconsciously curling her fingers with his. 'Yes. Thank you. The test isn't conclusive,' she added, grasping at straws.

'No. There will be much to discuss with Beth and Jason, and further investigations to authenticate the results with a DNA test for the delta F508 gene. If CF *is* confirmed, we can bring Lauren in as soon as possible to help with physiotherapy needs.'

'Yes.' Chloe nodded, scarcely able to take it in.

'You know early diagnosis means much more successful treatment and longer life expectancy. We start treatment and physio before there is lung damage, and refer to a specialist CF centre.'

Knowing she wasn't going to hold on much longer, she withdrew her hand from his and rose unsteadily to her feet, unable to meet his all-seeing gaze. 'Thanks for the information. Let me know when to be available to see the Morrisons.'

She turned and walked to the door, one hand pressed to her lips to hold in the sob that fought to escape. Her free hand fumbled with the doorhandle. Just when she managed to open it, desperate to be alone, she felt Oliver behind her, his hand reaching past her to hold the door closed and then lock it. She froze.

'Chloe…'

The gentleness in that husky voice threatened to undo her. 'I need to go.'

'No. Come here, babe.'

Hands settled on her shoulders and turned her to face him. Her eyes widened in confusion, tears shimmering on her lashes, and she tried to blink them back, but a couple escaped, dropping onto her cheeks. He cupped her face, his thumbs brushing the moisture away. A shiver ran through her, and she

felt uncertain when he drew her closer, tucking her head against his chest with one hand, his other arm curling around her.

'Oliver?' She held herself stiffly in his embrace.

'You're upset. Take a few moments. Let me cuddle you.'

Being held like this should have spooked her—would have done had it been any man but Oliver. Wrapped in his embrace she felt both anxious yet safe. Beneath her cheek she could feel the steady, calming beat of his heart. To her surprise, she began to relax, allowing her hands to rest at his waist, her fingers feeling the play of muscle beneath firm flesh through the thin fabric of his shirt. Another few moments and instinct had her leaning into him, her arms sliding around him, while his free hand stroked her back, and his husky, whispered words soothed her. She had no idea how long they stayed that way, but gradually she felt calmer, stronger.

Although he relaxed his hold, Oliver didn't let her go, but he pulled back far enough to look down and meet her gaze.

Embarrassed, Chloe bit her lip. 'I'm sorry.'

'Never apologise for caring.'

'I'm a professional, I—'

'You are also human. And you're so good at your job because of how you feel about the mums and their babies.' Sincerity and understanding shone in his brown eyes. 'It's been a difficult couple of days. This news about Timmy, on top of the emergency with Angela, was bound to affect you. The day it doesn't is the day any of us should stop doing this job.'

Aware he was still holding her close, that her body was responding in unfamiliar ways, Chloe found the strength to place some much-needed distance between them. His nearness addled her senses and turned her brain to mush. She more than liked him, was coming to trust him, but she still felt nervous of all the new and unknown sensations assailing her.

'I'm OK now.'

Oliver frowned, unconvinced, but he allowed her to retreat. 'Are you sure?'

'Yes. Thanks.' She managed a smile, grateful for his support. 'I have to get ready for the well-woman clinic.'

Something she didn't recognise crossed his expression as he looked down at her. 'All right. I'll talk to you later, babe,' he promised, tucking a stray wisp of hair behind her ear, his fingers lingering for a moment before he dropped a firmer kiss on her mouth, then stepped back.

Chloe let herself out of the room, jogging up the stairs to her own office where she sank into her chair, one fist pressed against her chest. Why did she feel so strange? Yes, she was upset about the news of Timmy Morrison's positive test, but Oliver had been empathetic, helping her over the initial shock, and he had managed to ground her again. He had been right— she would have hated to find the report on her desk, cold, with no warning. Sharing it with him, knowing he cared too, had made it easier. What she found less easy to understand were the raging emotions she felt when she was with him, the way her body reacted when he touched her.

Somehow she got through the evening, grateful that the clinic was busy. Oliver had been right, it had been a hell of a week. He had understood her, but she knew she took things too personally with her mums and babies. She couldn't help it. She became so involved in them and their lives, but it often cost her emotionally. Unfortunately her duty at the clinic meant she couldn't see Oliver, or Lauren, that evening. She would have liked to have talked to someone, she reflected as she walked home along the harbour front to her cosy cottage in Fisherman's Row.

She liked her home. It was the first place she'd been able to call her own. The first place where she felt safe and settled. After greeting Pirate and Cyclops, she fed them, then went upstairs to shower, washing the stresses of the day away before

changing into a cool top and shorts. Padding back down to the kitchen, she made herself a sandwich, then sat in the living room with the patio doors open and tried to relax.

She went to bed early, but felt restless and edgy, as well as uncomfortably warm. Her window was open, but there was scant breeze off the harbour to ease the sultry night air. When the phone rang, startling her, she picked up the receiver, hoping none of her mums-to-be had a problem.

'Hello. Chloe MacKinnon.'

'Hi, babe.'

The throaty voice sent a prickle along her spine. 'O-Oliver! Is something wrong?' She propped herself up against the pillows, frowning with confusion.

'I wanted to see how you were feeling,' he explained. 'Did I wake you?'

'No, it's too hot to sleep. I can't stop thinking about little Timmy,' she admitted after a pause, something about the dark and the connection she felt with Oliver making it easier to admit her worries.

'I know. Sometimes things are horribly unfair.' She could tell by his voice that he genuinely cared. 'We'll find a time between our appointments tomorrow when we're both free and we'll talk to Beth and Jason together.'

'Thank you.'

They discussed the Morrisons a while longer, then moved away from work, talking comfortably about anything and everything. Chloe snuggled down, relaxing, a smile on her face as Oliver's husky voice and rumbly laugh sounded in her ear.

'I missed seeing you tonight,' he told her softly some time later.

Biting her lip, Chloe gripped the receiver tighter, affected by the warm intimacy of his voice, longing for him knotting her stomach. 'Me, too.'

'Yeah?' She heard the smile in his voice, thought she also

heard the faint rustle of a sheet. Was he in bed, too? The image made her even hotter. 'We'll do something nice together at the weekend.'

'I'd like that,' she agreed, all too quickly, the prospect of spending time with him bringing a rush of excited anticipation.

'Do you think you can sleep now?'

She *did* feel languorous and at ease. Just talking with him had done that for her. It had been what she had needed without even knowing it. But Oliver had. 'Yes, I think so. Thank you for ringing.'

'No problem. I've enjoyed it,' he assured her.

'Me, too.' So much so she didn't want it to end. 'Goodnight, Oliver.'

'Goodnight, babe. Sweet dreams. I'll see you in the morning.'

When the click sounded in her ear, indicating that Oliver had hung up, she felt stupidly alone, but also had a warm, fuzzy, fluttering inside her tummy.

She had only known him a few weeks, but she was discovering how much she had misjudged him at the beginning. He wasn't the fast-living playboy gossip had suggested, but an instinctive, fantastic doctor, and a man who treated her with infinite patience, caring and sensitivity. She had never once felt threatened, pressured or unsafe. And as for his kisses... Oh, my! Oliver made her feel things she had never felt before, stirred things inside her that she wasn't sure how to handle. She just knew she didn't want them to stop.

CHAPTER SIX

'I'M SORRY. I'd forgotten about today.' As Chloe glanced up, Oliver saw regret in her eyes. 'We don't have to stay long, but I promised Eloise I'd come by.'

'Don't worry about it, babe. We've had a great weekend...and I have plans for later,' he added, his voice dropping as he murmured in her ear, close enough to feel her quiver in response.

Dressed in denim shorts and a loose cotton shirt knotted at the waist, which left her midriff bare, Chloe looked good enough to eat. His hunger for her only increased with every passing day. Resting one hand at the small of her back, enjoying the feel of her super-soft skin under his palm, Oliver guided her along the beach towards the spot where the informal barbecue party was well under way.

'Remind me again what we're celebrating.'

Chloe smiled up at him. 'Eloise Hayden and Lachlan D'Ancey's engagement.'

'He's the local police chief?' Oliver asked, his gaze scanning the gathering for people he knew.

'He lives in Penhally but he's based at the station in Wadebridge,' Chloe explained. 'He met Eloise, an Australian forensic pathologist, when she came over last month to give a second opinion on a surfer's death.'

Oliver nodded. 'I heard the talk, but I've never met Lachlan or Eloise.'

'They are really nice. There's Eloise, talking to Kate. Shall we say hello?'

'Sure.'

As Chloe led the way, he reflected on the last couple of days. Friday had been difficult, meeting the Morrisons and breaking the news about Timmy's results. But Beth and Jason had been strong, drawing on the support and encouragement Chloe had given them. He knew better than anyone how the news had affected Chloe, and he was so proud of the care and compassion she offered to her patients. If the next round of tests confirmed that Timmy did have cystic fibrosis, he knew that the family would have first-class support from Chloe, Lauren and himself, as well as whatever specialist advice could be offered to them.

After the success of his Thursday night phone call, speaking to each other last thing before they went to sleep had become a habit. Even if he had only just parted from her, they still talked for a few moments on the phone. It was special…and increased even more his growing need to be with her, to not have to leave her at all.

On Saturday, after morning appointments, he and Chloe had gone for a ride on their motorbikes, then had spent the evening cuddled up at her cottage, watching a DVD, talking, drinking wine and doing a lot of kissing. They were winding up the intimacy and the passion, with deeper, hotter kisses and some tantalising, teasing touches. He made sure he left her wanting more, but it also drove him insane with his own desire for her. Faced with Chloe's increasing confidence and eagerness, it was becoming ever more difficult to keep a tight rein on his control. But he wanted her to be ready, to ask for what she wanted, to need him as much as he needed her.

He had never been that into kissing before. It was too

intimate somehow, and past relationships had been more about instant gratification—on both sides. The full joy of devoting time to kissing, without rush and pressure, had passed him by. Until now. He could kiss Chloe for hours, days…for ever. Knowing he had to take things slowly with her brought everything back to basics, to endless hours of foreplay and hot, sexy, incredibly intimate and satisfying kisses. It was like nothing he had ever known before. There was no demand to perform, no haste for fulfilment. The drawn-out loving, leading to the blossoming of Chloe's sensuality, was reward in itself. For now. If he felt this charged from kissing her, he'd probably combust when he finally made love to her.

Plans for today had changed when Chloe had remembered the beach barbecue. Oliver was just content to be with her, whatever the circumstances. It was a major advance that she was unconcerned at them being seen in public as a couple. He cared about her and he wanted people to know that. In staking his claim, he was taking a risk, putting himself on the line, but, as he discovered more every day, Chloe was worth it.

After being introduced to Eloise and talking with her, Kate and Chloe for a few minutes, Oliver accepted Eloise's invitation to head to the barbecue buffet table and fetch some refreshments for himself and Chloe.

'I'll catch up with you in a few minutes,' he promised, leaving her with her friends.

Chloe watched Oliver saunter with deceptive lazy grace across the sand towards the food table where Lachlan was in charge of the barbecue. Oliver looked equally stunning in the faded jeans and body-hugging T-shirt he wore today as he did in the smart clothes he wore for work. She turned back to find Kate and Eloise watching her, knowing smiles on their faces. Chloe fought a blush.

'Any improvements in the situation with Nick?' Eloise

asked, and, although thankful to have escaped questions about Oliver, Chloe felt sorry for Kate. Eloise was the only other person who knew about Jem's real father.

'Things have settled down a little at work.' Kate managed a smile, her gaze straying to Jem, who was playing beach cricket with some friends. 'But Nick isn't ready to face the reality that Jem is his son. I don't know if he ever will be.'

Chloe looked around the assembled group. 'Is Nick not here?'

'No.' Kate's disappointment was obvious. 'He's gone to France for the weekend with the twinning committee. They have meetings in Normandy.'

They chatted for a few moments, then other people claimed Eloise's attention. Kate went to talk with Lucy and Ben, smiling as she cuddled their baby daughter, Annabel, whom she had delivered in difficult circumstances last Christmas. Chloe wished her friend could be as content in all aspects of her life. Turning away, she looked for Oliver, seeing he was still at the food table, talking with Lachlan, Dragan and Melinda. As she headed in that direction, she bumped into Eve Dwyer.

'Hello, Chloe, good to see you.'

'And you, Eve. How are things?' she asked the older woman.

'I'm fine. A bit tired of the commute to Newquay,' she admitted. 'I'll be so glad when a practice nurse vacancy comes up here in Penhally.' Eve paused a moment, glancing around to check they were not being overheard. 'Is the rumour about Rachel Kenner and Gary Lovelace true?'

Frowning, Chloe nodded. 'I'm afraid so. Poor Rachel. Gary treated her terribly.'

'How is she coping?' Eve asked, ever the compassionate nurse.

'She was very frightened, especially about facing her

father,' Chloe admitted. 'But you know how lovely Reverend Kenner is, and how much he cares for Rachel.'

Eve nodded, looking distracted. 'So he's supporting her?'

'Very much so. I'm seeing her regularly and she's determined to keep the baby while still following her dream to be a teacher,' she told her, explaining about the aunt and uncle in Plymouth.

'That's good.'

Chloe caught an edge in Eve's tone and realised the other woman looked pale and strained. 'Eve, are you all right?'

'I'm fine.' Her gaze slid away and she redirected the conversation. 'That family. Tassie is the only one with any goodness in her.'

'She's lucky to have your care and support,' Chloe praised, admiring of all Eve was trying to do for the troubled young girl.

'Tassie's not had much of a start in life. But even at ten she plans to be different from the rest of them, to use her brains to make a good life for herself. I want to help her.'

Eve still looked troubled and again Chloe voiced her concern. 'Are you sure you're OK?'

'Don't worry, Chloe. Just a shadow from the past,' the older woman murmured cryptically.

Before Chloe could question her further, Oliver arrived at her side, handing her a plate of food and a drink. 'Here we go, babe.'

'Thanks.' Chloe introduced him to Eve. The other woman seemed eager to leave, so Chloe had to let the subject drop. 'That was strange.'

Distracted, Oliver took a bite of his fish. 'Hmm?'

'Nothing,' Chloe murmured, watching Eve walk away, her shoulders hunched as if she carried the weight of the world on them.

Her worry about Eve dissipated as she and Oliver talked while enjoying their food. Afterwards, they mingled for a short

time, and Chloe was supremely conscious of Oliver beside her, touching her, one hand at the hollow of her back, warm against her bare skin. The pad of his thumb dipped under the waistband of her shorts and traced tiny circles at the base of her spine…devastating, enticing, strength-sapping touches. So simple, yet so seductive. Her legs felt shaky and there was a heavy knot in her stomach. All she could think about was how wonderful the weekend had been, how amazing it was to kiss him, how much she wanted to be alone with him again, how special it had become that his voice on the phone was the last thing she had heard the last three nights before she had fallen asleep.

'Ready to leave, babe?'

His voice was a husky whisper in her ear, his warm breath fanning her skin, sending tingles of awareness through her whole body. She met his sinful dark gaze, feeling hotter than ever, and nodded. 'Yes.'

He bestowed on her the kind of smile that always made her breathless, then took her hand, linking their fingers. After they had said their goodbyes, he led her back along the harbour front to his car and before long they were heading out of town.

'Why are we here?' she asked a while later as Oliver pulled into the parking area at a watersports centre a short way along the coast from Penhally.

'Knowing how you love motorbikes, I have an adventure planned.'

'What kind of adventure?' Anxiety gnawed in the pit of her stomach.

He slanted her a glance, dark eyes sparkling with mischief. 'I'm taking you jet-skiing.'

Chloe forced herself to climb out of the car. Part of her wanted to experience the thrill of riding a jet-ski, but she couldn't get beyond the fear that gripped her. She didn't want her past to keep impinging on the rest of her life. In the time she had known Oliver she had faced many of her demons but…

Her footsteps slowed, her heart thudded under her ribs. What was she going to do? How could she tell Oliver?

It took a few seconds before Oliver realised that Chloe was no longer walking with him towards the beachfront office where they would pick up the two-seater jet-ski he had hired. If Chloe enjoyed their outing, he planned to buy her a present—a single-person machine like his so they could go out on the water together. He turned round, noting the paleness of her face, the shadow of fear in her wary green eyes. Hell. He'd done something wrong. Walking back, he took both her hands in his.

'What's happened?' He searched her gaze, could feel her shaking. 'Talk to me, babe. Tell me whatever it is you're feeling.'

'I—I'm scared. Of the water. I nearly drowned once.'

'Damn, I'm sorry.' Oliver wanted to kick himself. Instead, he wrapped her in a gentle hug. 'I had no idea.' He pulled back enough to look into her eyes, seeing the uncertainty in their green depths. 'I didn't mean to upset you.'

'You haven't. It's not you. It's *him*.'

Confused, he lightly rubbed his hands up and down her bare arms. 'Him?' he queried, trying to make sense of what she was saying.

'My father.'

When she exhaled a ragged breath, he led her off the path towards a low wall. Sitting next to her, he slipped an arm around her, his free hand holding one of hers. 'Tell me.'

'I was about seven. I never understood why he went into rages, what put sudden ideas in his head, but this day he marched me down to the rocks.' Her fingers tightened on his and Oliver cuddled her closer, feeling icy cold despite the heat of the day. 'I'd never swum. My mother was always scared and kept me away from the water, and though I loved the beach, I suppose her fear rubbed off on me. Something set my father

off, and he said I could learn to swim or drown.' Chloe's voice wavered. 'He picked me up and tossed me in. I did nearly drown. A couple of nearby fishermen pulled me out. They threatened to tell the police but my father insisted it had been an accident and persuaded them to keep quiet.'

Horrified, he didn't know what to say. 'God, Chloe.'

This was another confidence, another sign of her coming to trust him. But it was also another piece in the jigsaw that her father was responsible for the horrors of her childhood. He hated it that he had made her face something upsetting when all he had wanted was for her to have fun this weekend.

'I'll cancel the booking. We'll go somewhere else,' he reassured her, startled when she pushed against him, her head shaking vigorously.

'No!'

'Chloe?'

She turned to face him, grasping his hand. 'I don't want to let him win, Oliver. I don't want to be afraid of things because of him for the rest of my life. You've opened my eyes to so much recently. You must think I'm really stupid,' she finished on a whisper, ducking her head.

'That's the very last thing I think of you.' His heart swelled with emotion. He couldn't bear to imagine all she had been through, couldn't bear to consider what else her father had done to her, what more he still had to learn about her childhood. Holding her close, he stroked her hair. 'I think you're amazing. And I'm so proud of you. Whatever you want to do, I'm here to help. Whenever you're ready to talk, I'm here to listen.'

She raised her head, disbelief and hope warring in her eyes, a shaky smile hovering at her mouth, making him want to kiss her senseless. 'Oliver?'

'Yes, babe?' He cleared his throat, his voice sounding raw to his own ears.

'Take me jet-skiing.'

* * *

She had to be crazy. Chloe choked down a nervous laugh. Here she was in a wetsuit and impact buoyancy vest about to face one of her nightmares. She was frightened. But she trusted Oliver—and what she had told him was true. She didn't want to spend the rest of her life being afraid, didn't want what Lauren had said to be true…that her father was still ruling her life from the grave. Oliver had changed her. He gave her strength and courage. She *was* scared, had no idea where all this might lead, but she was tired of living in the shadows.

'Chloe, look at me.' He cupped her face, raising her gaze to his. 'You can change your mind at any time.'

Her chest was tight and she felt sick, but she shook her head. 'No.'

'We're going *on* the water, not *in* it. There is no way on this earth that I would let anything bad happen to you.'

'I know.' She believed it, believed the earnest sincerity in his dark eyes as they looked deeply into her own.

'Trust me.'

Feeling this was now about far more than a ride on jet-ski, she tentatively placed her hand in his, immediately feeling enveloped by his gentle strength. Oliver sat her in front of him, his arms reaching round her to the controls, cocooning her in his protective embrace.

'OK?'

She nodded, trying to bank down her fear of the water, relaxing a little as he nuzzled her, pressing a kiss to the sensitive hollow below her ear. They started slowly, easing out from the shore, the water calm and smooth along this stretch of coast, for which she was heartily thankful. It didn't take her long to get used to the unfamiliar motion and, to her surprise, she began to enjoy it, feeling incredibly safe with Oliver watching over her. After a while he drew to a halt and they drifted for a few moments, the engine idling as they looked back towards the spectacular Cornish coastline.

'All right, babe?'

Nodding, she glanced round to smile at him. 'I'm fine. Thank you.'

'Thank *you*—for trusting me.' Before she could say anything, his mouth met hers in a brief but stirring kiss. 'Ready to move on?'

Sensing that there was more than one meaning to his words, Chloe's insides fluttered in nervous excitement. 'Yes,' she told him shyly, earning herself the kind of dimpled smile that would have weakened her knees had she not already been sitting down.

'Faster?'

'Faster,' she agreed, feeling warm and giddy with happiness at his carefree laugh and the glowing approval in his eyes.

They had a fun time. It was exhilarating, riding with Oliver, the spray hitting their faces. And always she felt safe, never sensing he was taking risks or trying to play the macho show-off. When they finally arrived back at the shore, Oliver slipped off, holding her steady and seeing her gently onto dry land. Then she did something she had never done in her life. She spontaneously hugged him, carried along by pure joy and emotion, the freedom from a part of her past that had held her back for so long. Could she now move on and let go of the other chains that bound her?

She couldn't think about that now because Oliver's arms closed around her, holding her close, making her all too aware of him, the strength of his athletic body pressed against her, the heady masculine scent of him. Her smile faded at the look in his eyes…intense, fiery hunger. Then his head lowered, his mouth taking hers, and she surrendered to the magic of his kiss.

'I hear you're something of a hero.'

Oliver's eyes opened at Chloe's words and he smiled tiredly. 'Hardly.'

He'd been more relieved than ever to leave work, dash to the flat for a quick shower and change of clothes, and then meet up with Chloe to enjoy a quiet meal at her cottage before relaxing on the sofa. Taking her hand, he shifted his position and drew her towards him, encouraging her to sit on his lap facing him, her legs straddling his. Grateful to hold her close, he breathed in the familiar scent of sunshine and fresh, fruity apples, feeling settled and grounded with her in his arms. Meeting her gaze, he saw the concern in her green eyes as she brushed a wayward fall of hair back from his face before resting her hands on his shoulders. He was encouraged that she was so comfortable with the new intimacy that had continued to build after their passionate kiss following their jet ski outing several days ago.

'I came back from house calls—one of which was to Avril Harvey, by the way, and she and her daughter are doing fine— to hear you'd had a run-in with Nick,' she prompted.

'That's good news about the Harveys.' His smile faded as he answered the other part of her comment. 'As for Nick, he didn't want me going out to see Henry Ryall, said we'd wasted enough time on the man, that there was nothing wrong with him.'

Chloe frowned. 'That doesn't sound like Nick. He can be difficult, but he puts patients first.'

'I know.' Oliver's frown mirrored Chloe's. Nick was still stressed and edgy. Clearly the problem with Kate had not been resolved. 'Anyway, he's been out to Henry's farm more than once in the last month, so have Dragan and Adam. No one found anything wrong with him. They'd all done everything by the book, there was no reason to believe that Henry was sick,' he admitted, recalling Nick's arguments. 'The consensus of opinion was that Henry was sad and lonely having recently lost his wife…'

'But?' Chloe raised an eyebrow, as if knowing that wouldn't be good enough for him.

'I don't like writing people off too soon. And I can't explain it, but I had a hunch, one I didn't want to ignore. Nick told me to go and waste my time if I wanted to.'

'You were right, though, and it wasn't a waste of time.'

Sighing, Oliver ran his hands down her back to her delectable rear end, pulling her even closer. 'It was a complete fluke that I happened to be there at that precise moment.'

'Having weak tea and stale biscuits,' Chloe teased, making him smile. He'd discovered Henry's infamous idea of 'refreshments' for himself.

'I'd checked Henry's notes, spoken with Dragan, Adam and Nick. Henry had reported banging his head twice in the same place in the last weeks, but they'd all done the right examinations and checks and could find nothing wrong with him,' he explained, the fingers of one hand finding the gap between the waistband of her jeans and the bottom of her shirt, enjoying the feel of satiny skin. 'Henry couldn't give a clear picture of what was wrong, just that things weren't right, that he felt foggy and was still having headaches. He seemed fine when I first got there and I thought maybe Nick was right and I *was* wasting my time.'

'But you weren't?'

'No. I did the same examinations, checked the reaction of his pupils, tested if he could balance on one leg, walk in a straight line, could touch the end of his nose with one finger with his eyes shut…all the usual things. I monitored his blood pressure and gave him a thorough health check. There was no sign of anything amiss.'

Looking puzzled, Chloe sat back and watched him. 'So what happened?'

'We were talking, I was getting ready to leave, and suddenly Henry's mouth was moving but no sound was coming out.' He shook his head, still unable to believe the timing of it, wondering what would have happened had Henry been alone and

unable to raise help. 'One moment he was speaking normally, the next he was looking bemused and frightened, unable to speak.'

'Wow.' Chloe's eyes widened in amazement.

Smiling, Oliver tucked a strand of hair that had escaped her braid back behind her ear. 'It was bizarre. But something I'd seen before. I took Henry straight to hospital, they did a CT scan and discovered a small bleed in his brain. He's having an operation to repair it and he should make a good recovery.'

'How could that happen?'

'Sometimes with a head injury you can have this slow, tiny bleed that causes no outward symptoms for a time. It didn't help that Henry hit his head twice in the same place in rapid succession. No one could have known. There was nothing to alert Dragan, Adam or Nick, no reason for them to send Henry for further tests. As I said, it was pure chance I happened to be there.'

Chloe dropped a kiss on his mouth. 'I'm glad you were. Lucky Henry. And I hope Nick was apologetic.'

'He was.' Oliver couldn't resist giving her another kiss before he continued. 'To be fair, he waited on at the surgery for me to get back from St Piran to talk about it. That's why I was late.'

'I'm just glad Henry is going to be all right.'

'Me, too.' He raised his free hand to cup her face. 'And I'm glad to be here with you now.' Brushing the pad of his thumb along the fullness of her lower lip, he held her gaze. 'I desperately want to kiss you.'

Creamy cheeks turned rosy as she flushed and her voice was breathy. 'Do you?'

'Oh, yeah!'

'OK.' She smiled, sinking against him. Her mouth was honey sweet, so eager and welcoming that he was instantly lost, his control on the ragged edge.

* * *

Chloe couldn't hold back a whimper of needy excitement as she lost herself in the taste and feel and scent of Oliver. They had spent every moment they could together since the jet-ski outing on Sunday, and she was feeling closer to him than ever. As well as increasingly frustrated when he kept calling a halt to their ever more passionate kisses before she wanted to stop. She was impatient for more…she just wasn't sure what *more* was, or how to persuade Oliver she was ready. He was so determined to take things slowly. She was also unsure what all this meant to him. His care seemed genuine but, as she had mentioned to Kate, was she just a diversion for Oliver? Did he plan to stay in Penhally Bay?

Reluctantly, she pulled back from the kiss, seeing his eyes darken with a desire that matched her own. One of his hands rested on her back under her shirt, sending heat permeating throughout her body. She wanted his hand to move. Wanted to touch him, too. Licking her lips, noting the flare of response in his eyes as he watched her, she shifted even closer, bringing their bodies more intimately into contact. Her own eyes widened as she felt the undeniable evidence of his arousal. Nervous, not sure how far she wanted to take this, she hesitated.

'Chloe?' Oliver's voice was rough and she was excited that she could affect him like this.

'About my lessons.'

A smile dimpled his cheek but the hungry look in his eyes didn't fade. Her pulse skittered as his fingers began a gentle caress up and down her spine. 'You're not enjoying them?'

'You have to know I am,' she protested, unable to prevent herself pouting at him.

A chuckle rumbled from his chest. 'But?'

'I'm ready to move on to a more advanced level.'

'I see.' The fingers on her back stilled for a moment. 'And what do you expect the next steps to be?'

Faced with the intensity of his gaze and the smoky rough-
ness of his voice, some of her nerve deserted her. 'Um…I
don't know. I just feel…'

'Tell me what you feel, babe,' he encouraged when she
paused, distracting her by nibbling along her jaw.

'When you kiss me and touch me, I feel all tingly and achy
and heavy.' Long, thick lashes lifted and she couldn't look
away from the heat in his dark gaze. She swallowed, searching for the right words to explain. 'I don't want you to stop as
soon as you do. I need you to touch me in other places…and
I want to touch you, too.'

She was surprised and pleased when Oliver drew in a ragged
breath. 'Are you sure?'

'Yes.'

Sinking her fingers into the thickness of his hair, she kissed
him with eager enthusiasm, unable to get enough of him. When
he sucked on her tongue, drawing her into the hot sweetness
of his mouth, it was so erotic and inflaming that she feared she
would explode, need tightening almost painfully inside her.
Pulling back a few inches, she looked down, her fingers
shaking as she began to inch up the fabric of his T-shirt,
exposing a flat stomach with a narrow trail of dark hair disappearing beneath the waistband of his jeans. She pushed the
fabric higher, revealing a toned abdomen and broad
chest…olive-hued skin, supple flesh and hard muscle. Helping
her, he pulled the T-shirt over his head and for a moment she
just studied him, heat prickling along every nerve ending. He
was beautiful. There was no other word to describe the masculine perfection of him. Hesitating, she spotted the dark ring
encircling the bicep of his left arm.

'You have a tattoo.' Surprised, she investigated the narrow
barbed band usually hidden by his clothes.

'I have two,' he told her.

Her gaze met his, seeing the amused mischief in his dark brown eyes. 'Where's the other one?'

'You can look for it another time.'

Disappointed, she frowned at him. 'Why not now?'

'Because my control is finite,' he warned her with a wry smile. 'And if I'm going to survive this next lesson, no way are you going anywhere near my other tattoo.'

Her heart skittered, her mind racing as she wondered just where it was. 'Oliver…'

'No, babe. Not now.' He shifted as if uncomfortable, again making her aware of his arousal. 'Today we both keep above the waist.'

Capturing her wrists, his gaze holding hers, he slowly brought her hands to his chest. She closed her eyes, savouring her first feel of him, warm and firm, his heartbeat under her palm as rapid as her own. Her lack of expertise didn't appear to bother him and he deftly tutored her, guiding her natural responses, showing her how he liked her to touch him. Soaking up every new experience, each new texture, she brushed her fingertips over the brown orbs of his nipples, shocked at his reaction, his stifled groan, the way his body tightened.

'That feels good,' he told her huskily, allowing her to explore him at will but stopping her if she tried to dip below his waist. 'May I touch you, too?'

Her whole body quivered with nervous anticipation. Unable to find her voice, she nodded, her breath catching, her heart racing as Oliver slowly but surely undid the buttons of her shirt one by one. The backs of his fingers brushed against her skin, setting off little fires of sensation. Shaking, she bit her lip as he peeled the shirt away, sliding it down her arms, his breath catching as he took in the sight of her full breasts encased in a green lacy bra. She enjoyed wearing nice underwear. Like growing her hair long, it was a throwback to her youth and her father's control, a way of thumbing her nose at him, refusing

to let him dominate everything in her life. The clasp at her back parted with a deft flick of Oliver's fingers and a mix of embarrassment, fear and excitement churned inside her as he slowly drew the straps down her arms, baring her to his view.

'You're perfect, Chloe,' he praised, his voice raw.

As his fingertips skimmed her ribs, his tanned skin looked exotic against the creamy paleness of her own. He leaned in to kiss her, lingering a while before his lips grazed away from her mouth to trail down her throat. His hands rested on her sides, while her own grasped his shoulders as she trembled, on the brink of something she didn't understand, yearning for his touch, yet scared, too.

'Oliver?'

'Slow and easy, babe,' he whispered, his voice seductive, low and husky, his breath warm against her skin as he nibbled round her neck. She started as his tongue tip tickled across the web of faded scars that fanned down to her shoulder. 'Did your father do this?'

Too lost in the moment to care what else she was revealing, she curled into his touch. 'He hit me and I fell through a glass door,' she whispered, feeling the sudden tension in Oliver's body, aware of his simmering anger on her behalf before he took a steadying breath and gentled again.

He raised his head to meet her gaze. 'Chloe…'

'Let's not talk about it now.' She didn't want to spoil this incredible moment with thoughts of her father.

After a pause, Oliver nodded, but his reluctance was clear and she knew they would have to talk at some point. Later. Much later if she had her way. She sighed as his fingers began to whisper over her skin, feather-light touches that teased and tingled and aroused.

'Your skin is impossibly soft, so warm and silky and smooth,' he told her, his voice dropping to a husky murmur. 'I love touching you.'

When his thumbs brushed the undersides of her plump, firm breasts, Chloe thought she would never breathe again. Then his hands covered her flesh fully for the first time and she was sure she had died and gone to heaven. She bit back a cry, her fingers tensing on his shoulders as she instinctively arched to his touch.

'Any time you say stop, Chloe, I'll stop.'

His murmured promise registered through the hazy fog of pleasure enveloping her, but she didn't want him to stop. Not yet. Not when this felt so fantastic. She closed her eyes, unable to focus on anything but the caress of his hands as he shaped her, his questing fingertips exploring nipples that had peaked to hard, sensitive crests. A moan escaped. She had never known anything like this. She couldn't believe the way her body was reacting, the way her breasts felt fuller and heavier, every sensation spearing deep inside her. And when Oliver touched her with his lips, lightly lapping his warm tongue around and over one nipple before he gently suckled it inside his mouth, she jolted, her body writhing in his arms.

It was so overwhelming, so new and scary and wonderful, that she pulled back. 'Stop.' Her voice was thready, mixed with confusion and doubt, yearning and desire.

Oliver immediately withdrew, and at once she regretted that the word had been pulled from her so unexpectedly. She hadn't meant it. Not really. Now she missed his touch. Surprising them both, she wrapped her arms around him, relishing the closeness, the feel of her breasts pressed against his bare chest. His hands stroked her back and she buried her face against his neck, breathing in his masculine scent, unconsciously rubbing herself against him.

'Chloe.'

She ignored the warning in his rough voice. This felt so good. The ache she had told him about had intensified between

her legs and she instinctively pressed herself against his hardness. Oliver groaned and put some distance between them.

'Enough now, babe.' He sounded tense, and she raised her head to look at him, seeing colour flush across his cheekbones, strain etched on his handsome features.

'Did I do something wrong?'

'Hell, no. But this is getting out of hand. It's too soon for you…and my control is at breaking point.'

Intrigued, she smiled at him. 'Really?'

'You're wicked!'

That seemed not to be an entirely bad thing as he was laughing. However, he gently but firmly eased her away from him, drawing her shirt back up her arms, unsteady fingers re-fastening her buttons before he pulled his own T-shirt back over his head. All too soon, he was lifting her off his lap and rising to his feet.

'I think it's time I said goodnight.'

Chloe heard the regret in his voice, felt her own sense of sinking disappointment, but at the same time she knew he was right. She wasn't yet ready to ask him to stay. There were things she had to come to terms with inside herself before she was free to move on, and she knew she had to open her past to Oliver and confide in him before she took the irrevocable step of letting him take her to bed.

Her body alive and buzzing, she walked him to the door, enjoying a last, lingering, passionate kiss before he left. Sighing, Chloe locked the door and leaned back against it, unable to comprehend how her life had changed so drastically in the few short weeks since she had met Oliver.

Slipping into bed some time later, she lay back against the pillows, disinclined to pick up her book. Would Oliver ring as he had done every night for the last week? How did he really feel about her? She couldn't believe how selfless he was, how

patient, but was that because he really cared or because he wasn't that affected? He'd certainly felt aroused that evening.

Just thinking about touching him, having him touch her, sent a wave of heat washing through her. She couldn't help but wonder what it would be like to go further—what would have happened if she hadn't had a second of nervous panic at the overwhelming but unknown sensations and stopped him. Her body still tingled, her breasts felt sensitive, her blood was still zinging through her veins, but she felt a restless tension, an ache deep inside that needed fulfilment.

She was so lost in reliving all the new experiences that she jumped when the phone rang. Smiling, she snuggled down and reached for the receiver, welcoming the prospect of hearing Oliver's voice one more time before she slept.

CHAPTER SEVEN

'COME in young man. Let me get a look at you.'

Hiding a smile at the barked command, Oliver walked further into the neat-as-a-pin living room of the bungalow in Gull Close, situated on the other side of the river from Bridge Street. Occupied by Gertrude Stanbury, the former headmistress of the local school, whom everyone had warned him was a tyrant, the home had a small garden beyond the open patio doors and a view of the water. Squatting down to eye level with the rotund figure propped on the sofa by a multitude of pillows, and one each under the knees that were giving her such trouble, he introduced himself.

'Hello, Ms Stanbury, I'm Dr Oliver Fawkner, the new GP.'

'Humph.' One small arthritic hand shook his with a surprisingly strong grip, while sharp grey eyes gave him the once-over. 'You need a haircut. Never would have tolerated that in my school. But you're a handsome devil, I'll say that for you. Are you any good as a doctor?'

The smile he had been trying to hold in escaped. 'Thankfully my other patients seem to think so,' he told her, still holding her hand, taking immediately to the bullish, white-haired lady who was clearly sharp and shrewd and, if the glint in those eyes was anything to go by, had a sense of humour lurking under the surface bluster.

'I suppose you're here to prod and poke me about.'

'And to tell you that we've heard from the hospital. Your operation for the first knee replacement has been brought forward to the third week in September.' Gently, he checked the sixty-seven-year-old over, pleased to find her blood pressure was stable. Aside from the arthritis, which severely reduced her mobility and caused her considerable pain, she appeared to be in good health. 'The consultant will write to you directly but you can always call on us if you need more information or if there is anything else we can do.'

The tyrant-in-disguise patted his hand. 'I'll be glad to get it over and done with.'

'Once you are home again, Lauren Nightingale will be by to help you with some gentle physiotherapy to get you moving and mobile until they can do the second knee,' he explained, sitting back on his heels, taking his time to ensure there was nothing else she needed.

'Talented girl, Lauren,' she muttered with a frown. 'Always good at art. Clumsy as a mule, though, and as stubborn with it. No doubt she'll try and bully me.'

Oliver chuckled. Gertrude Stanbury was priceless! He could just imagine her as the formidable headmistress ruling her school with an iron hand and caring heart. 'Lauren's very good at her job. She'll take care of you. Now, is there anything else I can do for you today? How's the pain?'

'Bloody awful. How do you think?' the woman riposted, but her eyes gleamed and he could tell she was enjoying having someone to spar with.

'I'll take a look at the medications you're on and see if there's anything else that will make you more comfortable until the operation.' Taking both her hands in his, he turned them over and carefully inspected them. 'Any more deterioration with your hands or wrists?'

She looked down, hiding her eyes, but he'd seen the flash of worry in them. 'I get by.'

'We want you to do better than that. I'll investigate some alternative ideas to help you keep active and reduce the pain,' he promised, jotting himself a note on her file. He'd mention it to Lauren, too.

'Would you mind bringing me a fresh jug of chilled water?'

The question was polite but the command was clear nevertheless. 'No problem.' Smiling, Oliver rose to his feet and took the empty jug from the table nearby.

'My daily will have left another one ready in the fridge. Bring yourself a glass. I want to talk to you.'

Checking his watch, Oliver headed to the kitchen. He had one more house call to make before returning to the surgery for his afternoon list and a mountain of paperwork, and while lingering with Ms Stanbury would mean he'd miss lunch, he didn't mind. Having discovered from Lauren that the girls were planning a night out to see some film or other, he'd persuaded Chloe to go and enjoy herself. He'd miss her like crazy, but it was important that she keep up with her own circle of friends.

After last night, when he'd nearly lost the last remnants of his composure, it might be a good idea to cool things for an evening to give him a chance to shore up his ragged self-control before faced with the temptation of Chloe in the flesh again. At least he could look forward to talking with her on the phone at bedtime. Tomorrow, Friday, he was planning a beach picnic after work and the weekly midwifery meeting. If sea conditions permitted, he could do some surfing while Chloe relaxed, then they could eat and talk before he walked her home.

As for the weekend—well, he hoped to spend as much of that with her as possible. Whatever few lingering doubts remained about what he was getting into so soon after his

return to Cornwall, he had come too far with Chloe to back off now. Aside from the ever-present physical desire, he genuinely liked her. She made him happy. The more he knew her, the more he agreed with her friends that Chloe was special. When he was with her he felt contented, whole, alive and charged with a buzz of excitement he had never known with anyone else. And he wanted to help her overcome her past.

He took the full jug from the fridge, refilled the empty one and set it in the coolest part to chill before returning to the living room.

'Anything else I can get for you while I'm here, Ms Stanbury?' he asked, handing the woman a glass of fresh, cold water.

'Call me Gertie. And do sit down, young man.'

Oliver grinned. 'Thanks. What did you want to talk to me about?'

'Word has it you're seeing our Chloe.' Shrewd grey eyes assessed him. 'I hope you're not going to break her heart.'

'So do I, Gertie.' Given how deeply he was becoming involved and how little he knew of Chloe's own feelings, he hoped *she* wasn't going to break *his* heart either. Pushing the niggling concern aside, he met Gertie's gaze. 'I shall do everything I can to never hurt Chloe in any way at all.'

The elderly woman gave a satisfied nod. 'I can see you mean it. Good. What that girl needs is someone to cherish her.'

'Do you know Chloe from school?' he asked, unable to resist some gentle prying.

'Yes, indeed. She was a first-class student.' A reminiscent look crossed her face. 'I was so glad to discover how well she had done for herself. When she ran away…'

The words trailed off, but Oliver's gut tightened, his attention sharpening. 'Chloe ran away?'

Gertie paused for a moment, sipping her drink, and Oliver

remained silent, tense and unsettled as he waited, impatient to hear what the woman had to say.

'I don't think anyone knows the extent of what went on in that house.' A shiver ran through her and Oliver felt chilled as the implications of her words sank in. 'I so feared for that poor child. And for her mother. Chloe's father was an evil man.'

'Why did no one do anything?' It was a struggle to keep hold of his temper and disgust at the thought of Chloe and her mother being left at the hands of such a bully.

'There was never any evidence. Chloe's mother denied everything, refused to leave him…Chloe herself would never talk. Too scared to, I suppose, poor mite. Everyone was frightened of him. You hardly ever saw Chloe or her mother outside the house. Thank goodness she was allowed to attend school.' Gertrude shook her head sadly. 'I tried to take an interest in Chloe. As I said, she was an avid learner but she had such a reserve about her and she didn't mix well with people. She ran away when she was sixteen, after her exams. I never knew what happened to her, never expected to see her again, but she must have kept in touch with her mother somehow—I guess through Lauren.'

Sitting forward, Oliver rested his forearms on his knees. 'When did she come back to Penhally?'

'After her father died, four years ago, Chloe returned to care for her mother. She worked locally as a midwife, then joined the surgery when Dr Tremayne and his then partner, Dr Avanti, opened the practice here,' Gertie continued, setting her glass aside, grimacing as she shifted her arthritic body into a more comfortable position. 'When her mother died eighteen months ago, Chloe sold the old house and bought the cottage in Fisherman's Row. I don't know how many people had any inkling back then what went on behind closed doors, or what that girl's life was like. It was well hidden. But I saw enough every day at school to be concerned. My biggest regret is that,

although I tried, I couldn't make a difference. Now…well, I am just so proud of Chloe for making a success of herself. She deserves to be happy.'

Oliver felt sick to his stomach. He wanted to tear Chloe's father apart piece by piece—would have done had the man still been alive. Yet even from the grave her father cast a shadow over Chloe's life, one Oliver desperately wanted to lift. He needed Chloe to trust him enough to tell him about her childhood herself. Only then could he really reach her, really begin to help her put the past behind her.

Meeting Gertie's gaze, seeing the understanding in her eyes, he nodded. 'If it's in my power, Gertie, I shall do all I can to make sure Chloe's future is a happy one.'

'A quick word with everyone if I may,' Nick announced, standing in the staffroom doorway at the end of a busy Friday.

Oliver had left the surgery some while ago to answer an emergency call from the lifeguards to attend an injured tourist on the beach, so Chloe sat next to Lauren. She'd been looking forward to heading home as soon as the midwifery meeting was over, but had been delayed with Rachel Kenner. The girl had needed reassurance and Chloe was trying to see her as often as necessary to give support and advice. Her father was busy with arrangements for the annual remembrance service in August, when the town gathered by the lighthouse in memory of the victims of the storm that had claimed so many lives, Nick's father and brother and Kate's husband James among them.

Chloe was meant to be joining Oliver on the beach for a picnic supper. Given that she had been out with Lauren and Vicky yesterday evening, and today had been so hectic, she had hardly drawn breath, much less spoken with Oliver, she was more than eager to see him. Their phone conversation last

night had been brief. She had been late home and sleepy, while he had sounded distracted.

'As you know,' Nick said, his words diverting her from her thoughts, 'I went to France with the twinning committee last weekend. It was a successful visit and things are moving on apace. It should be an excellent venture for Penhally, especially for tourism and business connections. For our part, Dr Gabriel Devereux will be joining us in the practice for a year, and although he won't be able to begin work until autumn, he is coming over shortly for a couple of days to look around. I hope everyone will make him welcome.'

There was some general muttering, but it was one of the practice nurses, Gemma Johnson, who spoke up. 'Have you met him? Does he speak English?'

'His English is perfect—he did some of his training in London—and from all I've heard, he's a highly respected doctor,' Nick confirmed.

His gaze swept the room. Chloe noted how he looked longest at Kate, a frown creasing his brow, the shadows in his eyes suggesting he was still having problems coming to terms with the enormity of the news about her son Jeremiah. *His* son, as it turned out. Chloe wished for a happy ending for them all.

'Dr Devereux will stay with me on this visit, but I've agreed to help him find somewhere suitable to rent. I know Oliver has been comfortable in the flat in Bridge Street, but that was for the short term,' Nick continued, and the reality that Oliver's stay in Penhally might be over all too soon sent a shock wave of alarm and disappointment through Chloe's body. 'If anyone has any ideas, I'd welcome them.'

Lost in thought, Chloe was only half listening as Lauren spoke up. 'What about the Manor House?'

'Isn't that already occupied?' Nick queried.

'Only until the end of August,' Lauren confirmed. 'But the Bartons are going to be away in South Africa for another two

years at least. I've heard nothing about new tenants—and given that I live in the Gatehouse Cottage at the end of the drive and have the spare keys, the solicitor always keeps me informed and asks me to check on things. The house is comfortable, furnished, not too grand, and conveniently situated. I'm sure the Bartons would welcome renting it to someone on a year-long let. Especially someone recommended by and attached to the surgery. They are more interested in the quality of the tenant and keeping the house occupied and in good order than in asking for some ridiculously high rent.'

Nick offered a rare smile. 'Thank you, Lauren, that sounds excellent. Could you let me have the contact details for the solicitor? If it can be arranged, and if the house is available, perhaps Dr Devereux can have a look while he is here to see if it will suit his needs.'

'Yes, of course.' Frowning, Lauren reached for her bag and fumbled through it to find her address book. 'I have it here…somewhere.'

'Thank you, everyone,' Nick said. 'Have a good weekend.'

People rose and began filing out, talking among themselves, but Chloe waited for Lauren as they had planned to walk back to town together. Lauren was going to meet Vicky, while Chloe wanted a quick shower and to change her clothes before heading to the surfing beach to find Oliver…and the picnic he had promised her. She was so hungry.

When Lauren was finished and had handed over the details Nick wanted, Chloe turned to leave, noticing Kate ahead of her. She was about to say goodnight when Nick spoke again.

'I appreciate this, Lauren.' His took the piece of paper, then his voice firmed. 'Kate, could you wait a moment? I'd like to have a word.'

Chloe saw the shimmer of wariness in her friend's eyes. 'Yes, of course.'

Hesitating as Lauren went on ahead, Chloe searched Kate's

gaze, feeling anxious about leaving the older woman. But Kate smiled and nodded imperceptibly, and she had no option but to say goodnight and follow Lauren downstairs. Even so, her worry for Kate remained.

Kate tried to appear unconcerned as she was left alone with Nick. True, since she had confronted him at home he had been civil to her at work, but the tension remained between them. Their old friendship was in tatters. She tried so hard to understand him; despite all the upset, blame and guilt over Annabel's death, Kate was sure that Nick had still not properly grieved for his wife. On top of which he had found out about Jem in the worst of ways. She wished that had never happened but it was too late to turn back the clock. And however unrequited her love, however hopeless the situation seemed, she could not regret having Jem in her life.

Meeting Nick's watchful gaze, she struggled for composure. 'You wished to talk to me,' she prompted, managing to keep her voice level.

'Yes. Sit, please.' She did as she had been bidden, while Nick closed the door and then sat opposite her, looking uncomfortable. Legs braced, he rested his elbows on his knees, his hands clenched together. 'I know it's rich of me to ask, given the recent difficulties between us, but you have been—and still are—invaluable to the practice.'

'Thank you.'

The praise surprised her. Nick was not often one for compliments or showing his feelings. That he had said anything, especially in the current circumstances, created a warm glow inside her.

'I know your role here has changed since you ceased being practice manager and returned to midwifery, but I would be grateful if you would be among the few to come for lunch to

meet Dr Devereux, to welcome him and help familiarise him with the practice and Penhally Bay.'

Kate swallowed her disappointment. She should have known Nick would only want to talk with her about work. 'I see. Who else will be there?'

'I was thinking of asking Dragan and Melinda. As incomers themselves, and originally from continental Europe, I thought they might have useful insights for Gabriel.'

'That's a good idea,' she acknowledged, realising how hard Nick was trying, that this was important to him—and maybe important to them in the longer term.

'Lucy and Ben will be coming, too, and bringing baby Annabel. I want to keep it informal. A barbecue, I thought. I...' The hesitation lengthened, then he raised his head, the expression in his eyes cautious. 'I have no objection if you wish to bring Jeremiah.'

Kate sat back, considering his words. Jem would attend as *her* son—she read that much between the lines. Part of her was downhearted, and yet she recognised the gesture for what it was...an olive branch of sorts. She couldn't expect too much too soon. Maybe if Nick saw Jem again in a social setting he would feel some draw, even if he was far from ready to acknowledge him as his son. It was less than she had dreamed of, but more than she had hoped for in recent weeks, so she accepted the hesitant step forward.

'All right, Nick,' she agreed, calling herself all kinds of a fool for allowing his answering smile to affect her so. 'We'll be happy to come and meet Gabriel.'

'Thank you, Kate, I appreciate it. I'll let you know when I have confirmation for the date of his visit.'

The edge of relief in his tone and the slight relaxing of his tension gave her a measure of hope that the future might not be as bleak as she had feared.

* * *

Chloe sat on the sand, her arms around her drawn-up knees, enjoying the early evening sunshine and the sight of Oliver surfing. Even though the beach was still busy and many people were in the water, she had picked him out straight away, instinctively drawn to him, admiring even from this distance the impressive athleticism of his six-foot-three inch frame, his supple movements, as if he were at one with the waves. The swell wasn't huge, but he caught the next crest, twisting, turning, weaving, as he rode the board back towards the shore. Moments later, he was wading through the shallows, his board tucked under his arm, his free hand pushing wet strands of hair back from his face.

Oh, my! Chloe thought she might self-destruct at the sight of him. All that bare, olive-toned skin over lean muscle dotted with water droplets. Strong shoulders, broad chest with a light dusting of dark hair arrowing down in a narrow line over an impressive abdomen, tight belly and disappearing under the low-slung, body-moulding, wetsuit shorts he wore. And she could glimpse part of the second tattoo he had mentioned. Sited off-centre, below his navel and over his right hipbone, the top of it peeped out from the waistband of his shorts. She couldn't distinguish what it was but, remembering how wonderful it had been to touch him two nights ago, she was filled with an eagerness to explore that body further.

Finding it hard to draw breath, Chloe struggled to swallow the lump lodged in her throat when her gaze clashed with his. His lips parted, his eyes darkened, and then he smiled. That slow, sexy, dimpled smile that melted her insides and made her forget her own name. He dropped to his knees beside her and leaned in to give her a lingering kiss.

'Hi, babe.'

'Hi.' He smelt of sea, sun and man. 'Sorry I'm late. Nick held us all back to talk about the twinning thing. Some French

doctor is coming over in a few months to work in the practice for a year.'

'Yeah?'

Oliver seemed interested but not concerned, and her fertile imagination conjured up reasons why the arrival of an extra doctor didn't bother him. Was there room at the surgery for both Oliver and Gabriel? Was Oliver planning to extend his current contract? She had taken Kate's advice and had asked Oliver about his return to Cornwall. He'd been open about his desire for a different kind of life, his need to settle, and she had hoped that had meant he would stay in Penhally itself.

She had also been surprised and moved that someone as self-assured and confident as Oliver had insecurities about himself. He'd explained how he had never been able to shake off the playboy reputation or the family name, that people judged him on those rather than the person he was. She had felt guilty because that was exactly how she *had* first seen him. Now, though, she thought of him very differently. And she didn't want him to leave. As she was struggling with her confused emotions, her stomach gave an audible rumble and Oliver laughed, rising to his feet again.

'Sounds like I need to feed you,' he teased, picking up his surfboard. 'The car is nearby so I'll head back to fetch the cooler. I won't be long.'

'OK.'

Chloe watched him go, admiring his rear view. Sighing, she dropped her head on her knees, thinking about comments made by Vicky last night when they had been out at the cinema. Comments she had tried to banish from her mind.

'I sometimes wonder if there's any oestrogen in your body,' Vicky had complained.

Taken aback, Chloe had frowned. 'What do you mean?'

'Well, you have the scrumptious Oliver Fawkner panting after you and you don't seem to be doing anything about it.'

Warming to her theme—subtle and tactful not being in her vocabulary—Vicky had continued. 'A holiday fling is what you need. No commitment, just some fun with a guy who knows how to please a woman. I'll have him if you don't want him!'

Vicky's words upset her now as they had last night. Lauren had intervened, and had later taken her aside and told her to take no notice. 'You know what Vicky is like. She doesn't mean any harm. And she doesn't know about your past.'

Which was true, Chloe acknowledged now. But she didn't want to think of her relationship with Oliver as some meaningless fling, and she was worried because she had no idea how *he* viewed their time together. She had no experience of this kind of thing, her feelings were so new and beyond her understanding. After Vicky's comments, and now with the news that Gabriel Devereux would be coming from France, she couldn't shake off the nagging fear that Oliver might not be serious about her, that he might move on. From her if not from Penhally itself.

'What's wrong?'

She glanced up, so lost in thought she had been unaware of Oliver's return. 'Nothing,' she answered, managing a smile, her gaze travelling over him.

He had changed out of his wetsuit into ordinary cut-off denims, topped with a short-sleeved shirt he had left unbuttoned, allowing her a glimpse of his delectable torso. Her hands itched to explore him again. Her own body yearned to feel his touch. Setting the cooler down, he sat beside her and began taking out an impressive array of food. The sight of the treats in store, including some of the Trevellyans' blue cheese she loved so much, had her stomach rumbling again.

She felt a new edginess, a tension, as if they had reached a turning point. But maybe that was inside herself. She had decisions to make, and she knew if she wanted to take things further with Oliver she needed to face up to the demons that held her

back. For now, though, she would enjoy his company and their picnic…time enough later to gather the courage to confront her memories of her father and confide in Oliver about her past.

The picnic had been a success and, as always, he adored being with Chloe. But Oliver sensed something had been different this evening. At times she had seemed distracted, focused inward, and a flicker of unease gripped him as he followed her inside her cottage. For a moment she stood with her back to him, looking out of the window, and he couldn't wait any longer to hold her. Closing the distance between them, admiring her curves in her sleeveless, knee-length dress, he slid his arms around her waist, nuzzling her neck as he drew her back against him.

'You're very quiet tonight, babe.'

'Just a bit tired,' she murmured. 'It's been a hectic week.'

He frowned, not entirely convinced by her explanation. 'Do you want me to go home and let you get an early night?' He'd be disappointed to cut short his time with her but he didn't want her fatigued.

'No.' She wriggled in his hold, turning to face him, taking him by surprise when she wrapped her arms around his waist and buried her face against him, her words muffled. 'No, don't go.'

Something wasn't right. He tightened his hold, raising a hand to stroke her hair. 'I missed this last night.'

'Me, too.'

'But you had a good time?' he asked, hearing an edge in her voice.

She burrowed closer against him. 'It was fine.'

'Did someone upset you?'

'No.' He didn't believe her but she changed the subject before he could question her further. 'What have you been up to the last couple of days?'

'Actually, I met an old friend of yours,' he told her, deciding to take a chance and offer her an opening to confide in him.

She pulled back to look up at him. 'You did? Who?'

'Gertie.'

'Gertie?' He smiled because her puzzled frown looked so cute. 'I don't know a Gertie.'

'Gertrude Stanbury. Your old headmistress.'

This time he laughed aloud at the expression on Chloe's face, her eyes widening, her mouth dropping open in shock. 'You called Ms Stanbury *Gertie*?'

'She asked me to. She likes me.'

'Obviously.' Chloe shook her head, a genuine smile curving her mouth. 'You're such a charmer!'

He manufactured a hurt look. 'What did I do?'

'We were so in awe of her at school,' she reflected with a reminiscent frown. 'Her rule was law. Nothing got by her.'

'She did say I should have a haircut.'

'I bet!'

Oliver regarded her for a moment. 'You think I should cut my hair?'

'No!' She sounded horrified at the prospect, but his smile faded as her fingers sank into the thick strands at his nape, tightening his gut and increasing his arousal. 'I like it. I just meant Ms Stanbury would have commented on it.'

'Yeah, she had quite a bit to say for herself. She's very fond of you,' he added, watching her carefully, controlling his own emotions as he recalled the tale the older lady had related.

'Really?'

'Mmm.' He slipped his hand under the fall of her hair and trailed his fingers over her silken skin. 'She said she used to worry about you, and she's very proud of your success.'

A welter of emotions chased across Chloe's green eyes, ranging from alarm to surprise. 'Oh. What else did she say?'

she queried, a new wariness in her voice, her body tensing in his hold, her arms loosening from around him.

'She told me how much she regretted being unable to help you, to make a difference. She said you ran away.'

'Yes.' He could feel her trembling before she moved away from him, wrapping her arms around herself. 'No one could have helped.'

Oliver was disappointed by her withdrawal, even though he had expected it. He felt nervous himself, concerned he was pushing too fast, unsure how best to reach Chloe, to encourage her to open up to him, to convince her it was safe to do so. Taking her hand, he led her to the sofa and sat down. Expecting her to keep her distance, he was relieved and delighted when she cuddled up against him.

'My father was a controlling, vindictive man.' Oliver held his breath as Chloe began speaking, wanting to protect her, hoping he was strong enough to help her through what was to come. Cradling her head on his shoulder, he kissed the top of her head. 'I don't know what had turned him that way but he was paranoid about things and he had very set rules and ideas. Nothing was ever good enough for him. The slightest thing would send him into a rage.'

'Was he an alcoholic?'

Chloe shook her head, turning more fully into him, her hand resting on his chest. 'No. He didn't need a drink to lose his head, to be violent. He did have a drink, on occasion, but not often. He had cut my mother off from her family and friends before I was even born. I don't know if I have grandparents, cousins or anything.'

'Why did he do that?' he asked when she paused, his fingers tracing soothing circles on the back of her neck.

'Like I said, it was all about control. He brought her here when they married. She knew no one, wasn't allowed to work, to go out without him, to have friends. He had to be in charge

of her whole life. And mine when I came along,' she added, a quiver in her voice, and Oliver closed his eyes. 'He was physically, emotionally and verbally abusive to us both…sexually abusive to my mother.'

'But not to you?' He didn't know how to get the words past the painful lump in his throat.

'Not to me. Not that,' she confirmed softly.

A sigh of relief escaped him. Not that the rest she had suffered hadn't been bad enough. He couldn't bear to think of Chloe left vulnerable at the hands of such a man—her own father who was meant to protect and nurture her.

'What happened, Chloe?'

'Sometimes, when I was very young, if he decided I'd been bad, he'd lock me in a cupboard, often for hours. Later he'd use his fists,' she admitted, and he could hear the remembered fear and pain behind her words.

'Didn't your mother do anything to protect you?' Despite seeing cases during his medical career, knowing of people who stayed with their abusers for various reasons, he didn't have his rational doctor head on now because this was Chloe and personal, and he felt angry, aching for her. 'Why didn't she leave him?'

Chloe drew in a ragged breath and he shifted them so they were lying on the sofa and he could hold her more securely, keeping her close and safe. 'I feel bad, guilty, because I often hated her, blamed her for staying,' she whispered, and he felt the wetness of her tears seep through his shirt.

'No, babe,' he protested, desperate to get through to her, to not have her carry this burden. 'They were the adults. Their responsibility, their duty, was to care for you. You have nothing to feel guilty about.'

For a few moments a tense silence stretched, and he wondered if she would continue, if he could bear it if she did. They had not turned the light on and, as dusk fell, the darken-

ing room gave a privacy that appeared to encourage the sharing of secrets.

'I think my mother was so brainwashed, her self-esteem so shattered, that she couldn't think for herself,' Chloe explained, a deep sigh torn from her. 'She said she loved him once, that it was her duty as his wife, that you made allowances, even that he didn't mean it. But he *did* mean it.' Anger and disgust rang in her voice. 'He enjoyed the control, the domination. His rules were strict and often contradictory. He demanded that my mother remain feminine and attractive for him, yet he criticised her for her appearance and accused her of trying to attract other men.' Almost by instinct, she pressed closer, as if seeking the comfort he was so desperate to give her. 'Once I became a teenager, his anger focused more on me, on putting me down, challenging me, finding fault. Apart from school, I wasn't allowed out. I couldn't have friends, wear nice clothes, make-up, jewellery, perfume. Then he started accusing me of flaunting myself for men, of being just like my mother.'

'Chloe…' Her name escaped as a groan. He felt helpless, unable to imagine the horror her life had been, furious that no one had helped her. And he could see how the groundwork had been laid to make Chloe subconsciously deny her sexuality and attractiveness—and mistrust men. 'Was there no one you could talk to?'

She shook her head. 'He had us so well isolated. And he made it clear what he would do if we ever told anyone. I hated him, Oliver, and while I felt sorry for my mother, wanted to stop her pain, I began to hate her, too, to disrespect her for not doing anything. And yet I did nothing myself, was just as cowardly and afraid of him.'

'What could you have done on your own? As a child, with no adults stepping in to care for you?' he interjected. 'Don't blame yourself, babe, please. It is not your fault. And you most definitely were not, and are not, a coward.'

He understood now why Chloe's past experiences made her wary and cynical about relationships, love, marriage, men. Frightened, she had protected herself by shutting down the part of her that would allow desire, believing it led to hurt and abuse and the surrendering of control, of her very self. He was angry and distressed at all she had endured, but so proud of her for all she had achieved despite it, for having the courage to face it, to share it with him, to let him close to her. It was a special gift, one he hoped he deserved. To know he was the first man she had ever trusted, had ever allowed to kiss her, hold her, touch her... It was humbling, overwhelming.

'What happened to make you run away?' he asked, his voice rough with emotion.

He felt her shaking and hated himself for causing her any further upset. 'It was after my exams, when I was sixteen. I came home from school to find my father waiting for me. He started accusing me, saying he had seen me flirting with a man outside school. It was crazy. I'd spoken to a boy, a classmate, about an exam for less than a minute, but nothing I said made a difference. You didn't answer back, didn't challenge his perception of things. He...' She halted, her voice breaking.

'It's OK,' he whispered, his chest tight, stroking a hand up and down her back. 'You don't have to tell me.'

'I do. I need to.' Oliver's own shuddering breath mirrored hers. 'He said I had to be taught a lesson.' Again she paused and he heard the determination in her voice. Turning more onto his back he drew her on top of him and she pressed her face into his neck. 'It was Lauren who found me hiding after I had escaped his attack. She and Vicky were three years ahead of me at school, so not really friends with me then. Lauren had left home after A levels, moving away to do her physiotherapy training, but she was back for a week's break. I was a mess. Bleeding and bruised. He'd hacked all my hair off with scissors. I was so scared, so angry. I felt guilty leaving my

mother, but I knew I could never go back there. I believed he'd kill me one day.'

'God, Chloe.' Shocked, his hold tightened and he wished he had been around to protect her, get her away.

'Lauren took me to her home. Thankfully her parents were out. Did you know she was adopted?' she asked, confusing him for a moment with the change of tack.

'No,' he admitted, getting his head together. 'I didn't know that.'

'Anyway, Lauren cleaned my cuts, found me clothes, fed me, got part of the story out of me. Then she gave me money, made some phone calls to a women's group she knew through college, and found me a safe place to stay away from Penhally. No one else knew where I had gone, at least to begin with, but I kept in touch with Lauren and she passed on news about my mother. The shelter helped me get on my feet and find a way to pursue my goal to be a midwife. When I was twenty-three, I heard my father had died and that my mother needed someone. I came back and felt strangely detached. I couldn't grieve for him, and I had confused, ambivalent feelings for her, but I needed to do it, needed the closure. She was a broken woman, her mind was scattered, hardly in touch with reality. We never talked about what happened. As for Lauren, I returned the money eventually, but I can never repay her for all the rest.'

'You are amazing, babe. Strong and brave.'

'No, it was just self-preservation,' she refuted, sounding sad. 'Years ago my mother told me I'd understand one day. But I'm never going to be like her, never going to endure what she did for love.'

Her words troubled him and showed him the journey was not yet over. Cupping her face with his hands, he tried to see her in the darkness, to give her his strength, assure her he was sincere, prove to her she could trust him.

'That wasn't love, Chloe. Not at all. You're not your mother…and I'm not your father.'

She didn't answer, but neither did she pull away. Instead, she rested her head on his chest and slipped her arms around him. He held her long into the night, seeking guidance for the best way to help her, stunned, overcome, even more in awe and in love with her than he had been before she had trusted him with the horrors of her childhood.

For a moment he froze, realising what he had just admitted to himself. He hadn't planned it, hadn't expected it to happen so soon, but this whole gamut of feelings and emotions had grown and deepened over the weeks and he was in love with Chloe MacKinnon. In some ways he was stepping into the unknown as much as she was, experiencing all this for the first time. Chloe deserved the best—he prayed that could be him.

He felt the full weight of responsibility for what he was taking on, for what this meant for Chloe's sake. But he knew with an utter certainty and finality that he didn't just want to be the first man Chloe let into her life, he wanted to be the *only* man. The man to claim her heart, the man to cherish her and love her and care for her…for ever.

If only she would let him.

CHAPTER EIGHT

HER Saturday lunch-time parents' class over, Chloe headed out to Lauren's cottage and wandered around her studio, admiring the selection of paintings her friend had available for sale. When she decided which one she wanted, there would be the usual good-natured debate about the cost, an argument Chloe was always determined to win, convinced that Lauren should not make over-generous allowances for her friends. In truth, she loved all Lauren's work, but this painting had to be extra-special because it was for Oliver.

Just thinking about him made her warm and tingly, although thoughts of last night, of facing up to the past and revealing the full extent of her father's cruelty, had a chilling effect. Confiding in Oliver had been one of the most difficult things she had ever done. Not because of the way Oliver had reacted. Far from it. He had been wonderful…tender, considerate, protective and supportive. She had felt his anger, but it had been *for* her, and she had never felt anything but safe with him.

For the second time she had fallen asleep in his arms, only to wake up that morning to find herself alone on the sofa, a light throw tucked around her, a pillow under her head, and his note propped on the coffee-table, waiting for her. She'd had appointments and her lunchtime class, while Oliver had had morning

surgery, so she had not seen him yet today, but she had done a lot of thinking.

That he believed in her made her feel good, and thinking of his words, his reasoning, had helped ease her long-buried guilt. Oliver was right. None of it had been her fault. Her parents had failed in their responsibilities to protect her. She had not been to blame for her father's anger, or for her mother's choices. Sharing the burden with Oliver, telling him things she had never told anyone else, not even Lauren, had brought unexpected but welcome inner peace, a letting go. She refused to allow her father any more influence on the rest of her life.

She wanted to do something for Oliver to show her appreciation. Something tangible that, should he decide to leave, would be a reminder of her and his time in Penhally. That he might go was too painful to consider. It would soon be his birthday and, knowing how he admired Lauren's work and loved the local landscape, it had seemed an excellent idea to buy one of her paintings for him.

'Have you found something you like?' Lauren asked with a smile, handing her a glass of chilled fruit juice.

'Thanks.' Chloe took a sip of the drink and turned back to the array of work with a sigh. 'I love them all. That's the trouble.'

Her friend laughed. 'I appreciate the compliment. Perhaps I can help. Where are you going to hang it?'

'Actually, I'm not. It's a present…for Oliver,' she admitted, blushing.

'Really?' Lauren's smile widened. 'That's great. I'm so pleased for you, Chloe.'

'It's his birthday in two weeks' time. I want to thank him—and I want him to have something to remember me by if he leaves Penhally.'

Lauren frowned. 'What makes you think he might leave? He wants to settle down, doesn't he?'

'He's said nothing about staying or extending his contract at the surgery.' Sitting down, she confided her fears to her friend. 'I told him about Gabriel Devereux arriving from France in the autumn, and Oliver wasn't the least bothered.'

'The surgery is getting busier all the time, especially with the ongoing expansion, and could easily carry another GP or two. Lucy is still on maternity leave and Dragan will be cutting back when Melinda has the baby. And with Ed and Maddy having recently chosen hospital work in St Piran over staying at the practice, there is space for Oliver and, later, the French doctor for his year's placement. Probably another nurse, too. You're really smitten with Oliver, aren't you?' Lauren added after a pause, sitting beside her.

'Yes.' Chloe met her friend's gaze. 'But I don't know how he feels. And I have no experience of this sort of thing. What if Vicky's right and this is just a fling?'

Lauren waved her comment aside. 'Vicky was talking nonsense, and you know it. Oliver cares about you, Chloe. We can all see it. And we can all see the difference in you, too. You're blossoming. It's fantastic. You've come such a long way in the last days and weeks. Don't get cold feet and turn back now. Oliver is good for you—and believe me, you're good for him. See where it takes you, go for what you want.'

'I don't know.'

'Hasn't he shown you how different he is? Has he ever pressured you, scared you, tried to change or control you? Has he ever said he's leaving?'

Confused, Chloe shook her head. It was true that Oliver made her feel things she had never felt before. Things that were so unfamiliar but which made her heart beat with excitement and brought incredible sensations to her body. But he had always left the choice to her, had respected her, never pressured her.

'What I feel is scary...but exciting,' she admitted.

'You are learning what it is to be a woman, desired by a sexy

man. Go with it. You won't be sorry,' Lauren reassured. 'Now, about this picture.'

Dragging her thoughts back to the matter at hand, Chloe stood up again and returned her attention to the canvases. 'Are you trying some new techniques?' she asked, noting subtle differences in Lauren's new work compared with older pictures.

'No, why?'

Surprised at the edge in her friend's voice, Chloe glanced round and saw Lauren frowning in puzzlement, almost squinting as she looked at her own work. A flicker of unease curled inside her as she remembered Oliver's questions about Lauren's clumsiness. Could there really be something wrong? Unwilling to consider it, sure her friend would say something if there was a problem, Chloe tried to set her disquiet aside. Perhaps she was seeing changes in the paintings that weren't there.

'All the pictures are amazing, Lauren. But with Oliver's love of the sea, I'll settle on this magnificent coastal landscape,' she decided, preparing herself for the battle ahead to ensure Lauren took enough money for her work.

Oliver glanced at his watch and wondered when Chloe would be home. He hadn't seen her since last night, when leaving her had been almost impossible. After a busy morning at the surgery, when his clinic had overrun he had sent her a text and discovered she was with Lauren for the afternoon and having a meal with her friend. Having told her he was home if she wanted to meet up, all he could do was wait. And worry. He understood if she was feeling awkward after last night's talk about her past and knew she might need some space. But he wanted to be with her. He still felt shaky, sick about all she had suffered, angry that no one had helped her. Until Lauren. Thank goodness she had been there to help Chloe get away to safety.

As for his own feelings for Chloe, well, he loved and wanted

her more every day. He had never spent so much time with a woman, being with her, getting to know her, talking, laughing, dating…all without sex getting in the way. He enjoyed it. Because it was Chloe. Not that he didn't want to make love with her. He did. He ached for it, and hoped they'd get there before he expired from unfulfilled desire. In the meantime, everything about her fascinated him, and the slow build-up of the physical side of things was exciting, and heightened the anticipation.

That she had been completely unaware of her own body's needs and desires was amazing, but awakening her to intimacy, sharing the journey with her, was the most incredible experience of his life, an honour and a privilege. He could kiss and touch Chloe for ever. Yearned to do so. It took every atom of self-control he had not to rush things. Tamping down his desire, his urgent need to know her fully, wasn't easy, but he was determined to do this the right way for Chloe. Nothing had ever felt this special. Being with Chloe made his world a better place. He wanted her, needed her. But it was too soon to tell her. He had to be sure of her feelings for him and where she saw this going before he made a public commitment. What scared him was that Chloe might never be ready to consider love, marriage and for ever.

He paced the small rented flat. In a week or so he would have to vacate it, make long-term plans about work and living arrangements. He glanced at his watch again. Was Chloe home yet? Should he ring her? He dragged his fingers through his hair, caught in an agony of indecision yet knowing the next move had to be hers.

Chloe stored Oliver's painting safely in her spare room. The end of July was approaching. She hoped he would stay, but what would happen if he didn't? What if he left and she never experienced being with him in the fullest sense of the word

because she had been too cautious, too cowardly to take a chance and go for what she knew deep down inside she wanted?

She couldn't imagine ever feeling like this about anyone else. Couldn't imagine ever allowing any other man into her life the way she had Oliver. Because she trusted him. Trusted him not to be like her father, not to hurt her, control her, abuse her. If she gave herself to him now, he would take a big piece of her heart and soul if he left, and she might never be the same again. But if she didn't… Lauren was right. No one knew what tomorrow would bring. And she would forever regret this missed opportunity if she didn't take it.

Her mind made up, she left her cottage, thankful not to meet anyone as she made her way to Oliver's flat. As she walked, she thought over the last weeks, the way she had grown in confidence thanks to Oliver's patient care. They had progressed from those first awkward kisses, when she hadn't known what to do, to the most amazingly erotic, deep, drugging kisses that knocked her senseless and set every part of her aflame. Then there had been some pretty serious petting. She felt hot and achy just thinking about his touch…and being able to touch him.

Despite rejecting Vicky's ridiculous suggestion that she use Oliver for sexual experimentation, Chloe *was* curious. Not because she wanted to see what sex was like on a general level, and certainly not to use Oliver. She could never do that. This was about Oliver himself, the need she felt for him alone. The thought of stepping into the unknown was scary. But she had reached the point where she was even more scared *not* to explore where this might go. He had awakened a long-dormant part of her. It was him she wanted. Badly.

Shaking with nerves, she hesitated outside Oliver's door, reaching out to ring the door bell before her remaining courage deserted her. It was several moments before she heard the turn

of the lock, then the door opened. She had been on the point of walking away, losing her nerve, but she froze, her gaze locked on Oliver, taking in the wonder of the man. She looked slowly up long, tanned, muscled legs to where a pair of skimpy, faded denim shorts hung low on narrow hips, the button unfastened. The tattoo above one hip bone was almost fully visible—vaguely it registered that it depicted a lone wolf. Her gaze followed the narrow line of dark hair from the gaping waistband, up over a taut belly and toned abdomen to the perfectly contoured chest, broad and muscled, olive skin marked by the two orbs of bronze nipples.

Slowly, he raised one arm and braced it on the doorframe above his head, the rippling play of muscles and the tattoo banding his bicep distracting her. She felt hot enough to melt into a puddle at his feet and couldn't drag enough air into her lungs. Biting her lip, she forced her gaze to continue up the strong column of his throat, over a jaw darkened with the shadow of a day's stubble, past sensual lips that held such sexy promise until her gaze clashed with his. Rich brown eyes…sinful, liquid, hot with a sexual need that both excited and frightened her. Part of her wanted to run away. The rest of her couldn't move, wanted to stay, needed to touch him.

'Chloe?'

The smoky voice pushed her over the edge. She pressed a closed fist to her sternum, terrified she was going to hyperventilate or faint or do something equally embarrassing in front of him. A ragged breath shuddered through her.

'Is something wrong, babe?'

She shook her head, unable to speak. Vulnerable, she tried to convey through her eyes why she was here. Her heart rate doubled as awareness stilled him. His own eyes darkened impossibly, his expression growing hotter, even more intense, and his lips parted a fraction as if in silent invitation and anticipation. He said nothing, just lowered his arm and held out his

hand to her. Trembling so badly she could barely command her limbs to obey, she took a jerky step forward and placed her hand in his, sealing her fate.

Warm, strong fingers closed over hers and drew her inexorably closer. She stepped over the threshold, deafened by the pulse racing in her ears, drawn by the unquenchable ache deep inside her. The sound of the door closing and the lock turning was loud in the electrically charged silence.

Helpless to halt her own fate, Chloe surrendered herself to Oliver's will.

Oliver couldn't believe that Chloe was there, that she had come to him, but he read the need in her eyes, felt it in the quiver of her body, the frantic race of her pulse. He wanted her as he had wanted no other woman. He ached with it, ached to back her up to the wall and take her, hot, hard and desperately. But he knew he couldn't do that. Not yet. Somehow he had to get a grip on his raging desire before it slipped out of control. This was Chloe's first time, and whatever it cost him to wait and go slowly, so be it. He was going to make this as special and memorable an experience for her as he could. Later there would be time to indulge in more carnal, urgent pursuits and introduce her to exciting new experiences. Later…

Not yet breaking the silence between them, he led her to his bedroom, more than grateful he'd stocked up on some condoms in the last few days in the hope that this precious event might happen. His hand held hers lightly. He wanted her to join him of her own free will, to make the decision herself. As much as he longed to sweep her up in his arms and tumble her to his bed to ravish her, this had to be Chloe's choice. The first time had to be right. Halting beside the bed, he turned to face her, his heart swelling with affection at the look in her eyes…a sliver of fear mixed with determination and longing. He was so damn proud of her.

'Are you sure this is what you want, Chloe?'

'Y-yes. If you do.'

'Hell, yes!' Feeling raw with need, he gave a rough laugh at her doubt. 'You have no idea how badly. But this time is for you, babe. If I do anything you don't like, you tell me. If you want me to stop, you say so. OK?'

She gave a shaky nod. 'OK.'

Holding her gaze, he released her hand and slowly began to undo the buttons down the front of her sleeveless, multi-coloured sundress. 'First we'll get this off you. I can't wait to see you properly. You're so beautiful, Chloe. I want to touch you and taste you all over. You always remind me of food,' he murmured, brushing his lips along her neck.

'Food?'

'Mmm.' He nuzzled against her, his tongue flicking out to sample her skin. 'You smell like green apples, sunshine and fresh air. Your skin is as smooth and pure as cream, you taste as sweet as honey, and your mouth and nipples are as succulent and juicy as strawberries. I want to eat you all up, Chloe. I hunger for you…and it's never going to stop. You are a feast I shall never have my fill of.'

'Oliver…' Her whole body trembled in reaction to his words.

'Let me love you, babe. Let me show you how beautiful you are, how special desire and passion and making love will be between us.'

'Yes.'

She whimpered, swaying as he peeled off the dress and discarded it, revealing her lush curves covered only in lacy green bra and panties. Heat seared through him. His nostrils flared. Sucking in a strangled breath, he fought to keep to the plan, despite how painfully hard and desperate he was for her. To distract himself and boost her confidence, he kept talking to her, praising her. His own hand shook as he reached out and

traced the outline of her bra and panties with his fingertips, watching and feeling the reactions of her body to the light touches. A flush of arousal warmed soft, ivory skin, her nipples hardened further, pushing anxiously against their lace covering, and her flesh rippled as she shivered in anticipation.

'You can touch me, too, Chloe. I want you to. I long to feel your hands and mouth on me.'

Guiding her palms to his chest, he left her to explore, loving her curious, enthusiastic touch. He reached round to unfasten her bra, allowing the perfection of her breasts to spill free. Full, firm but soft, they filled his hands and she moaned as he shaped them, his thumbs grazing over the tight, swollen, sensitive peaks. She arched towards him in response, her own fingers tightening on his flesh.

Chloe was so reactive to his touch. He couldn't wait to turn weeks of seductive kisses and lingering foreplay into the real thing, imagining how much pleasure he could bring her. Resisting the temptation to linger on her breasts just yet, he knelt in front of her, sliding his hands down her hips. Leaning in, he nuzzled the rounded swell of her belly, breathing in the scent of her. His heart thudded, his body tightened even further. Slipping his hands round to cup her delicious rear, he held her still for him as he explored her navel with lips, teeth and tongue. She gasped, squirming against him, and he felt her legs giving way. Supporting her, he eased down her panties, his gaze drawn to ivory thighs and the apex of them where a triangle of soft dark curls arrowed down to the core of her femininity. He laid her gently on the bed, moving to straddle her, his knees on either side of hers, keeping his shorts on to maintain some much-needed distance so he remembered this was for Chloe and didn't end things in an instant.

Running his hands up her body, he leaned in to kiss her, giving her more of his weight, rubbing his chest across her breasts as she wrapped her arms around him and opened her

mouth for his tongue. She tasted amazing. His own body shook as her hands tentatively explored, her nails grazing down his spine, threatening to tip him over the edge. He drew back, concentrating on her needs.

His fingers stroked the baby-soft skin of her thighs, sliding higher as they parted for him, dipping between, feeling her heat and growing excitement. Her hold on him tightened and he drew his head back to watch her, seeing the flush of arousal colour her face, her eyes turning darker and unfocused. Her breaths were rapid and ragged as he brushed his fingers over her, getting her used to the sensations before touching her more intimately. She felt incredible. He sucked in his own shuddering breath, sure he was going up in flames at any moment.

'Oliver?'

She sounded uncertain at what she was feeling. 'Easy, babe,' he soothed, taking his time as he stroked her, slowly parting her and exploring deeper.

Unbelievable. She was perfect. So hot and wet. And tight, he discovered as he carefully pressed one finger inside her. He used the pad of his thumb to circle and brush across her sensitive clitoris, and she gasped, squirming on the bed, clutching at him.

'What…? What's happening?' she cried on a half-sob.

'Trust me. Just let go.' She was so close. He could feel it in her, the building tension. Carefully he added a second finger, rhythmically stroking inside her. 'Go with it, Chloe. Let it happen. It feels good, doesn't it?'

'Yes! Please…Oliver!'

She tightened round his fingers and he took her through the release that gripped her, holding her close, revelling in the cries pulled from her as she clung to him, surrendering to what he knew was the first climax she had ever experienced. He made sure to extend and prolong the sensations for her.

Watching her pleasure was incredible. It overwhelmed him to share this with her, to know he was the one to make her feel good, to make her come apart. And this was just the beginning.

Easing his fingers from her, he softly stroked her trembling thighs and belly, brushing kisses across her flushed face. 'You were amazing, babe. Did you like it?'

Nodding she turned her face into his neck, hiding, her arms wrapping around him.

'Don't be shy with me.' Her flesh quivered as his fingers resumed their light stroking along her inner thighs. 'What you felt that time will only get better, Chloe. When I use my mouth on you. When I'm inside you and we come together.'

He gave her a few moments to adjust, then he began kissing her again, building up her arousal a step at a time as he slowly inched his hands and his mouth down her body, worshipping every part of her, lingering at her breasts before continuing his journey to her navel, then lower. She froze in shock the first time he touched his mouth to her most intimate flesh but he gentled her through, encouraged by the responses of her body, her sighs and moans, the way she writhed beneath him.

'You can't,' she gasped in shocked delight.

Oliver chuckled. 'Sure I can.' And he proceeded to show her how.

'Oh, my! Oliver!'

'Come for me, babe.'

He kept her on the brink for as long as his patience could bear it, then led her over the edge to her second orgasm, this one even stronger and more intense than the first. He kept his tongue and fingers moving, intensifying her pleasure, loving her cries, her uninhibited responses. As after-shocks rippled through her, he released her long enough to shrug out of his shorts and reach for a condom, cursing his shaking fingers as he wrestled to extract it and roll it on. Soon it would be time.

He'd needed Chloe to climax a couple of times, wanted her

so hot and wet and needy that she would be relaxed and boneless enough that she wouldn't have the time to worry or the strength to tense herself when he took her virginity. He was scared. He'd never been anyone's first man before. He didn't want to hurt her, ever, and he'd tried everything he could think of to make it as easy and good for her as possible. She had been so tight to his fingers and he shook with wanting, imagining how it would feel to be inside her. Chloe was so special. Looking down at her, limp and replete, a small smile curving her mouth, he knew it was now or never.

Chloe struggled to open her eyes as she felt Oliver's hands lift her sated body and slide a pillow under her hips before gently setting her down again. Why was he doing that? His fingers stroked her thighs, parting them before he eased between them. She felt languid, every part of her quivering with sensation after the indescribable pleasure of two amazing orgasms, and it took an effort to raise her hand and run her fingers up his chest and throat to cup his jaw. The faint rasp of stubble was an exciting caress against her skin. His earthy male scent teased her, aroused her. Heat shimmered off him and she met his gaze, saw the intent in his eyes, the flare of colour across his cheek-bones.

Oh, help. It was going to happen.

She wanted it, but she was scared.

Before she could voice her concerns, his mouth took hers in a searing kiss, deep, seductive, hotter than hot, dragging her back into oblivion. Nothing existed but Oliver and the way he made her feel. His hands and mouth brought her back up to full arousal. Every part of her was straining for release. She felt achy, empty, needy. Oliver sank the fingers of one hand in her tousled hair, meeting her gaze, his eyes hot with desire. He moved to her and, as she felt him poised for the first time, her hands instinctively grasped at him.

'Relax, Chloe.' His voice was hoarse. He teased kisses at the corners of her mouth, his tongue tip stroking her bottom lip. 'Trust me.'

Slowly, so slowly, he entered her. She felt the unfamiliar pressure. It went on and on as he pressed inexorably forward. Her breaths were coming in ragged gasps, her heart racing madly. For a moment he paused, but before she could tense or prepare herself, he thrust forward again, firmer, surer. The pressure intensified and she felt a sense of impossible fullness. She'd expected pain but there was nothing more than a brief sting before it was gone.

He paused to allow her body to accommodate him. 'Are you OK, babe?'

'Yes,' she managed, although 'OK' didn't seem to cover the magnitude of it.

'Is it uncomfortable for you?'

She shook her head in response to his rough, raw question. The sensations were amazing. His own breathing was as ragged as her own, then he groaned, his hold tightening as he began to move, slowly at first, and then with less restraint. The friction was exquisite. Her fingers dug into the slick flesh of his back. Sobbing, unable to help herself, she curled around him, her hips rising to match his rhythm. Oh, this was fantastic! She loved it. She wanted more. And something far greater than she had already experienced was clamouring inside her.

'Please, Oliver. Please…'

Oliver fought to retain control, to go slowly, to make this first time right for Chloe. But it was impossible not to react to the way she responded so naturally and eagerly to him. Her scent, her taste, the feel of her opening to him, accepting him, welcoming him into her body, was the most incredible thing that had ever happened to him. She fitted him like a glove. He couldn't hold on. He had to move. As she clutched at him, pleaded with

him, instinctively wrapped her legs round him and tilted her hips, sending him deeper still, she pushed him over the edge. His control snapping, he upped the tempo, unable to hold back any more. He bound her to him and gave himself up to the unbelievable bliss of making love with Chloe MacKinnon. She met and matched his every demand, crying out as he took her higher and higher, until the moment when she flew with him over the precipice, freefalling into the abyss as her release triggered his and unimaginable pleasure shot him spiralling into oblivion.

He had no idea how long it was before he managed to stir himself. He had to be crushing her. Keeping her with him, he carefully rolled them to the side, tightening his hold, needing her close. Always. He had to be dead. He couldn't breathe, his heart was thundering far too fast. Only it wasn't enough. Not nearly enough. For ever wouldn't be enough with Chloe.

Forcing his eyes open, he focused on her flushed face, wiping tears from her cheeks with unsteady fingers. 'Chloe, are you all right? Did I hurt you?'

'No. Not at all. It was… Wow!' A naughty smile sparked her green eyes and curved lips rosy and swollen from his kisses. 'I loved it,' she admitted with a shy laugh. 'Can we do it again?'

Ecstatic, he hugged her and gave a mock groan. 'Help me. I've created an insatiable monster!'

'If you don't want to, I understand.'

'What?' Alerted by the uncertainty in her voice, he rolled them over, cupping her face in his hands. 'Not want to? Are you crazy?'

She bit her lip, making him want to do the same, to taste her again—all over. 'I just thought…'

'Thought once would be enough? Hell no, babe. You can unthink that idea. No way am I ever going to have my fill of you or do all the things I want to do with you.'

* * *

Oliver's words fired new arousal through a body she thought must surely be sated. She couldn't believe she was here with him, that after so many years of locking her sensual side away, Oliver had breezed into her life and so easily broken down the walls of her prison—a prison she hadn't even consciously known existed. Now she knew what she had been missing, but she also knew it wasn't sex per se, it was Oliver himself. She wanted to travel this erotic journey with him for ever.

'Don't move,' he instructed, rolling off her.

'I don't think I could.'

Smiling, she watched as he left the room, presumably to dispose of the condom. She closed her eyes, trying to capture and relive every moment of the most earth-shattering experience of her life. She felt exhilarated, charged, buzzing with life and yet deliciously spent. Her eyes opened as Oliver came back into the room, unselfconscious about his nakedness, and she revelled in being able to look at him in all his naked glory. He was superb. When he knelt on the bed beside her and she realised what he was going to do, she tensed, feeling embarrassed.

Leaning down, he kissed her. 'Let me take care of you, babe.'

A blush stained her cheeks and she closed her eyes, surrendering to him as he used a warm, wet flannel to wash between her thighs. She felt tender, but not unpleasantly so. When he had finished, he surprised her again, lifting her up in his arms and carrying her from the room.

'Where are we going?' she murmured, feeling sleepy.

'I've run a warm bath for you. I don't want you getting stiff and sore.'

Touched by his kindness, she pressed a kiss to his cheek. He set her on her feet beside the bath, cupping her face to bestow a lingering kiss on her lips.

'You get in. I won't be a minute, then I'll scrub your back!'

Smiling, Chloe pinned up her hair and lowered herself into the fragrant bubble bath, the lavender scent relaxing her. Oliver soon returned and slipped into the bath behind her, wrapping his arms around her. For a while she enjoyed resting back against his chest, disinclined to talk. As the water began to cool, Oliver reached for the sponge, soaped it, and took his time working over every inch of her.

'What about my turn?' she complained when he rose and stepped out of the bath.

'Next time.' The devilish smile he sent her as he shook out a towel and held it ready for her made her glow inside with renewed desire. 'I have other plans for you now.'

When he led her back to the bedroom, she discovered he had changed the sheets and again felt a mixture of embarrassment and gratitude for his thoughtfulness. She gasped as he tipped her onto the bed and followed her down, relishing the feeling that this was Oliver let off the leash of the self-control he had maintained until now. He was an amazing man and it hit her for the first time that she'd fallen completely in love with him. Oh, hell. But she didn't have time to fret over the revelation because Oliver's hands and mouth were taking her back to paradise.

In the days that followed, Chloe spent every spare moment she could with Oliver—and every night with him in his bed or hers. Lauren and Kate had noticed the difference in her, claiming she was glowing. Oliver was certainly teaching her things she had never imagined and she was a more than willing pupil, growing in confidence to explore his body and give him pleasure in return.

As she waited for her next patient to arrive, she couldn't stop her mind drifting to Oliver. It always did. The last month had changed her life. *Oliver* had changed her life. She had never been so happy, never felt so free, so content, so whole. But she

was scared it wouldn't last. Nothing had been said about any kind of future. Oliver had never discussed his plans for when this contract ended or his flat lease expired, and he had never said how he felt about her, not in words, even while he loved her with his body. She had been equally careful not to betray her own feelings for him, but she very much feared she had given Oliver more than her body. She had given him her heart and her soul.

She had gone into this with her eyes open, so she had no one to blame but herself for falling in love with him—something she had claimed she would never do. But until Oliver, she had never known what love was. Now she did…and it just might break her heart.

CHAPTER NINE

'A QUICK word before you go out to your house calls?'

Oliver looked round at Nick Tremayne's words, halting on his way towards the front entrance of the surgery. 'Of course.'

Puzzled by the request, wondering what Nick wanted to talk to him about, Oliver followed the older man to his consulting room and closed the door.

'Sit down, Oliver.' The senior partner's relaxed manner and rare smile eased Oliver's wariness. 'You're probably aware there are changes afoot in the practice,' Nick began. 'My daughter, Lucy, headed up the plans for expansion before she went on maternity leave. When the alterations are finished we'll have a broader capability to treat minor injuries, plus there will be X-ray facilities and a plaster room. Various other services will be more in-house, including Lauren having a better physiotherapy space to see more patients here.'

'Everyone's very excited about the new facilities,' Oliver agreed.

'Good, good. The workload is continuing to increase for us all, and not just during the tourist season. Initially, your contract was temporary, but your experience suits our needs and will benefit us even more when the expansion is complete.' The older man paused, his gaze assessing as he sat forward and rested his elbows on the desk. 'How would you feel about

staying on in Penhally Bay? You've fitted in here, the patients like and trust you, and the staff find you a pleasure to work with. Lucy may not come back to work full time for some time, and Dragan would like to be flexible and reduce his hours when Melinda has their baby. Even with Gabriel Devereux coming over from France for a year in the autumn, we'll need another doctor. We've discussed things, Oliver—myself, Lucy, Dragan and Adam—and we'd like to offer you a full-time post and a junior partnership.'

He felt dumbstruck! When he had first decided to come back to Cornwall, he had hoped to settle down, and the opportunity to stay on permanently suited him down to the ground. Possibilities ran through his mind. Part of him wanted to accept Nick's offer on the spot, knowing he had finally found a place to call home, one that offered the kind of community-based medicine he loved. But another part of him urged patience and caution. He needed to share this with Chloe, to have some sense of what the future held in store for them, and if he had a chance with her long term. If Chloe didn't want him, he wasn't sure he could stay here, to see her, work with her but not touch her and be with her.

For the first time in his life he was in love. He had laid himself bare to Chloe, was totally vulnerable in a way he had never been before. Physically, things just got better and better between them, and she was an avid learner, eager and enthusiastic to experience everything. Emotionally, he felt on shaky ground. For him it was serious. But he had no clue about Chloe's feelings. She had never spoken of them, had never asked about his own. Neither had she asked him about his plans. So many times he had wanted to tell her he loved her but he had held back, scared of her rejection.

Old hurts and doubts nagged at him and he couldn't help but remember the way he had been used so often before. He had never been so uncertain, or so dependent on another person

for his happiness, his very existence. Did Chloe see beyond the playboy image to the person he was inside? Could she get over her past and come to love him? He needed answers before he could give Nick a decision.

'Think about it and let me know in a few days,' Nick said now, clearly taking his silence for reticence.

'I will. Thank you, Nick. I'm overwhelmed—but delighted.' Rising to his feet, he shook his boss's hand. 'I just need to be sure of a couple of things before saying one hundred per cent yes.'

A knowing glint appeared in Nick's eyes. 'I understand.'

As he headed out to complete his house calls, Oliver already knew what he wanted. To accept the position, to put down roots in Penhally and make a life with Chloe. To love her, marry her and cherish her. For ever. What would she say when he told her he loved her? Could she care for him as he did for her? Or was he making a mistake in pinning all hopes for the future on her?

'How did the barbecue go?' Chloe asked when she met up with Kate for a quick cup of tea before the final antenatal clinic of the day began.

'It was good.' Kate smiled, helping herself to one of Hazel's home-made biscuits. 'I have to say that Gabriel Devereux, the French doctor, is absolutely *gorgeous*! Dark skin, dark hair, dark eyes. Charm personified. And that accent!'

Chloe smiled. 'Sounds like you're smitten.'

'Unfortunately I'm fifteen or twenty years too old.' Kate chuckled. 'Lucky Lauren, though, having him as a neighbour when he arrives for his year's placement. He loved the Manor House and Nick is making the arrangements for the long-term let.'

'That's good. And what about Jem? Was everything all right?' Chloe asked, concealing how much she had worried about Kate and her son attending Nick's welcoming event for the French GP.

Sitting back in her chair, propping her feet up, Kate looked thoughtful. 'It actually went well. Nick has always known Jem, of course, just not that he's his father,' she explained, lowering her voice even though the staffroom was empty. 'At one point Jem fell over, grazing his knee, and it was Nick who took him indoors to bathe it. I was desperate to go, too, but thought it best to leave well alone. Neither of them said anything but, with at least four other doctors in attendance, I took it as a step forward that Nick wanted to do it himself.'

Chloe hoped Kate was right. It would be good if Nick did come round. Even if he decided not to publicly claim Jem as his son, he could have a friendly relationship with the boy, be an influence in his life as a role model. And she knew Kate would be happy if her own friendship with Nick could return to its former footing, even if her love ultimately remained un-requited.

'How about you and the lovely Oliver?' Kate queried, her eyes twinkling.

Fighting a blush, Chloe thought again of how special he was, how her life had changed because of him. 'It's good. More than good.'

'Why do I sense a but?' Kate sat forward again, a frown creasing her brow. 'What's worrying you, my love?'

'We've just not talked about anything. You know, whatever this is between us. Not beyond taking things a day at a time. I'm terrified he'll move on soon and this brief interlude will be over,' she admitted, her stomach tightening.

'Oh, Chloe. Perhaps Oliver is being cautious because he knows what a big step this is for you,' she suggested, and it was Chloe's turn to frown as she considered her friend's words. 'This is new for him, too. Maybe he needs to hear how *you* feel.'

Chloe thought over what Kate had said as she returned to her room and prepared to greet her first patient of the afternoon.

If only she had some idea how Oliver felt about her, if he planned to stay, she might have the courage to take that extra step and confess how much she loved him.

Never willing to stint on patient care, Oliver forced himself to set his thoughts about his own future aside, but he longed to return to the surgery and see Chloe. The afternoon seemed to drag, but he was soon on his final home visit.

Edith Jones, one of Lucy's patients, lived in a bungalow in Polkerris Road. In her seventies, Edith had endured a tough year. On top of her heart problems and suffering a minor stroke, she had fallen in her home and split her kneecap in two. Since she had returned home from the hospital after initial rehabilitation, the district nurses and a GP visited her regularly, and Lauren was involved in her care, helping her remain as mobile as possible. Oliver had visited Edith a couple of times and was thankful the elderly lady was maintaining Lucy's original advice to change her diet and reduce her salt intake.

'Anything else I can do for you today, Edith?' he asked, packing away his things, satisfied with the results of his examination.

'No. Thank you, Dr Oliver.' She sent him a gentle smile. 'It's a bit of a struggle, but I'm coping, and everyone is very kind. I'm relieved to be able to stay in my own home with my own things around me. Sarah Pearce, my neighbour, is an angel. And I have my cat for company.'

'Call any time if there is anything you need.'

Reassured that Edith was settled, he took his leave. The journey back to the surgery was short and, when he pulled his four-by-four into the car park he saw Lauren getting out of her Renault.

'Hi, Lauren,' he greeted her, balancing his pile of patient notes and his medical bag while locking the door.

'Hello, Oliver.'

'I've just seen Edith Jones. She seems to be doing well.'

Walking with him towards the entrance, Lauren nodded. 'Yes, she is. I'm going in twice a week at the moment.'

They walked into the reception area to be greeted by Sue, the head receptionist. Oliver smiled and set his notes down on the counter for them to be filed away, then accepted the bundle of phone messages Sue handed him.

'Thank you. Anything urgent, Sue?' he asked, flicking through them.

'No, I don't think so. I do have one urgent call for you, though, Lauren,' she continued, handing over the message. 'Can you call back straight away?'

Lauren frowned at the note. 'Of course. I'll do it now.'

'Vicky is here—she said she was meeting you. She's upstairs, talking with Chloe,' Sue explained.

'I'm going up,' Oliver told Lauren, eager to see Chloe himself. 'I'll let Vicky know you're back.'

'Thanks, Oliver.'

Filled with urgency and a sense of purpose, Oliver left his medical bag and his phone messages in his consulting room then headed for the stairs. At the top, he rounded the corner. Chloe's door was open, but as he heard her and Vicky talking he hesitated outside, frozen to immobility, unable to believe what he was hearing. Blindly, he put out a hand to brace himself, feeling as if his heart was being dug out of his chest with a blunt spoon, leaving him bleeding and battered.

'Is that beard rash on your neck?' Vicky grinned, perching on the desk and leaning closer.

'No.' Chloe fought a blush, determined to hide the truth from Vicky. It was just as well she couldn't see the other places on her body that carried the faint mark of the delicious caress of Oliver's stubbled jaw. 'I was in the sun too long.'

Vicky's grin widened. 'Sure you were! So you and Oliver

are finally doing the wild thing, like I told you to. I knew my plan would work. Having him around for a few weeks was bound to liven up your boring sex life.'

'Thanks.' Her ironic riposte was lost on Vicky.

'What's the stud muffin like in bed? I wouldn't mind finding out for myself when you've finished with him…if he sticks around long enough.'

Chloe's hands clenched to fists in her lap as she tried to hide her anger, wishing Lauren would hurry back and rescue her from this torture. The very thought of Oliver with anyone else twisted her insides with pain and jealousy. She liked Vicky…usually. The woman wasn't spiteful, but she was incredibly tactless, leaping in without thinking. No way was Chloe going to leave herself or Oliver open to Vicky's brand of loose talking. And no way did she want Vicky anywhere near Oliver.

'You haven't been stupid enough to fall in love with him, have you, Chloe?' Vicky continued, flicking her fringe—today her hair was green—away from her eyes.

'Of course not,' she lied.

'Well, that's a relief. We all know he's not that kind of man, so it's no use you starting to think wedding bells or anything. That's why he was so perfect for your summer fling.'

'So you said.' Chloe ducked her head to hide her hurt, wanting to yell that Vicky had no idea what kind of man Oliver was. She knew there was no point in explaining, the other girl would never understand how wrong she was. 'Let's forget it, Vicky. It's not important.'

She just wanted Vicky to go. She knew how sensitive Oliver was about people falsely labelling him as a playboy and she was disappointed and cross with Vicky for doing the same thing. She wanted to protect Oliver, to stand up for him, but at the same time she didn't want Vicky spreading rumours and gossip around Penhally about her relationship

with Oliver. And she certainly wasn't going to confide to Vicky how she truly felt about him, not until she had told Oliver himself and knew what his plans were and if she stood any chance with him. Vicky knew nothing of her past and would never comprehend what a huge step she had taken in trusting Oliver and finding love with him. It wasn't something she wanted talked about or mocked, however well meaning the teasing might be.

Oliver leaned against the wall, a tight band around his chest preventing him from breathing. Something inside him died and a void opened up. A dark, cold void where just moments ago there had been hope and love and the feeling that maybe this once he had met someone who saw beyond the playboy exterior. He had thought Chloe was different. Apparently not. He stepped into the room, bitter hurt and betrayal swirling inside him, mingling with anger at himself for being such a fool and at Chloe for not being all he had thought she was.

He had tried not to worry that Chloe had said nothing about her feelings, had not wanted to spoil the perfection of their days and nights together by pressing her too soon, by revealing his love for her. He had worried that she might never get beyond her past, and yet he had still gone ahead and laid himself bare to her, committing himself body and soul, leaving himself more vulnerable than ever before.

That Chloe had discussed him with her friends, had been using him as a temporary playboy for some sex education and a holiday fling, hurt more than he believed possible. He was devastated. All his dreams and plans, fledgling ones that had taken real flight after Nick's offer earlier, now crumbled to dust around him.

In the moment before Chloe or Vicky noticed his presence, he drank in the sight of the woman he had so wanted to believe in but who had hurt him beyond bearing. She glanced

round then, shock and guilt in her expressive eyes when her gaze met his.

'Oliver! I—'

'Vicky, Lauren is waiting for you downstairs,' he interrupted, somehow managing to force the words past the tightness in his throat.

'Oops! Didn't see you there.' With an irritating giggle, Vicky slid off the edge of Chloe's desk. 'Thanks. I'll see you later.'

A tense silence followed her departure. Feeling as if the floor had been pulled out from under him, he thrust his hands in his pockets and forced himself to look at Chloe. 'Nick offered me a permanent job in Penhally.'

He watched as her face lost colour and renewed shock widened moss-green eyes. Clearly this wasn't the pleasant surprise he'd wanted it to be and she'd meant what she'd said to Vicky—she didn't love him, had never expected more than a few nights in his bed before he moved on.

'You're thinking of staying here?'

'Of course, that doesn't fit in with your plans, does it, babe?' Hurt brought a sarcastic edge to his voice. 'You and Vicky had it all figured out. I was a not entirely repulsive *stud* you thought you could use to satisfy your curiosity about sex for a night or two because it wouldn't matter to me.'

Chloe stared at Oliver in horror. The icy chill of his voice was matched by the expression in his eyes, eyes devoid of their normal life and warmth.

'That's not—'

'I heard what you said.'

'Oliver!' Hazel's urgent call from the direction of the landing prevented Chloe making a rebuttal. 'We have an emergency outside. Can you come?'

'Of course.' He cast Chloe one searing look before turning away. 'I'm done here.'

The finality of the words cut Chloe to the quick. 'But—'

Chloe watched through a film of tears as Oliver strode away, his footsteps retreating down the stairs as he followed Hazel. Slumping against her desk, her whole body shaking in reaction, Chloe wrapped her arms around herself. Damn Vicky. Just how much of their conversation had Oliver heard? It must have sounded bad. And on top of that, instead of responding with the joy and hope she felt at the thought of Oliver staying, the shock and confusion of the last moments had made her reaction slow and lukewarm.

What was she going to do? So inexperienced at this kind of thing, she had made a mess of everything. Because of her past, she hadn't believed she could be happy, that what she felt for Oliver was real, that it could work. Had not believed he could love her. But his pain had been obvious. She would never forget the look in his eyes. The knowledge that he now believed she had used him stung.

'Chloe, what the hell is going on?' Lauren demanded, rushing into the room and closing the door behind her.

Tears trickled down her cheeks and her voice shook. 'Oliver's gone. It's over.'

'Vicky told me what happened. She's an idiot.' Lauren handed her a tissue and slid an arm around her shoulder. 'So will you be if you let Oliver go. Damn it, Chloe! You have to go after him.'

'No.' A sob escaped. She thought she had known what pain was like but this was worse, much worse. 'I can't. He'd never believe me now.'

Lauren cursed. 'I was there when he followed Hazel downstairs. He was devastated. I've never seen anyone look so broken. You love him, Chloe, I know you do. Don't let it end like this. It's too important, for both of you. He doesn't know what Vicky is like, he didn't understand you were trying to

protect him from gossip. He's not a mind-reader. You have to explain.'

'I've been too scared to tell him I love him.' Chloe's throat closed and her chest crushed with hurt. 'Now it's too late. I let him down.'

'*Tell* him.'

'What if he won't talk to me?' she whispered through her tears, scared she had driven Oliver away for good.

'You won't know until you try. Make him listen,' Lauren advised. 'He's hurting now because he loves you. You love him. What have you got to lose?'

Nothing, Chloe realised as her friend left her alone to think. She had already lost everything that mattered to her. A fierce mix of need and hurt and anger swirled inside her. She was angry with herself for handling things so badly, angry with Vicky for interfering, angry and disappointed that Oliver hadn't given her the chance to explain. It hurt that he hadn't believed in her enough. But why should he? She'd never told him how she felt, had taken everything he had given her these last weeks but had still doubted. After what he had overheard, followed by her reaction, what else was he to think?

Lauren was right. She was the only one who could change that. Oliver was worth fighting for. She gathered up her things and hurried down the stairs, upset to discover that Oliver had left. The emergency had been a suspected heart attack and he had gone along in the ambulance to St Piran with the critically ill patient. No one could tell when he might be back.

Unwilling to hang around the surgery, she went home to shower and change her clothes. After feeding the cats, she paced her small living room. Several times she phoned Oliver's flat but there was no reply, and his mobile was switched off. When her phone rang, she jumped and rushed to answer, hoping it was Oliver, swallowing her disappointment when she discovered it was not. It was Kate.

'Are you all right, Chloe? What's going on with you and Oliver?'

'I don't know.' Her voice trembled with tears. 'He overheard me talking to Vicky this afternoon. She can be so persistent and thoughtless. I told her a few fibs. I was trying to stop her gossiping, but now Oliver thinks I have just been using him. It isn't true!'

'I know that, my love. So will Oliver when he's calmed down,' Kate reassured her, but Chloe knew it wasn't that simple.

'He told me that Nick had offered him a permanent post. Oh, Kate, I was so shocked, so stunned to discover he had heard me and Vicky, that I reacted badly. I didn't get the chance to explain, and now he believes there's nothing between us, that I don't care. And that's my fault, too, because I was too scared to tell him.'

A heartfelt sigh from Kate increased her anxiety. 'He's going, Chloe. I was here at the surgery when he came back from the hospital fifteen minutes ago. He told Nick he didn't want the job, that there was nothing for him to stay for.'

'No!'

'Go to him, my love. It doesn't matter who is more at fault, you are both hurting and you need each other. If you don't talk to him, you will always regret it,' Kate counselled, reinforcing Lauren's advice. 'Make it right, Chloe…before it's too late.'

Knowing there was a wealth of meaning behind Kate's words, empathising with her friend's difficult situation with Nick, the man she had loved for so long, Chloe made her decision.

Oliver tossed clothes into his bags, trying to use anger to mask the bitter lance of terrible pain. How could he have been so stupid? Chloe wasn't different at all. Like everyone else, she had seen the outer package, the reputation, and not the man

inside. His gut ached at the knowledge she had used him as some kind of sex tutor. And he would never forget the look of shock on her face when he had told her he was staying. Clearly she didn't want him. He had read everything wrong and now there was nothing for him in Penhally Bay.

A furious pounding on the door had his head snapping up. He hesitated. He wasn't on duty. Indeed, he had a few days off to decide if he even wanted to see out his contract here. But what if someone was in trouble? Hell. He ran a hand through his hair and stalked towards the door. Throwing it open, he froze when he saw who waited outside. Chloe. Her hand, raised to knock again, fell to her side. Before he could react, she pushed past him.

'What do you want, Chloe, another quick tumble in bed before the playboy leaves town?' He hated himself for the words and tried to close his mind to the hurt clouding her green eyes.

'No. That wouldn't be enough.' She folded her arms across her chest and fixed him with a glare. 'I'm here because you didn't give me a chance to explain and I'm not going to let you judge me and leave without me saying my piece.'

Unwanted amusement and affection welled inside him at her bravado. He'd never seen her so riled before. It was cute. No, he— Before he could formulate his thoughts and raise his defences again, she launched into her attack.

'Do you seriously think, with my background and having waited until the age of twenty-seven, that I would suddenly turn into some kind of sexpot who is going to sleep with anyone for the sake of it? Yes, Vicky made some stupid comment when she found out you were interested in me that I should go for it. But that's Vicky. She doesn't know about my past. She certainly doesn't know me if she thought I could ever do such a thing.' She paused a moment, dragging in a lungful of air. 'And neither can you if you believe it, even for a moment. I didn't

come on to you, chase you. You courted me. And it was only when I came to know you, to like you, to trust you, that I began to wonder if maybe you were someone special, someone who made it worth my while to confront things that terrified me and open myself up to experiences I had shut out of my life because I was so scared. You think I would have just jumped into bed with anyone?'

She was shaking with rage and hurt. All the fight went out of him as every word she said hit home and he acknowledged how badly he had behaved, how horribly he had treated her. Yes, he did know her better. He just hadn't allowed himself to believe it could be true that he had found his perfect soulmate, that she could ever come to love him back, that there could be a happy ever after. Just when it had all been falling into place, everything had been shaken up and he had allowed his own insecurities to get the better of him, to believe the worst of her.

'Chloe…' He tried to swallow past the lump in his throat and find his voice. 'I'm sorry.'

'So am I.'

Tears shimmered on long sooty lashes as he closed the gap between them. 'I was so dumb.'

'Me, too.'

'Can you forgive me, babe? Please?'

'Oliver—'

He rested the fingers of one hand over her lips, not wanting her to reject him as he deserved, needing to say his own piece while he had the chance. 'I should never have paid heed to what I heard. I was just so stunned, so hurt when you told Vicky you didn't love me.'

'Vicky means well, but she's the biggest gossip in Penhally, Oliver, and she has zero tact. I didn't want her telling all and sundry our private business. I was angry with her for judging you, for being so shallow, but I knew she would never listen, never understand, so I let her ramble on. No way was I going

to tell Vicky, of all people, about my feelings—not when I hadn't even had the courage to tell you.'

'Chloe,' he murmured, stepping closer, a glimmer of hope challenging the darkness inside him. 'When I came back to Cornwall, I was jaded, fed up with people using me because of the family name, the money, my so-called playboy lifestyle. Sure, I liked to have a good time, to enjoy myself, but no one saw *me*. The person inside. Not until you. I was drawn to you from the first and the more I came to know you, the more I knew you were special, and I dared to allow myself to believe.' He cupped her face, breathing in her fresh apple scent. 'Nick sprang the junior partnership on me and immediately I had all these plans and wanted to share them with you. But I had no idea how you felt. When I heard you talking and it seemed to have all been some grand scheme for a fling between us, I let the hurt and fear get in the way of my common sense and all I knew about you. I was scared because I thought I had been a fool to think someone like you could possibly care about someone like me.'

'Someone like you?' she challenged, her own hands lifting to grasp his wrists. 'A fantastic, caring doctor, adored by his patients, young and old, male and female? Someone like you, who is good and kind, funny and intelligent, selfless and giving? Someone like you who saw *me* when no one else had, and who cared enough to wait, to gain my trust, to spend so much time getting me through the scary moments and awakening me to all I was missing by not setting the past behind me where it belongs? Someone like you, who changed my life…who made me really feel alive for the first time? That someone like you?'

'Yeah.' Love and desire glowed inside him at the sincerity of her words.

'Oliver, I don't care about your bank balance. I don't care about Fawkner Yachts. It wouldn't matter to me who your

family were as long as they loved you and were proud of you. I'm proud of you. And I love you. I should have told you before, but I was scared, too. Scared you would leave soon and I'd never see you again. Scared none of this meant to you what it did to me. You stole my heart, you made me believe in romance and love and for ever. You even made me like sex,' she added with a shy laugh, a blush staining her cheeks.

'Chloe…'

Her eyes full of vulnerability, she stepped back a couple of paces and pulled the tie holding the fabric of her floaty dress together. She let it drop, revealing barely-there silk and lace bra and panties. Every part of him sprang to attention. OK. Any moment now he would remember how to breathe. That or pass out. Dear God…

'I've never seduced a man before.'

He filled his lungs on a ragged gasp. 'You're doing one hell of a good job,' he managed, his voice hoarse with love and admiration and desire.

'Am I?'

'Oh, yeah.' Given how hard he was and how close to embarrassing himself. 'Don't move.'

He reached for the phone, his fingers shaking as he felt for the keys and dialled a number, his gaze never leaving Chloe's.

'Nick? It's Oliver Fawkner. If the offer for the junior partnership still stands, I'd like to accept. Thank you. Yes, I'm sorry about that, it was a misunderstanding. I've just discovered that I have everything to stay for. All I'll ever need is right here in Penhally Bay.'

As he replaced the receiver, he saw joy dance in Chloe's beautiful green eyes, along with a whole host of feelings that mirrored his own. To think he had been so foolish to risk throwing this away. 'Now, you said something about seducing me.'

'Yes. That.'

'Don't let me stop you,' he invited, his fingertips brushing across the rounded swell of her breasts over the top edges of her bra, enjoying the tremor that rippled through her.

'I was kind of hoping you might take over at this point.'

'I don't know. You're doing so well.'

'Really?'

'Don't you know you had me on my knees from the moment we met?'

She shook her head, looking shy yet bold, sexy yet uncertain as her fingers began to undo the buttons of his shirt. 'I only know you didn't give up on me, didn't let my past and my fears chase you away.'

He moaned as she freed his shirt, leaned forward and closed her mouth over one sensitive nipple. Not wanting to be left out, he deftly unhooked her bra and tossed it away, filling his palms with her firm, full, soft flesh.

'How about we do the seducing together?' he suggested hoarsely.

'Good idea.'

'We'll do everything together, Chloe, for the rest of our lives. I'll do all I can to make you happy and I'll love you for ever. If you'll let me.'

'Yes.' She whimpered as his thumbs brushed over taut nipples. 'I will. If you'll let me love you for ever, too.'

'I think I can manage that.'

Her fingers fumbled with the fastening of his jeans. 'Starting now?'

'Hell, yes!' He kissed her, long and hard and deep. 'What say we shock Vicky and make it another wedding for Penhally before the year is out?'

'Lauren is right. There definitely must be something in the water!'

He nipped her earlobe. 'Is that a yes?'

'Of course it's a yes!'

'I already have a present for you,' he told her with a teasing smile, thinking of the jet-ski he'd ordered.

Green eyes sparkled with mischief as she looked at him. 'Funny. I have a present for you, too. It's at home. I hid it in the spare room. It's for your birthday, but I was going to give it to you if you left…to remember me by.'

'As if I could ever forget you.' He groaned, pulling her close. 'And I'm never leaving, babe.' As curious as he was about what she had bought him, amazed and touched that she had done such a thing, he had other things on his mind right now. 'Presents can wait until later.'

'Whatever did you have in mind?'

Laughing, he swung her up in his arms and carried her to the bedroom. He set her back on her feet, grimacing when he saw her pained expression as she looked at his half-packed luggage.

'Like I said, I was dumb.'

'You can still pack.'

He froze at her words. 'What do you mean?'

'Your lease here runs out any day.' Shy invitation shone in her eyes. 'I was thinking… Maybe you'd care to move in with me?'

'I'd love to. And down the line, when we decide about a family, we can find a new home together that we can grow into. With the cats, of course.'

'Perfect.'

'No. You're perfect.' He tipped her on to the bed and stripped off the rest of his clothes. 'Do you think, knowing you—and your background—that I ever would have embarked on a relationship with you if all I had wanted was a quick, meaningless tumble before I moved on again? You're not a quick tumble kind of woman, Chloe. If I'd only wanted one night, I would never have touched you. I would have walked away. But I came here to settle down, to meet the right woman for me, and

I soon knew you were the one. You are a forever kind of woman. My forever woman. It's happened quickly, but I love you. And I've never said that to anyone before. I know this is all new to you. If you need time to be sure, that's fine, I understand. But I'm only going to love you more each day.'

Tears filled her eyes, threatening to spill past her lashes. 'I am sure. I love you, too. So much. I just can't believe I'm enough for you.'

'Babe, you are everything.' He joined her on the bed, dipping his head to steal a hot kiss. 'And it'll be my pleasure to prove it to you every day for the rest of our lives.'

She wriggled out of her panties. 'Starting now.' It was half question, half demand, her voice throaty with arousal.

'This very second.'

He fulfilled his promise, as he planned to fulfil all his promises to her, now and for all the years that lay ahead of them. How could he be this lucky? He was the happiest man alive, and if he had his way, Chloe was going to be the most satisfied woman in Penhally Bay. Hell, the whole world!

Linking his fingers with hers, holding her gaze, he united them, starting them on their journey to paradise together, joining not just their bodies, but their hearts and their souls…for ever.

Midwives' Miracles

About the Authors

After completing a degree in journalism, then working in advertising and mothering her kids, **Robin Gianna** had what she calls her awakening. She decided she wanted to write the romance novels she'd loved since her teens, and now enjoys pushing her characters toward their own happily-ever-afters. When she's not writing, Robin's life is filled with a happily messy kitchen, a needy garden, a wonderful husband, three great kids, a drooling bulldog and one grouchy Siamese cat.

Three-times Golden Heart® finalist **Tina Beckett** learned to pack her suitcases almost before she learned to read. Born to a military family, she has lived in the United States, Puerto Rico, Portugal and Brazil. In addition to travelling, Tina loves to cuddle with her pug, Alex, spend time with her family and hit the trails on her horse. Learn more about Tina from her website, or 'friend' her on Facebook.

Margaret McDonagh can't remember a time when her nose wasn't buried in a book. She read avidly, but always knew that she had to write. In 2005, after twenty years of writing novellas for My Weekly Story Collection and Linford large print, plus serials and magazine short stories for The People's Friend, her manuscript was accepted by Mills & Boon. She has been writing novels ever since! You can contact Margaret via her website: www.margaretmcdonagh.com